WISE MEN

WISE MEN

STUART NADLER

THORNDIKE PRESS
A part of Gale, Cengage Learning

GALE
CENGAGE Learning·

Detroit • New York • San Francisco • New Haven, Conn • Waterville, Maine • London

GALE
CENGAGE Learning

LIBRARY OF CONGRESS CATALOGING-IN-PUBLICATION DATA

Nadler, Stuart.
  Wise men / by Stuart Nadler.
    pages ; cm. — (Thorndike Press large print peer picks)
  ISBN-13: 978-1-4104-5927-5 (hardcover)
  ISBN-10: 1-4104-5927-6 (hardcover)
  1. Interracial friendship—Fiction. 2. Family secrets—Fiction. 3. Identity (Psychology)—Fiction. 4. Large type books. I. Title.
PS3614.A385W57 2013b
813'.6—dc23   2013007008

Published in 2013 by arrangement with Little, Brown and Company, a division of Hachette Book Group, Inc.

Printed in Mexico
2 3 4 5 6 7 17 16 15 14 13

For my wife

All love is in great part affliction.
— MARILYNNE ROBINSON, "WILDERNESS"

PART I

ONE

In the spring of 1947, when I was twelve years old, a passenger plane crashed near Narragansett Bay. It was a small craft, newly built, operated by a nascent aviation outfit called Boston Airways. Color photographs show that the nose and tail of the plane were painted the yellow of a girl's Easter dress. Because of this, in the hangars where it was stored, its name was *Bunny,* or *Chickadee;* both names are listed in the official testimony. The intended flight path that afternoon had the plane headed first to New York and then to Miami, and then, if weather permitted, back along the edge of the Atlantic to land in Baltimore.

Lately I've begun to collect artifacts from the crash: a shard of the captain's seat belt; the sleek, burnished blade of a cracked propeller; the top flap of a carton of Fatima cigarettes, remarkably well preserved, a greasy, spectral fingerprint smeared across the red crescent moon of the logo. Filed away on a computer, I have recordings of the few radio transmissions that exist. The pilots are calm before their death. I'm not ashamed to admit that I've listened to them dozens, if not hundreds, of times. Everything in my story depends in some way on this crash.

Takeoff: eight past noon, out of Logan. Estimated arrival: half past one.

Sixty people were on board, fifteen of them were children; no one survived.

At the time of the crash we were living in New Haven. I was out in the yard when a man pedaled by me on a bicycle. He was in a gray suit and a black felt fedora. "Plane's gone down outside Providence," he said, slowing to tell me the news. He had a calabash pipe in his teeth, and the smoke from it was sweet, like apples cooking. "Guess it took off out of Boston and couldn't get airborne. Just sort of floated above the trees all the way down into Rhode Island." He put up his hand flat into the air and made a nosedive with it, his voice adding to the effect. A moment later, he was gone, off on his bicycle, the tails of his sports coat fluttering up as he wheeled away.

My mother was standing in the kitchen. I

could see her from the lawn. There was a square window framed by a wheat-colored curtain. She had the glass open, bugs at the screen, a breeze frittering at the fabric. Her cheeks were flushed. Steam in the kitchen from a kettle. Maybe a trace of cinnamon, baking, from the stove. Only two months earlier she'd celebrated her thirtieth birthday, but if you were to look at her straight, and in good light, you'd think she was a college girl. For the occasion my father had bought her a fake sapphire ring, a solitary costume stone set up on a pewter band; it'd cost him three dollars and she hadn't taken it off since.

When I came in to tell her, she already knew. The radio was on, a man's voice, grave, full of baritone. He rattled off what was known at that point, the plane's type, its supposed location upon impact, the assumed number of fatalities.

My mother — and I have always remembered this — became angry at the news.

"How can something that large just fall out of the sky?" she asked me. She slapped at the linoleum with her open hand. She'd been frying an egg. Her ring clapped the air. "All those children! Who is flying these things!"

■ ■ ■ ■

My father's connection to the crash was
tenuous. A man on board had been the
brother of a classmate of his. There were
telephone calls, so many of them, and then
a frantic hustling on my father's part that
culminated two weeks later in an office near
Hartford, where he agreed to represent ten
of the affected families. By then my father
had collected enough information to believe
he had a case: there was evidence that
executives from the airline knew the plane's
engines were damaged; at airports along the
coast, word had spread of lazy safety up-
keep, mechanical ignorance, pilots capable
of flying a six-ton bomber but unfamiliar
with the relative delicacy of such a small
aircraft. One night before it all really started,
I found him at our kitchen table in his
underwear, blueprints and memos and
cigarettes scattered in a mess. It was a new
plane, and apparently something this new
shouldn't have crashed. "Can you win?" I
asked. He moved to make a space for me at
the table and asked me to sit down. "What
do you see?" he asked, pointing to the
diagram of an airplane engine. "Gibberish,"
I said. "Squiggles." He laughed. "Me too."

He wasn't the best person for the job, something he likely kept to himself. He had been an ambulance chaser before all of this — your average slip-and-fall-and-sue attorney — and if for any reason my mother needed to get ahold of him in those days, her best bet was to search the waiting areas of the city's emergency rooms, where, invariably, he was sure to be camped out with his coffee, his cigarettes, and a stack of his business cards. His arrogance was often mistaken for the genuine artifact: skill, or competence, or some combination of the two. His strategy was to charge only a small retainer fee, enough for us to pay our rent and to eat and occasionally to see a movie. In return he demanded a larger-than-usual portion of any potential winnings. He claimed that it would be difficult to emerge with a victory. The arrangement, he told his new clients, was a safe bet.

The number of plaintiffs grew. These calls came sparingly at first, waking us at night, a bereft mother sneaking away to call my father while her husband slept; a PFC in the army, stationed in Okinawa, whose father had died and whose brother could not be reached. Letters arrived. Two Cuban women had stood waiting at the airfield in Miami, unknowing, before word arrived.

15

The abbess of a Connecticut orphanage wrote, claiming to represent one of the children; the girl had been on her way to New York to meet her new parents. With every call the case became larger, the potential purse of damages fuller, the bustle in our small rented house busier and noisier and filled every night with the whispered idea that maybe, possibly, if things went perfectly, if the judge saw something the right way, or if the opposing counsel decided to take a certain tack, we — it was always *we* — might win.

The first press photograph of my father was published in the *New York Herald* in August 1947. It shows him emulating one of Hoover's G-men: a fedora tipped low, covering his face; a fussy double Windsor; black jacket, black pants, black belt, black shoes; an Old Gold cigarette on his lip; a charcoal Chesterfield trench coat and a leather briefcase.

"What do you expect to happen here?" a reporter is quoted as asking him. "Are you hoping to bring down the entire passenger aviation industry? Do you expect us to revert to the railroads to get around? Is that what you want, Mr. Wise?"

"Bring down!" my father answered, laugh-

16

ing. "What a terrible choice of words!"

My father was a handsome man. All my life people had said this to me, but I had never really seen evidence of it until he began to appear in the papers: his thin face, pointed cheeks, a cupid's smile, a rumor of white in his widow's peak. The first time we saw his picture in the news, my mother told me that publicity made a man more beautiful. She put her fingers down onto a photograph of him. "His eyelashes," she said. "Look. He's got the eyelashes of a lady." The attention didn't surprise my father. He had a certain glint in his eyes that seemed to imply he'd expected something like this all his life.

Lucky for him that in those days the class-action suit seemed revolutionary. The idea that big business could put lives at risk without recourse seemed to tap at some primal suspicion seeking a new home after the war. People love an enemy, and without the Germans or the Japanese, my father was smart to cast Boston Airways the way he did. In an article in the *Times* later that same summer of 1947, he actually paints it that way. "Left unchecked, this is the biggest threat to civilian safety since the Blitz."

His partner's name was Robert Ashley. They'd met as infantrymen in Cherbourg, where Robert had saved my father's life, an act that forever placed him in Robert's debt. Afterward they enrolled in law school together. Robert was a kind man, taller by a head than anyone I had ever seen, a pale and gawky Kansan with a flat accent, a taste for rye whiskey, and a reputation for kindness that did well to offset my father's often repellent brashness. As far as I could tell, Robert's primary responsibility was to keep my father's worst impulses — and he had so many of them — in check. It is worth noting that there are no photographs of Robert from this period, no interviews, only the nominal mention in the firm's name: Wise & Ashley. In my research, he is largely absent. He is a shadow in the court transcript, often interrupting my father's questioning.

A typical interjection, taken from the first week of courtroom proceedings: "My colleague is motioning to me, Your Honor. I apologize. Allow me a moment."

The trial seemed to go on forever. I was twelve when the plane crashed, thirteen when we won the first round, and seventeen when the appellate process was exhausted. Because my father needed to be closer to the court of appeals in New York, he decided to move us all out of New Haven my senior year. He rented us a house in a town called Wren's Bridge, a bedroom community a half hour north of Manhattan. I hadn't wanted to go. In New Haven I'd pitched for our middling excuse for a school baseball team. My best friends filled out the rest of the infield. I was popular in the way that most pitchers are popular, and I had for those few seasons something of what made my father so effortlessly confident in a room full of strangers. When people put their confidence in you, it's not so difficult to let some of that hope and faith and trust change the way you act. I figured that if I was lucky, after graduation I'd get to play baseball in one of the less competitive collegiate divisions or that I would join the army, the way my father had. Leaving New Haven, leaving my friends, my ball club, that infield — all of it devastated me. I was seventeen, and devastation came easy.

Our new house was plain, decent, set on a quarter acre of crabgrass. Our lawn was sloped like a shallow soup bowl, and in the winter it flooded with rain and snow and then froze so thick, my mother could skate on it. We were, I'm sure of it, the first family of Jews on our street. Occasionally I was teased by some boys eager to get a rise out of me by chanting something about ovens or Germany, or by throwing pennies at me and daring me to fetch them. It was the fall of 1951. People are sometimes surprised to hear me say these things, but wars do nothing to end the cruelty of boys. In my first week there, I got myself into a half-dozen fistfights. In most of these I managed all right; in only one did I get my lip split and my nose cut open. This isn't to say that Wren's Bridge wasn't a nice town. It had some good places to eat, a passable movie theater, and from a high peak called Traverstock you could see the tip of something that sort of resembled the very tallest point on what some people claimed might be the Empire State Building. The people there were nothing if not exact.

And on the far west side of town, about as far from our house as possible, there was an indoor skating rink where on cold days you could get on the ice for a small fee. If you weren't half-bad, you had a good chance of impressing some girls. I had my first kiss there, against the visitor's penalty box, with Pauline McNamee. Of course, the twelfth grade was late for a first kiss, but I didn't let on to Pauline. Before she kissed me, I'd had a sinking feeling that she liked me because she knew who my father was, that she'd seen him in the papers looking serious and important and blathering on about engines or mechanical failures. I was right. Afterward, as she pulled away, and while there were still strings of our saliva connecting us, she asked if she could meet him. "Maybe just once? Nobody knows this, but I really want to be a lawyer when I grow up. I just *love* Perry Mason."

Soon after I started school in Wren's Bridge, I was drafted into our debate club. Again, this was mostly because of my father's reputation. I was a lousy debater. I'd wanted to play baseball, but we'd arrived too late for me to grab a spot on any of the teams, and so most afternoons, when our practice sessions ended and I'd exhausted myself with weak exhortations on Stalin or Trujillo or Happy Chandler, I went over to the Warren Fields and watched the local American Legion team practice their fungoes. All I'd ever wanted to do was to play ball, or to watch it, or to find some way to be around it. But everything in Wren's Bridge centered on our lawsuit. For those first few months, my father did nothing but work and litigate and argue and appear with some regularity in the press. I wanted to go back home to New Haven. So suddenly I'd gone from being a normal, even popular, kid to being the son of a loudmouth, rabble-rousing attorney. I could divide all the people I knew into two camps: those, like Pauline McNamee and my debate coach, who wanted something from me, who wanted some of the sheen of my father's fame to rub off on them; and everyone else, who saw the groveling and brownnosing, and decided because of it to hate me, or to ostracize me, or to throw pennies at the back of my skull while I tried to walk home.

I missed New Haven, the toughness of our neighborhood, all the Italian guys who lived on our street and hung out on their porches, shooting the shit and betting their paychecks on the Giants game. I missed the big arch of the New Haven Railroad headquarters, where the pigeons liked to roost, and I missed the stinking river weeds on the Quinnipiac. I hated Boston Airways, that their plane had crashed, that my father had taken the case. Soon, things began to crack. I stopped seeing Pauline, stopped keeping up with my assignments, and I picked a fight with the boy in my class who pitched for the high school team. I wanted what he had — his varsity letter, and the chance to throw every third day. We were in the cafeteria. I tripped him. When he got up to challenge me, I hit him in the teeth with a decent jab, walked out of the school and up a few blocks, to a spot on Adams Street, where I hailed a taxi. Ten minutes later I boarded a train to New Haven.

My father was the one to fetch me that day. When he found me standing in the cold on Elm Street, shivering in my car coat, searching for a familiar face, any familiar face, he laughed. He was proud of my gumption. I'd been standing on the corner by the Triumph Theater, staring at the movie bill for *High Noon,* Gary Cooper brandishing his pistol. Apparently, I'd been sold out by the guy I'd clobbered, and my father had come to get me not even a half hour after I'd gotten off the train.

"I know you hate it in town," he said once we were in the car. "But you can't just up and leave when things get tough."

I turned up the radio. I'd been listening to him rehearse his arguments in the kitchen all year. He used my mother as his jury. Whenever he talked to me, I couldn't help but think he thought of me as his opposing counsel.

"I don't care," I said. "I think you should let me re-enroll here in New Haven. I'm old enough. I can live on my own."

"I don't think that's happening."

"Why's that? It's a perfectly fine city. And

I like it. We all used to like it."

I despised him for moving us. This was the beginning of everything for him and me. All of our trouble came from that one decision. And I think he knew it before I did. He shifted uncomfortably in his seat. What he wanted to say, which is obvious to me now, was that New Haven was too small for him. Already he'd begun to field offers from the big white-shoe Manhattan firms, the kind of places that sent over a baby-blue Lincoln Cosmopolitan, just for you to borrow, just to see how it would be if you were part of the company. He was happy to have the attention. That much was easy to tell. Each successive offer brought with it all sorts of celebrations in the house. Cheap champagne that they drank from coffee mugs, because all we had were coffee mugs. Or bottles of Moxie soda. Or just a dinner of spaghetti and meatballs one time on Mulberry Street. My mother seemed wild at the notion that her lifetime of near poverty was over, or nearly over. What was actually over for us was our life in New Haven, and as we rode away, I had to stop myself from turning around to see it pass behind me.

For a long while we drove in silence, down through the Connecticut River Valley, through Bridgeport, into Stamford and then west, where we crossed the Hudson at Wren's Bridge and glided slowly back home. The sun set behind us. I remember it as a spectral sunset, full of heat, like all of New England had somehow caught fire. Beyond our car, and my mother's ring, my father owned one suit, two pairs of loafers, a knockoff English wristwatch, and his old service revolver. Everything else, even the food we ate, was bought on credit. Everything in our lives hinged on the idea that his case was impossible to lose.

"What would you do if, say, you were to have more money than you'd ever thought possible?" He asked me this as we rolled up to the house. My mother was sitting on the front steps in a striped housedress, smoking a cigarette fitted into a short, stubby black holder. More and more, I saw her begin to assume these small affectations of what she believed aristocracy might be like. Being wealthy, I knew even then, was just an idea for her. She'd never known a rich person.

I shrugged. "I'd buy tickets to some ball games," I said.

Beside me, my father tried to suppress his eager joy. "How about a gift, then? If I were to get you a gift. Anything you wanted. Anything. What would it be? Would you like a trip overseas? Or how about a car?"

He wanted me to go bigger, so I did. "How about a baseball team?" I asked. He laughed. Then I laughed. "You asked me, didn't you?"

Robert Ashley came out onto the front steps then. He had a copy of the newspaper in his hands. My father was on the front page, a photograph of his face set beside a picture of that Boston Airways plane. Robert smiled, flashed us a thumbs-up.

"What's he so happy about?" I asked.

"We're getting close. That's what."

One week later, while I sat through a discussion of John Keats and his tuberculosis, our principal came into my class, whispered something into my teacher's ear, and then navigated the rows of wooden desks to hand me a small envelope. He had a delirious smile on his face, as if he'd only just finished a laughing fit before coming to find me. The letter was handwritten and had only two words on it: *We won!* I knew right away what it meant, of course, and because the kid beside me stole the card and passed it around to all my classmates, so did everyone else.

Hours later, the news had spread, and while I was trying to eat my lunch in the cafeteria, a crowd gathered around me. My name is Hilton Samuel Wise — named after each of my grandfathers — but I have always been known as Hilly. That afternoon in the lunchroom, everyone around me began to clap and say my name — *Hilly, Hilly, Hilly* — as if I, and not my father, had done something extraordinary. When I left that day, walking the short distance back to our house on Hamilton, I turned at the curb to look back at my classmates, some of them lingering around to watch me go. Pauline McNamee was there, waving. So was Anthony Jackson, the pitcher for the school team whom I'd punched a few weeks earlier. They'd all gathered to see evidence of what had already spread around our school in that cunningly quick way of a good rumor: the Wise family had won.

In my research, I've come across a printed interview from Thanksgiving 1952. I will reproduce its most interesting section below.

Q: What happens now, Mr. Wise? Will you continue to take on the airline industry?

A: (*Laughter*) If they continue to keep me interested.

Q: Do you think you are the most famous young lawyer in America?

27

A: Famous? I don't know how those things work. Who measures? I'd like to meet this man. Are you him? Are you that man?

Q: *What about the best? Are you the best lawyer in America?*

A: No. Definitely not the best. I didn't do anything special here. There are men like me in every city. I'm not even close to the best.

Q: *The luckiest?*

A: How about the richest? How's that? Print that. I'm probably the richest. That's probably true.

Between 1948 and 1952, hundreds of airplanes crashed across the globe. Some of these were military aircraft. Some of these were cargo planes, the only passengers onboard the skeleton crew required to bring the plane from one place to another. But a good deal of these were commercial aircrafts carrying innocent, unsuspecting passengers. Out of these disasters, my father became the lead plaintiff's attorney in dozens of class-action lawsuits similar in design and scope to the one that had ruined Boston Airways. He had found a strategy that worked, and people wanted him on their side. Rather than battle in court with him, the enormous corporate defense firms hired to represent the affected airlines offered settlements as quickly as my father filed suit. They wanted nothing to do with him. The money came fast, and it was huge. We were rich.

What I remember is the instant accumulation of wealth: overcoats from Harrocourts; shoes from Dunbartons; silk ties from Saks or Bloomingdale's; shoes straight from Italy, delivered by parcel; a pashmina from Afghanistan for my mother; a walking cane cut from Brazilian wood for my father, something he looked at, laughed at, and then put away until he said he might need it. There were steaks at Honey's on Fifth; lobster at Nero's; caviar from Zabar's in the tin at midnight; spaghetti and clams at Lucitti's. There were my mother's cigarettes from Nat Sherman, arranged in the colors of the rainbow, held in a pewter clapping case. She smoked, always, from violet to red, right to left, like the text of the Torah. There was a silver-plated revolver, bought for my father by Robert, and then a matching one, except in gold, bought for Robert by my father. I remember a leatherbound collection of Heraclitus, Herodotus, Sophocles, in the original Greek. I don't have a memory for what came when, and to whom it went. But there was more. There were furs, I know, never taken from the box. They were still there twenty years later, sitting in storage in the basement of Bergdorf's. There was art: Chagall. We are Jews, and so we bought Chagalls. There was jewelry: bracelets fitted with Ethiopian turquoise; diamonds mined from West Africa; hematite strung up on a flossy gold necklace, imported from New South Wales; Chinese jade; pearls pried loose from Bora-Bora oysters; Siberian lapis lazuli; gold-rush nuggets dug from the earth at Mount Shasta and melted into rings.

There were also houses. First, there was the house on Riverside Drive, which my father allowed my mother to choose: a freestanding beast off 107th Street that had belonged once to a Turkish tobacco magnate — so much white marble; one enormous parlor, fit with a Venetian chandelier; a half-dozen fireplaces; and a limestone patio with a view of the flatlands in Edgewater. My mother thought that corner of Riverside was the prettiest, with the park out front, all of Manhattan to the south, Jersey to the west, and, from the roof, a gray-green hint of the Atlantic Ocean.

Because of this house, I'm a New Yorker,

quick to anger, difficult to shake, able to pass unmarked through a crowd, capable of simultaneously managing a sandwich, the 7 train, and a detective novel. But because of what my father bought next — the big thing, the best thing, my favorite thing, the only thing he ever really demanded we buy — some part of me has always felt most at home in New England. Then, men like my father gave their houses names the way they gave their dogs names, but for whatever reason — ignorance, stubbornness, a rare show of modesty — he never did this. He made the purchase over the telephone, and I remember that when he hung up the receiver, he turned to me, and said, "My grandfather milked cows in the coldest, worst part of Poland, Hilly. Now your grandchildren are going to have their own goddamned piece of the American coastline to call home." And then he leaned back, took off his glasses, and laughed. He slammed his fist down against the table. It was as if he'd just pulled off a magic trick. "What do you say, Hilly? How do you like that?"

Two

The first time we saw the house in Blue-point my mother screamed. We'd parked in the driveway, the tires loud against the pebbles underneath. She stepped out of the car, looked at the house, the ocean behind it, the white gulls circling overhead. Then she edged her sunglasses down to the point of her nose and let out an astonished yelp. Her reaction delighted my father. He had one foot up on the running board of the car. The engine was still going.

"Pretty damn good, right, Ruthie?"

She turned to him, one hand over her mouth. He was beaming. He jumped off the car's runner. "I knew you'd like it," he said.

Bluepoint was a town on the far edge of the flexed arm of Cape Cod, a sanded dot on the map between Wellfleet and Truro. We'd driven up from Wren's Bridge that morning, making the trip in less than six hours. The house was simple, just a small two-bedroom saltbox. The shingles were stained so that the wood looked wet. The front door was red. The grass needed cutting. There were mosquitoes. All in all, it was the sort of house we saw every day in Wren's Bridge or New Haven, but still, as we stood on the rocky driveway, my mother yelped.

He turned to me. "What do you think?"

I shrugged. "Not bad," I said.

"Not bad, Hilly? It's far better than that! It's a hell of a lot better than not bad!"

The yard was big enough for a baseball game. This was something I liked about it. The street was quiet but dusty. The air was filled with salt, and the wind had teased my hair up above my head. My father was dressed in what amounted then to his summer uniform: a gray vest, a pair of slacks, and a white oxford-cloth shirt with the sleeves rolled up to his elbow. Except for the vest, I was dressed in exactly the same clothes. It was the end of June 1952, six weeks after the Boston Airways case had closed for good. In a few months, I was supposed to start classes at Dartmouth, and my father was trying to groom me, or train me, or make it so that when I went out into the world with his name, I didn't embarrass anyone. Dartmouth was something he'd arranged for me. I didn't have anything close to the grades to get in. But still, he was famous now. He wanted his son in the Ivy League, and that's where I was going. He'd tried to get me into Yale, to get me back to New Haven, but evidently admissions there had some standards of decency they weren't willing to compromise.

He put his hand on my shoulder and led me to the bluffs that sat above the beach. I knew the ocean mostly from New Haven, where Long Island Sound abutted the city, everything gray and unforgiving, the horizon marked by hydroelectric plants. We stood there together for a few moments at the edge of our lawn, where the earth gave way to a slope of loose sand, and then a sharp bluff, and then the Atlantic. He pointed toward a spot down the beach where the grass had been cleared, the ground tilled up. A small white house, very much like ours, sat dappled by sun. "Robert's going to live there," he said. He still had his hand on my shoulder, and every few moments he muttered to me, "What do you think of this, son?" I shrugged again. I was seventeen, and I didn't understand what it meant to own a piece of the beach, the status of it, the way it would make people think of him. If the early part of his life was a battle, this

34

house marked his victory. He wore brow-line eyeglasses then, and I saw him take them off and fold them into his hands and wipe at his eyes.

At some point a pod of dolphins appeared on the surface of the water, their silver hides emerging in small crescent-shaped ripples. My father slowly put his eyeglasses back onto his face, and then, having straightened them, took a step toward the sea, first test-ing the firmness of the eroding shoreline with the toe of his loafer and then standing with his head craned forward.

"They're not real," he said, turning to me, grinning, and then laughing. "They can't be, right, Hilly?"

"Why wouldn't they be real?" I answered. "It's the ocean, isn't it?"

"Nah," he said, shaking his head.

"They're clearly real," I said. "What's wrong with you?"

He wasn't listening. He went one step farther out onto the silty ledge. He was afraid the ground would give way, and he reached out for me to steady him. The sea grass came up to his knees. Each of his steps disturbed a cloud of gnats. He peered out. "Nah," he said, turning to me. "Definitely not real."

"Do you think somebody put fake dolphins in the sea — just for you?"

He smirked. He was putting me on. Every day was a show for him. "It's pretty, right? I hope you like. I got it for all of us."

By then, my attention had shifted to a small two-story garage out behind the house. It was a bright day, and I could see inside to the second floor, where a finely dressed black man was standing, watching me as I was watching him. I managed a weak wave, and after a long moment, he waved back.

My father saw that I was waving.

"Didn't think they'd actually do it," he said. He still seemed giddy from seeing the dolphins.

"Do what?" I asked.

"The sellers threw in their boy."

"Their what?"

"Their *caretaker,*" he said, fluttering his hands in front of himself to indicate that I was supposed to understand that he wasn't sure which term to use. Servant. Butler. Housekeeper. Valet. He was walking back to the front of the house. Then he looked over to me. "They told me they thought he might move. Also said he might stay. I said, let him stay if he wants to. If he's good, I'll take him on. Don't know how much work he's gonna get cleaning up after us three, though. But, he's cheap. And by cheap, I mean very cheap."

We came back around to the front of the house, where my mother was still standing beside our new Cadillac. She had her sandals in her hands. I went ahead to tell her about the dolphins. When I was younger, she used to take me to an aquarium near New Haven. She loved that sort of thing — tapping at the glass to see if the fish would move, hearing small facts about each new species. She'd always seemed so much like a kid when we went to an aquarium or a museum, her curiosity rising up in her. That was the best part of having a young mother: she remembered what it was like to be excited by something new.

In the sun, wearing a brand-new coat and shoes and jewelry, she seemed so pretty. She'd curled her hair for the drive, and it was still hanging in tight ringlets. That was when I noticed that she'd never stopped screaming; she'd only stopped doing so aloud. Her hand was up against her mouth. What I'd first thought was her happiness — she screamed a little at everything in those early years: a good chocolate cake, a baby in a stroller that smiled at her, every mention of my father in the newspaper — I saw now was actual fear. She lifted her hand to

37

point at the house.

"What is it?" my father asked. He began to run to her. "Ruthie?"

I saw it before he did: resting on the window's ledge, just inside the living room window, was a dead cat. It was a big cat, a fluffy tuxedo cat, obviously a pet, and it had died with its paws against the glass, as if the poor thing had been trying to push itself out of the house before it lost its struggle. Because we were there, my mother felt the liberty to scream loudly now. "It's a cat! A house cat!" She stumbled forward and slumped despondently on the hood of the Cadillac.

My father and I looked nervously at the window. Neither of us was very good with animals, and neither of us wanted to go move a dead cat. This much we could communicate to each other without words.

"Probably a present from one of my admirers," my father said finally. "Don't you think?"

"What in the hell," I offered.

"I can't believe they left her here," I heard a man say. He was the black man I'd seen above the garage. He was running toward the house, moving quickly. He was wearing fine gray slacks and a white dress shirt, which he began to unbutton.

"I told them not to do it," he said, taking my father's keys. "I told them I'd find her a home."

A few moments later he wrapped his shirt around the cat as a makeshift body bag. It was a Sunday morning, and he was, I realized, dressed for church.

His name was Lem Dawson. He was a small man, with tiny hands, chewed nails, a corona of white hair from temple to temple, and a hint of the South in his vowels. He was a smoker, and his clothes betrayed this whenever he passed by me. It had been his responsibility to prepare for our visit, and to do so he'd turned the soil in the gardens, putting beach plums into the ground, pink tulips, and white hydrangeas with blossoms as big as softballs. Because the locks had been changed, he said that he hadn't been able to stock our refrigerator with the jams and freshly prospected littlenecks he said we would love. He said this to us when we met him, his hand out to shake my father's, an overture my dad refused. "What's a little-neck?" my father asked. "Is that a kind of chicken?" My mother refused to shake his hand, too. All she wanted from him was that he check the house twice over for any other abandoned house pets. "Please," she said, still quivering. "Make sure it's clear."

The house itself was spare, white, the floorboards bleached, the back windows open to the water. Salt air in the kitchen. Twin wicker settees in the living room, a shipman's lanterns on a side table, a tide chart, two years old, folded on the lip of a broken radiator like a road map. We went back into the kitchen, where my father stood, one hand on the stove's handle, one on his belt, breathing vigorously, his nostrils flared. "I really like this house," he said, and then he took his shoes off, and then his socks. He rolled his pants up above his knees while both Lem Dawson and I stood and watched, and then he walked out through the back door, leaving it open, his feet in the high grass, mosquitoes buzzing as he went. I saw him stand out on the shore for a while, looking blankly at the sea before he disappeared down to the beach.

My mother was on the telephone with Robert, who had stayed behind in New York to close up the rented houses in Wren's Bridge, and who was planning to come north the following week, carrying with him everything my mother had just bought for our new home: French linens, new breakfast china, the paperback romance novels that she would love no matter her level of wealth, and all the heaps of beach clothing she'd picked out from Abercrombie & Fitch. I could hear her in the hallway off the kitchen. "It's fine here," she was saying. "But it's in the middle of nowhere. I told him we should go to the Catskills. That's where everyone else is. Arthur thinks he knows everything. Oh, Robert, I'm bored already. And there was a dead cat. Have I told you about the cat, yet? Maybe you should send a car for me."

I was left alone in the kitchen with Lem. He'd changed his clothes. He leaned back against the counter, a blue work shirt unbuttoned, a stained white undershirt on underneath, khaki trousers hitched above the ankle, green-and-blue striped socks, a pack of cigarettes in his hand. He had a thin mustache, as delicate as if he'd drawn it with a marker. He saw me, looked down to his hands, and then raised his eyebrows.

"Your papa let you smoke?" he asked. "Or does he think you're too young?"

I shook my head. "No. I probably shouldn't."

Still, he held out the pack for me. I looked out to see if my father was nearby before I grabbed one.

It was our first conversation. Even then,

Lem could see how much sway my father
held over me.

THREE

That first week was brutal, heat in waves from the steel girders on the boat docks, the birds dunking their heads in the onrushing tide to cool themselves. Inside, our new house sweltered. Even with the windows open, we had no relief. My mother grew quickly irritated, first with the heat, and then with the house itself. Having decided that she disliked the furniture that had come with the place — all the wicker and the white wood end tables and the nautical bric-a-brac — she set off for Boston to buy something that fit her style. Whatever that style was; until now she'd never had the money to really know. She'd always loved home decor magazines, collecting them when we lived in New Haven and keeping the pictures she liked in a series of carefully organized paper folders, but our house was nothing like the ones she'd seen in *Better Homes and Gardens* or *House Beautiful,*

those open rooms full of Tiffany lamps or
wax-dripped candelabras. This was rustic. It
was spare. Some of the windows were
painted shut. The bugs near the sea bothered her. So did the scent of seaweed, and
the faint tracks of loose sand that were suddenly everywhere. My father, though, had
none of these problems. He'd installed
himself in one of the bedrooms on the
house's second floor, a room to which he'd
taken so much paperwork, an antique roll-
top, an Underwood Universal, and a loud
electric fan. He had Lem place a fresh bowl
of iced water under the fan every hour. At
first my father called him by his name, the
way he'd call after a bartender he knew: *Mr.
Lem Dawson! Mr. Lem Dawson!* But on the
last day of that week, when we were all waiting around for Robert and my mother to
come, he lost his patience. From then on he
called Lem *Boy!*

Regarding Lem: our first night in the
house, my father pulled me aside and told
me to stay away from him or, if I couldn't,
to keep to myself around him. I wasn't supposed to let Lem know anything about us.
Not our sudden wealth, not our family history, not our address in New York, not even
that we were Jews. He said this to me in the
front room. It was dark. My father was

drinking. He claimed that he was concerned about his privacy. Bluepoint wasn't a popular vacation spot for somebody of my father's new social status, but it made a great deal of sense, he told me, if what you wanted was to be left alone. "You want to be left alone?" I asked him.

"When I'm here, I don't want anybody to be able to find me."

"Why's that?" I asked.

"Because sometimes men just need a place to go. To retreat. To be away. That's why I bought this place." He told me that Bluepoint appeared so infrequently, even on good maps, that a man determined to find us might not even be capable of doing so. But I knew that what my father was truly worried about was having someone like Lem, which is to say a Negro, living so near us, carrying with him all of what my father considered to be the various indignities of a man of his race. He didn't need to tell me that he was worried about being called upon to serve as an attorney for an aggrieved black man; I could see it on him. There was a noticeable hitch in his voice whenever the subject of Lem was raised, a breaking point in his speech, his apprehension becoming clear. My father, for all his apparent gifts, his certain, precise locution, his big, brash voice, his ability to sway a jury, never learned to wear his circumspection well. He believed such a thing — this was his word of choice, and by *thing* he meant involving himself in any small way in the matters of the struggles of black Americans — was a trap he wouldn't be able to extricate himself from. He'd said as much to Robert Ashley once, in New Haven, when Robert had wanted to take on a black man as a client. "The last thing I need are these people after me for help. God knows how they are when they know someone's on their side. Everything's a fucking church sermon." Still, he kept him on. My father liked having somebody to do things for him. He liked ordering people around. My father thrived on control.

For all of his abilities, he had no general skills as a parent — no ability to cook, other than to open a can, something he did with a serviceman's utility, cleaving the lid whole with the knife he'd been given in the war. And for a while that first week, with my mother in Boston, we subsisted that way, on condensed soup for lunch and dinner, even in the heat, just the way we'd done in New Haven when we couldn't afford any better. Because of the heat we ate outside at a badly worn picnic table off the patio. It was red as a Radio Flyer, chewed at by wood beetles, flanked only by one bench, so that we had to eat side by side. It was the only time in our life that we did this. Lem offered to make our meals. He was a decent cook, he said, and could make for us food far better than a scalding bowl of tomato broth. "That's what I'm here for," he said. To which my father replied: "I haven't figured out exactly why you're here."

Most of the time we ate in total silence. I tried to talk to him about baseball, about how the Red Sox were faring now that Ted Williams was off in Korea. I even tried to talk to him about what I wanted to study when I went off to Dartmouth in the fall, but he couldn't be bothered to pay much attention to me. He had other cases coming up, other clients. Planes kept crashing, law suits kept arriving. There was work that needed to be done on the house, on Robert's house. There were people constantly calling to talk to him, to interview him, to ask him for legal advice. There was my mother to worry about. And there was Lem, always at the edge of our meals, hovering, waiting for my father to give him direction or orders. The tension between all of us — between Lem and my father and me — was clear and uncomfortable. Every meal seemed to make it worse, the quiet between us deepening, Lem watching us in silence from a cinder-block bench he'd fashioned outside the garage.

This all began to change our second Sunday at Bluepoint. My father was awake earlier than usual. The weather had cooled finally, and fog from the bay had come across to the sea side of the Cape. Robert Ashley was coming that afternoon with my mother. He'd called the night before and suggested that we put some flowers around the place to spruce it up. "That might make Ruthie feel better about all this," he told my dad. "She might stop saying that you made such a big mistake buying this place." Early that morning my father walked out into the backyard, up the rickety catwalk staircase that led to Lem Dawson's apartment, and knocked loudly on his door. He wanted Lem to drive out into town, buy the flowers, come back, and do the plantings. I'd have done it myself if he'd asked. I had my license now, and I was itching for the chance to drive my father's new Cadillac, or to do anything, really, other than the very little I was doing. Lem answered the door slowly, as if he already knew that his day was about to be ruined. I was down in the yard, watching all of this. It'd taken me a few tries, but

I'd finally hung a tire from the backyard poplar. Even though I hadn't pitched my last season in high school, I still figured I had a decent chance to make the squad at Dartmouth. It was, after all, the Ivy League. How good did I really need to be?

Lem had music going. Piano, trumpet, an insistent high hat. He was wearing a suit. I heard my father's voice. "What's this? Where do you think *you're* going?"

A car pulled up to the house just then. It was a Packard, most of the name carved out over the grille — the second *A* was missing. Its muffler was dislodged from the undercarriage, and as it slowed to park behind my father's Cadillac, the bottom end of the car scraped against a high bump in the ground. At the wheel was a black man about Lem's age but with large, round eyeglasses, a dark suit, and a thin gray tie. Beside him was a young woman in a wide-brimmed white hat. My father grabbed hold of the railing. "What's the big idea, boy? You throwing a party at my house? You call the whole goddamned NAACP over for a clambake?"

They got out of the Packard, the young woman shielding her eyes from the sun and then resting her back against the car door, her hands set nervously behind her. She had on a halter-neck dress, red with small white

49

spots, her shoulders bare. My father slapped a closed fist against the banister. Everyone looked up, and I saw the man, his arm on the hood of the Packard, laugh quietly to himself. My father disappeared into Lem's apartment.

The man at the Packard scoffed again and then turned his attention to me. "What are you trying to do?" he asked. He adjusted his eyeglasses with the point of his finger.

"Trying to get it through the tire," I said, holding up the ball.

"That's it?" The man laughed. "That's not hard."

"With a curveball," I said, trying to make what had been an impossible task sound relatively simple.

"Might hurt your arm if you do it wrong," he said, walking toward me. "You know that, don't you?" He reached out to touch my shoulder slightly, and instinctively, at the glancing contact, I looked up fearfully to see if my father had seen. I was relieved he hadn't.

I blew air through my teeth. Of course I'd never heard anything about hurting your arm. I was a hack of a pitcher. Real pitchers were artists. I was the worst kind: a pretender. "I know," I said. "Everybody knows that."

The door to Lem's apartment was still open. It was clear they were arguing, even though by now my father was making sure to lower his voice. He'd come out onto the landing, looked out at the water, and then turned back to Lem. His fists were clenched, and periodically he pointed down to the flower bed or to the piles of mulch or the back porch, which was strewn with birdseed and leaves. I heard my mother's name uttered, and then Robert Ashley's name, and then I saw my father look at his wristwatch, as if to say that there wasn't much time left in the day before they arrived together.

I'd made my way over to stand beside the girl. She was pretty, and dressed up, and I wanted to talk to her. I'd been out at the beach for a week, basically in the middle of nowhere, with no one to talk to but my dad. She looked about my age, and about as uncomfortable to be here as I did. While I was standing there beside her, the man took our picture with a small camera.

"Would you put that damn thing away," she said, shooing him away with her hand.

"What? You two make a good picture," he said, smiling.

She looked at me. "He won this stupid camera playing poker."

"Twenty-one," he said. "Not poker."

"Now he's shooting off pictures every five seconds," she said. "Thinks he knows what he's doing with it."

"Fine," he said, putting the camera back inside his car. Then he turned to me. "If we can't take pictures, let's see the boy go at it, then."

"See what?" I asked.

"Your curve. Show me what you got."

"Oh, I don't know," I said. "I'm just practicing."

He came and took the ball. "You can't do it. You're bluffing me. Let me show you how to do it."

"That's Charles Ewing," the girl said as he went away. She'd come toward me, walking slowly, just as Charles stalked off with my ball. She seemed less interested in me than she was in the view behind me — the sea, the dunes, a blue tarp the team of carpenters had left on what was to become Robert's house. After a moment, she sighed, her shoulders rising and then falling. "You never heard of him, have you? Before this minute, you never heard of a guy named Charles Ewing, right?"

"No," I said.

"Thought so," she said.

"Should I have heard of him?"

"You like baseball?"

I nodded. And then laughed a little. "I *love* baseball."

"Then you ought to know Charles Ewing," she said. She pursed her lips doubtfully. "According to him, that is."

Charles was walking deliberately across the grass. He was, I realized, counting off sixty paces.

"He's always trying to prove himself," she said, snickering. "Even to kids."

"I'm not a kid," I said.

She looked me up and down. I was in short pants, bare feet; my hair hadn't been cut in weeks. "You could've fooled me," she said, smiling.

Although I was usually terrible at this sort of thing, and although it seemed impossible to me, the thought crossed my mind that she might be flirting back at me. "So what? Is he your father or something?" I asked.

The sun was in her eyes. She put up a hand to shield herself. Her expression was suspicious, her head tilted away from me, an infinitely small calibration of doubt. She smiled in a way that I took to mean that he might have been her father, but even if he was, it was none of my business.

"You all live here?" she asked, looking beyond me now, out at the water.

"Yeah," I said.

She raised an eyebrow. "So all of this is yours?"

I turned. "Not all of it," I said.

"But a lot of it?"

"I guess."

"Damn." A high, long whistle split between her teeth.

"My father's a lawyer," I said.

"He a lawyer for a president or something?"

"No," I said.

"He famous?" she asked.

I nodded. "Kind of."

"That's what I heard," she said. "On the way over here, I heard we were going to see some famous person's house. That's why I bought myself a new dress." She ran her hands down from her neck to her waist like a showroom model. This was supposed to be a joke. I realized this a moment too late, and she smirked dismissively at me. I guess I had overlooked what were obvious signs of wear in her outfit: loose threads, a tiny hole on the hem, a soft, dull stain at her navel. It wasn't a new dress at all. Her shoes were worn, the buckle on her left foot assisted by twine.

She pointed down toward Robert's house. "That your place, also?"

"That's my father's colleague's house," I said.

"He famous, too?"

"Not as much," I said.

Then she whistled again. "Y'all got an entire corner of the world, don't you?" she said, smiling, her teeth showing finally. Her hair moved — she had it tied behind her with a white ribbon — and when it did I could smell the sugar in her shampoo. "That must be nice."

I felt so quickly incapable of moving at the proper speed, or at any speed, really, as if by smiling at me, she'd actually took hold of my ankles or my shoulders. This had happened before, in Wren's Bridge with Pauline McNamee. After she'd kissed me, I'd just frozen stiff. She'd wanted to kiss me again, had even leaned in to do it, but I couldn't. I was stuck, in shock. Now it was happening again. She was saying something to me, but I'd missed it. I was thinking about the fact that she was clearly, undoubtedly flirting with me, and that I was clearly flirting with her. Now she'd noticed that I was in a daze, so she repeated what she'd said. "It must be nice to be that *rich*," she said. What I wanted to say in response was that two years ago we'd been living in New Haven in four rented rooms; that this, our corner of the world, was so new that I still woke up in the morning thinking I was elsewhere. But I didn't do anything except blink foolishly at her. She was like a comic-book villain: by looking at me calmly she'd obliterated any trace of my intelligence or charm or wit — really, any trace of my personality.

Finally, she stepped toward me — a wonderful moment of terror — and put her hand on my shoulder.

"What is it?" I whispered.

She pointed behind me, out to where Charles was standing on the grass, tossing the ball in his hand. I was standing between him and the tire.

"You're in his way," she whispered.

"Oh."

"Yeah." She grinned. She knew I was a wreck. "I think he wants to show you how good he is."

"Right," I said.

"First thing you want to do," Charles called out to me, "is disguise the pitch in your hand."

"Oh please," the girl called out. "Stop giving a lecture to the boy."

"I got ten that he misses," I said.

"He won't miss," she said. "Unfortunately for all of us." And then, to Charles: "You're a show-off!"

He turned and scowled. "I'm gonna show him how to throw this thing right. His daddy sure not doing it." He looked up over his left shoulder at Lem's apartment. My father was still inside, and periodically the sound of his angry, recriminating, exacting voice came down onto the lawn. At this, Charles let out a burst of cocky laughter, and then, a moment later, he whipped a blazingly paced curveball across the grass, his windup as perfect as an illustration in a textbook, his arms clasped behind his head and then pumping in front of his chest. The kick of his right leg propelled the rest of his body, his chest perpendicular to the ground for the briefest instant. The ball sailed toward the tire — there was never a doubt it wouldn't ace the thing — with such speed that I took a sharp, shocked breath at the sight of it. And then, just as it seemed the ball had begun to rise a bit high, the speed of its trajectory lifting it on the wind, the pitch broke, just like someone had swatted it out of the air. It was the finest pitch I'd ever witnessed.

Above us, my father and Lem appeared on the staircase. Now Lem was dressed in his coveralls and his work shoes. Charles saw this and then looked down at his feet before he quickly and wordlessly walked back to the Packard. The girl lingered for a moment, looking out at the water, and then up at Lem with what I knew was an expression of deep disappointment. When she walked past me to get back to the car, I asked her quietly what her name was.

"Savannah," she said. She didn't look me in the eyes. "It was nice to meet you." She lowered her head and gave me half of a humiliating curtsy. "Sorry we disturbed your day."

My father went off toward the house before the Packard left, Charles backing up down the long drive, his muffler once again scraping the dirt. Savannah had pulled the brim on her hat down on her face. To hide, I figured. At the sight of the car backing up, Lem cried out to my father.

"It's Sunday," he said. "Least you can do is let a man go worship."

My father turned, one hand on the handle to the patio door. "Least you can do is shut the fuck up and do what I'm paying you to do. How's that?"

I stood for a long while, holding the baseball. Lem eventually took his shears and got onto his knees to begin pruning flowers.

"Who were those people?" I asked. "Are they family?"

He rolled his eyes. "I got things to do, Hilly. In case you haven't heard."

"Is she your niece or something? Savannah?"

He seemed surprised that I knew her name. "Look," he said, the points of the shears in his hand sharp, new, and polished. It was hot. Already he had sweat on his forehead, perhaps from the weather, perhaps from arguing with my father. He lowered the shears so that they were pointed at me. "I got orders to get back to work. So how about you leave me alone."

FOUR

Most mornings my father was at his desk by eight. The racket of his Underwood would wake me. He was always typing. A mile down the shore, Robert Ashley was doing the same thing. His house was a twin of ours except that he lacked a telephone connection. Apparently, when the houses were being built, the local telephone company had balked at trying to run a line that far out toward the water. Because of this, dozens of times a day my father called Lem to his office to hand him a sealed envelope, or a stack of papers, or sometimes a box of documents, with the instructions to run it over across the beach to Robert. And Robert did the same, exchanging my father's papers with a set of his own, so that all during the morning and early afternoon, I could find Lem running their mail back and forth. They typed on carbon paper, so every document existed in double, one for each of their files. For Lem, the trips between the houses weighed twice as much as they should have.

He took the beach path, which at that point included a boardwalk built from rickety blue planks. When the boardwalk ended there were rocks and sand. The road between our houses was paved, but Lem claimed that it was shorter to go by the beach. He'd make the first of his trips quickly, running down the slope behind our house and off toward Robert's back door. Lem kept a key to Robert's house on a ring he had clipped to his belt. He ran because he had other chores to do — he cooked breakfast for my mother, he tended to the gardens, he folded linens, he did our laundry, he cleaned our bathrooms, he straightened our various messes, and he unpacked whatever it was that my mother had bought that week. There were, just in the first month alone, nearly two dozen deliveries: beach furniture, wicker picnic baskets, hats from Paul Stuart, tweed from Oxley & Hawlings, tubes of zinc oxide from Leifbaums, boxes of Florida oranges, insect repellent, English gin, Old Gold cigarettes, crates of Dewar's, Christofle stemware, and furniture from Florence Knoll. Even though Lem was a very good runner, by late in the afternoon, after he'd done the trip a dozen times, I'd find him exhausted, sweating, crouched at a low crook among the dunes where he thought nobody could see him. I knew that the arrangement made Robert uncomfortable. I'd see him out in the yard, watching Lem run, something close to remorse on his face, a glass of water waiting in his hand. But my father didn't care whether Lem was tired or whether making a grown man do something so ridiculous was beneath his stature. When I complained to him and said that perhaps Lem might be better off using a car, or at the least a bicycle, my father laughed at me. "First off, Hilly, I offered him the Cadillac. My new Cadillac. *And* a bicycle. I even offered to buy him a motorcycle. He turned it all down. Says he likes the outdoors. Likes the water."

"He was just being nice," I said. "Obviously he needs *something.*"

"*Nice?* What does that even mean? Either you want a bike or you don't. It's not that hard a concept to get."

"It's cruel, making him run like that."

"So, you're telling me I've got the one colored boy in all America who can't manage a simple run, Hilly? Men like him got an engine. Only thing that stops them is their laziness. And that's congenital, Hilly. It's my job to get him moving. And if you catch him slacking, it's your job, too."

After a month of watching Lem struggle under my father's orders, I found myself in such a position. I heard him struggling as he came up the bluff. The last bit near our house was the toughest, purely and steeply uphill. He had a crate in his arms the size of an apple box and, on top of that, a pile of envelopes balanced in two stacks. All of them were emblazoned with the familiar square art deco logo of Wise & Ashley. It was the *W* that had become so iconic: the two columns on either side, like glass skyscrapers rising, their serifs like balustrades, the connection at the center marked with a barely perceptible pearl.

Lem glared at me, panting.

"Hi there," I offered.

Another long moment. His eyes on me. I wondered what was darker: his irises or his pupils. I had iced tea beside me. The glass sweated. He'd brewed it that morning. His brow flickered.

"How about grabbing something," he said.

I saw his fingers flex beneath the box.

"Uh —" I stood up. Instinctively I looked to see if my father was watching me. This was certainly not allowed. Helping Lem.

Helping any man like Lem. The curtains at my father's window stirred in the sea breeze. They were new curtains, of course, bright blue, stitched from fine cotton, ordered from Wanamaker's or Bloomingdale's or Saks. Maybe even from Paris; Printemps. There was the faint murmur of my father's radio; he listened to the news all afternoon.

"Just take the box, at least," he said.

"You made it all this way," I said. "It's just another few steps."

"Can I have a sip of your iced tea?" he asked.

I looked down at my cup. The imprint of my lips was clear on the glass. I hated acting like this.

"I might be getting sick," I said. I held it in my hands. "But I guess, if you need it."

He turned around toward the house, also trying, it was clear, to see if my father was watching us. Finally, when Lem was content that my father was, as usual, locked in his office, or drunkenly examining all the new things my mother had bought, he dropped everything onto the ground. He put his hands onto his knees.

"Are you OK?" I asked.

"Oh, now you're interested?"

"I was interested before," I said.

"Usually, when someone asks for help, a

man gives it."

I was quiet. He had the box between his legs. The letters had become shuffled. There were perhaps a dozen of them. Droplets of sweat fell onto the top envelope in a crisp, wet rhythm. That would make my father angry — the sweat, the drops. Lem continued to suck for air. Behind him there were birds out over the water. Far out, there was a lighthouse, visible only on the clearest days. Sun had burned through the clouds in stripes. It was a gorgeous afternoon, and this was a beautiful place to sit to see it; it occurred to me that maybe he took the path by the beach to be closer to it all.

He arched his back. "Your damn father's got me running every other minute."

I frowned. "Sorry."

"He's trying to kill me."

"I doubt that."

"No," Lem said. "He told me. He said: 'This case is going to get so tough, I might end up killing you before summer's over.' "

"He was joking," I said.

Lem tried to right himself, thought better of it, and clutched again at his knees. "Said he'd need to shoot me if I pulled up limp. Like I'm a goddamned horse."

"It's a joke. Trust me."

"Is he watching me? Turn and see. He

watching me?"

I turned. My father's office window was empty. "No," I said.

"All right, then," he said, looking at his wristwatch, "I'm gonna get a glass of water. Change my shirt. Then I'll get this to him."

"Maybe you should do that after you deliver the letters," I said.

He scoffed at me, stood up, and went off toward his apartment, grabbing the box with his hand, and then the letters, his feet heavy on the staircase, the wood creaking beneath him, the entire structure swaying in the light wind.

"Why are you taking it all upstairs if you have to bring it back down?" I asked.

He turned and smiled. "Your dad says I'm not supposed to let this out of my sight. He also said he might shoot me. So, you do the math."

He moved slowly, hunched, every step an effort. As he got to the top of the staircase, wind blew some of the letters down onto the ground. Lem hadn't noticed. I went to fetch them. Beside the logo of Wise & Ashley was a simple red stamp: BROOKLYN.

Brooklyn stood for a case my father and Robert had that year against the New York City Subway System. A man named Rooney had lost his foot on the tracks beneath Flatbush Avenue and was suing the city over what he and my father claimed were dangerous working conditions. The case involved a dump truck's worth of paperwork, and most if not all of what Lem ferried back and forth that summer were documents my father and Robert called the Brooklyn Pages. Often, he'd call Lem into his office to give him a new stack, and say something like, "Another slim volume to add to the Brooklyn Pages." By the second week of the summer, the volume of the traffic involving these pages grew. And as I stood that day on the beach, with those envelopes that the wind had blown off Lem's stack, I worried for him. If any of these envelopes went missing, my father would go ballistic. "Lem!" I yelled, calling up. "You dropped something."

I turned to see my father's window. The shades were pulled.

"Lem!" I tried again, before climbing up the stairs.

I went slowly at first, afraid of what I might find, or of what might happen to me if I were found. His apartment was a small space, with two rooms, each of them without any furniture aside from a mattress and a row of bookshelves. In neat, orderly piles set up beside his bed, he had his clothing arranged by color. Through the open bathroom door, I could see a duplicate of the uniform my father required, hanging on a hook. In his kitchen, behind a louvered window that looked down onto the yard, he had a row of Christmas cactuses, each of them a different shade of red.

"Got those in Mexico," he said, coming up from behind me, seeing that I was captivated by them. "A few years back. Nice, right?"

I touched my finger to a thin point on the cactus nearest me. "When were you in Mexico?" I asked.

He smiled. "A few years ago. 'Forty-seven and 'forty-eight. Good country. Big. Hot as hell."

"What were you doing there?" I didn't know how to ask him whether he'd been in Mexico doing what he was doing here, working as another man's servant, just the way he was for my father, but he seemed to understand this.

"I'm no professional houseboy, Hilly. If that's what you're getting at."

I blushed. "I didn't say that."

"You wanted to," he said. He had on a fresh shirt, white, crisp, the color of a bleached sail, and he buttoned it slowly.

"I did not," I said.

He grinned. "Fine. You were thinking it,

though."

On the wall beside me was a photograph of two people I assumed were his parents: his elderly mother and father, standing in coveralls against a whitewashed barn, their expressions flat and serious. Tacked above this was a photograph of an older woman, a white woman with white hair, holding a house cat. He pointed at the cat.

"Recognize her?" he asked.

I squinted. And then I put my hand over my mouth. "Is it?"

He nodded. "Name was Ernest," he said. "Funny name for a girl cat, isn't it?"

"Funny name for a cat, period."

"Funny lady," he said.

"Who is she?"

He buttoned his shirt, then folded the cuffs up above his elbows. "Lady Henckin," he said. "She's who lived here before you. I met her in Mexico. And she brought me here. It's a long story with a sad ending, so I'll just cut it right there."

"Why's it sad?"

He shrugged. "Well, y'all live here now," he said. "That's why."

I laughed. He was always joking and laughing, and I had simply expected this to be another one of his jokes. But he had begun to lift my father's box of documents off the ground and had turned to the door when I called him back.

"Wait," I said.

"What now, Hilly? I got things to do. Your daddy probably wants me to go change the oil in his car or something."

"Why were you in Mexico? What were you doing there?"

"I was trying it out," he said.

"What do you mean, trying it out? Trying what out? What does that mean?"

"Trying it out. Seeing if I liked it."

"Liked it for what?"

"For living there. For being someplace else. Other than where I was from."

"Which is where?"

He paused, put the box down. I was exhausting him.

"Georgia," he said, slowly. "Macon, Georgia. You heard of it?"

"Of course," I said. I pointed at the photograph of the elderly couple. "These your parents?"

He shook his head. "Grandparents." I thought he might say something about them, but he wouldn't even look at their picture.

"So you were thinking of just *moving* to Mexico?" I asked. The concept seemed ridiculous.

"For a minute," he said, and then he seemed to laugh quietly to himself. "It didn't last long. Believe it or not, I actually prefer it up here."

"*Here* here?" I asked.

"Up until a few months ago," he said, "yes."

"*Up until a few months ago,*" I repeated. "Until we moved here?"

"Exactly."

"What were you *really* doing in Mexico?" Now that I was in his apartment, I wanted to know more about him. We'd been here a month, and I'd watched him run up and down the beach and do countless errands for my mom and dad. But there was more to him. I knew it. I'd seen it in him when Savannah and Charles Ewing had come by that day, and I saw it now.

He pointed beyond the bookshelf, to a space on the floor where a large leather portfolio and a smaller black box lay against the wall. They were unmarked, and, like everything in Lem's apartment, they were immaculately clean.

"What are they?"

"My paintings and drawings are inside. Paintings in the portfolio. Drawings in the box."

I laughed mockingly. "You paint and

71

draw? That's what you were doing in Mexico?"

"Do you ask so many questions because your father's a lawyer? Or is that just something you do on your own?"

I went to open it and he stopped me.

"No," he said. "You can't open it."

"Why?"

"The work's not finished."

"So?"

"A real artist doesn't show work that's not finished."

"Oh," I said, laughing. "So you're a *real* artist?"

"Are you being smart?"

"I just didn't expect it from you, that's all."

He leered at me. "What's that's supposed to mean? I don't look like a real artist?"

"I don't know what a real artist looks like, I guess."

"Probably not a man that looks like me, though, right?"

"Oh, come on. I didn't say that."

"Well, you got my life story now."

"So," I said, "are you any good?"

"Why are you so interested all the sudden? I've been here a month with you, and you barely said hello."

I could have told him that my father had

told me not to have anything to do with him. But I had the sense that Lem already knew this.

"Just because my father's the way he is," I said, letting the thought hang for a moment, "doesn't mean I can't be friendly. Or friends."

This made him laugh. "All right. Let's get going, Hilly." He waved me to the door.

"No," I said. "I'd like to see what's in there. Come on. Please. Show me one. I'm interested."

He bit his lip. "I can't," he said.

"I'll pay you," I said.

"You people and your money," he said.

"Are you nervous about what I'll say?"

"I just don't do that," he said.

"Do what? Show people your paintings?"

He shifted uneasily. "I'm a perfectionist," he said.

"So nobody's ever seen it?"

"Lady Henckin did."

"She was the only person? You've only shown one person?"

"Pretty much."

"That's crazy! You're *nervous*," I said. "Admit it. Show me. I'll be nice."

He shook his head. "Not gonna happen."

"So. What happened to her?" I asked.

"Cancer. Got her lungs. At least, that's

73

what I heard." He touched his hand to his chin. He had the hint of a white beard growing. "One day they left. Changed the locks on me. Then you showed up. That's basically what happened."

"Why'd you show her your paintings and nobody else?"

"She was nice," he said, shrugging.

"I'll be nice."

"You're not as nice as her."

"How do you know that?"

"You wouldn't give me a sip of your iced tea."

I blushed again, but this time, I could tell the effect was more pronounced, an itching redness up from my neck to my brow. Seeing this, Lem cocked his head and winked pitifully at me. "After she died," he said, "I thought I'd move. Thought I'd go somewhere new. Go to Paris. You ever been there?"

"Paris?" I asked. "As in Paris, France?"

He nodded. I blinked. Lem lit a cigarette. They were hand rolled and smelled hard and crisp. He offered me one, grinning slyly.

"Other people are doing it," he said. "Going to France. People like me."

"Is that so?" I asked.

He stood beside me, nodding and looking out toward the window, full of its usual view: the sky, striated with clouds, bruised blue at its edges; the white dunes; daisies near the porch, planted close to each other, like sisters; paint chipping from the house. The light was on his face, the smoke from his cigarette escaping him slowly.

"You think you'll just move out to Paris, be some fancy French painter?" I asked.

"Sure beats being here, being your father's carrier pigeon." He didn't turn to look at me. "I'd done every sort of job a man can do. Cooked, cleaned, built houses in Atlanta, lugged fruit in California. I shot armadillos for two weeks in Texas. And I *like* armadillos. But this, Hilly, this is the worst."

"Then leave," I said.

"Not that easy," he said. He shook his head. Every word came out slowly. "Not that easy."

"He's gonna get Robert a phone. It'll get better," I said.

"I don't understand why they don't just work in the same office," he said.

I smiled. "My father hates having people around. I don't know if you've noticed that."

He laughed. I looked for a place to ash my cigarette, and he gave me a small dish.

"Really, though," I said, "I'm sure Robert will get a phone."

Lem narrowed his eyes at me when I said this. "I'll believe it when I see it, Hilly. Besides. I got a plan. I won't be here long. I'm getting out. Gotta do what you gotta do. You know?"

Beneath us, my father walked out onto the deck, a tumbler in his hand. We both watched him. He wore white trousers and a navy collared shirt. It was past noon. He was looking out at the ocean, and the wind was on him; he looked content. Lem grunted. I watched my father a while longer. He squinted out at the water. Ever since Boston Airways, there was always so much trouble in his expression, as if he expected at any moment to have to fight to fend off thieves.

"I read that your father knows the name of every person in that crash," Lem said. "Is that true?"

It surprised me to hear Lem mention the case. I'm not sure why I supposed that he wouldn't have heard of my father, or why, once we'd moved to Bluepoint, Lem wouldn't have done some of his own research. Especially here. The Boston Airways flight had cascaded right over Cape Cod before it crashed in Rhode Island.

"That's probably bullshit," I said.

This made him laugh. "You think so?"

"Half the stuff in those articles people write about him is bullshit," I said.

"People say all that money he's got is nothing but blood money," Lem said.

I must have looked blankly at him. "I don't know if that's true," I said. "Someone hired him. He did his job. That's the system we have."

In the window's reflection I saw Lem raise his eyebrows when I said this. He didn't want to engage me in an argument any more than I wanted to engage him. He left the room for a moment, to refill his glass or to change his pants, and when he did, I wondered why I'd come to my father's defense so quickly. This was the way it went between fathers and sons, I figured. No matter the disagreements, no matter the undesirable trace of yourself that you saw in your father, sometimes there was still a pull to loyalty. It was an instinct to unlearn. I could still remember the very beginning of it all, when he'd had me sit down at the kitchen table and look over the blueprints of that plane.

If I'd wanted to, I could have looked at Lem's paintings then. The box was sitting there. The portfolio was resting against the wall. The room was empty. But I wouldn't do it. Instead, I got up to look around his

room. Everything seemed assiduously organized: the linens on his bed had been
creased with hospital corners; his floors
didn't have any dust; his windows were so
perfectly clear that the point at which the
glass ended and the outdoors began seemed
somehow inexact. I looked at his books.
Most of them were books about painters.
On a small wooden desk was a pile of writing paper, a black pen, and a rubber stamp,
which I turned over. It had his initials, *L.
D.,* the letters square, firm, respectable.
Beside all of this was an Underwood typewriter, black, fairly new, just like my father's.

That was when I saw, at the bottom of a
pile of papers at the corner of his desk,
beside a small black jewelry case, the clear,
unmistakable *W* in the logo of Wise & Ashley. It was the torn mouth of an envelope,
the teeth of the paper calling attention to
itself. I looked behind me for Lem, heard
him in the kitchen, the water running, a
glass chiming, rinsing. Quickly, I pulled at
the envelope. Two came with it. Both had
already been opened, both were addressed
to Robert, both were done so in my father's
drunken, smeared, left-handed penmanship.
I looked back again. More water, Lem's
footsteps, the sound of a dish towel coming
off cheap plastic rollers. So gently, I puck-

ered open the envelope. The look of the type from my father's Underwood was something I knew well. He wore a ribbon down to its last moments, so stingy, even when he was so rich; the sentence was short and the type was faint, streaked.

I saw only this: *By now you know that people are trying to poach me.*

"Hilly," Lem called out. I dropped the letter. "I gotta get going."

FIVE

Newsreel footage from the period shows my father with a limp, which is something I don't remember about him. To see it now raises my suspicions. It's a stiff-legged thing, his right leg locked at the knee. There were footraces at the North Atlantic Yacht Club most weeks. We joined because my father didn't have a choice. For a man of his stature, with his money, it would have appeared unseemly to reject their invitations, and my father, if nothing else, had become a slave to social conventions since Boston Airways. (That my father was a Jew and that the club's unofficial stance toward Jews was not something anyone would consider kosher didn't seem to matter to him. My father was famous. What club doesn't want a famous member?) Quickly after he joined, they made him governor. The footraces came about spontaneously, usually at the bad end of some drunken bragging. He didn't always win these races — I have photographs that show, clearly, Robert Ashley besting the field by a good distance — although club journal reports from the time indicate that he did win more than a few. That he could win a race with a bad leg leads me to believe that the limp was something he affected when in the presence of someone truly distinguished. Plainly put: I think he was faking it.

A short news clip of my father from the summer of 1952 shows him beside an associate of Jack Kennedy, at that time the congressman from Massachusetts's Eleventh District. Kennedy, in '52, was a few months away from running against Henry Cabot Lodge for the commonwealth's Senate seat and had sent an emissary to curry favor with my father — a needless trip, for my father was a conservative in the most stringent sense: aggressive in his stance toward Communism, aggressive in his stance toward regulations of the market, and aggressive toward what he considered the cowardice of liberalism. This was a secret, of course. My father had become something of a liberal hero since bankrupting Boston Airways, protecting the little guy against huge corporate interests. But to mention Franklin Roosevelt in his presence was to arm my father unnecessarily with an hour's worth of anger against the man he liked to call the Dictator from Hyde Park. To mention Kennedy — both his father, the ambassador, whom my father tolerated despite his advocacy of European appeasement, and the son, who was considered widely, especially on the Cape, to be a gallivanter — was to see my father at his most gleeful. This, he liked to say, laughing, is what our future opposition looks like. And by *this,* I think he meant the specter of a young Jack Kennedy: lanky, promiscuous, wildly juvenile.

In the clip, my father is joking with someone off camera — my copy of the film doesn't contain the original sound, just a post-production voice-over wondering about the congressman's future plans. My father has a wide, easy smile and is terribly young and, in some ways, very awkward. He's wearing a brown hat and at a certain point is shown walking beside Kennedy's guy, limping, his left foot dragging, swinging, landing softly. This is at our home, and there are beauty shots of the sea, the back face of our house, my mother at thirty-five, wearing a white summer dress and a scarf, smiling, waving, playing with someone's golden Labrador. Everything to her is still new and wonderful.

My father is on camera, speaking for only a moment. He is walking, limping. This time, it's his left leg. Asked whether he has any aspirations to seek government office, he answers flatly:

"The money isn't anywhere good enough."

Interesting to me, though, is a fleeting image of Lem Dawson. With the film strung up on an editing table, it's possible to slow it enough to see Lem emerging from his apartment door. The camera is panning quickly across the yard, a reporter exclaiming: *Saturday saw a visit from the Kennedy camp to the new beach house of New York attorney Arthur Wise.* Lem is, for the instant, caught unaware of the scene. He's in his coveralls and has a straw hat on his head. He seems to be in a rush. He has a stack of letters in his hands. No one had bothered to tell him what was happening that day. This is the only picture of Lem that I know of.

When the men from Silver & Silver came to Bluepoint that August, I sat on a bank of cinder blocks outside Lem's apartment to watch their limousines park in the dirt oval by the main house. There were two cars, black, as long as hammerheads, their engines whirring softly before they cut out. My father had told me to get out of the house. "Make yourself sparse, Hilly," he'd said. He didn't want me around when these men came inside. But I knew better. He was nervous. Silver & Silver was the largest corporate defense firm in America. Just in the first months since the Boston Airways suit was finalized, they'd negotiated big settlements with my father. They'd come to Bluepoint to woo him to their side. They were tired of losing to him, tired of handing him so much money.

They'd sent four men to do the recruitment. Each of them was impeccably dressed. They all wore shined oxfords and dark wool suits, despite the heat. And they'd all brought gifts: bottles of whiskey, a crate of cured Providence sausages, a basket of Tallahassee navel oranges, and a bouquet of Dutch ice-hued orchids. My father greeted them warmly. He knew most of them from the courtroom. It was always odd to me that, no matter how fiercely they battled, they all got along with one another. Some of it was respect — the way boxers hug after a fight. But some of it was genuine. When I watched my father hug Jerry Silver, and clap him on the back, and show him the house in pretty much the same way he'd shown me the house two months earlier, I could see that he thought of Jerry as his friend. Still, I knew he wasn't going to take the job. Even though he hadn't said anything to me, I had the feeling that my father was never going to go work for somebody else. He had everything he wanted now. No matter how much they offered him, they had nothing to offer him.

I went out to Lem's apartment, and we shared a cigarette outside on the cinder blocks. From where we were, we could see everybody, but they were too busy looking out at the ocean and the house to notice us. Jerry Silver was the most garrulous of the bunch. It was his father's firm. He had a dark crew cut and a loud Bronx accent.

"That man's been shaking your father's hand for two minutes," Lem said, laughing into his fist. "He must really want your father to feel appreciated."

I nodded. "Smart man."

We'd all been warned of their arrival a week earlier. My father had gathered us in the dining room. Robert had wanted my father to turn them away without notice, the same way he'd been ignoring all of the letters that came to our house asking for legal advice. Robert was a true liberal and thought that what the big defense firms did was immoral; part of the crash settlements always involved a refusal to accept blame. But at least some of these men had worked in the highest levels of the government, and most had access to America's largest corporations — their client lists, their political contacts, their tips about stocks and bonds. It was a delicate balance: he wanted to reject them but have them leave thinking only the best of him.

While the men met — my father and Robert and the lawyers from Silver & Silver — Lem took me out for a ride in the Cadillac. We left without telling anyone. Lem was allowed to use the car only to do errands like picking up groceries or garden supplies. So long as we came back with a bag of food from the store in Wellfleet, we were fine to take the car anywhere we wanted. I didn't think much about going with Lem. I think my father would have wanted me to think twice, or to think whatever it was about black people that he thought. But ever since I'd heard that Lem was a painter, ever since I had heard that small part of his life's story, I thought I knew something about him that nobody else did. I might have even understood him. I thought we might even be friends. So I went. It was easy. I had nothing else to do. I just got in the car, and we were gone.

Lem seemed apprehensive at first. He was worried, I'm sure, about crashing the car. The roads were slick with sand. But then, on the stretch between Truro and Wellfleet, where the road is flat and the dunes are high and there is the thick, heavy stench of the sea, a curtain of salt and brine, he opened it up, really swelling the engine, the radio going, Big Boy Crudup singing "That's All Right," the speedometer rising, the windows down, wind bearing in on my face, and everywhere inside myself I felt the undeniable thrill of speed, speed at its reckless, foolish, idiotic core. After a moment, he slowed down and laughed to himself.

"It'd be a crime if your father had this car and never once got it going the way it's supposed to."

We emerged near Wellfleet Bay, the grassy swampland scorched by summer, the scaly oaks thin like pencils and filled with squirrels and doves, the roadsides marked every quarter mile by oystermen shucking and polishing and squirting lemon halves. I'd been up and down this road dozens of times since we'd come out to the Cape, but with Lem Dawson everything familiar became new. I sat up in my seat, took a cigarette from the pack of Fatima Golds skittering on the dash, struck a match, and took a searing inhalation.

In a clipped voice Lem told me we were going to a hotel called the Emerson Oaks. "To see some friends," he said. And then, forming the most minute, arrogant, amused smile: "You're gonna have to start getting your own pack soon, Hilly."

The Emerson Oaks was a summer resort in a town called Fairmont, fifteen miles inland, neither on the bay nor on the ocean but stuck in the dead-land middle ground of the inner Cape, the very territory my mother had lately begun to call by all sorts of terrible, unfair names. (It's worth noting that my mother, after only a month, had become nearly unrecognizable in her attempt to appear effortlessly rich. The scorn of being seen as nouveau riche, with all its attendant foolishness, its gauche sensibilities, scared my mother, even if she didn't understand exactly why someone might have these opinions. Her tack was to become overly negative, full of false conviction, and occasionally cruel. Thus, the inner Cape, a perfectly beautiful place, with immaculate lakes and gorgeous dunes — where the Kennedys lived — was suddenly beneath her.)

The Emerson Oaks wasn't itself a large hotel, but a series of small cottages set up in the woods and rented out each summer to Boston union men who couldn't afford a beach house. From the street, I could see only the very top of the crest of the building that housed the Emerson's dining room. It had a blue roof, an odd choice, peaked like a wizard's cap, a perfect triangle, under which were four windows paned in squares of eight. A dirt path led us in a winding arc by the cabins, where I saw, in a short span, a man and a woman lying out on their beach towels, a pair of boys snapping each other with a wet wound-up shirt, and a group of teenage girls in canary-colored one-pieces, sitting on the green rotted planks of a picnic table, licking vanilla ice cream cones.

Each cabin had at its back door a small clearing of grass, sun bleached and white as hay. Some residents had brought with them soaking tubs, plastic pools, volleyball nets that sagged in the wet earth or a strong breeze. There were wooden crates out in the high weeds, filled with ice and long-necked beers, and there were smothered campfires, still smoldering hours after day had broken. The cabins themselves were small, shuttered with black planks of louvered maple, their roofs made from pitched plywood affixed with cheap stick-on shingles painted to look like brickwork. We drove slowly. The ground had been paved once but was worn now, the drive nothing but huge lumps of loose concrete interspersed with windblown beach sand. I had my arm out the window. It felt good to be away from home, to be out exploring. The stereo was on low, a man's deep voice advertising a Kenmore air conditioner. I could hear kids out on the grounds but couldn't see them. Between each cabin there were a few trees, the trunks as tall as buildings, packed so tightly that little light came through and hit the ground. Everywhere there were pine needles as sharp as knives, so hard and brittle and cooked from the sun that as we drove, the loudest sound was the noise they made when our tires rolled over them. There was a man-made lake with a sad, halting fountain at its center, the water spurting rhythmically from its spout. On the water there were docks shaped like *Y*s.

I worried that Lem was lost. The car was moving as slowly as possible without the engine stalling. He had himself perched over the wheel. By now, the pines outnumbered the cabins, and the buildings we passed were badly worn, clearly empty, badly neglected. A spider's web — so intricate, so enormous, so ingeniously erected — stretched across the entryway of one cabin, spanning a big red Dutch door. I could see it briefly as we passed, when the light was perfect, the thread clear for only an instant: fleeting, flossy, brilliant.

"You know where we're going?" I asked.

"It's the last one," Lem said. "That's where we're going."

I'd thought that the road we were on was a big circle, but instead I saw that it was a long and curving dead end. Its last structure — a tiny white cabin without a roof, without glass in two of its four windows, and with a piece of plywood in place of a front door — was the one we'd been looking for. The roof looked as if it had been blown off. Where it should have been, only a loose blue tarp hung, secured to the frame of the cabin by what seemed like tabletop vises. There were shingles in the grass, and shingles resting on a stack of lobster traps as high as a tall man, and shingles strewn across the road. A rusted Ford the color of a cranberry sat on blocks, its tires scattered on the lawn, awaiting some inventive use.

"You wait here," Lem said to me, cutting the engine. He looked at me, perhaps trying to see whether I was frightened by the poverty. I wanted to tell him that I hadn't always been the person I was now, dressed in silly madras shorts and a collared Brooks Brothers shirt. Being poor isn't something to be proud of, but I hated to be misunderstood. And it seemed somehow worse to be looked at as a rich guy, effete, lazy, incapable of anything, rather than as a poor guy, which was what I'd been most of my life. Lem got out of the car, leaving behind his cigarettes. I stayed behind, edged myself up in my seat to get a better look. The front steps, I noticed, were resting in the pine needles beside the lobster traps. Close by was a bucketful of nails. I'd been wrong: the house hadn't been wrecked or blown apart; it had never been finished.

Savannah answered the door. It had been a month since we'd met; she seemed younger somehow. Her hair was done up in braids, and she wore blue jeans cut off above the knee, no socks, a white T-shirt with a red smear across the chest that I figured must have been paint or nail polish or maybe lipstick. In the sun, she was black, very black, darker than Lem by several shades. She smiled. Her teeth were perfectly straight. Her relief at seeing him was so clear that I felt it nearly ten yards away. I opened the car door to join them. She sighed when she saw me. I couldn't tell if she was glad to see me or annoyed.

"I came to check on you," Lem said.

"I'm fine," she said. "You don't need to come look in on me."

"Are you sure?"

She nodded. There was a radio on in the cabin, the signal not quite full. Her right knee had a bandage across its center. It was your standard adhesive bandage, peachy-cream in color, but on her it was so garish, so mismatched. She looked over at me then, seeing that I was staring. She was effort-lessly pretty.

"Why are you here?" she asked me.

"He's my friend," Lem said.

"Your friend, or your little boss?" she said.

"You know who he is," Lem said quietly.

She smiled at me, raised her hand, and then affected an English accent. "I apologize I don't have tea and biscuits to offer."

"Come on now," Lem said.

"He do whatever you order him to do?" she asked me.

I stiffened. "I'm not his boss," I said.

"Quit it," Lem said.

"I'm fine, Lem," she said, softer now, urgent. "Now get on and go."

"Where's your dad at?" he asked.

"He's out."

"He was out last time."

"He's always out. What's new." She put her hand on her hip.

Because the front step was missing, there was a gap between where Savannah stood and where we stood, an effect that made her a good deal taller than us. Inside, three buckets sat in a row on the floor directly behind her, blue, plastic, the sort you bought filled with nails at a hardware store. Lem took a step forward.

"I thought you got the plumbing fixed," he said.

She sighed. "It *was* fixed. Now it's broken."

"You need to call the landlord."

"The landlord knows how we live."

"What about the roof?" he asked.

"It's nice at night," she said, looking up. "You can kind of see the stars through it. It's like a tent."

I laughed at this and immediately felt bad. But Savannah smiled at me in a way that wasn't unkind. She seemed to me to be making the best of a sorry situation.

"You need me to call him for you?" Lem asked.

"This place is perfectly fine for us," she said. "We all don't need a house by the ocean so we can make pretty pictures."

Lem took a step closer. "Can I come in?"

She blinked twice. Despite her bravado, it seemed clear to me that she wanted him to come in, or for him to take her with us in the Cadillac — she'd looked over at the car a few times now, wondering perhaps if she could stow away in the backseat.

"Let me up," he said.

She shook her head.

Lem put his hands in his pockets. "Sweetie," he said.

"What?"

"You got food?"

"I'm *fine.*"

"You got something to eat?"

"I told you."

"You look skinny."

"You look ugly," she said, her eyes wet.

"Here," he said, taking from his pocket an envelope. "Take this. Don't give it to your pop. This is for you. You got it?"

She took the envelope. "He gonna find it."

"Hide it, then."

"He still gonna find it. He got a nose for money."

I thought of my father's unused stuff — his guns, his coin collection, the furniture, the useless jewelry, everything in immaculate shape, still as clean as a whistle. I could sell it.

"I'm gonna leave now," Lem said. He looked at his watch. "I gotta get back."

"You sure?" she asked, her voice high.

He reached up and took her hand into his, first his right and her right, and then both of her hands cupped in his, as if they might begin to pray together. "You know I got a telephone now," he said. "Right?"

She nodded.

"I gave you the number, right? You just go to a pay phone. Call me collect."

"I got it," she said.

"Anything happens," he said.

Again, a small nod. She lifted her chin slightly, bravely. Lem let her hands go.

He turned and went to the car quickly, brushing my shoulder, nearly knocking me over. He was crying, I knew. A small whimper had escaped him. I was left there alone, staring at Savannah, her envelope full of money, her bandaged knee. She looked at me straight for a moment, and for a crazy instant I thought I should reach out for her hands the way Lem had, but she looked away.

"Come again," she said cheerfully, stepping back into her house, suddenly covered in shadow, the door shutting.

■ ■ ■ ■

We went home the same way we came, this time in silence, the moon beginning to show opposite the sun, both in the sky at once. Rain threatened for a minute, the clouds over the sea full and black, and then just as quickly the sky was made clear by the heat. Gulls swarmed. Canada geese, in an arrowhead; one hawk, hunting, floating, and then, as we passed, nose-diving for something: a jet turned down and crashing. Lem drove slowly, both hands on the wheel. Billie Holiday on the car radio, soft, singing "Pennies from Heaven." He hadn't said anything since we'd left, and there was little evidence in his expression that anything extraordinary had happened at all.

"Was that all your money?" I asked.

He smiled. "Why? You gonna pay me back?"

"It was a lot of money," I said, even though there was no way for me to know this aside from the general width of the envelope.

"You think it's all the money I got, 'cause I couldn't have much money, right?"

"No," I said. "I just know my father doesn't pay you much."

97

He laughed, his cigarette bobbing. "You're right about that."

It was near seven at night. The light was gray now, dim, the air thick with fog, sand blown off the dunes settling on the high grass like snow in summer. The men from Silver & Silver would stay for dinner, I was sure. My father would probably lure them in, allow them to think for a few hours that they had him, that they'd gotten him on their side, before he cut everyone loose. I had begun to figure out the devious designs of my father's personality: it was a perfect balance to strike, to allow them to think that he'd do it, he'd join them, if only circumstances would allow it. He'd done the same thing to us when we'd moved to Wren's Bridge, allowing me to think that it was only temporary, that we'd go back home soon, when all along he'd had other ideas. For Silver & Silver, he'd stand at the threshold of the front door, smiling as they climbed back into their limousines, allowing them to think simultaneously, What a good guy, and, What were we thinking, trying to get *him* to join *us*?

"Her dad's no good," Lem said abruptly. "There's not much more to it." He seemed to want to light another cigarette off the one he'd already lit. Sunlight was in the stubble of his beard. "Her idiot father couldn't come up with a better name. Just named her after the place she was born."

She had seemed so confident that day, I thought, out in her church clothes. *Y'all got an entire corner of the world.* It stung now to think of it. "How do you know her?" I asked.

"She's my niece," he said. His voice was soft, steely, hopeless. "Her mother was my sister."

"Why are they living like that?" I asked.

He sighed. More birds above us. A man on the shoulder in shorts, walking three retrievers. A group of girls walking to the water at Truro. Lem exhaled loudly. "That's not really an easy question to answer, Hilly."

"She looked like she wanted to come with you. With us."

A sharp wince. "I know," he said.

I sat up. "Maybe we should go back, Lem. She didn't have any *plumbing.* How is that even possible?"

He put his hand on my forearm, left it there for a moment — a moment of shared contemplation, anxiety, pain — and then took it away.

"That girl is *my* business," he said. "You understand that."

"You took with me you. That makes it my business, doesn't it?"

"Listen," he said, his voice rising. "You keep out of my business. I keep out of your business. All right?"

"What does that even mean?" I replied, my voice rising as well. If he wanted to argue over it, I would argue.

But Lem merely pointed ahead, through the windshield. We were pulling up to the house then, the bruised sky behind the roof, every lamp on the ground floor turned on, bright, golden. My father and the lawyers were sitting in the front room. Their bodies were dark cutouts against the light. If it had been a secret that we had taken the car, it wasn't any longer: my father was looking out at us. I couldn't see the details on his face, the contours of his expression, evidence of his happiness or his displeasure, but I knew it was him. The shape of my father's body was unmistakable to me, as it is, I imagine, for any son. Lem stopped the car, took the keys into his hand.

"Don't tell your father we went to see her," Lem said.

"What do I say?" I asked.

He looked up at the roof of the Cadillac, as if the answer were printed there. "I don't know. Say I took you to the library."

I laughed. My schoolbooks had gone unopened that summer. "He'll know that's a lie. We didn't we get any groceries, either. He's gonna know something's up."

"Say I took you to the movies." He was exasperated, nervous now. Maybe it was the notion that my father might not be so happy to have had Lem take his car.

"What movie?" I asked.

"Damn it," he said, turning to me, scowling, his eyes still red from crying. "I don't fucking care, Hilly. Make something up. Tell your old man I fell asleep. Tell him I'm so tired from picking up after his ass, I fell asleep."

He slammed the car door. My father turned, then everyone else turned, and then, so clearly, I could see so many faces, all the lawyers, my mother, in a blue linen shirt, so many eyes tracking Lem's small, stooped, nervous body walking across the grass to his apartment. The sound of the door closing had gotten their attention. I stayed in the Cadillac for a while. Lem had left the keys in the ignition, which was something my father liked to do, and I stayed in my seat, the radio tuned to an evening baseball game — Sox, Indians, a repeat of the '48 pennant. By now, Boston was a ghost of itself, with so many ballplayers off fighting in Korea. I loved to hear Curt Gowdy call the night games. There was something about his voice that always helped put me to sleep. Usually I'd put it on the small radio I had in my bedroom, the speaker right beside my pillow, but tonight, with the lawyers in the house, I had to stay in the car.

And then my father woke me up, his hand tapping on the glass. I had been dreaming that it was me in that house at Emerson Oaks, and Lem coming to see me. Behind my father, on the front steps, the guys from Silver & Silver were waiting, looking in at me.

"Get up and say goodbye to our guests," my father hissed. He was blazingly drunk, one eye larger than the other, a great, frightening smile showing his teeth stained by whiskey and coffee, meat wedged in the crook between his gums and one of his incisors.

"I fell asleep," I said stupidly, blinking at my father.

"No shit you feel asleep," he said. "Get up and do what I said."

"What time is it?" I asked. The radio had gone off-line, just a mess of static. It was dark outside, the moon covered by clouds, the water quiet, great hovering hordes of mosquitoes behind my father's head.

"Two," he said.

"Two in the morning?"

My father laughed. "It's certainly not two in the afternoon, Hilly."

I closed my eyes. "I fell asleep," I said again, and then I shook my head, trying to wake myself. I could smell the afternoon's cigarette wafting off me — all of Lem's cigarettes that afternoon — and my father, instantly, could smell it too.

"You smell like an ashtray," he said.

"It wasn't me," I said.

Behind us, I could hear a big voice, a voice from the Bronx. "This your boy, Wise? Tell him not to be scared of us. Or — no. Tell him we got his phones tapped. Tell him we've been listening to his every waking thought."

There was raucous, senseless laughter. My father pulled me up by my shirt but did so in such a way that it likely appeared to his visitors, his colleagues, that I'd shot up on my own. I was still growing that summer, caught in the middle of a terrible, uncomfortably late growth spurt that would leave me only a hair's breadth shorter than Robert Ashley, who was looming behind everyone, still near to the house. I caught his eyes first. He was the only person who still had on his necktie, and he looked a bit sad to be a part of this: the drunkenness, the sad charade of luring these men to Bluepoint. It

103

occurred to me at that moment that Robert hated these men. He thought it was important to defend people who had nothing, who had lost everything. Unlike my father, he saw great honor in that kind of work, not just a quick path to big money. He nodded at me, slightly, and I nodded at him.

"Hilly," my father was barking. He had his arm around Jerry. "This is my new friend."

"Your new *great* friend," the man insisted. "Introduce me properly, Art."

"This is Jerry," my father said. "He's an important man."

"Not as important as your dad here," Jerry said.

I shook his hand. "Good to meet you."

"You look like your old man," Jerry said, smiling at me, gripping my hand for too long, just as he'd done to my father hours earlier.

Jerry wore his hair back across his head, slicked into a wet, oiled sheen. He had a huge forehead, sloping down through his nose, crooked, with a bump like a knuckle. A skinny striped tie looped around his neck, unknotted, blowing in the sea breeze.

"Your father was telling me all about you in there," Jerry said.

"Is that so?"

"Says you got a sense of your own purpose in the world," Jerry said, a line that yielded laughter from my father, and also, I noticed, from Robert Ashley. "Maybe you can work him over. Get him to join up with us. He may not realize it, but we're the major leagues."

"I don't know how much I can help," I said. "He's awful tough to convince."

Jerry laughed. "You don't need to tell me that," he said. "I've been trying to get him signed up all night. Thought if I got him loaded, I'd have a better shot."

My father stumbled. What followed was a short, inescapably awkward moment as my father tried to right himself. It was a joke at first, a nod to his lack of sobriety, but then it became grueling to watch — my father stumbling, one knee in the grass, his cap falling off, his hair in his eyes, a line of spittle from his mouth to the lawn. No one went to help him. Perhaps everyone was already too drunk to move. Or perhaps my father had done what he always did, which was to create around himself such an attitude of inapproachability that no one would dare to touch him. My mother stood facing me, her arms crossed against her heart, imperious and matronly. She wanted everyone gone, the evening over, all of us in bed, the next morning to come quickly.

My father began to laugh at himself, and then everyone began to laugh at him. The noise became so great that the lights went on in Lem Dawson's apartment, a fact that seemed to delight everyone. The laughter grew raucous. "We've woken the Big Black Wolf," someone said. "Run!"

Robert Ashley came down off the porch and tried to silence everyone.

"He's trying to sleep," Robert said. "Let the man sleep."

More laughter: apparently Robert had become the funniest thing on Cape Cod that evening.

"Did you hear him?" my father cried. "The black fellow's trying to sleep! Boo-hoo!"

Six

Over those next few days, I began to gather all the surplus that had collected in our house. We'd been at Bluepoint six weeks by then, and already the place was filled with what Robert, with his usual prudent, upright Kansas disdain, called our junk. With my mother out of the house as often as possible, and my father upstairs in his office, I had almost no supervision, and so the task was easy: loaves of white bread, canned preserves, littlenecks, turkey breast, cocoa, boxes of General Mills cereal, Campbell's, Heinz, Hershey's, a basket of apples, and a frozen ham sent by my father's new client in the Brooklyn case, a token of his gratitude. (My father, though eager to renounce all the limits of kosher dining, was still afflicted by a superstitious aversion to pork. The ham had greatly offended him and had become a joke between him and Robert.) The spending at that point had become so reckless that there was no inventory of what was bought and what was consumed and what was wasted. My mother bought things. And then my father bought things. And sometimes they bought the same things. Making a real inventory might have been something Lem could have done if my father hadn't continued to run him into the ground. Even my mom, whose effort to try to love her life here had so quickly become eclipsed by her boredom, paid no attention to the urgent way I rushed between the pantry and the driveway, loading everything into the backseat and trunk of her Fleetwood. I stole everything. I didn't care what I took. We didn't need what I was taking, and someone else did.

All of this, of course, was for Savannah. I kept picturing her cabin, and especially those buckets. It all began to haunt me. With every trip I made out to the Fleetwood, carrying an armful of junk, I thought of something new she might need, and this something, whether it was pots and pans, or toilet paper, or insect repellent, or magazines (because she deserved some entertainment, didn't she?), was usually something we had piling up in our house.

The plan was relatively simple, and as I waited for the right time to make the drive from Bluepoint to the Emerson Oaks, everything, so suddenly, brought to mind her poverty, her bandaged knee, the way she had grasped for Lem's envelope full of money with the simultaneous sense that she shouldn't and yet she should. My father had taken to putting up an American flag every morning, and the sound of its grommets smacking the flagpole made me think of the creaky hinge on the door Savannah had held open with her toe. Wind lifting the canvas over a cord of firewood behind the house suddenly became the sound of the tarp flapping against the roof beams of their cabin. In *Life* magazine that month, there was a series of photographs of young ballerinas dancing in a window in downtown Independence, Missouri, Harry Truman's hometown. They were simple pictures, charming, and all the girls seemed relatively happy to have their hands on the bar, to have been photographed in their tights and tulle. My only thought was whether this was something Savannah might like. A newspaper advertisement for a local bakery showed a three-tiered wedding cake. What about this? Would Savannah like this? A trio of speckled birds nested outside my bedroom window for a few noisy days. I hated them. They were loud and seemed to do nothing but chirp at each other and break apart worms in their beaks. But still I asked myself the same question: How about these? Would she like these? I was prepared to get her anything.

The drive to Emerson Oaks took longer than I expected. At the rotary in Orleans, I went in the wrong direction, crossed the Sagamore, and was nearing the outskirts of what Bostonians call the South Shore before I turned and headed back. Even though I'd had my license for a year, I had driven only twice — once in Manhattan, when my father was too tipsy to park his Cadillac properly, and once on a somewhat sentimental trip my mother and I had taken to New Haven in order to see the old place. I had, I discovered, a heavy foot, something that unnerved me. Speed as a passenger is something far different from speed as a driver. Because of this I made the trip slowly. It was a Thursday evening. Robert Ashley had somehow met a woman — Emily Baines — and had invited her over for a dinner at his house. Never one to miss a potential coupling, my mother had managed to invite herself over. It fell to Lem to do what my father called "working the party," which meant acting as waiter, bartender, and janitor. He'd appeared on the lawn wearing a cummerbund and a black jacket and feeling, he told me later, mortified.

It was still light when I arrived at Emerson Oaks. Summer in Cape Cod seemed to have a monopoly on daylight. As I got out of the car, I saw Charles Ewing standing a few yards from the cabin's front door. He had two pieces of a fishing rod in his hands and was trying, I guessed, to fit them back together.

"What do *you* want?" he called out. He wore a white tank top and tan work pants. He was a remarkably skinny man, scrawny, even. His collarbone jutted out, two tiny columns. Now it seemed even more amazing that he'd been able to throw that curveball so well, so fast, with so much English on it.

"I came to bring you some things," I said eagerly.

"Who said we need things?"

"Uh . . . I just . . ."

"You think we're a charity case?"

"I didn't say that."

"You don't think I can get things?"

"I'm just trying to be nice," I said.

"Yeah? Nice?"

I reached through the open passenger-side window and grabbed what I could. "It's just

111

bread and jam and stuff."

"You working for some sort of organization?" he asked. He put the fishing pole down. "Some church group send you?"

"It's whatever you want it to be," I said. This was something I'd rehearsed. I'd figured he might say this to me, or something like it. I was proud I'd come up with something like that to say back to him.

Savannah came out of the house then. She was in a tank top like her father's. In fact, it might have been one of his. It hung past her waist, almost to her knees. I could see the outline of her brassiere beneath the fabric. She put her hands on her hips.

"We don't need any of this," she said, jumping down from the front door, bridging the distance where a staircase ought to have been. She came up to the car window and peered inside. I was tempted to look with her. I'd lost track of everything that I'd stuffed into the backseat.

"There's more in the trunk," I said.

"Who told you to do this?" she asked. "Did Lem?"

"No," I said.

"He know you're here?" she asked.

"Course not," Charles shouted. "Giving things to you is his job. Ain't it? You don't think he'd let that lawyer's boy start buttering you up, would you?"

She looked at me. I felt the urge for some reason to touch her wrist, just her wrist, not any other place on her body, which was, I saw now, a beautiful body, different from the bodies of the girls at my school, more delicate somehow. Her wrist, though, was what had my attention. It had a mark on it where a doctor might put his fingers to search for a pulse, a raised welt like the club on a deck of cards.

"All right," she said. "Get on, now. Take it back."

"Look," I said, "you don't know how my father is."

"I read the papers," she said. "I got an idea."

"No. That's not what I meant."

"I know you guys are richer than the Rockefellers. You don't need to come all this way to tell me that."

"He just buys this stuff. Half the time he doesn't even remember why, he's so drunk. The other half, he doesn't realize he already has what he's buying. Like this," I said, opening the front door, reaching for a gallon of milk. "We have six gallons of milk in our house right now. Six. He doesn't remember that he keeps calling the milkman. Our milk guy is basically the happiest milk guy in America."

She pursed her lips. "I can't take that."

"Yes, you can," I said, lifting it out. It was still chilled. We were talking so softly. "Here. Just take it. It's yours. Otherwise it'll spoil."

"It'll spoil anyhow," she said.

"It won't. It's fresh. I took the freshest bottle."

"We don't have a refrigerator," she said. "Or an ice chest."

"Of course you do," I said. The thought seemed ridiculous to me. Who didn't have a refrigerator? I looked behind her toward the cabin. Its door was open. Again: those buckets.

She shook her head. "Listen —" she tried.

"OK, fine," I said, unwilling to be refused. "Then here." I reached for the bread, the rice, the macaroni, the jam, the cans of cooked littlenecks, the jars of peaches. I put it all on the ground at her feet. "Here. You don't need a refrigerator for *this*. For any of it."

Her eyelashes were suddenly wet. "Please."

"Wait, wait, wait . . ." I reached in toward the far edge of the backseat, where I'd stuffed a few of the scarves my mother had bought in Boston and never even taken from the packaging. I held up what I considered

the nicest scarf for Savannah. It was red, with a thin yellow band at either end. It was the kind of scarf you wore to the Princeton game. "I figured it must get cold here," I said.

"At night," she said quietly.

I put it in her hand. "It's soft," I said.

Savannah bit down on her lip. What was only a hint of tears was now a full barrage. I wanted to ask her if she still had the money Lem had given her, but somehow, I knew she didn't, and that her father had taken it, and that it was gone now. I got all of this from her tears.

"I can't," she said finally, waving her hands over the car like a magician, shoving the scarf back into my hand. "Any of it."

"Take it," I said. "It's wool."

She felt it and laughed a little. "It's cashmere," she said.

"That's a kind of wool, isn't it?"

"What am I gonna do with this?" she said. "Wear it with my overcoat?"

"Sure," I said.

She laughed more and kicked at the dirt. "That was a joke. I don't have an overcoat. Obviously."

"Well, fine. Joke about it. Cut it up, make it into a sweater. I don't really care."

"Why're you doing this?" she asked.

"All this junk is just sitting around in our house," I said. "Collecting dust. Ten days from now, there's gonna be a whole new pile of junk. More scarves. More food. More milk."

"And what then?" she asked. "You gonna come by with all that, too?"

"If you want," I said.

"Your father is gonna get so angry when he finds out. I've seen him get angry," she said. "You remember?"

I laughed. "He's just like that."

"Every day?"

"Only when he drinks."

She seemed to like that I'd said that. "Dad and Lem have names for him."

"Like what?" I said, smiling. "Like what? Tell me!"

"Oh," she said, placing her hand flat against my chest for a brief moment, as if she wanted to push me away. Her fingers were long, and her nails had chipped yellow polish on them. I had never seen a girl with fingernails painted yellow before. "I don't know you well enough yet to let you in on that kind of secret."

I blushed, either because of her hand, or because of the way she'd intimated that I might indeed get to know her well enough at some point that I might learn some of

116

her secrets. Suddenly, nothing mattered more to me — not my father, not what was in the car, not the fact that I'd just driven nearly sixty miles without any permission. I looked down at her hand, and then, inexplicably, I reached out and put my hand on top of hers. She pulled away so quickly that I thought I'd hurt her.

"You flirting with me?" she asked.

"No," I said. "No way."

She grinned. "You are. You're *flirting* with me, aren't you? Is that why you came all this way? Is that why you brought all this?"

"No," I insisted. "You've got the wrong idea."

"Oh, I do, huh?"

Charles started to come toward us. He had both pieces of the fishing rod still in his hands. He saw me looking at it and then held it out to me. Savannah straightened, and whatever anger or suspicion she held toward me was quickly replaced by something altogether different. Her father, like my father, held such sway over her that his emotion was the emotion that mattered most, his gravity the gravity that took precedent.

"He found this fishing rod," Savannah explained, the muscles in her jaw clenched. "He thinks he's gonna start fishing out all

117

our meals from the ocean. All of a sudden he's Captain Ahab."

"I don't know who the hell Captain Ahab is, but I don't get what's wrong with a man who wants to fish. Fish are just out there. Free for anybody to get. I don't see why I shouldn't be able to get some. Maybe I'll get so good, I'll get a boat, go out farther, get some big fish. Bluefish. Then maybe you'll change your tone."

Savannah *tsk*ed quietly.

"I like to fish," I offered.

"Yeah? What for?'

I was lying, of course. I hated being out on the water, hated that when I closed my eyes after a day at sea I could still feel myself rocking, swaying, tilting. Being out on a boat seemed like something rich people were supposed to be good at; I was horrible at it.

"Any fish is good fish, right?" I said.

He laughed and clapped me on the back. "Any fish *is* good fish," he said. Then, to Savannah, he grinned. "See? Our little rich fella here understands."

"Don't say stupid things like that," she said.

"*That,*" Charles told me, "is my life right there. Raise a girl up, give her everything, feed her, take care of her best I can, *sacrifice,*

118

then she calls me stupid. Life in a nutshell."

I reached for the fishing rod. "Did it snap?"

"I found it like this," he said.

"If you want, I could get you a new one," I said.

"Why you want to do that? You don't even know me."

"I know you can throw a curveball."

"At least someone does," he said bitterly.

"You should try to play professionally," I said. "There's all sorts of ballplayers like you. Larry Doby. Hank Thompson. Dan Bankhead, Roy Campanella, Don Newcombe —"

"Players like me?"

"You know. Jackie Robinson."

"You wanna know something about Jackie Robinson?" he asked.

"Sure," I said, although I was pretty sure I knew what there was to know. If there was a subject I was better suited to talk about, prompted or not, I don't know if one existed.

"Before all y'all knew him, before they put him in a fancy movie, I knew him," Charles said.

"Oh, please," Savannah said, rolling her eyes.

"Quiet, girl."

119

"It's the same story over and over and over and over," she complained.

"You play with him or something?" I asked.

"Really," Savannah said, looking coldly at me, "you don't want to know. 'Cause the next time you see him, he's gonna forget he told you, and then he's gonna tell you again. And that's just gonna keep happening. Forever."

"But I do," I said. "I *do* want to know."

"Three times," Charles said, stomping the ground with his heel and then holding up his last three fingers, the way a ballplayer would. "Three times I faced him. Three times I turned him around with that curveball I showed you. Buckled the guy's knees. *Buckled.*"

"*Buckled,*" Savannah said, imitating him, wiggling her head the way her father had.

"See, I started out in Kansas City. Played on the Monarchs. Played with Satchel."

"Satchel?"

Charles shook his head. "You think you're an expert? Satchel Paige. Played with him there. Pitched the lights out. I mean, just crushed fellas. Threw shit nobody could hit. I could go eight or nine any night you needed. Then, after that, went down to Birmingham. Played on the Black Barons.

Piper Davis. Ulysses Hollimon. All sorts of fellas down there. Checkers Lauren."

"Who?"

"Checkers. Younger than me by five years. Just a sweet kid. Crazy swing. Kid could hit a marble, he was so good. Even Willie Mays."

"Really?"

"Young Willie Mays."

He smiled to himself, remembering this. So suddenly I was in awe of him.

"What was he like?" I asked.

"He was like Willie Mays, but really young," he said, laughing.

"This is incredible," I said.

"One night while I was living down there, took a drive up to meet a nurse I met in Savannah. That's where this one comes into the picture," he told me, rubbing her hair with his hand. "Named after the city she was born in."

I smiled at both of them. I loved hearing this. All summer, I'd been poring over an old baseball almanac I'd found on one of the bookshelves in the house, left there by the last owner, almost like a present for me. I was this book's perfect reader — it was full of just numbers, averages, statistics, the sort of arcane effluvia that I'd somehow always keep in my brain. But none of the

121

stuff Charles had just told me was anywhere in that almanac, in any column, or box score, or chart that spanned the history of the game. Its absence suddenly felt criminal.

"Finally," he said, "I went back out, tried a year with Chicago American Giants. This was only a few years ago. But they buried me in the bull pen. Never really got out much."

"You're young," I said, because he did look young. "You could still play. I saw you throw."

"You saw me throw *one* ball."

"Still!"

"I'm thirty-six," he said. "Thirty-seven in November."

"That's young," I told him.

"Not for a ballplayer."

While we talked, Savannah started to look at what I'd brought over. After a moment, she gasped, put her hand to her mouth, and ran into the house. The doors of the car were open. And so was the trunk, where I'd stashed the frozen ham. I could hear Savannah crying from inside the house.

"What did I do?" I asked.

He walked around to the back of the car and saw the ham. "Oh," he said. He said it again. "Oh."

"What? What did I do?"

"It's nothing, son," he said kindly. "Just should have asked me before you did all this."

"No," I said. "Clearly I've done something. Usually, when you make a girl cry, you've done something."

He smiled slightly and nodded. Then he reached in and took the ham into his arm. Wind blew at the ribbon. "Her mother used to tell her we were gonna have a good, proper Christmas together. For once. Eat a ham like that. With the ribbon and everything."

In my blind stupidity, I still didn't understand. I put my hand out and took the ham. "What should I do?"

Charles looked back at the cabin. We could both hear her crying inside.

"Go home," he said. "Forget about us. That's what you should do."

SEVEN

When I came back, I went looking for Lem. The party was still going on. I didn't know whether he was there or not. It was dark now. The only light near our house came from the moon, which was dull, covered by clouds, and which seemed to hang so low that it might as well have been propped up on the lip of our chimney. Far off and across the dunes, Robert's house was bright still, his dinner party in full swing. I called out for Lem, said his name twice. The air was cool and wet. When I got no response, I walked to the edge of the lawn, put one foot onto the rotted planks where the boardwalk began. I tried again. The side of Robert's house had two windows, one of which was his kitchen window and was lit now in bright white, as if his new female friend, Emily Baines, had brought with her some capacity to turn his normally dull home — he had a taste for dark brown leather, stained oak, deeply hued Persian rugs — into something stark and new. Even from hundreds of yards away, I could see the figures of my father and Robert and my mother and someone who I figured was Miss Baines through this window, drinks in hand, their silhouettes clean, cutout, and recognizable to me. But none of these was Lem's. I figured that by now my father might have let him off.

I checked Lem's apartment, but he wasn't there. Instead I found a small table covered in paint jars, brushes, rags, two palettes with daubs of dried color. Beside that, a small plate and a half-eaten peanut butter sandwich. Near the window was his kerosene heater. On another table, there were six empty bottles of orange Crush. By his bed, his shoes were aligned perfectly. In the kitchen, his dishes were clean, one new-looking pot hanging from a hook. By the window, he had an illustration of a puppy, torn, I could see, from the *Cape Cod Gazette*. It was an advertisement: FREE PUPPIES. On it, Lem had written in blue ink: *Ask Mr. Wise.* Resting against the wall was his leather portfolio and his box of drawings, everything sealed and zipped up, all the art hidden from view. I didn't dare to open them, even though I knew I could have. Back in his bedroom, I looked at the picture of his grandparents and did some quick math. The picture alone looked twenty years old. Maybe more. And their faces, their wrinkles, the general weariness in their eyes, a certain exhaustion in the way they seemed to be holding their breath, made them seem near seventy. "Ninety years," I said aloud. Which would have made the year of their birth about 1860. Macon, Georgia; Lincoln's election year. More than likely they'd been born slaves.

Eventually I grew bored and left. I took the beach path rather than the road. Down at the water, it was immaculately dark. The moon on the sea did only so much. I walked with my hands up in front of me. I could feel my skin puckering, water spraying me, gulls keening. As I got closer to Robert's house, I heard music playing, a saxophone and then timpani.

I knew at his best, Lem could do the trip back and forth from our house to Robert's in thirteen minutes, and that included whatever time he spent in either house, receiving orders from my father or Robert, taking their parcels, their boxes, their paper folders. Subtracting that dead time, I figured that he could make the trip in six minutes or so. But ten minutes into the walk, I was not even a quarter of the way there. Suddenly I saw how tough this really was, how great an act Lem put on when he came up the hill near our house. The boardwalk beneath my feet betrayed some loose planks. From that point, where the last piece of wood gave way to a series of boulders covered with green algae that looked like the hide of some shelled reptile, I could see only the peak of the roof on Robert's house. I took off my shoes and walked on the wet sand. I'd worn my best pair to see Savannah. The shore, for a few minutes, was flat and easy, and it was nice to feel my feet in the surf. The tide pulled at my toes. Slowly, my vision adjusted to the darkness. The ground was dappled with newly minted holes where the waves had torn rocks out from the earth and brought them back into the water. I stopped when I came to the dunes. There were two of them, each as tall as a school bus. I turned back. I couldn't see our house now. Desiccated shells from hermit crabs were everywhere, strewn by the wind and tide. Or perhaps this was just a place they all came to and couldn't escape. I climbed the first hill slowly, slipping down a few times and succeeding only when I really dug my toes into the ground.

As I came to the peak, I stopped and

sucked for air. I turned back toward our house. Everything was still dark, but now I could see the outline of it, the frame, the general modesty of the whole thing, the basic, crafted simplicity. Really, it was just an average wood house, only right on the ocean. I tried to see it the way my father saw it — as a trophy, as something to show off to his friends. What did the men from Silver & Silver think when they saw it for the first time? Was it impressive? Modest? Shabby? What would President Truman or General Eisenhower think if he came? Or any of the Kennedy boys? Robert had a weather vane bolted to the roof beside his chimney, and I could hear it whirling madly in the breeze. And then I looked down, preparing my route to the bottom of the hill before I crested the next.

Beneath me, Lem Dawson was sitting against the sand, neatly hidden between the dunes. My father's leather bag was open across his lap, and he held a ream of papers in his hands. He seemed bewildered by what he was looking at. I was quiet. My breathing was measured, exact. As I watched silently, Lem read. To get enough light he lit matches, burned them down until the flame licked his fingers. I saw him read three or four pieces of paper. He handled each page very carefully, placing it facedown against the briefcase when he was finished. And with every new sheet, he seemed more puzzled.

Finally, I cleared my throat.

When he saw me, he flinched and scrambled to his feet, scattering papers and then trying inelegantly to retrieve them. The wind threatened to take them up over the dunes.

"Damn, Hilly. You scared me."

I didn't answer. He was filing the papers back into my father's bag, doing it quickly, trying to be discreet, as if I wouldn't notice. He was terrified that I'd caught him. That was clear.

"What are you doing all the way out here?" he asked. "Is everything OK? Is something going on at the house?"

"What've you got there?" I asked. "Some mail?"

"What?" he called out again, clasping the bag shut, looking up to me. "It's nothing."

"Doesn't look like nothing," I said, walking down the hill toward him. "I'm pretty sure you shouldn't be reading those papers, Lem. They don't belong to you."

Lem wiped at his forehead. He looked imploringly at me. "I wasn't reading anything."

"Oh, come on. I'm not stupid. I saw you."

"Hilly?" he asked. "Please. You *didn't* see. You didn't see *anything.*"

He tried to leave, to walk back toward his apartment. When I reached for the bag, I clipped his back, and he fell awkwardly into the dune, face forward, his nose going into the wet sand before his shoulders and his knees.

"Just give me the bag," I said.

I stood over him. The bag was opened now. I could see the type from my father's Underwood. His signature flashed at the bottom of one page, looping, jagged, ugly. "This isn't yours!" I yelled. "This isn't your job!"

"Don't tell on me, Hilly," he said pitifully. He got up on his knees. He grabbed my foot. "OK? Please don't tell. I was tired. I was just sitting here. And I got bored. I'll forget everything I read."

He let go of my leg, grabbed the bag, offered it up to me silently. Wind blew at the leather. A page was jutting out of the corner of the bag, crinkled.

I started to leave, and he called out for me.

"Hilly?" he asked.

I turned. "I don't even know what to say to you right now, Lem."

"We're friends, right?" he asked. He started to come to me, and I put my hands up. "I've been good to you. We're friends."

"No," I said. "I've been good to *you*."

I turned my back on Lem and made my way to Robert's house, shouldering my father's bag, hurrying away from Lem. I hadn't expected this — to find him that way, to see him doing something so stupid. And I hadn't expected to act the way I had. Here was that loyalty again. A moment earlier, I'd been rushing to tell Lem about my visit, to tell him how proud I was of what I'd done. Now this: I didn't know whether to tell my father or to keep what had just happened a secret. When I got to Robert's, I saw that everyone was out on the front patio, so I let myself into the living room through the back door. Robert was the first person I knew to own a television. He liked everything loud, and when I turned on the set, the ball game came across the line with a boom. My father, by that point, was very drunk. It was likely near ten at night, and he'd been drinking since before noon. I could hear him through the walls, and evidently he'd heard me. When he found me, he squinted in my direction rather than looking straight at me. His eyes were very dark. Finally, he straightened himself and pointed to the television. I thought of how Lem had fallen into the wet beach, the way sand had stuck to his face. I had my father's bag right next to me on the couch.

"What's the score?" he asked.

"Six–two," I said. I still hadn't been able to catch my breath. "Red Sox."

He seemed to be licking something from the inside of his mouth — a bad taste, some food stuck to his teeth. "OK, good." Then he laughed. "Or is it good? I forget. Who do you root for now?"

I looked behind me, worried that Lem might come to the window. "Boston," I said.

"Why's that? You ever even been to Boston?"

"I don't know why," I said. "Ted Williams, maybe."

"Does he still play?"

"Yeah. He does. He's in Korea, though," I said.

My father wrinkled his nose and grunted. "*Korea.* That's a shit storm right there."

I looked at him. He seemed, impossibly, to be in a kind mood, a rarity these days. "You think I'll go to Korea?" I asked.

"Honestly, Hilly, I hope not. You're a good kid."

"Good kids don't go to war?"

"Good kids don't come home from war," he said.

" 'Cause they get killed?"

He nodded. "That, yes. But also, they just don't come back the same way."

"*You* fought," I said. "Is that what happened to you?"

He let out a short bark of a laugh. "That might be something to have asked my father," he said. "I can't answer that for you."

He put his hands in his pockets. Then, finally, he saw his leather bag beside me on the sofa. "Hilly" — his voice rising — "what are you doing here?"

I didn't have a good answer for this, and I'm sure that my father — my exacting father, on whom nothing was lost — noticed that I was trying to concoct some truth out of thin air. But what he was really asking me, I thought, was why I had his bag with me. I thought of Lem — his pitiful, frightened face.

"I got tired of waiting around in our house," I said. "Thought I might watch television."

"Where'd you go in the car?" he asked.

"What car?"

He sighed. Nothing ever escaped him. "My Cadillac. The car you took tonight."

"Nowhere," I said.

"Nowhere?"

"Just to get a burger. And see a movie. Nothing big."

"What happened to all the things you had in the car?" he asked.

"The things?"

"The junk."

I stiffened, sat up on the sofa, nervously fiddled with the buckles on his bag. "I don't know what you're talking about," I said.

"You're the worst liar I've ever seen, Hilly. You've been running back and forth to that car all week. You didn't think I noticed?"

I didn't know what to say. I saw now how ridiculous I was to think he wouldn't have seen me. He was looking at his bag. By now, he must have seen that a piece of paper was sticking out from beneath the clasp.

I touched the bag with my hand. "I thought you might need it," I said.

"You got some of the Brooklyn Pages there?" He motioned for it with his head, a small tilt. "Why don't you give it to me."

As he reached for it, my mother came into the room. Unlike my disheveled, drunken father, she still looked coolly elegant, in a black dress and white pearls, carrying a glass of red wine. Behind her, Robert was reaching for her arm. He'd clearly been rushing after her.

"Arthur," she said. "Arthur."

My father turned to her.

"Is this true? Is it? Is what Robert just told me, is it true?"

"What're you nattering about, Ruthie?"

Then my mother saw me. In such a short time, she'd become unrecognizable to me. When I was young, we used to listen to music together in the front room of our house in New Haven. She loved Chicago rhythm and blues, and especially the guitar, and we used to root for cloudy days so we might get a stray radio signal bounced our way from the Midwest. She was a terrible dancer, but I loved to watch her dance in our kitchen. She would push aside the tables and the chairs, and she would say, "Look, Hilly, look," and she would sway her arms and her legs. She was probably making everything up, all the steps, and the dances, and the names that she gave to them. This was ten years ago. It was such a short time in which to have changed so much. Now here she was, all dressed up in pearls. There was music on Robert's stereo — plinking, tuneless, middling jazz — I knew she would have hated only a few years earlier.

"Ruthie, please don't," Robert was saying.

"That kind man," my mother said. "The

Irish fellow with the foot. Is it true what Robert just told me?"

My father smiled. "He doesn't have a foot, Ruthie. You can't call him the Irish fellow with the foot if he hasn't got one."

My mother slapped my father's chest. "Is it true?"

"The case wasn't going anywhere," he said. "So we took the offer."

"But, but, but . . ." My mother searched around for a place to put her wineglass. Behind her, Emily Baines appeared. She was pretty, younger than my mother, supremely uncomfortable. She was wearing a green dress. "But Robert . . . Robert told me that the offer was *garbage.* That it was a *garbage* offer. Isn't that true, Robert?"

Robert shook his head and reached for my mother's arm.

"Good going, Bob," my father said.

"Is it?" my mother asked.

"It's a goddamned truckload of money, is what it is. That Irish fellow is gonna be able to buy himself a golden foot if he wants to. Heck, he can buy himself a gold slipper to put his gold foot into."

"But Robert said it was *garbage.* Said you could have won loads more if you went to trial."

"You don't have enough shit?" my father

136

asked. "You're hurting for more shit to buy?"

"Not for me," she said, wounded. "For the Irishman."

"He's gonna be fine," my father said. "Just fine. The guy's been living on soda bread and cabbage his whole life. Now he's gonna have hundreds of thousands of dollars in the bank." He wiggled his foot. "He was an idiot in the first place to not hear that train. I mean, who can't hear a subway car coming?"

"Arthur, that's a terrible thing to say," Robert said.

"It's true, Bob," my father said. "The city's case was better than ours. I knew it. The union knew it. Our guy was an idiot. I mean — you've met him. Tell me he's not an idiot."

"Art," Robert cautioned him.

"The guy brought me a *ham.*"

"He didn't know you don't eat ham."

"He should have."

"Did you tell him that you didn't eat ham?" Robert asked, clearly worried. This was the sort of ridiculous, crazy thing my father always wanted to do, and the sort of thing that was Robert's job to stop.

"Of course I did."

He shook his head. "You're kidding me. A

fucking ham? That's why you wanted to stop working on the case and accept the settlement?"

My father laughed. "Look, at the end of the day, Bob, I don't see why it's the city's responsibility if the guy's too stupid, or too deaf, or too much of a drunk, to hear a goddamned subway car coming."

Robert threw his hands in the air. Hearing my father say this clearly came as a shock to him.

"But why would you cut the case loose?" my mother persisted.

"We've been on it for too long now, Ruthie. I'm tired of it." My father looked as though he couldn't have cared less about the Brooklyn case. "I need to do better work. Bigger work. I'm tired of doing this liberal bullshit."

"Then why didn't you say yes to Jerry Silver?" Robert said.

My father turned toward Robert.

"What's in it for me, Bob?"

"Money. Isn't that what you want? That's what's in it for you."

"It's not just money," my father said. "Of course *you* would think it was about the money."

He'd let the word *money* stretch, adding an extra breath to it, or an emphasis that made everything somehow more sinister than it needed to be. My father looked to me and scoffed. Robert might have saved his life in Cherbourg, might have helped him escape enemy fire, but as a lawyer he was second-rate. This was what my father seemed to be telling me when he scoffed. He expected me to laugh with him, but I stayed quiet.

"You just didn't want to be Jerry Silver's second," Robert said finally.

My father nodded. "You're damn right I didn't want to be his second. Screw Silver and Silver."

" 'Cause Jerry's younger than you."

" 'Cause I'm *better* than him. And because I'm nobody's second. I have a second. *You're* my second."

There was a long silence. A window was open to the beach. High in the trees there were crows cawing. My father walked over to a chair and tried to sit. He missed the seat, stumbled for a moment, and put one knee onto the ground, as if he'd decided to stop and pray. Robert took my father's drink from his hand and poured it into a houseplant.

"Why don't you hit the sack, Art?" Robert said.

"Why's that?" my father said, turning

over, lifting himself into the chair. Then he pitched his voice upward, like he was talking to a baby, or a puppy. "I hurt your feelings, Bobby?"

"You're getting unruly. That's why."

"I'm just speaking the truth to God's ears," he said, singing the words.

Robert Ashley laughed at this.

"What's so funny, Bob?"

"You get really stupid when you're drunk."

"How stupid do I get, Bob? Tell me."

"Why don't you just get up and go to bed, huh? Let's spare the family a big scene."

"Why don't you suck my dick, Bob," my father said. He started to unzip his fly. "Here. That's what you want, isn't it?"

All of this shocked me. I tried not to show it. At that moment my mother and Emily began to back into the kitchen. Robert didn't seem bothered.

"OK, Art," he said. "Get up."

"Oh, shove off, Bob."

"Get up, Art." Robert said. "You're going to say something you truly regret."

"Oh, I will?"

"It looks that way," Robert said. He smiled at my father, which seemed to me to be an impossible gesture of faith in him. "And then where will you be?"

"I'll be right over there," he said, pointing

out the window. "In my goddamned fucking chair. In back of my goddamned house. With my little goddamned slice of the ocean to stare at. That's where I'll be."

"Let's get you to bed," Robert said, trying to lift him up.

"Get your hands off me."

"Don't cause a scene," Robert said. He said it like a warning.

"We're among friends," my father said. "Just speak your mind. Do you have something you want to tell me, Robert? The boy won't care." Now he regarded me. He looked positively threatening, I thought. "You won't care, will you, Hilly?"

"I do," Robert said. "I care. And I want you to get up on your feet and go to bed before we have any more trouble."

"You thought they wanted you, didn't you?" he said. "You did, didn't you? Is that why you think they came? For you? You didn't know they were only here for me? You probably had a little speech prepared! Isn't that rich!"

"How many times do I have to tell you, Art, that I'm happy doing this kind of work?" he said. "You want to go, go!"

"Oh, everybody knows you're upset over it."

"I'm fine, Art. If you want to switch sides,

141

go. You want to start fucking the little guy, be my guest."

"We're better than Silver and Silver. *I'm* better than Silver and Silver. That's a fact, Bob. I can't just toss away our reputation because some asshole twerp from some fancy white-shoe firm comes over and tries to woo me. It's a snow job. Didn't your father ever teach you the difference between a good opportunity and a bunch of bullshit?"

Robert stood over my father, bent at the waist slightly, like a cocktail waiter expecting to receive another order. They appeared to me as if they might start whispering to one another. My father crossed his legs at the ankle. He had on long white pants and leather loafers, which he wore without socks. He smiled at Robert. It was an ugly smile: a big, mocking thing.

"Oh, what do you want from me, Bob? I came over to meet your little girl here. She's awful nice. Awful nice girl. Is that what you want me to say? It's true. She's a lovely girl. She's got on a lovely green dress. Is that good enough?"

Robert appeared genuinely confused by this. He tried again to lift my dad from his seat.

"You'd have fucked up whatever case they

gave you, Bob," my father said.

"OK, Art," Robert was saying. "That's enough."

"Whatever it was. You'd have ruined it."

"Please, Art. Get up."

"Jerry wasn't here for you," my father said. "He was here for me. Everybody knows that. They were just *entertaining* you. They were just being *polite*. Even my dumb nigger knew that."

"Hilly," Robert said, turning to me. "Help me get him up."

I stayed where I was. I felt like the whole of the last few years was coming to a head right here in Robert's living room.

"I turned them away because I'm going to do what they do, and do it better. Why the hell not?"

"Because what they do is evil," Robert said.

"Evil! Ha! You're a little boy! Evil!"

"Art, cut it out."

"Fuck you, Bob. How's that?" My father said it again, slowly, spit flying everywhere. "Fuck you. How's that sound? That good enough for you? Fuck you."

Robert threw the first punch. The punch landed square against my father's teeth, knocking a slot cleanly out of his smile. (The next morning, Lem Dawson would recover the tooth, wrap it in tissue, and leave it on my father's desk.)

My father tried to get up, and when he couldn't, he called out to me for help.

"Hilly, get me on my feet," he yelled.

I didn't move. A part of me wanted Robert to tear him apart. My dad looked at me. He was on his side. His face was red. A trickle of blood on the carpet. He said it again.

"Help me up, Hilly."

I backed away. A few minutes ago I'd basically pushed Lem into the sand because I was coming to my father's defense. Now that it mattered, I found that I couldn't get involved. I stayed stuck where I was.

"Damn it, Hilly. Get me up so I can clean his clock."

"I'm not getting involved in this," I managed, finally.

"Get me up, Hilly. My friend here needs a lesson taught to him."

I held my ground. "No."

"Hilly, get me up so I can lick him one. Come on, Hilly!"

"I can't," I said. "I'm sorry."

"*Now* you're sorry. *Now?* You'll be sorry. How's that? I'll get myself up. And *then* you'll be sorry."

But he didn't get up. Robert pulled him

up — and hit him again. Robert seemed to snap at some point. Perhaps it was because for so many years he'd been degraded, his confidence eroded, chipped at, stolen; for years his had been the face in soft focus in the *Times,* his name an afterthought. I could see the tension welling in Robert's face, and in his arms. Robert had kept his military physique, something my father had let go by that point, and I was shocked at the speed and the crude force with which he dispatched my father. When my father was finally on his feet he knew what was coming, and for a split instant, standing against the living room wall, a photo of Iwo Jima behind him, he seemed for the first time like a small boy to me: his eyes widened, he tried to put his hands up, and he whimpered.

There was a series of blows, perhaps six or seven, all of them to the head. Robert had backed my father up into the corner of the room. I remembered at that moment all the stories my father had told me of Robert's heroism in the war, and I could see evidence, however crudely, of his instincts. I thought of the way I'd tried to beat up that pitcher at Wren's Bridge High. Robert had my father blocked the way a true fighter traps his opponent against the ropes. His footwork was pristine: he stepped into everything, and he moved so lightly. His punches were exact, crisp, and punishing. My father was likely unconscious by the last of them, although up to that point he'd been merely grinning. It was an odd, sadistic grin, and it sickened me to see it.

Robert seemed to realize what he'd done only after my father crumpled to the floor. By then, Lem had appeared to try to end the fighting. He didn't look at me when he came in. Not once. My father was bleeding from both eyes, his nose, and his lips, and when Robert saw this, he began at first to weep; then he clapped his hands over his mouth in shock, and then — and I will never forget this — he ran away, down the steps, across the patio, and out over the lip of the shore, crying the entire way.

Later, I brought cotton balls and alcohol from the first aid kit Robert kept in his kitchen to the second-floor bathroom, where my father was seated on the toilet, his shirt off, his face swelled, cuts over both eyes, blood on his pants. He had his army flask on the floor, next to his feet. My mother was crying, pressing a damp washcloth to his wounds. Garbled noises came out of my father's mouth. He was trying to moan, but it hurt him too much to do it right. His head lolled on his shoulders, and as I stood watching, he rested himself against the tile backsplash.

The door was ajar slightly. It was a small bathroom, the walls painted a dull, muted orange. All of Robert's house was dull in this way, as if he wanted nothing to rouse the flat, steady Kansan inside of him. There were two sconces on either side of the sink, the light warm against my parents' skin. My mother was on the floor. Her black party dress was up over her knees. On the vanity, she'd put all her jewelry — her pearl necklace, her gold bracelets, earrings, a brooch. The floor was slick with water and hydrogen peroxide. I stood near the door for a moment so they couldn't see me. My mother's hands were shaking.

"Do you need to go to the hospital?" she asked.

"*Wha— ?*" he asked. His head rested against the tile.

She asked him again, and once more he didn't give an answer. Finally, she screamed at him in a way that he couldn't ignore, her hands clutching at his cheeks. Only then did he seem alert. *No.* I hadn't heard her yell at him like this since I was young, when we were living in New Haven, before we were rich. I turned to leave, clipping my arm against the doorjamb.

My father turned toward me. "Is that Hilly?" he asked. He tried to get up. My mother put her hand flat against him. "Hilly? Is that you?"

"I'm here," I said.

"Bring him in here," he said to my mother.

"I'm right here," I said. "Can you see me?"

"Of course I can't see you," he said. "Look at me."

With his full attention trained on me, his face — swollen, red, stained with blood — was such a shock that I couldn't look at him.

"I brought you alcohol," I said.

"A drink?" he asked.

"No," I said. "The other kind. Rubbing alcohol."

He sat forward. He kicked over the flask. Scotch spilled on the floor, on the hem of my mother's skirt. I held out the alcohol and the cotton balls.

"Here," my mother said, reaching. "Give it."

My father grabbed the bottle of alcohol. He held it up to his face, trying to read it. His glasses had been ruined.

"Are you OK?" I asked.

"No," he said.

"Did he break anything?"

"Besides his hand?" my father asked. "I don't know. I'm gonna shoot him when I'm better."

"Art," my mother said.

"No. I'm gonna find him and kill him fucking dead. Nobody treats me like that."

"He was crying," I offered.

"*He* was crying? Of course he was crying. That figures."

To see him this way — shirtless, bloodied, woozy, talking about killing the man who had prevented the Germans from killing him — was as unsurprising as it was terrible. They each had been so silently disappointed in the other for so long: Robert in my father's spending, the gradual, moneyed shift in character, the notion that he would "switch sides," and now his abdication of the Brooklyn case; my father in Robert's modesty, his primness, the idea that beneath his steadfast propriety lay a withering disapproval.

"Do you want me to do anything?" I asked.

"When your father calls for your help, you do something," he said, slowly. He tried to get up. My mother sat him down. "You help him. You *always* help your father. You *always* come to him when he needs help."

"I didn't want to get involved," I said. I

put my hands in my pockets.

"You are involved. You're my son. Because you're my son, you're always involved."

"Arthur." My mother tried to reason.

"When a man is being pummeled, when he's being punched, when another man is scratching your father like a girl, you step in," he said. "That's your responsibility."

"Well, I'm sorry," I said.

"You humiliated me," he said. "You made me look like a fool, Hilly."

"Arthur, leave the boy alone," my mother said.

She was on her feet — without shoes, just her pale, ordinary feet, white and freckled beneath Robert's bathroom light. Her dress was wet with my father's blood, and she didn't care. This was my mother, I thought, my real mother, the woman from New Haven, the woman who had been cooking and angry when the Boston Airways flight went down. The other woman, the woman who had been a perfect party guest just an hour ago, loaded down with jewels, woozy on gin, was someone who up until now I hadn't realized was something of a stranger to me.

"Hilly," she started to say, "let me deal with this. Let me deal with him. Why don't you go downstairs, try to find Robert —"

"Did you like that," my father asked her, "the way he took it to me? Did ya like that, Ruthie?"

"Shut up, Art. God, you sound like a monster."

"Hilly," he said, turning back to me. The way his face was damaged, it looked as if he were squinting at me. He grabbed at my legs. His blood smeared the fabric of my pants. "Why'd you let it happen, Hilly? Why'd you let him humiliate me?"

"I didn't do anything," I said. I took a long breath. "Robert humiliated you. I just watched."

It took a moment for this to register with my father. He hated that I didn't see him the way the rest of the world saw him. I didn't care that he was famous now. I hadn't ever cared. My father reached for his flask, took a swig from it, then threw it at me, hitting me square in the jaw. I backed up beyond the door, clutching my face. It startled me more than it hurt.

"OK then," my father said, shutting me out of the room. "See what happens the next time you need anything from me, Hilly."

EIGHT

I walked home along the road. It was past midnight now. The moon was covered by clouds. Wind pushed against the shore. The bugs were gone, and so were the birds. There were crickets somewhere. My eyes grew used to the dark, and from the road I could see the ocean, the shape of the waves, and in the opposite direction I could see the furry quills of the cattails rustling. I couldn't walk out here without thinking of Lem. Our house was still dimmed at the end of the path. Lem's apartment, though, the peak of which I could see now, was warm with light. I scuffed my feet in the dirt, thinking of how he'd turned down our offers of a bicycle, or a car, so that he could walk near here, near the water. Now I understood: I thought of him, of what I'd caught him doing, of the plain anguish of his guilt, the way he had so many of my father's papers in his hands. As much as I wished for a decent explanation, I knew what I'd seen. It made sense to me. His existence here on Bluepoint had been, for so long, quiet and steady and uneventful, with his books and his paintings and his photographs, and then suddenly we had arrived, bringing with us all of our profligacy, our wild arguments and secrets and tempers, our crude sense of his position in our lives. I wondered whether, if our situations were reversed, Lem's and mine, I'd have done anything different. And thinking about it in this way, from Lem's perspective, caused me to feel a grave sense of regret at the way I'd treated him. I rubbed at the welt growing on my chin. My father's flask had bruised me. This, I thought, wincing at the pain, was what I had defended, what had caused me to push Lem into the sand: a man who thought it all right to hurl a hunk of pewter at me. I stopped on the path. The closer I got to Lem's house, the worse I felt. The most grievous part of an evening like this was the knowledge that the morning would come eventually, and with it, a new brightness on our sins, all of ours: Lem's, mine, Robert's, and especially my father's.

A few minutes later, I heard a car's engine behind me. A pair of headlights strobed across the gravel. I could tell by sound alone that it wasn't a car I knew. The engine from Robert's car was smooth. And the Fleetwood sounded as if it had within it a parade of drummers, everyone beating in time to the pistons. The car behind me slowed, the engine humming as it pulled alongside me. It was a Packard. The hood was missing its ornament. Before she rolled down the windows, I knew it was Savannah. A map of the outer Cape was opened on the dash. She reached to turn the stereo down. Gershwin was playing: clarinets, timpani, cymbals.

She leaned across the seat. For a moment it seemed that she didn't know what to say. The expression on her face was one of confusion, as if she still hadn't figured out why she'd come all this way. The silence was so long — she just stared at me, blinking, and I did the same — that I wouldn't have been surprised if she'd suddenly thrown the car into reverse and driven home.

When she finally did speak, her voice was quiet, hoarse, as if she'd been yelling all evening. "I was really hoping that was you," she said.

I looked around. We were alone. I knew that fact with certainty, but still, I checked. I went to the car slowly, nervously, and put my hands on the lip of the open window.

"What would you have done if it wasn't me?" I asked.

"If it was your father?" she asked, giggling slightly. "I don't know. Maybe I'd have hit him."

I managed a weak laugh. "He's already in rough shape tonight," I said.

This comment passed without notice. Maybe she knew somehow. Maybe Lem had called the pay phone at Emerson Oaks, told her what Robert had done to my father. She was smiling. She had gloss on her lips, I noticed. I was crazy about her. I knew it then. Beside her on the seat was a pile of some of the clothing I'd brought her.

"And if it were Lem," she said, uneasy in her seat, edging closer to the open window, still giddy, I suppose, that she'd gotten here to Bluepoint at all, "I guess I'd have ducked and turned around."

"So you came here for me?" I asked.

"I hope that's all right."

"It's so late," I said. Beside me, in either direction, the path dissolved into darkness. Wind against the dry leaves in the bushes made an anxious chittering noise. When she stopped the car, the water once again became the loudest thing. Far off, there was no evidence of traffic on the county road. We were alone, but still, I hated to think what would happen if someone discovered us.

"I didn't want anyone to be awake," she said. "That's why I left so late."

"Did you get lost?"

She pointed at the map. "I can read a map."

I tapped the roof of the car. "Is this your father's?"

"He bought it new," she said. "In Birmingham. Said they'd told him he was bound for Milwaukee. He'll probably lose it soon in some card game. But yeah, it's his."

"Milwaukee?"

"The big league. The Majors. The Milwaukee Braves."

"Why didn't he mention that?"

"He threw nine pitches, that's why."

"What do you mean?"

"They called him up. He threw nine pitches. And then they cut him." She shrugged, as if this were something I shouldn't find as sad as I did. "He says if he'd known how it'd turn out, he'd have bought something used. Something cheaper."

There was rust over each wheel well. Both tires were missing their hubcaps. The interior handle on the driver's side had been cracked and was held together with what looked to me like fishing twine.

"It's dangerous to be out right now," I said, "isn't it?"

"For you? Not so much," she said.

"You know what I mean, Savannah."

"I don't know," she said. "I guess."

"You shouldn't have done this." I pointed at the clothing. "I gave it to you because I wanted to."

"I thought you brought it all over because you didn't need any of it." She put one hand on the clothing. "I thought you said that your folks just shop and shop and shop, and they don't even know what they're buying."

"I did," I said. Then I shook my head. "They do."

"Well, I came to thank you."

"Totally unnecessary," I said. "I didn't do it to be thanked."

This made her smile. "Please."

"I wasn't flirting with you."

"You weren't?" she asked. Her feelings seemed to be hurt.

"Unless —"

"Just because I live where I live doesn't mean I can't recognize a boy being sweet on me."

"Being sweet on you," I said, smiling. "Is that what I was doing?"

"Listen," she said. Again, she seemed to

test her thoughts before uttering them. I could almost watch them flash and fail in her. Finally: "I just think I acted badly. I guess I'm not good at accepting all this charity."

"No," I countered. "I shouldn't have come over. It was wrong of me. I should have asked if you needed anything."

"Who would you have asked?"

"Lem?"

She laughed. "My father was right. He thinks it's his job to look after us."

"Maybe I could have asked your father," I said.

She scoffed. "I think you know how he'd have answered you."

"I'm going to buy him his fishing rod," I said confidently.

"Please don't," she said.

"Why? That rod he has is broken. He'll never get it to work."

"I hate fish. If you get him a new rod, all I'll have to eat is fish. Every day."

"You're living in the wrong place if you don't like fish."

"Believe me," she said, very seriously, "I didn't want to come here. I fought it the whole time."

I stepped closer to the car. Now my whole side was pressed against the passenger door.

"Where were you before this?" I asked.

She shook her head again. "I'm not getting into my whole life story with you."

"OK," I said.

She touched the clothing again. "Thank you, Hilly."

"It was nothing. Really. It wasn't anything big," I said.

"But it was. You saw our house. It's not even a house. We had a house once. That's a cabin. A shed, really. Not even a shack. You saw. My dad keeps saying he's gonna get it fixed. It's embarrassing even to have Lem see us that way. He's got it made out here. But then you had to come with him."

For a few moments I was quiet. What happened now, I wondered?

"You never answered me," she said quietly. Her voice had changed. I realized that it was the sound of her being nervous.

"What do you mean?"

"Is it all right that I came?" she asked. "Are you glad?"

It had been Savannah's idea to sleep in the Packard. I told her it was risky. Not only because my father would have tried to kill us if he caught us — me first, Savannah second — but because he'd notice my absence in the house at some point the next morning. He would notice everything, however damaged and bruised and bloodied Robert had left him. Savannah, though, was adamant. It was near two now. She was exhausted, and so was I. The drive back to the Emerson Oaks at this hour was sure to attract notice. A black girl driving without a license at midnight without getting stopped was lucky enough. And at my suggestion that we sneak into our house, or into Robert's house, she insisted that it was safer to park the car beneath a tree somewhere on the property and sleep until the sun rose, at which point she'd drive home. The car, she told me, was big enough to hold both of us. "I sleep in the back," she said. "You sleep up front."

We parked at the end of the path to Lem's apartment, where a copse of tall firs provided a decent semblance of privacy. She wanted to see what the water looked like at night, she told me, and she grabbed my wrist, her shoes in her free hand, and walked barefoot across the tall grass. The only sound was the lapping crash of the ocean. When we reached the one large tree in the clearing west of our home, a hulking bent birch, its bark peeled and encased in wind-sprayed salt, she stopped me, her hand flat against my heart. The moon was still covered by clouds, and the surface of the water was dark, murky, shapeless. When she took her hand away, I felt cold.

"Don't," I said, taking her hand.

"You're sleeping up front," she said again. "I'm sleeping in the back."

"But we're not going to sleep now," I said.

"Oh, you're going to get me in trouble," she said. She was smiling so broadly. And so was I. For a moment I dared myself not to look away when she looked at me. I wanted just that small thing, to not flinch, but I couldn't. When she looked my way, I pretended to look out at the water, to find something interesting out in the waves.

"You bored?" she asked.

"No," I said, "not at all."

"Boys always seem to get bored around me."

"I doubt that," I said.

She sighed. "It's true. Most of the time, at least."

"Boys you drive all the way out to the beach to see? Those boys always seem to be bored?"

"Now you're flirting with me," she said, laughing. "*That,* I can tell."

"I made you cry earlier," I said.

"Oh please. Let's not talk about *that.* About me crying. Let's talk about this house

161

of yours."

We both turned around to look out at the house. We were down at the edge of the beach. Weeds poked up through the sand. The way we were standing there on the beach, it was like we were spies, or burglars, getting ready to ransack the place.

"When this is all yours," she said, "which one will be my room?"

"Oh, you want to play that game?"

"I like an ocean view," she said. "That's something you might want to know."

"That's fine. I can handle that."

"I can't believe you just live there like this," she said. "That you just wake up every day and the beach is here."

"It's not bad," I said.

This made her laugh. "Hilly, this is *amazing.*"

When she turned back around, I lingered for a moment. Looking out at the house, I wondered when my parents would go home, when Robert would return, even when Lem might discover us.

"How about I show you something?" she said, and then she pulled a sewn doll from her purse. It was near six inches long, woven in white and cream-colored yarn, with a round face, a jagged stitched mouth, a floppy-brimmed blue cap, and two black flecks of stone for eyes.

"What do you think, Mr. Wise?" she said.

"Did you make this?" I asked.

"With my mother." She shrugged. "She made these when she wasn't washing up at the Emerson. She wanted to get good at it, maybe sell them to a toy store on commission."

"On commission?" I asked.

"It's when you sell the store something, and then the store sells it to customers, and you get a cut."

I had the doll in my hand. I wiggled its small head in Savannah's direction. "I know what it is," I said.

"Then why'd you ask?"

"To hear you talk," I said.

"Oh gosh. Can you stop being sweet on me for one second?"

"I'll try."

"Lem is my mother's brother," she said quietly. "Or he was."

"She died, didn't she?" I asked.

She nodded and then reached for the doll. By the way it flopped in her hand, it seemed as if it were struggling as she took it. "This was one I tried to do myself. It's got a messed-up mouth. I'm not good with my hands. Not like her. She was so good. She could just do this so easy. So quick."

163

She dug into her bag and retrieved two other dolls. These were perfect, clearly done by a person with skill, and I saw nothing to distinguish them from the dolls sitting on the shelves of the toy shop in Wellfleet.

"You just carry these around?" I asked.

"Yeah," she said, "sometimes. My mom kept them in a box in the house. The box was the only thing that didn't burn up in the fire," she said softly. "It was weird. It was just there, not a thing on it. After the fire department left, I went in, and it was basically the only thing of hers I got back. These little guys."

"I didn't know it was a fire," I said.

She made a small, disappointed noise. "Lem doesn't tell you *anything,* does he?"

"No," I said. I had three dolls in my hand now, surely the first and only three dolls I'd ever had in my hand. "I guess not."

"It was awful," she said. "Fires are awful."

She smiled at me. The clouds were above us and there were no stars and I felt perfect to be there with her.

"Do you like them?" she asked.

"They're nice," I said.

"Nice for a doll. That's what you mean?"

"No. There's nice because they're yours," I said. What I didn't say was that I loved hers the most. Hers was beautifully imper-

164

fect. Perfection was boring.

"You like living here?" she asked. "In this place? This town? Sounds to me like y'all are always arguing."

"Lem tell you that?"

"I think he tells me more than he tells you."

I thought of the letters and wondered what this meant.

"My father is busy. And anxious about things."

"I know."

"There's this law firm. They want to hire my dad. But he had this other case, this guy without a foot, and that was sort of taking up his time."

"A guy without a foot?"

"He got it cut off by a train."

"That's nasty."

"Well, everything sort of went wrong. Now everyone's angry."

"Sounds fun," she said.

"I guess." I took a deep breath. "It's pretty here, but I like the city more, I think. It's slow here."

"I *am* making you bored," she said. "See?"

She leaned forward. She wore a simple silver necklace, and as she moved, it tapped against the skin on her clavicle.

"You ever see anybody famous in New

York?" she asked.

"Once I saw Clark Gable."

"Oh," she said. Obviously she wasn't a fan. "Nobody better?"

"I don't know. My mother thinks she sees people all the time. Like, she thinks she's always seeing Judy Garland or something."

"I love Judy Garland," she said.

"Yeah, but it's never her. It's always someone regular. Some ordinary woman walking her dog."

"That's funny."

"My father knows famous people. But they're usually lawyers and people from the government."

"How about any musicians? Or painters? Does he know anyone like that?"

"Well, I know Lem Dawson. He's a painter. You ever hear of him?"

For a few minutes we sat down on the edge of the beach and watched the water and the moon. I felt brave enough to put my hand on her hand, and then she put her hand on my leg. For a moment I thought she was going to kiss me. I was sure of it, and I thought she was sure of it, and then, either because she got scared or because she thought I was scared, she got up and started walking back to the car.

She began to talk: "My mom, it was like

nothing bothered her. She'd go to work at that awful place, the Emerson Oaks, and she'd be hauling the laundry and hauling the trash, and she'd be polishing the dining tables, and the whole time she'd have these guys from the city coming on to her, or squeezing her on the backside, or walking up and whispering some crazy shit in her ear, like, 'Oh, I like the taste of chocolate.' And you know, she just shrugged it off. Every time. Me: I'd have stabbed somebody. But her? She just came back home, made me dinner, acted happy. She had to make two dollars for every one, just 'cause she knew my dad would gamble it or waste it somehow. I just thought we were on our way out here. You know, everybody gets a bad move. A mistake. Coming here was ours. Lem told my mom there was work to be had. That the people'd be better here than they were in Savannah, or in Atlanta." She stopped and looked back at me.

"Are they?" I asked.

This was the loudest I'd heard her laugh. "Dumb people live everywhere, Hilly." She kept walking. We were almost back to the car. "Her whole life she just kept following my dad around. Go to Macon, watch him play ball. Go to Birmingham, watch him play ball. Go to Richmond. Go to Cincinnati. Go to Cape Cod because her brother told her to. She just never did anything she wanted to do. Then, boom. Fire starts in a dining hall. That's it."

We were going through the brackish beach weeds. She had her shoes in one hand, the hem of her skirt in the other. Her hair wasn't much longer than mine, but she'd tied white baby's beads to the ends of her ponytail, and as she ran they clapped against her neck.

"You wanna know a secret?"

"What's that?" I whispered.

She got to the car first and leaned up against the door. She waited until I was next to her before she answered me.

"You have to promise not to tell," she said.

"Fine," I said. "I promise."

"No," she said, all the easy joy in her face suddenly gone. "Seriously. I'll come and find you. I'll hurt you."

"Oh, will you?" I said. I felt brave enough now to put my hand onto her shoulder without much of a thought. Her eyes narrowed with amusement as I did it.

"You're a bad flirt, Hilly Wise."

"I think every girl in my school knows that. This is well established."

She laughed. "What kind of stupid name

is Hilly, anyway? Whose dumb idea was that?"

"It's short for Hilton."

"Still," she said, "it's kind of dumb."

"Don't Southern boys have names like that? That's what my dad always told me. That people would hear my name and think I was from the South."

She still hadn't moved. Her body: long and brown and gold. "They teach you rich white boys about the South in your fancy schools?"

"They teach us some," I said.

"I can't even imagine," she said. "I bet it's all just peach trees and horse races and funny accents."

Of course, what I wanted to say was that we learned about slavery.

"What's your big secret, anyhow?"

She turned and opened the car door. When she answered, she was facing away from me, and her voice was quiet.

"I'm gonna run away," she said.

"What? When?" I asked.

"I don't know. Soon. Me and Lem."

"Really?"

She nodded. "Really."

"Tell me when. I'll come."

"You will, huh?"

"Well," I said, trying to be funny, "I guess

it depends where you're going."

"Who knows? Somewhere else. Some-where nice."

"I don't believe it," I said. I kicked at the dirt. "Not at all."

"You don't believe it? Or you don't want to believe it?"

I couldn't think of how to respond to that. She was sitting on the passenger's seat of Charles's car. Her bare feet were on the sandy ground. The door was open. A thin sheen of sweat had emerged on her fore-head. Even though it was night, it was warm and muggy, the weather over the ocean stalled. She looked down to her shoes, hang-ing by their straps in her hands, and then up at me defiantly.

"I like being with you," she said.

What a thing to say! Somehow she had the confidence to utter this. There was no one around, not a soul within earshot, but still I swiveled to see if anyone had heard her. She laughed at me.

"Anyone ever say that to you?" she asked.

"Of course."

"Any *female*?"

"What makes you think that nobody has?"

"You just look it," she said. "That's all."

I thought to protest, but she had me. I threw my hands up. She reached into the car and put on the stereo. A man's voice, smooth, easy, sweet, and then a saxophone. I must have strained to see if I recognized who was singing.

"It's Nat King Cole," she said.

"Of course."

"Do you know who that is?" she asked.

"Sort of."

"Well, you either do or you don't," she said, and then she sighed. "I don't know why I like you, Hilly Wise. You're kind of skinny. You're not really that bright. You got a crazy man for a father running around, yelling at everybody. Plus, you got pimples."

"All of this is so nice of you to say."

"You're damn stupid, actually," she said, shaking her head. "If I had your money I'd be a genius. A real genius."

I laughed and looked back over my shoulder, toward the house. "Should I go? Or do you just want to keep me here and insult me?"

She reached for my hand and pulled me into the car. "Maybe I'm the stupid one."

The first thing she said to me when we were in the car was that I shouldn't try anything too fast on her, and then, not even a moment later, after she had kissed me only twice, she pulled away and whispered into my ear that Lem Dawson was standing outside, in the grass. We both grew very still. "This is fine," I told her. "This is fine. He's my friend," I said. She frowned. "He's not your friend," she said sadly. "You his master, idiot. He's your boy."

As I got out of the car, I heard her mutter under her breath, "I was right."

And that was the last thing I heard her say.

NINE

A storm came through that evening. It swept sand up onto the grass from the beach, shaking the oak trees free of their fat, salt-sprayed leaves and tossing my father's newly planted white hydrangeas onto the lawn, their blossoms lying across the grass like baseballs with their hides beaten off their backs. I lay awake in my bed, unable to sleep. It was four in the morning. Our house was still empty. I kept thinking about Savannah — her long fingers, brown in the bleed-off from the Packard's headlights, darker at the knuckles; the pale underside of her palm. Lem had taken her up into his apartment. She'd gone wordlessly, obediently, without once looking back. A few times I got up out of bed to look out the window and see if I could get a glimpse of her in his windows. But I couldn't. Everything there was dark. How were they possibly asleep? How could anyone sleep after a day like that? I was still awake two hours later when my father came home. He was drunk again, or drunk still, and I heard him crash into our dining table. It was stacked with long-stemmed wine-glasses left out by my mother earlier in the day. Robert Ashley was with him, too. I heard Robert's small, anxious voice, straining to control my dad's temper. It was warm, and I stayed there on top of my sheets, with the windows open, the loud crash of the sea unable to drown out my father's voice. Even from up in my bedroom, I could make out Robert's insistent, whispering apologies and my father's full-throated protests, and then at some point the unmistakable sound of my mother's coffee percolator beginning to boil. The last thing I heard before falling asleep was Robert Ashley imploring my father not to worry. "You need to relax, Art," he said. "The case is over. We settled."

When I finally woke up, late the next morning, I looked out the window to Lem's apartment. He was out near the cinder blocks, smoking a cigarette. When he saw me, he waved me down to join him. The lawn was a mess: a branch from a pine tree had been severed by the wind and tossed like a javelin through a glass lawn lantern.

There were shards everywhere, and pine needles; and in four large pieces, like a pumpkin split by an ax, there was the lantern, lying at Lem's feet.

"Wow," I said. "Look at all this. I must have slept through the worst of it."

I walked across the grass to him, smiling, trying to act as if he had no reason to be angry with me. I figured we were even: I'd caught him, he'd caught me. He was leaning against the garage, a garden rake beside him and a pack of Old Golds resting on the pile of stacked cinder blocks.

"You almost got yourself killed last night," he said.

"That's how you greet me? No *good morning*?"

"If Charles found out about that, about you two, he'd have killed you. I'm talking murder. Straight murder. He'd have cut your head off."

"Decapitation?" I said, a rising note of incredulity in my voice. "That's what you're threatening me with?"

"Please, Hilly. Don't act dumb. Not with me. I've seen this before."

I sat beside him and took one of his cigarettes. The ground was a mess of them. He'd been awake for hours, I guessed.

"Where is she?" I asked.

175

"I'm not telling you," he said.

"Oh God. You're not her father. Just tell me where she is."

"I'm her uncle."

"Is that the same difference?"

He got up and stood over me. He thought I'd be intimidated. His hat was canted on his head, a sharp, dark shadow on his face.

"Damn it, Hilly, you need to promise me, right here, at this moment, promise to God, that you'll keep away from her."

"I don't know what you think I was doing," I said, "but you're wrong. I know what I saw you doing last night. I think we both do. So why don't you tell me where she is, Lem?"

He turned his back to me. I saw his shoulders sink. He pointed up above us to the catwalk staircase. "Just for the night," he said.

That she was only a few feet from me was a relief. She'd slept in his bedroom, probably, that small space, the walls the gray of a sparrow's belly, with that window that looked out onto the patio. He'd have given her the bed and slept on the floor.

The heat wasn't bad yet. I figured it was ten-thirty, maybe eleven. I blew smoke out above us. I tried to act like someone confident and older, someone very much like my father. "It was just a kiss, Lem. One kiss. That's all it was."

He shook his head. "You know that if someone else caught you, they'd fuck *her* up, not you."

"No one's doing anything like that," I said.

"Listen to me," he said. "They'd *fuck* her up. You get me? That's how that works, Hilly. Nothing people hate more than what I saw last night."

Lem occasionally cussed in my presence, and I should have been used to hearing him talk like that. This was different, though, and if I didn't understand it by the expression he wore — his face was gravely tired, the lines beneath his eyes pronounced in the harsh light — I did by the fierce urgency in his voice. He slammed his hand into the wood shingle beside me.

"You get what I'm saying, right?" he asked.

"This isn't Mississippi," I managed. "People here aren't like that."

"Don't matter. You're an idiot if you think it matters a damn bit that we're up here in Bluepoint."

I looked up at his apartment, hoping for a glimpse of Savannah.

"That girl's got no one looking after her," he said quietly. "You understand how that is?"

"She's got her father," I said. "That's better than nothing."

"You don't know him."

"Still better than nothing," I said. I thought of Savannah's doll, the broken mouth, its jagged sewn smile. And then I thought of Savannah, rummaging through the burned remnants of what had been their house, finding it in her mother's box.

He laughed mockingly at me. "I didn't think you'd be the kind of guy to take advantage of your situation, Hilly."

"What are you talking about?"

He glared at me. The whites of his eyes were yellow. "I work for your father. She's my niece. That's a compromising situation. You understand?"

"It was her idea," I said. "She came over on her own. She likes me. I like her. It's really not that complicated a situation."

"She just wants someone to help her. Look after her. You got more money coming your way than anyone your age in this country. You get that? Does that make sense to you?"

"I don't think this has anything to do with money," I said.

It was clear the moment this left my mouth that I was unsure about it. I thought of Pauline McNamee kissing me at the

Wren's Bridge ice rink. How she'd started in about my father right away. When had a girl my age ever really wanted to kiss me? Savannah had said it herself: I was skinny and pimpled, and I wasn't very bright.

Lem took a cigarette from the pack. He seemed to study it before he lit it.

"You like her?" he asked me, his voice quiet.

I nodded quickly. Of course I liked her. I was filled with pity for what had happened to her, for what she had seen, for how she lived — those buckets — for how she had lost her mother, and because of all of that, I wanted to keep her safe: I was seventeen.

"Girl like that, in a situation like that, with her mother, with my sister, getting burned up like that: a girl like that's bound to do all sorts of foolish shit, Hilly."

He was pointing at me. He was a big man when he wanted to be, and to have him standing over me like that, in anger, was plainly intimidating. I backed up two steps, a short distance that he made up by taking two steps toward me, his finger still jutting out at me.

"Try putting yourself in her shoes," he was saying. "Try imagining for a minute, Hilly, what you'd do."

"What are you saying?" I asked.

179

The sun was in Lem's eyes, and he put up a hand to shield himself. He took a step closer to me, suddenly in shadows. There were only a few inches between us. He put both hands on my shoulders, like he wanted to shake me until I heard him clearly.

"I'm saying that her mind's not in the right place. She knows that if something changes, if her father decides he wants to go try to be a ballplayer again, God help us, she's going to be out on her own. Sixteen. No momma. No way to earn money for food. Nobody knows this like she knows this. You understand now, Hilly?"

I managed a weak grunt.

"You think I can take care of her?" he asked me, his voice growing louder. "You think your daddy pays me enough money to feed another person? You think I can get her clothes for school? Or her books? You think I can even get her a bus ticket south so maybe she can get back to her grandmama? Do you?"

"My dad pays you money," I said.

"Eight dollars a week," he said. "Eight."

I blanched.

"That's right." He nodded.

"W-w-well," I stammered, "I thought you were both running away, anyway?"

I knew this startled him. He shuddered a

180

little and fiddled nervously with the brim of his hat. Of course I understood what he meant, however much it hurt to hear it, and after a moment I got up from where we'd been sitting and walked to the cusp of the shore. The tide was low. I could see straight to the seafloor where the water was shallow; there were hundreds of tiny worn stones smoothed by the current. For a while I stood there and considered what Lem had said to me. I couldn't admit to him that Savannah was only the second girl I'd ever kissed. And I couldn't admit that I wished he hadn't come to interrupt us. But neither of these facts mattered much in comparison with what he'd said. My father was always warning me not to be taken advantage of. Whenever we were in the car together, driving in Wren's Bridge, or driving down Park Avenue in a hired Lincoln, he'd say this to me: men in his position were always at risk for being taken as fools. Because I was his son, and because he was my father, he wanted me to know this, and I had to know how to recognize when someone wanted something from me simply because of who I was. I'd always laughed him off, out of arrogance, and out of what by then was a deeply held belief that my father was a cruel, petty, stupid man. Now I felt for the first time the terrible possibility that my father had been right and I'd been wrong. Perhaps Savannah had come to me seeking protection, in a way, from a situation that for her had become especially precarious. I couldn't say that, had events been reversed, I wouldn't have done the same thing. Survival, I knew, was a fickle thing: no one ever cared about scruples when it came to making it to the next day.

We were a few yards down the beach. I looked back to Lem's apartment. There was a rustling behind his laundry, a billowing in the linens on the line. The wind turned his work shirts momentarily pregnant. It was her. She was there, above me, lurking. Smiling. Her hand went up slowly, a short, bashful, testing wave.

Then Lem was gone. Above me the lights flickered on in his apartment, and my father was walking across the grass to talk to me. He'd scared Lem off. I was positive that he'd have no memory of my refusing to intervene in his fight, or of hurling his flask at me. I knew him this well. His face was badly bruised, and swollen, although far less so than it had been a few hours earlier. As he drew closer, he took his car keys from his trousers and tossed them at me.

"How about you take your old man for a

drive, Hilly?"

I caught the keys easily, one-handed, all of them clanking in my palm. "Are you sure?" I asked.

"I can't really see," he said. He thrust his hands into his pockets. He squinted at me. "And I need to do some things inland."

His skin was flushed, and he was sweating, even with the cool breeze from the water. He closed his eyes for a moment longer than normal, and I decided that he was still drunk from the evening before. A small dolphin pendant dangled from the key ring. It was an unusually decorative flourish for my father. I thought of the dolphins we'd seen when we first arrived here.

"What about Robert?" I asked. "Can't he drive you?"

"I think he's still broken up about giving me this beating," he said, pointing at his face.

"Right," I said.

"He's sensitive like that."

"How does it feel?" I asked. "Your face, I mean."

"Doesn't feel good, Hilly," he said. Then he pointed at his car. "So, what do you say? When was the last time we just went out for a drive?"

I turned to look up again at Lem's apartment — the small louvered window and the wooden ledge behind it, where he had his row of potted Christmas cactuses. On the ground near his front door were dozens of cigarette butts, evidence of how long he'd waited for me to show this morning, and of just how angry I had made him.

"You want to ask him permission to go?" my father asked, laughing. "You want me to call him down and see if he thinks it's all right if you go out for the afternoon with your father?"

"No," I said, "that's not necessary."

"Are you sure? You don't sound sure. Let me see what old Lem Dawson thinks about the idea."

The Fleetwood was parked in the gravel beside the garage, two arching conifers nearby providing decent shade. It was exactly where I'd left it last night. I walked without a word across the grass and into the driver's seat, struck up the engine quickly — a deep, thunderous sound, my foot on the gas, a cough of exhaust breathing through the tailpipe. I had the door open. My father was standing, looking out at the water. I called out to him, but he didn't turn. He shifted his feet and put one hand on his hip. There were big, broad sailboats out on the water, and there were,

184

someone had told me, whales passing through on their migration north, or south, whichever it was. We were at the far edge of the continent. Out east, beyond my father, there was the ocean, and there were the great cities of Europe, and beyond that there were the small villages on the Baltic Sea where his own father had been born and where he'd been forced to flee. I had no idea what my father was looking at, exactly, not then, not on any of the days during which I caught him looking off at the water like that, his eyes narrowed, a serious, mournful expression on his face, but I've always thought, as I did at that moment, that he was thinking of his father, whom I knew only as a little man in a brown topcoat, small, black eyes beneath a great white brow, his hand on the rusted hood of a Studebaker Big Six — one photograph in a gilded frame, which my father kept at the corner of his desk. While he was alive, we couldn't communicate. My grandfather never learned English well enough to have a real conversation. My grandfather, that little, sweet man, would never have believed how successful his son had become.

When my father turned around, he seemed glad to find me in the car, and soon I had us off the gravel path on Beachside

Grove and out onto Route 6, where the dunes between Bluepoint and Truro were shrouded by mist. My father crossed his legs at the knee, his right foot dangling over the center console. He grew nervous and began to fidget with the stereo dials. His searching brought nothing. It was a cloudy morning, the sky cluttered with heavy, cottony cumulus clouds, and the radio this far out on the narrow arm of the Cape was a mess of broken signals. Occasionally there came the scratchy sound of a man's voice, a preacher's, or an announcer for a ball club, listing names I'd never heard of; briefly there was the momentary swell of a string orchestra, the first trilling notes of some symphony I didn't recognize. My father couldn't be convinced that slamming his fist against the face of the radio did nothing to affect the reception.

He had on a new watch. I noticed it then as we drove, and as the light struck through the windshield, glinting off his wrist. It was big and gold, and when he saw me looking at it, he told me that it was a gift from a client. "Cartier," he said, tapping its front face with his fingernails. "Supposedly this piece of shit costs more than this car. You believe that, Hilly?"

"If you say so," I said.

"It was a thank-you gift from a client."

"You must have really helped him out," I said.

My father laughed in a way that I knew to be fake. "I kept him out of prison," he said, "so he owed me."

"Really? How'd you do that?"

I looked over to him, and he seemed for a moment as if he wanted to tell me exactly what I'd asked. His nervousness was always most evident in his extremities — his fingers wiggled; his hands reached to straighten the fabric on his knees.

"I can't tell you that, Hilly. You know that." Then he saw me staring again at his wrist. "You want a watch like this?"

"That's OK," I said.

"No," he said, taking off his watch. He put it next to me, on my seat. "It's yours. I have enough watches. You keep it."

"Really?" I said.

"It's there. Take it. Leave it. Whichever you want."

"Isn't it expensive? Why would you give me something that expensive?"

"It's just money, Hilly. You get it, you spend it. It's just how it is. You can't take it with you. It'll all be yours eventually, anyway."

My father's wealth, I had begun to realize,

surpassed what most men considered to be normal. Occasionally, I caught something in his behavior, or in his posture, that seemed to me to be close to shame: shame for his good fortune, or an accumulated shame for the misfortune of others. His childhood had been lived a hair's breadth above poverty. And now this. At seventeen I wasn't sure exactly how wealthy we were. All I knew was that we had started off without anything, the three of us happily striving in our bungalow in New Haven, and now I was driving my father's Cadillac, opening it up on Route 6, the speedometer climbing as effortlessly as the second hand on my father's new watch. Beneath my feet the car hummed, and when the transmission shifted, I could feel the possibility in the engine.

We passed by a second set of high, smooth dunes. These were larger and more impressive than the first, and for a brief moment we were alone with them, just our black car and all that sand.

"It's like the moon might be," my father said as we passed. He was squinting out the window. His voice was thin, high, almost wistful, a rarity for him. "Don't you think?"

"I'm not sure I know what the moon looks like," I said.

He turned to me. I had one hand on the wheel — my right hand — and I had my left knee jutted up in just such a way as to keep us straight. This was how Lem had driven.

"Two hands, Hilly."

"There's no one on the road," I said. "It's empty. It's just us."

"Do what I say," he told me.

I put two hands on the wheel. We were headed south, toward the rotary at Orleans.

"So, what did you think of the way Robert took out your old man?" he asked. "Pretty brutal, huh?"

"I think he got in some lucky shots," I said.

"Nah." He laughed. He touched a long, rough gash on his cheek. "There's no luck in doing this to somebody."

"It's gonna scar," I said.

"Maybe the women will like it."

"Is that what you want?"

"You always want the broads to notice you," he said.

"How'd he learn to fight like that?"

"In the service," he said.

"Is that how he saved your life?"

He nodded. "Something like that."

"Why didn't you take the job with Silver and Silver?" I asked.

He touched his fingers gingerly to his face.

"I'm not talking about that with you, Hilly. That's none of your business. Frankly, it's none of anyone's business right now except Robert's."

"Are you really going to switch sides?"

"I'm a lawyer. There's no such thing as a *side* except for the side I'm on. It's not a sport."

We were passing by a row of closed seafood shacks. There were young men out in the driveways, loading in the morning haul through the kitchen doors. The harbormaster's truck was parked in the clearing, its bed filled with lobster traps and a stack of wooden clam barrels. I caught my father looking lustily out the window at the trucks and the stacked traps and at a pair of boys out in the grass, taking a hose to the long wooden boiling vats. Just the sight of this seemed to make my father happy, and when he began to interrogate me, he did it with a smile.

"Last night," he said. "You went out in the car. You go see that Negro girl?"

I felt his hand on the back of my headrest. "Who?"

"That young girl. The pretty colored one. The one that Lem has in his apartment. The one who was here last night?"

I knew enough about this to lie. "I think

you're still a little drunk."

He grinned. "I saw you this morning," he said. "You were arguing with Lem."

"We weren't arguing. We were talking."

"He was pointing at you, Hilly. I saw it."

I don't know how it became clear to me that we weren't going anywhere in my father's Fleetwood, but at that moment I knew that he'd given me his car keys so that we could speak freely in that perfect way that an automobile makes possible: we could talk without looking at each other.

"It wasn't what it seemed like," I said.

"Didn't he point at you?" he asked.

"He may have. But we were just talking."

"About what, Hilly?"

"Oh, I don't know," I said, thinking at that moment of Savannah — her shy wave — and all of Lem's clothing drying on the line.

"You were just talking to him," my father said. "How could you not know what you were talking about?"

"It was probably about baseball," I said.

"That's what you usually talk about, isn't it?" he asked.

"It is. Sometimes. He has a friend who was a ballplayer."

"No kidding. Like Jackie Robinson?"

"Sort of. Actually, he struck out Jackie Robinson. A couple of times."

He whistled. "How about that."

"That's probably what we were talking about."

"*Probably?* Hilly, it was only a few minutes ago." He made a show of consulting his new wristwatch, taking the Cartier off my seat and tapping the glass face of it. "He was pointing his finger at you not even fifteen minutes ago," he said. "You're lying to me. Why would you do that, Hilly? What don't you want to tell me?"

"I'm being honest," I said.

"In my experience, Hilly, whenever someone says that, they're not being honest. They want you to think that. But it's a lie."

"I'm not lying."

"You had my bag yesterday. My leather bag. Why'd you have my bag?"

"Oh, who cares!" I yelled out, into the car. "You lie all the time. You fired your client because of that ham? Like you're some pious Jew!"

"What was the girl doing here last night? And where did you go with all that stuff you had piled up in the car last night? All your mother's clothing? And what was Lem saying to you this morning?"

My father was a professional. His lack of a reaction to my counterpunch was effortless. All good litigators possessed this trick,

I knew. It was an ability to redirect questioning, to take new information and craft a separate and effective line of attack. A great attorney was like a skilled battlefield general: able to survey a huge mess, some unexpected movement, and still make a clean kill. The truth was that if I told my father about Savannah, she'd be the one to suffer. I knew this implicitly. But I also knew — terribly, inevitably — that my father would get me to say *something*.

"You know, Hilly, I think we ought to just cut this out, and I think you should tell me what was happening."

"Nothing happened."

"It's an impossibility," he said.

"What is?"

"You and that girl."

"I don't know what you're talking about."

He frowned. "I know something about it," he said, and then he coughed. "Impossibilities, that is." He had both of his hands on his knees. Like he might be sick. "Do you understand what I'm telling you?"

"Why are so you convinced that something happened?"

"He told me, Hilly. That's why. Lem told me this morning about you and the girl, and I just think we ought to talk about it before someone gets in trouble."

"I don't believe you," I said.

"Well, he told Robert. But it's close enough," he said, and then he laughed to himself. "At some point this morning, Bob saw Lem out in the grass. So they had themselves a chat. Bob's a pretty nice guy. People tell him things. Lem would never tell *me* anything."

"I know," I said, bitterly.

"Show me at least a little respect, Hilly," he said. "I don't know why you think I'm some monster."

"You made him run up and down the beach all summer like he was a mule! You're a slave driver!"

"I didn't tell him to go that way," he said. "I offered him a car. I told you that."

"You should have made him take a car! You just liked seeing him suffer!"

"You're wrong, Hilly. I offered him whatever he needed. I told him all that running was foolish. But he demanded it. He likes the water, he says."

His voice was calm, and not wholly unkind, but I was immediately furious — at him, for bringing me out here, for knowing about Savannah. It wasn't yet noon. The sun was already high, and the air was warm. The roads were empty. "Pull over," my father said. "Next place it looks good, stop."

I wanted to tell him something other than what he knew to be the truth, which was that I had been caught kissing Lem's niece. I'd thought I would know what he'd say to me when he found out, and what would happen to Savannah, and I'd even thought I would know what awaited Lem because of it all. But I couldn't have. Being caught with Savannah was one thing. But what I hated most was that Lem Dawson, who had been my friend, and whose reputation and comfort and dignity I'd tried to protect, had been the one to turn me in.

It seemed so easy.

"What he told you is a lie," I said quickly. "I didn't have anything to do with the girl. He's trying to get out of what he's done. He's the one who's done something wrong."

My father grinned. He was only thirty-five years old. He didn't have a gray hair on his head. He had rolled down the window to let in some air. That grin: his straight white teeth flashing at me, one of them missing, all of them taunting my surrender.

"What do you mean, Hilly?" he asked. "What's he done?"

"I caught him," I said. I was looking out through the windshield at a patch of sea grass, still and unwavering, and at a squirrel furrowing around near the road, a nut in its teeth. "I caught Lem. Last night. He was reading your papers. The ones you and Robert send. The Brooklyn Pages. Your work correspondence. I yelled at him. I wanted to tell you, but he wouldn't let me. That's why I had your bag."

TEN

Not even three hours later he was gone. It was my mother who told me he was going, but it was my father who went up into his apartment, followed by Robert Ashley, the two of them glum-looking and dressed in black. Behind them were four members of the Massachusetts State Police, guns drawn. By then it was evening, and two lines of cruisers had parked on the front grass, their sirens on, blue light washing and then not and then washing on the side of the house. Rain loomed.

It would be days before I discovered what the charges were — theft of personal items — and another month before I learned that my father had refused to drop the charges, but I was there, on the lawn, when two troopers took Lem down the catwalk staircase, his arms cuffed behind him, his head down. He was dressed, just as he had been when I'd first seen him, like he was going to church, in dark slacks and a fine white shirt. He didn't look up to me, not when he passed me, not when I called out to him and tried to block the troopers from arresting him. My father, his face still bruised and swollen, had the officers hold Lem upright so that he could spit at him and punch him twice in the head with his balled fists. He screamed at Lem. *Where are the goddamned papers, boy!* Lem's knees buckled at the impact, and then the cops took him away. When the caravan of squad cars left, their lights flashing, sirens coming on, I saw his dark head bobbing in the back window of the last car, a fine silhouette.

Four months later, he was dead, killed in prison, a knife in the neck. I was at Dartmouth when it happened, but still I blamed myself then, just as I blame myself now. News reports on his death were, predictably, scant. One short mention of it occurred in the police blotter of a paper called the *Boston Mission,* in print for only three years, during the 1950s: *A prisoner named Lemuel H. Dawson was found dead in the visitors' area of the state penitentiary last night at seven in the evening. Dawson was reportedly stabbed. Authorities say that the room was crowded at the time of his murder. Police believe another inmate was the culprit.*

Right after they took Lem away, my father finally came into the house and looked at me solemnly. "You did the right thing by telling me," he said. And then Robert, his hands still bruised and wrapped in white bandages, put a soothing arm on my shoulder. "It's tough, kid. I know," he said. Then, clearly agitated, he pulled me aside. "We're missing the Brooklyn Pages. Most of them. Do you know where he might have kept them?" I shook my head. Of course I didn't.

For the rest of the summer the apartment sat empty. At night, when I couldn't sleep, I would look out at it. He'd lived there for nearly five years before we'd arrived, and so quickly we'd had him put in jail. This, I decided, was the true gift my father had, not a gift for oratory, or for managing the press, but for degrading those who disagreed with him, who crossed him. Lem had left the windows open in his kitchen so that mist from the sea could water his plants. Somehow, this always made me choke up.

As summer ended, my mother began to talk of her plans for the whole structure — the garage, the back patio, and the living space above it. She wanted to level it, she told me one morning over cold muffins and orange juice. This was the first hint that my parents were going to build something enormous on their land. Of course they wouldn't just stay in a small cottage. "I'd like a studio to paint in," she said.

"But you don't paint," I offered. "You've never painted. You probably couldn't even paint a circle."

"Well," she said, breaking open a muffin, "I might start. All sorts of ladies like me paint."

"Ladies like you?"

"Wealthy ladies, Hilly."

"Did you know he was a painter?" I asked.

"Who, Hilly?"

"Lem?"

"Mr. Dawson the houseboy? That fellow we had arrested?"

I nodded. "Yes. Lem the houseboy."

"Is that so?" she said, tilting her head backward, as if considering the notion on the face of the clouds. "No," she said. "I don't believe that. What makes you say that?"

"He told me so."

"Hilly, you're just making up stories now."

"Why is it so hard to believe?"

"I don't know," she said. "I guess I just never imagined it."

"He painted every day," I said.

"He showed you these paintings?"

"Well, no." I said.

"So how do you know if he was telling you the truth?" she asked.

"He was telling me the truth," I said.

"Was this before or after you discovered him with your father's papers, Hilly?"

I blushed and got up from my seat. "Let me go get them," I said. "The paintings up there. I'll show you."

"You can't go up there!" she cried, reaching across the table to stop me.

I had been silent on the matter of Lem until now. My complicity in the situation had gone unmentioned since the evening he'd been taken away, when a detective for the state police took a very brief statement from me, in which I merely said that I'd told my father I'd caught Lem reading something that apparently he wasn't supposed to read. Since then, every mention of him by my parents I answered with a steely sort of silence. At night, when I went to sleep, I tried to imagine him in prison, how much he might be suffering, and then I tried to discover an angle from which I was not guilty for his fate. Of course, I never came up with anything good to make myself feel better.

And then, two days before we left Bluepoint for the summer, a team of men came to empty his apartment, lining up all of

201

Lem's belongings on the lawn: his furniture, his bookshelves, his stacks of detective novels, a paper folder full of photographs, and of course his leather portfolio. It was a slow process, the men combing over every inch of Lem's belongings. I didn't know whether they were looking for the Brooklyn Pages or whether they were looking for something good to take home for themselves. When it was done, my father and mother were down the beach, at Robert's house. Perhaps the sight of a man's paltry belongings spread out on the grass, so much small stuff under such a big sky, made it clear how foolish we had all acted over someone who really had nothing that we didn't have in dozens.

At some point it began to rain, first lightly, and then, hours later, very heavily, so that the ground where the portfolio was resting flooded into small gullies, drenching the bottom of the leather, staining it, and finally toppling it, so that it lay in the mud, its zipper half-open. It was a fine piece of leather, surely expensive. I wondered how he'd afforded it. It was terrible to think of his paintings stained with water. So I went up and got them and brought them into the house. I was afraid of what my father might do if he saw me there, but I had to do it. At that point, I still figured that Lem would eventually get out of jail.

It took me almost a half hour to reach Savannah and Charles by telephone, and another ten minutes of pleading before they would agree to come. They had every reason to distrust me, something I admitted to them. But it was the paintings that brought them to the beach that last time. "He'll want them," I said. "You know he will."

When they came, Savannah got out first and went wordlessly to Lem's belongings, piling up what she could into the trunk. I followed her as she worked, trying to get her to look at me. None of it mattered. At one point, she whipped around and hissed at me. "You my little dog or something? Stop following me. Get. Get, doggy."

Savannah took the portfolio from the house, running it to the car. Charles was the one who found the box. I'd forgotten about the box. When I saw it sitting in the mud, so wet, I started to cry. When Charles saw it, he put his hands up against the wood on the side of the garage. His knuckles clenched, and then, slowly, I saw him lower his body, so that his forehead was resting on the top of his knee. His hat fell into the mud, and when he bent to retrieve it, I think he discovered the extent of the damage. He opened the top of the box. He gasped, cried slightly, and tried desperately to dry the top few pieces of paper, taking off his coat and reaching inside the thing to stanch the wet sketches with his jacket. "They're running," he cried, turning to Savannah. "They're running!" The wind blew some papers out onto the wet grass. Photographs and sketches and notes streamed out of it, too, everything blown out over the grass and the sea by the wind. I went out onto the lawn, determined to help, but Charles stood and put his hand up to stop me.

"Christ almighty, you need to get lost, boy. You hear me?"

When I threatened to keep trying to help, he cocked his head at me. At my foot was the photograph of Lem's grandparents. I picked it up and offered it to him.

"I ought to kill you," he said.

The last I saw of Savannah, she was bending to retrieve a metal box. It was a simple box, a small square. She wiped the rain off the lid and opened it. She removed something from inside, turned it over in her hand. I couldn't see what it was. She put everything into a brown paper bag she'd brought. And then she was gone.

■ ■ ■ ■

Part II

■ ■ ■ ■

ONE

A brick wrapped in newspaper. Glass everywhere. No witnesses. Nothing inflammatory about the paper, nor, really, about the brick — no words written on it, no note attached, no *Coloreds go home,* no *Not in my town, nigger,* no *This time a brick, next time a bullet.* No protests outside. No sit-ins. No prior record of intimidation, threats, altercations. No complaints to the local police, the state troopers, no reports filed in Washington with the DOJ. Nothing sinister, really, about the lease on the place, no kickbacks, no surplus taxes, no sweeteners, no handshakes out back of the town hall with the mayor — a man with a graveled voice, a whiskey nose, soft hands — no intimation of anything nefarious, really. No fire hoses here. No dogs. No photo spreads in *Life* magazine, no tributes in *Ebony,* nothing in the *Wall Street Journal* saying that those marching for their rights were asking for it, that they were communists, agitators, utopians. No midnight rallies on the town green, no torched crosses, no guys in white hoods just standing around on Main Street, trying to scare the shit out of you. Not here. No public proclamations from the steps of the YMCA, calling the black man a scourge, a cancer, a threat to their women, an instance of social leprosy; none of that. In fact, when the churches burned in South Carolina, in Georgia, in Alabama, in Mississippi, the school kids here raised money, cut a bank check, sent it to the NAACP, wrote cards in marker with cheery salutations like *Peace* and *Love* and *Respect FOR ALL.* After Dr. King's murder, a vigil was struck up on the green, housewives and children and all the men, out with candles. In the groceries, on the baseball diamond, in line at Kreutzer the butcher's, at the landfill, in the corn-fields, not even any whispering. Just the brick — thrown, someone said, from a moving car, through the front plate window of the town's only diner. Something about the speed of the brick and the serious amount of damage. Something about the way the brick landed. Something about the cut of the glass shards as they lay on the tile. You just can't wreck a window like that standing still.

This was where I'd found Charles Ewing, in a town called Ebbington, Iowa. It was the fall of 1972. I saw him through a hole in the tarp that covered the broken window at Foreman's Diner. He wore a black apron, a white work shirt, and red suspenders. From what I'd seen of Ebbington, it was little more than six stoplights, a crosshatch of avenues, a grocery with mums arrayed in the window, and a wasted, dust-dry baseball diamond called Gaithersburg Grounds. Of course, I thought. Charles would end up here, across from a ball field.

By the time I got there, a few days after the incident, police still had caution tape wrapped between the parking meters out front, and there was a stationary cruiser idling outside. Apparently, teenagers had tried to loot the place right afterward, steal Charles's toasters, his stash of whipped cream canisters for their nitrous gas. Someone on the street had told me this. The cruiser had its flashers going, muffler exhaust thick like wood smoke. It was midday, the sun white and weak. A wet banner hung across the street, advertising a parade for Halloween, still two weeks away. Children had painted ghosts and ghouls in yellow and orange. *Come get spooked,* it read. A poor choice of words, if only someone stopped to think about it. There was a Presbyterian church down the street, its wooden doors like the gateway to a castle, the steeple an upturned funnel. One officer was out in front of the diner, shivering. When he saw me, he came over.

"Hilton Wise," I said, flashing my business card with aplomb, as if it were a serious credential, an FBI badge. "*Boston Spectator.* I'm a reporter."

"You want to talk to him, then? Go talk to him, he won't bite. He's pretty ornery right now, but he won't bite."

Before I could answer, the cop had gone around to open the front door to the place, sounding a bell strung up on the hinge. Even though I knew otherwise, a part of me still doubted it was really him.

"Slim! Hey, Slim! Got a guy here from the paper. Some guy from Boston."

"No," I said, feeling a panicked sweat on my forehead. I thought to tell the cop that I'd seen what I needed to see, that I'd just turn around and head back home.

"I already talked to the paper," I heard Charles say. "Tell the paper I'm busy."

"Come on, Slim," the cop said, smiling at me. "He looks harmless."

A moment later, Charles was in the door-way, glaring at me. His clothes hung from him, all of it too large for his thin body. His grip on the broom whitened his knuckles.

"I got nothing more to say," he said. He was exhausted, sweat on his upper lip in beads. "Really. I don't want to be rude. But I got nothing to say."

And apparently neither did I. Twenty years of worrying and repenting had made me mute in front of him. I cleared my throat, took a pencil from my shirt pocket. I decided I wanted a pen. Then I decided I wanted a different notebook, a clean one. I flipped some pages back, smoothed them down, straightened my hat. I cleared my throat again for good measure. For a moment I thought I saw some flickering of recognition in him. I wasn't so different, I thought. Age had done to me what it did to everybody. But instead of recognition, what I saw on Charles's face was a clear but polite trace of annoyance. He didn't know who I was. He didn't remember me.

"Listen," he said, wiping his forehead, barely looking at me now, "I'm busy. Trying to get the place back open. We've been closed for a few days now. So —"

"Right," I said. "I'll come back."

He managed a faint smile. "Should be open tomorrow. Maybe the day after."

For five years now I'd worked as a reporter for a paper out of Boston, tracking down cases of racial intimidation, violence, voter suppression, anything that fit into what my editors liked to call the *race beat*. This was how I'd found Charles Ewing in Ebbington, Iowa. Part of my job was to scan the AP wire, the Reuters and McClatchy wires, the UPI dispatch, looking for incidents that might make a good story for my editors. I'd have been better served sticking around Boston. I knew this even then. We were two years away from the busing crisis, and already you could see the fault lines emerging, the heat building, animus bleeding out of the court queue, onto L Street. But there were better reporters doing that beat, and better papers. The *Spectator* was a decent daily, with a better-than-average sports section. That was what I'd started with at the paper. I had the job I'd always wanted — a ticket to every ball game at Fenway, a seat in the press box, permission to go into the dugout and interview anyone I felt like talking to. Eventually the games become boring. No matter how big a fan you are, no matter how much of a thrill it is to get to bump shoulders with, say, Joe Willie Namath minutes after Super Bowl III, when he's still got blood on his elbow, when he's only just booked it through the tunnel with his finger raised to the nosebleed seats, when you can still make out the imprint of the Baltimore Colts horseshoe on his leg, the initial boyish thrill of those games starts to fade. Part of the general contract of being a sportswriter, though, is the obligation to manufacture content whether the games demand it or not. When it got old and I felt like I was really losing my love for the games, I asked for a transfer to the national desk. To the *race beat.* Here I was.

At least once a week, I'd go through the big mess of dispatch papers and wire reports that piled up on my desk. This was four years after Dr. King had been murdered at the Lorraine Motel. The awful news kept coming. Occasionally you'd stumble on a good story that hadn't been picked up by any of the bigger outlets, and if you were lucky, you could earn yourself a decent byline for a few days. Of course, I was also looking for her. For Savannah. I was always looking. In twenty years, I hadn't ever heard from her. Not one letter, not one telephone call. I didn't really expect that she'd try to reach me. But I still wanted to find her —

to see what had happened to her, to see if she'd turned out all right, to see if she might forgive me for everything I'd done.

When I saw the news about Charles, I put in a few calls to the paper in Cedar Rapids. Iowa seemed an unlikely place for him to be. And Charles Ewing seemed like a common enough name for it to be somebody else. I asked them if they had a picture they could send, and when it came, his photograph was right below the fold in the *Gazette.* This was big news in that part of the world. The picture showed the broken window, the brick like a mortar shell resting in the mess. Beside the window, Charles stood in a suit and a tie and a hat. This, the caption, reported, was his place, his window.

Ten minutes later I dropped everything, booked a flight, and went to Iowa.

Why would somebody like *you* want to do something like *this*?

When we first started dating, this was what my girlfriend, Jenny, said when I told her how I earned my money. I took her through the progression step-by-step: sports reporter with a hankering to get more serious; an open chair on the national desk; the arc of unending racial violence across the Bible Belt and the upper Mid-west and New

214

England, and in California, and really just about everywhere else; and, I guess, a certain predisposition I held against the general, flagrant idiocy of bigotry. Jenny was a fourth-generation Baltimore Catholic with three brothers in Vietnam, one of whom — Jerry, broad-shouldered, supposedly an ace shot — was her twin. They hadn't waited to get drafted, didn't stand around at the Harbor Armory, pissing themselves about what number they might pull. They'd just gone in and enlisted without much consternation as to what the Pentagon might do, something she was constantly telling me, and a fact she was plainly proud of. She was a woman of varied tastes — ethnic food, crude humor — a woman who detested the foreign cinema so fashionable then. ("Why would I want to sit through another Bergman film when the last one was so cold, and quiet, and so *fucking* dreadful!") When it came to politics, she professed to be a fan of both Johnson and Nixon. Because of her brothers, she'd been hell-bent on supporting the mission, expanding into Cambodia, really just fucking torching the Vietcong, her logic being that expansion begat aggression, and the full weight of American aggression had, as she kept telling me, no equal in the world. She would pound her

215

fist into her palm to tell me this. Jenny had been the one to teach me that all politics isn't local, as Tip O'Neill would have it a few years later, but personal, and that party affiliation or ideology is eventually bullshit when every potential enemy incursion is aimed at the head of your twin brother.

But when it came to race, she grew quiet. I understood this. Nobody really wanted to hear about it anymore. This was why she put the question to me: *Why would somebody like you . . .* By *you,* I suppose she meant to point out my meekness, my squeamishness around blood or stories that got too gory; or perhaps she meant to point out my whiteness, which during a Massachusetts winter became even more pronounced. And by *something like this* — well, I suppose that didn't need much of an explanation. Nobody liked to talk about what Jenny called "all this terrible racial business," the last word pronounced, in her weird Baltimore accent, as *bizniz.* "Doesn't it upset you?" she asked, flipping through photographs I'd taken of a desecrated black graveyard in South Carolina. They were Instamatic pictures, taken not for the paper but for my own research, and she handled each one carefully, as if they were bound to become evidence in a trial someday. When she was done, she pushed them across the table. "I mean . . . this is just *disturbing,* Hilly."

I hadn't ever told her about Savannah. What would I have said? That I'd kissed her twenty years ago, that we'd tried for a minute to go to sleep in the same car, that I'd gotten her uncle arrested and that he'd been murdered in jail, and that in my head, all of these things were connected: race and lust and death? And even then, if I'd somehow managed to say this with even a shard of dignity — what then? How do you explain to someone like Jenny that my thinking of Savannah for so long wasn't a fetish? That I wasn't just flexing my newfound liberal muscles or trying to prove that not every white American was complicit in some systemic prejudice? That I wasn't collecting a stamp on the game board of female varieties: first a black girl then a Native American and then an Asian and then so on and so on? How does somebody explain something like that? I was always looking for Savannah's name to pop up on the AP wire. Always. I was always looking for her. Did I tell Jenny this? Should I have mentioned that whenever my editors sent me to, say, Cleveland, to report on the Indians–Red Sox games, the first thing I did was search the telephone directory for her name? Did I admit that once, having stumbled across a listing for an *S. Ewing* outside of Tuscaloosa, I'd skipped the Auburn-Alabama game, sat outside some poor man's house in a rented Cutlass Supreme, daring myself to ring his doorbell, and then, having fucked off and wasted a whole day, gone and filed a completely fabricated report on the Crimson Tide victory?

What I knew to be true was that I'd confused my curiosity for Savannah's whereabouts, my concern for her condition, with affection. I knew this without any doubt. Her specter muddied every relation I had. Jenny constantly pleaded with me to tell her what was bothering me, even when I wasn't sure that anything was bothering me at all. A typical interaction:

Her: What is it?
Me: What are you talking about?
Her: You were crying in your sleep.
Me: That's ridiculous.
Her: I was right next to you. I watched it happen.
Me: It was allergies. It's allergy season.
Her: Those are some sad allergies, Hilly.

The foolishness of all this, the sheer, pure,

juvenile silliness of it, didn't escape me. I'd
been with Jenny now for two years — a
lifetime, compared with the few moments
I'd spent lying beside Savannah in Bluepoint. I knew Jenny's family, what made her
laugh, which movies she liked to quote,
what her drink was, what her father had
been like. I knew Jenny's body, what made
her excited, what disgusted her. I knew
where to take her in Manhattan, which Italian places; what she ordered in a Chinese
restaurant; how she liked her burger cooked.
She'd moved in after nine months. On
Sunday mornings we'd walk down the
Esplanade to watch the rowers on the
Charles. Or we'd take a car west of the city
to shop at the farm stands in Lexington. I
knew nothing about Savannah, not even
what name she went under. But she'd
become stuck in my memory, regardless.
Just her. I certainly wouldn't tell Jenny this,
would I? Did I tell her that everyone else
after Savannah lost her shape, became
blurry; everyone else ran together? Come
up with any metaphor — a filmstrip burning up in the projector; a paragraph I could
not stop rereading; a record cracked and
repeating — all of them fit. Did I admit I'd
been thinking of her for so long that it
seemed sensible — reasonable, even — to

compare every new woman I met with Savannah? As if she were an ex-wife. As if she'd made me a widower. Even when I'd first met Jenny, there had been a moment when I'd thought to myself, *She's pretty, and she's sharp, but isn't Savannah better somehow?* I kept thinking that love, or whatever it was that I felt for her — affection, addiction, adoration; or maybe it was just obsession, plain and simple obsession — possessed on its own an intrinsic half-life such that one day soon I'd wake forgetting who she was, or what she looked like, or what, at sixteen, her laughter, and then later her fear, had sounded like. To the series of therapists and analysts and social workers who had the misfortune of listening to me, I displayed simultaneously a pitch-perfect self-awareness and a desperate urge for self-sabotage. No amount of talk could dislodge this. Surely the effects of love on the heart diminish over time, I'd thought. Such a moment of nothingness — just a kiss! — couldn't hold someone like *me* hostage.

But it had, and here I was, in little Ebbington, Iowa, hoping that I might convince her father to talk to me. Of course I wanted his forgiveness. This was as true as anything in my life was true. But what I really wanted was *her* forgiveness. She'd loved Lem in a way that she could never love her father, and I'd taken him away.

I was fairly sure that murder had no half-life.

I stood on the sidewalk outside the diner. I'd imagined this reunion before, of course, but we always saw each other by accident when I thought of it, not because I'd seen his name come across the AP wire and flown four hours to see him. Not because some bigot had thrown a rock through his window. Whenever I'd picture him, I'd see him alone on a street somewhere — in Chicago, or in Philadelphia. I'd see him at the movies or at a New York Knicks game. I'd see him in the airport lounge, waiting for a flight from Miami to Houston. He'd be the guy two tables over from me at the Iridium while some hack played "In a Sentimental Mood" in the wrong key, mucking up the sax line. In my fantasies he'd be prosperous because I wanted him to be. The man who'd lived in that cabin with those buckets, the man trying to put back together a severed fishing rod — that guy would definitely have been erased by time, replaced by someone successful, diligent, responsible, someone healed and bighearted. Because so much time had passed, and because my sins and errors had been committed in my youth, when I knew nothing, and because I had done what I had done out of insecurity and fear, Charles would find it within himself to say simply, *I forgive you, Hilly.* That's what I wanted. That's what I needed.

I was still outside the diner a few minutes later when the police officer told me to go. "Do what he said, buddy," the officer said. "Come back tomorrow. He'll be in a better mood."

Two

That Sunday, in October of 1972, my father appeared as a guest on *Meet the Press*. I have a recording of the broadcast, downloaded from the web. For whatever reason, my copy is without sound — an error in the transfer from film to tape to the tiny file at home on my computer, streaming now in my office as I write this, flickering, mute, everyone long dead but him. Everyone a ghost but my dad. His hands are locked at the knuckles, behind the folded tent of his name tag. Unlike the other guests, my father has no middle name. I've seen his birth certificate, held it in my hands. That section is blank on account of his father — *my* namesake — who believed that in America, brevity won the day, that two names bested three. Consider the founding fathers. Adams, Madison, Franklin, Washington, Jefferson. No middle names. So for him, just Arthur: Celtic for *bear,* Gaelic for *stone.*

Perfect for my father: *the stone bear.* And then, Wise. That name. He'd worn it better than I had. To me it was a lark, as ridiculous as anything, a source for mockery. How could the name Wise ever be uttered without it sounding like a joke?

This isn't early color television, but it might as well be. There is the saturation of his hair dye, singed, almost, by an overhead top light, black at the part, blacker than in 1947, the black hair of a boy, but on the body and face of a fifty-five-year-old. There is the rainbow of the peacock feathers on the NBC logo, the red matching the red of my father's pocket square. There is the glint in the diamond of his tie bar: a few thousand dollars there. There is the pinched flaw in his Windsor knot: immaculate blue silk, one of a closetful, fifty dollars each. Beneath the flimsy desk, he's likely to have on something Italian. Black Bruno Magli. One hundred dollars new in New York. What would become known as the OJ Simpson shoe. These were his favorites. There is the way his hands quiver as Lawrence Spivak begins to ask him something, his shirt cuff lifting. Nerves on national television; just a trace of sweat on his hairline; no French cuffs today. But there's the watch, Cartier, possibly the same one he tried to give me that day in

Bluepoint. He seems just as imposing to me on screen as he did in reality. Of course, he looks just like me. At a certain point his reputation should have faded. Men, even great men, have only a short moment when everything — luck, skill, ambition — works perfectly in concert. But not him. On tape, he is quite a good deal younger than I am now. But still. Your father is always older, always.

The picture cuts now to a photograph of a parked airplane. The edit is jumpy, the image coming on, then going away, then coming back, the V-hold straining. It's unclear to me if this was how the image was broadcast or if this is just how it was recorded, digitized, streamed to me. Again: the plane, stationary on a nondescript runway, a big jetliner, with a row of windows closed to the sun. A logo on the tail fin tells me that this is probably Sunbeam Air Flight 81. Takeoff out of Denver, 11:00 a.m., August 1972. Estimated arrival at LAX, 1:03 p.m. The plane was found in pieces in the Rockies, the cockpit six miles from the tail. His nickname has become Arthur Crash, but it might as well be Arthur *Cash*. Robert Ashley once wrote to me that if I were to look outside on an average day, an average clear day where you could see jets coasting by at forty thousand feet, and I picked out just one flight — any flight, like a kid picking just one card from a street magician — there was a good chance my father was making some money off it. Either because of insurance or some judgment on the airline, or because they had asked him to make sure they couldn't be sued the way Boston Airways was sued. Every jet wake: cash. Every sonic boom: cash. Every landing, smooth or not: cash.

Now: a shot of Nixon. There's a rumor that the president might make my father the head of the FAA. When I look closely, I can read the initials *FAA* on Spivak's mouth, and then there's my father's big, bright smile.

I didn't need to work. Not at the paper. Not anywhere. For nearly twenty years now, my father had kept an interest-bearing account for me in New York at McKinley & Sons. If I could dream it — a penthouse in Paris, parasailing in Puerto Vallarta, a villa fronting the clear sea of the Adriatic, a fleet of yachts, a ski chalet, an oil refinery in El Paso, even my own private baseball club, that thing I'd asked for so long ago in New Haven — I had the cash for it. If I'd wanted to, I could have walked into any of McKinley's branches in New York or Chicago and one of the McKinley boys would have been obligated to cut me a check on the spot. But shortly after Lem was arrested, I'd left for Dartmouth, and afterward, for the most part, I had little to do with my family or their money. They were in New York, and I'd settled in Boston. At the beginning, in my early twenties, I saw them on holidays. For my thirtieth, my father threw me a party at Honey's on Fifth, where at the end of the night, he tried to give me a beautiful waxed twin-cylinder Jaguar that he'd had parked out front. He'd dangled the keys in front of me. "Take it! It goes really fast! It's yours!" For my thirty-fifth he'd tried to give me a part of Wise & Ashley, which probably could have kept five generations of my grand-children afloat. But I took nothing. I wanted to work. If nothing else, he'd given me this. "It's waiting for you," my father said that night, after I refused him. He tried to give me a kiss on the cheek. I backed away. "It'll always be waiting for you."

For a while, out of duty or guilt or some combination of the two, I called him whenever I was in the city so we could meet for an awkward lunch someplace loud and conspicuous, someplace where we could be together but ignore the troubles between us. He hated the way I dressed, the work I did, the women I dated. But, more important, he knew that I considered him responsible for Lem's death, that this was the reason I'd never touch his money. He considered my forgiveness of Lem's crime a character flaw, evidence that at my core I lacked the strength of conviction that had made him such a success. My mother suffered the most from all of this. I had nothing against her, really. There were times when she'd drop the pretense and she'd seem to me to be the same woman she'd been before she got rich. The same woman I remembered dancing to the radio in New Haven. But she refused to think that my father could have had anything to do with Lem's murder, and I did. How could I not? He could have dropped the charges. After all, they were just letters. And then, that knife? Reports had it as a long knife, not some jailhouse shiv — a real weapon. How had a knife like that ended up in Lem's jail cell?

When I woke that Sunday in my hotel room outside Ebbington, this was the episode of *Meet the Press* airing on television, this last bit the part I remember catching: Spivak thanking everyone for coming, a quick shot of my father behind his desk, and then a word from their sponsors. I'd woken late, and I was groggy. Driving back to my hotel after I'd left Foreman's, I'd somehow ended up at the edge of a field miles away from where I needed to be. Two wrong turns had deposited me on a road so narrow that the side mirrors on my rental whacked at the planted corn edging the pavement. I was exhausted and still shaken from seeing Charles. Then a funny thing happened: the hills began to look like the sea. Indeed, the whole place looked like I had come upon Bluepoint somehow from an entrance I hadn't ever known of — some detour that cut across the country to the Atlantic. When the wind got at the peaks of the crop, I swore they were waves. A spinning windmill from a thousand yards was suddenly a lifeguard's chair; the curved spine on a farm sprinkler became the iron trusses on the Sagamore.

I had a message from Jenny waiting for me, slipped under the door while I slept. It read, simply: *Your boss told me where you were. Call home.*

Home: my street in Beacon Hill, the line of brick row houses that rose up Mount Vernon to the big old building where I had my apartment. It was a simple, small two-bedroom with a view of the Charles. When

I'd last talked to Jenny, I was at the office, arranging my ticket out to Iowa. She'd moved in because the lease on her apartment in Allston was up, and because I wanted to see her more often. I'd thought that if she were around more, then I might stop thinking about Savannah and she might replace whatever it was that made it so I couldn't stop thinking about her. Almost on cue, the apartment started to fall apart, as soon as she was there. The roof started to leak. The radiators needed an overhaul. Our landlord tried to patch it all up, but the problems kept coming: my television refused to change channels; my turntable ruined every record I tried to play; the refrigerator I'd been forced to buy stopped cooling the food and started spoiling everything I bought. Without my father's money, I couldn't afford to fix it all.

My hotel room in Iowa wasn't much better: spare, smoked in, the carpet worn through, marks on the wall where the headboard hit the paint. The bed was a twin, just big enough for a twelve-year-old. At the foot of the mattress was a writing desk, and beside that, an ashtray the size of a salad bowl. The curtains opened onto a slow-moving curl in the river, which was thin, calm, a felled tree crossing it like a makeshift footbridge.

Across the line, Jenny was hoarse.

"I'm exhausted," she told me. "I've been exhausted ever since you left. Just wiped out." She took a long, reedy breath, as if trying to sit up or to steel her strength. "I've been drinking coffee all day. And I can't wake up. Maybe you should come home. Maybe I'm sick."

I got up off the bed and walked to the window. There were people on the river-banks, fishing, and I wondered if they could see into my room. I hated that feeling — of being watched. At home, Jenny was the opposite. Because she'd grown up with broth-ers, she had a boy's notion of modesty, which meant that she had none.

"Maybe you should call my doctor," I said.

Our telephone was in the kitchen, but the cord went everywhere. I thought of her, barefoot, going from one room to another, swiping a finger through the dust on the mantel.

"What are you doing in Ohio?" Jenny asked.

"Iowa," I said.

"What, honey?" Her voice was a sweet sort of hoarseness; butterscotch.

"I'm in Iowa," I said, "not Ohio."

"What happened in Iowa? What could

possibly happen there?"

"Someone put a brick through a window."

"Hmmm. Black guy's window?"

"Yep."

"Stupid question: there are black guys in Iowa?"

I sighed. "There are. I just saw the window. Talked to some cops."

"Oh, Hilly, what are you *doing* out there? Is it dangerous?"

"It's not dangerous," I said. "It's just work."

"Are you sure? Don't make the wrong people angry. OK? Don't piss the wrong people off."

"I'll try," I said, doing my best to sound cocksure, tough, unshakable.

"Windows break everywhere," she said. "I'm sure someone put a brick through a window here today. In Boston. *Where you live.* I don't understand why you need to go so far away."

"I'm sure you're right," I said. "But I think I could get something good here." I went to the window again, pulled back the drapes, brown and starchy in my hands, like reams of burlap hanging on a rod. The boys on the river were out in T-shirts, despite the cold. Midwesterners were immune to the weather, I was learning. I needed a winter coat, and there were kids outside like it was the summer. "It'd be a think piece. How even the smallest, most peaceful towns are more like the big cities than we know."

"I'm not your editor," she said. "You don't need to convince me."

"I know," I told her, even though, of course, I felt I did. The hotel was called the Garden. It was my fourth hotel room that month. My job, if nothing else, kept me away from Jenny more and more. There'd been a time in my twenties when I'd lived like this: six cities in seven days; every meal alone in a restaurant; my editor's telegrams awaiting me at reception. Those first years, I took everything they threw at me: spring training, Ivy League football, high school hockey, even a stint in Barrows, Maine, for a rafting contest between two now-defunct girls' colleges. I was young, and I thought hotels were glamorous. Now, just walking through the front door, fiddling with the keys, having my credit card run on carbon paper — all of it exhausted me. The Garden felt like a hospital room. The sheets were stiff, musty, unwashed. This was a place you came to do secretive, shameful, terrible things. Why else would you come to Ebbington?

"There are more people in Brooklyn than

in the entire state of Iowa. Did you know that? I'm looking that up right now in the *World Almanac*."

"It's not surprising," I said.

"I hate being sick," she said, her voice breaking. "I'm afraid I might throw up. I hate throwing up. I'm so tired, it's like I'm walking in a swimming pool. That's how hard it is."

"Did you call the doctor? It's probably just a virus. You'll be better tomorrow."

A sigh. Quiet. Delicate. I imagined her adjusting the bracelets on her arm, something she did when she was nervous; she collected them. She liked plain gold bangles, and already I'd gotten her two. She had them going up both arms, halfway to the elbow.

"How long does it take to file a story on a broken window?" she asked, her voice suddenly higher. Maybe she was sitting at our kitchen table, wearing one of my old dress shirts over her underpants.

"I have to interview the guy whose window it is."

"Then?"

"Then, probably interview some more cops. Then get a few people on the street to tell me what they think. Then, I come home," I said.

From across the line I heard the sound of a kitchen chair wincing against the hardwood. We had a tiny galley kitchen, the sort of thing that made you want to do anything but cook. Even if our oven worked. It was hard to have two people in the space at once.

"When, Hilly? When does that happen? Like, tomorrow? Can you even fly out of Iowa? Do they even have planes there?"

I wanted to get off the phone, wind down the conversation, do that trick with your voice that everyone understands is the cue to end the call. I had to get into town, to see Charles. "I don't know. It happens when it happens. Listen, go to the doctor. Then call me to tell me what she says."

She cleared her throat. "Your father says I should go see *his* doctor. Some guy on Cape Cod."

"Did he call?" I asked.

Another prolonged silence. Now I could hear with certainty her bracelets clinking together. "Yeah. We talked for a minute. Is that bad?"

"He have anything interesting to say?"

"The usual," she said, chuckling. "Money money money. Plane crash plane crash plane crash."

"That it?"

"He said he was calling from a boat. Said

235

it was some fancy phone. Is that even possible?"

"Who knows."

"Said he was docked with some millionaire client of his."

"Makes sense."

"And . . ." She hedged. "He had a cake sent to the house."

"A cake?"

"Yes. A cake." She *tsk*ed her tongue. "It's something people eat for dessert, Hilly."

"What's my father doing sending you a cake?"

"I mentioned that when I was sick, my mother used to make me this vanilla cake with green frosting. So he sent me a cake. It has blue frosting. But it's close enough."

I laughed. "His assistant sent it."

"It was a nice gesture, Hilly. Very nice."

My father. I could see him out on a boat somewhere, six rum and Cokes deep, chatting up my girlfriend, thinking of a way to make me look bad.

"You shouldn't accept anything from my father," I said.

"Oh, I know the drill, Hilly," she said, feigning exhaustion. "I called some of the neighborhood boys over and made them test the cake before I ate anything. Nobody died."

236

I laughed. "You think that's funny."

"He's plenty nice to *me*," she said. "I don't get involved in any of your power struggles."

"He likes pretty girls. You were probably the highlight of his day."

"What would your mother think of that?"

"That's a good question, Jenny."

She'd figured out that I was Arthur Wise's son quick enough. A few magazine articles, a few photo spreads, and the mystery wasn't that difficult to unravel. It still isn't. She'd never pressed me about our relationship, and so I'd never really talked about him. She'd gotten it in her head that our major disagreement was over money; he wanted to give it to me, and I wanted to be more self-reliant. It was easier to let this slide than to explain everything.

Jenny went on: "He kept asking about the account," she said. "Said he could have Billy McKinley come by and talk to us if we were interested."

"What did you say?"

"I didn't know what to say. So I said nothing."

"That's good."

"Maybe you should just take it."

"You want it, right? That's why you're saying I should take it?"

"What if I do want it? Is that so bad? Money doesn't necessarily make you a bad person."

"No. But that much money magnifies whatever might be bad in you."

"What about poverty? What does poverty do?"

"We're not poor," I said.

"Tell that to our bed frame that keeps breaking," she said.

"I'll look at it when I get home," I said.

"Tell that to your crappy fridge. Or that showerhead you bought. Tell that to the crack in the roof that leaks water all over the place."

"That," I said, thinking about the roof, *"that's* the landlord's responsibility."

A small, humiliating scoff. "How much, exactly, is a shitload?"

"Excuse me?"

"He said that you had a shitload of money in that account. He asked me if I knew that."

"He did, huh?"

"He seemed very intent on me knowing that you had a shitload of money."

Of course my father would say this to her. To impress the girl I was with.

"I don't know how much is in it," I said.

"How could you not know?"

"I'm not interested in his money."

"Still. How could you not even know?"

"I just don't look. I'm not interested in being rich."

"You're lying."

"It's blood money."

"He told me you'd say that."

"That's rich."

"No. *You're rich.* Somebody else would have sued those airlines, Hilly."

"Maybe. But he did. People died and he got rich. There's no other way to see it."

"He seemed to think that you had a good deal of money in that account. He made this whistling sound. I don't know; when a guy like that whistles at money, I'm inclined to think that means a lot is really a lot. Like, millions."

"Well, he made it. He's fond of the things he makes. Like anybody. You'd whistle at a birdhouse if you made it, if you put it up in the tree and it looked good."

"What if I asked you to take the money?" Jenny asked. "What if I demanded that of you?"

"If I take even a cent, a *cent,* he'll expect something from me. He'll want me to be his little partner in crime."

"*Crime.* That's ridiculous. You're acting like a little kid."

"It's true."

"When am I going to meet him, Hilly? Two years now, and you haven't taken me to meet him."

"Jenny —"

"I want to meet him."

"Maybe when I get back."

"What are you *really* doing out there, Hilly?"

"I'm working. I told you. There was a window. A broken window."

"There's no other girl out there?"

I sat up. "Why would you ask that?"

"He said that maybe you were going to see another woman."

"Who did?"

"Your *papa.*"

I got up. My reflection in the mirror was startling. I'd turned thirty-eight a few months back, and almost on cue I'd started to notice signs of wear: raking arcs at my eyes, some white in my beard. Jenny said it all made me look smart and distinguished, but I knew differently. It was my father's face. I switched the telephone from my right ear to my left, and suddenly the conversation sounded different; even the sound of my voice seemed pinched, anxious. Did my father know why I'd come here to Iowa?

"He said that?" I asked. "He said that I was here because of another woman?"

"Maybe."

"Well, did he, or not?"

"He implied it."

"He's lying, Jenny. That's what he does."

"If you were —" she was saying. "I mean, if you were there because of some other woman, whoever it was, would you tell me?"

"Yes," I said. "But that's not why I'm here."

"Are you out there, wherever you are, because you've found someone else?" I heard her start to sniffle across the line, and I hoped this was the beginning of a cold and not the beginning of a tantrum. "Seriously?"

"No. I'm here for work. A man had his window broken by a brick."

"If you were lying about this," she said, "that would be awful. Awful to use a man's misfortune for your own benefit. And awful to lie to me. It already seems like you keep so much from me."

Another glance in the mirror at my guilty, red, stricken face. How had my father known?

Now Jenny was crying. And for a moment, she put down the telephone on the kitchen counter to fetch a box of tissues. While she was away, I could hear from across the country the muted noise of my apartment:

the teakettle brimming, steaming, skittering restlessly on the electric coils of my broken stove; the crackle of the dust-covered needle on my turntable. I had lived there now ten years, the longest I had ever lived anywhere, nearly a full decade longer than I had lived at Bluepoint. From my front steps to Boston Common, it was five minutes on foot; I could get from my bed to home plate at Fenway in twenty. I still liked the city then. Jenny and I went to concerts at the Tea Party: Bowie, dressed up like an alien; T-Rex; Serge Gainsbourg, doing the entirety of *Histoire de Melody Nelson.* We liked to go to the North End for cannoli and cappuccino. And to the Gardner Museum. Jenny's favorite painting hung there, Thomas Wilmer Dewing's *Lady in Yellow.* It was a simple picture, a woman in evening wear, sitting in a chair, a content expression on her face.

I could tell she was back on the line because I could hear her small, girlish whimpers.

"The mail came," she said.

"I'll be home soon," I said. I sat on the edge of my mattress, kicked off my shoes. "Call my doctor. Don't call my dad's doctor."

"But there's stuff for you."

"Leave it all on my desk."

"There's a note from him," she said.

"Fine. Go ahead," I said. "Read it."

"No," she said. "I would never read your mail."

Again, this made me think of Lem. "No. I want you to. Read it. Just so you know I'm not keeping anything from you."

The sound of an envelope tearing. Was this the same sort of envelope my father had used in Bluepoint, with the same logo, the logo I'd seen hidden away on Lem's desk? I felt my face flush. I couldn't remember the last time I'd seen my father. Either it had been last Thanksgiving or the Thanksgiving before, and even then it had been unpleasant.

"OK," she said. "It's, like, two paragraphs long. It's typed."

"OK."

"You want me to read it to you over the phone? What if there's something private in there?"

"Then you'll know."

"It's just some stuff about the money."

"See? It's always about the money."

She began to read.

There is the matter of your money, which, as you know, is still sitting in that same account with the McKinley boys. I'm

243

fine with it collecting interest, but just know that there are no strings attached. I made it for you, and both your mother and I want you to have an easier life than we did.

At this, Jenny cleared her throat.

"Is that it?" I asked quietly. "This is certainly not new."

"Maybe you should read the rest when you get home," she said.

"Now I'm curious."

"Well. Then he says, *I don't know why we can't seem to make peace, Hilly.*"

"Keep reading," I said.

"He says you can come home any time you want. At any moment. No questions asked."

"OK. That's enough. Put it down."

"And he says that he loves you. He wrote that. A few times." I heard her counting. "Ten, actually. He wrote it ten times. Until he ran out of paper."

THREE

I ran out of money the next morning. The problem started with breakfast. At a restaurant in town I'd ordered an omelet and coffee, and one of the waiters came over to my table to tell me that my credit card had reached its limit. That I'd found a place in Ebbington to take a credit card at all seemed to me to be a stroke of luck, an omen that my visit here might turn out well. I was off to a poor start. "They're telling me I need to cut it up," the waiter said as he held up my card and frowned dramatically. He was whispering across the breakfast counter. "But I don't like doing that." I had five cards, and this was the one I thought was the good one. "Let's pretend I did," the waiter told me, making a snipping motion with his fingers. "How's that sound?"

I kept my money at a small bank in Beacon Hill that advertised good personal service. But when I called over there, I wasn't met with the kindness they liked to advertise. "Mr. Wise, you can put in an application for an extension of your credit line," he was telling me, pronouncing the word *mister* with a drawn-out sense of disappointment, as if my filing such an extension were only a technicality and I had no chance to get any more money from them. "All right," I said. "Let's do that. How long does that take?" I could hear his impatient breathing across the line. "Usually a day or so," he said. "We file it with the main branch. Then we wait for their response. If I get it in before lunch today I can get it back before lunch tomorrow."

I sighed. "Expedite it for me. Can you do that?"

"And why would I do that for you, Mr. Wise? You owe us money."

"Because I'm asking you to?" I said, trying to sound as needy as I could. I heard him put the phone down on what must have been the counter. The bank in Beacon Hill still didn't have the technology to put anybody on hold.

I was in a telephone booth out on the edge of the hotel's parking lot. There was a perfectly decent phone in my room, but the sad fact was that I couldn't afford the charges the call would cost. Jenny worked waiting tables at a French restaurant not far from our apartment. On a good night, she could bring home twenty dollars in tips. With my salary at the paper, we had enough to make our rent every month and to occasionally entertain ourselves on the cheap. But that was about it. A few times over the years, I'd had the opportunity to do something bigger. An article I'd written about redlining in the Chicago suburbs had attracted interest from some editors in New York who wanted me to write a book. But who wanted to write a book? All of that work and effort and privation, so that someone might drop it in the bathtub or leave it at the beach? The truth was that I didn't want to stop working at the paper. If I did, I couldn't keep searching through the wire services for Savannah's name. She'd held me back. I was thirty-eight years old; I had a bad roof, a balky fridge, and five maxed-out credit cards.

The booth was squalid and hot, and the glass around me had been keyed up and scratched. Everywhere I looked, there were horrible things written. Trucks idled beside me. A wad of gum had been jammed into the loose-change slot. Postcards advertising a strip joint called the Spread Eagle were strewn on the ground. The cord to where the phone book should have been attached was severed and seemed to me like the broken live end of a power line. As I waited, a teenager knocked on the door. I'd thought it was someone waiting for the phone; already a few people had complained that I was hogging the line. The boy had a stack of flyers in his hand. He was young — thirteen or fourteen. At that age I've never been able to tell. He had on a cap for the local high school — a blue cap with a big, blocky *E* sewn onto it.

"Fund-raiser," he said. "Five bucks to see if you can hit Slim Ewing."

"Is this to help fix Charles's window?"

"Charles?" the boy asked. "Who's Charles? I'm talking Slim. Slim Ewing. Five dollars gets you an at-bat."

"How's it work?" I asked.

"You hit him, you get all the money in the pot. He gets you, he gets your money. So if you think you really have a chance, go late. When he's tired. Starts at four," he said.

The kid left then, stopping a few steps away to take a loopy practice swing at the air. It looked to me more like a golfer's swing than a ballplayer's. I looked down at the flyer. *Please come out to help repair Foreman's Diner.* And then, at the bottom: *An evening of fun with our local big-leaguer.*

He shouldn't have needed to raise money to fix his window. Insurance should have fixed it. If not, he should have had the spare cash to do it. But this was Charles, the same Charles Ewing I'd met in Bluepoint, the same guy I'd seen trying to put a broken fishing rod back together, the guy always looking for a card game, or a risky bet. I thought of Lem at that moment, how he'd told me that Charles was *no good.*

Finally, my banker got back on the phone. "We're prepared to extend you fifty dollars," he said gruffly. "But this is the last fifty dollars until you start making payments."

"Fifty dollars?" I cried. "How about a hundred. Could you possibly, possibly do a hundred?"

"I'm afraid this isn't a negotiation, Mr. Wise," the man said before hanging up on me.

Fifty dollars settled my tab at the Garden — two nights, one long call to Jenny, tax, my rental and its gasoline, and a copy of the *Cedar Rapids Gazette* delivered twice to my door — but left me with only ten dollars. I'd already used the twenty I always kept in my wallet for an emergency. Jenny called this my *power twenty,* to be used only when I was destitute. There'd been a hope that I could get a story from the trip out here and expense the whole thing. But this was too small to make a paper in Boston. Nixon's FBI wasn't coming to Ebbington. The Justice Department wasn't going to investigate a simple shopwindow. There were more pressing matters elsewhere. This wasn't Birmingham, Alabama, or Detroit in 1967, or Newark, or Washington DC, or Baltimore, or Chicago, or anywhere where people were going to riot. This was Ebbington, Iowa — quiet and green, with corn and soy everywhere. The people here seemed bothered to know that the news had come home, but now that it had, they wanted to forget about it. They wanted all of it gone. I knew this because I'd seen it everywhere I'd gone the last few years. The urgency of the matter had vanished. The young white kids were mad about the war now, or they were still trying to figure out how to design the perfect society, or they were handing out pamphlets for George McGovern, or they'd simply given up on politics and policy and were busy fucking each other and getting high. They certainly weren't here. My editors would balk if I came back with a story about a rock thrown through a diner window. Jenny was right. There were rocks going through windows in Boston. Who cared about Iowa?

The plan was to stay one more night. That's how much I'd given myself. As it was, Jenny wouldn't let me stay away much longer. She'd called me back an hour after our talk ended last night. "What about your mother?" she'd asked me. "Will you let me meet your mother?" The hour between our conversations had made her furious. At this, I stayed silent.

I wanted to tell Jenny everything. I wanted to tell her about the summer in Bluepoint, about Jerry Silver coming to recruit my father, about Lem Dawson running up and down the beach, about Lem's arrest and his murder in prison, about how he'd been killed during visitors' hours, about how no one seemed to have witnessed the crime, about how I thought my father had had everything to do with it. But Jenny wouldn't stop. "When was the last time you called your mother?" she asked me. Her own mother was at home in Baltimore, with three sons in Vietnam, so destroyed by anxiety that Jenny claimed she slept only ninety minutes a night. Jenny was constantly taking the bus to see her, bringing her cakes, bringing her jewelry from Filene's, bringing her makeup and magazines. "Did you even talk to your mother on her birthday this year?" And when I couldn't tell her the last

251

time we'd spoken, Jenny hung up on me.

As I stepped out of the phone booth, another young kid from the local high school stuffed a flyer in my hand, not seeing that I already had one.

"Come," the kid said. "Everyone'll be there. Everyone."

Gaithersburg Grounds had been freshly lined that morning. Even though there was no grass, even though the infield and the outfield were indistinguishable from each other, even though the flagpole out in center was bent at the top, as if somebody had tried to hoist up a Cadillac and the thing had buckled under the weight — even though all of this was true, they'd still lined the base paths, the batter's boxes; they'd hung bunting along the dugout fences, the outfield fences; they'd put out new, cushy-looking bases; and for the occasion, they'd built up a small mound for Charles to stand and pitch from, to show all of Ebbington that he still had it, that he could do to them what he'd done to Jackie Robinson. He was going to buckle them, make them fools, hurt their pride. By the time I arrived, the grandstands were full, people standing now on each base path. A few maple leaves, loose from piles raked back off the field, had blown onto the dirt, and a team of boys was running, laughing, trying to bag it all in paper sacks. A wire practice basket stood left of the mound, filled with new baseballs. It was a cool wet day, the air dense with humidity, the exact weather somebody who threw a good curve would pray to have for an exhibition of his talents. A municipal water tower stood fifty yards beyond right field, as tall as an ordinary Manhattan office building, painted the warm cerulean blue of the water in the Mediterranean. Inked onto its front were the words *Ebbington, Iowa,* and beneath that, *Home of the Spartans.* If you were to walk beneath it, as I did, waiting for this whole strange afternoon to start, you'd see that the front face of the thing had been dinged hundreds of times, welts like dimples, the paint chipping off the big Roman *I* in *Iowa.* Opposite the backstop, at the crest of a steep hill, Ebbington High School stood guard, a big, creepy, gothic building, WPA era, steps and steps and steps leading to an arched doorway, gargoyles perched everywhere like pigeons waiting out bad weather. The kids must come out and play here, I figured: afternoon home-run derby.

A hundred men had paid five dollars each to try to hit Slim. He'd be something like a human pitching machine; this would be like an evening at the batting cage. The replacement cost for the window at the diner had been estimated at five hundred dollars. This included an identical replication of the hand-lettered welcome sign that had adorned the glass before it'd been destroyed, something of which the town was evidently proud. They hadn't had any trouble raising the money. I'd learned this from a kid named Davis, to whom I'd promised ten dollars' worth of fast food to serve as my local stringer. This was a trick I'd learned from a few of my editors. Technically, of course, I couldn't pay for information. Journalistic ethics prevented me from doing anything like that, even though most everyone I knew did this in some way or another: sweetening your sources, my editor called it. Davis had a taste for a particular pizza shop, where working the register was a particular girl named Lauren Becker, russet haired, freckled in October like it was August and she'd spent the day at the beach. Lauren, it turned out, had a taste for boys who had a taste for things Davis didn't. He'd shown me a picture he had of her. In it, she wore a navy one-piece and stood in front of a diving quarry. She was gap toothed, cute, probably out of his league. And so for two large pizzas, a bucket's worth of soda — *pop,* in his flat local tongue — and my best efforts to tell Lauren Becker that my friend Davis was an indispensable cog in the larger wheel of civil rights, I'd made it his job to stand by my side, to be my gopher, to be my information man. Davis's dad was a cop in Ebbington, one of the first responders to *the whole window thing,* as he called it.

So while I waited and watched everyone line up to try to hit Slim — all the guys with their own equipment, so many weekend warriors with their aluminum Eastons, swinging, chopping, lining up invisible curveballs and following through — Davis pointed at each one and told me what I needed to know. Of a stocky man wearing regulation-style stirrups, Davis said, "That's McAfee, town librarian; played minor league ball *eons* ago. Basically he's got no chance unless he's the last guy and Slim is exhausted." A big guy swinging a handful of bats at once: "Checkers. Don't even know his real name. Works at the landfill doing something probably illegal. Story is that once he hit eight home runs in a Babe Ruth League game." Farther down the line, Davis pointed out the cops. "Chief's name is Sylvester." Then, peering at my notebook:

"That's his last name. Third-generation cop here. Don't think he's ever even tried to hit a baseball." His own father, Davis said, was the slender man in sweats out talking to a group of Boy Scouts. He looked bookish for a cop, a thin wash of hair combed across his head. "He got a chance?" I asked Davis, who shrugged. "I don't know. Maybe. He's got good eyes. So he won't fall for any of Slim's cheese." *Cheese* became the operative word for the next few hours, meaning simultaneously the break on a well-paced curveball, the slickness of a cutter, the clap of a fastball pushed by a guy waiting on something slower, or merely something good, as in, *Damn, that car, that's good cheese right there.*

To advertise the day, two teenagers milled around in the grandstand wearing sandwich boards. *Come see former Milwaukee Braves pitcher Slim Ewing! Come see OUR big-leaguer.* Davis told me that these were the Gaithersburg brothers, their grandfather the man for whom the park was named, some battlefield stalwart who'd come out of retirement to go fight the Germans in World War II even though he was clipping sixty. A modern-day Cincinnatus, I guessed. Their signs, with their insinuation that Charles was some glorified big-leaguer, made me instantly sad. Over the years I'd done my homework. Working at the sports desk for a decent newspaper afforded certain privileges, paramount among them access to some very decent research material — a library of tape, reams of microfiche, hundreds of thousands of box scores to pore over.

The bottom line on Charles's Major League experience was this: nine pitches on a day in Milwaukee in late 1949, three years before I met him, two years after the crash of the airplane that made my family wealthy, two years after Jackie Robinson started his first game in Brooklyn. He'd come into a game in September, the Braves already out of the contest for the pennant. I've come to believe it was a test of sorts. A way to gauge their fans. They were still a few years away from signing a skinny outfielder named Henry Aaron, and without much word to their beat reporters, or to anyone really, they'd signed Charles on a fourteen-day tender, flew him out from Birmingham, where he'd been their ace, where he'd been untouchable, where it was said that his pitches were unhittable. He'd been called out of the bull pen in the eighth, the Braves' starter having already blown the game. Their skipper would have gone out slowly to the mound, tipping his left hand, that being the sign for the southpaw — *Give me the lefty.* The game had been delayed for hours by rain, and when Charles made his debut, it was near two in the morning. It's doubtful anyone was there to see him except the guys on the field. There are no written reports of his participation, no indications that day in the *Milwaukee Journal Sentinel* that they'd breached the color barrier, just one line in a faint box score: C. EWING 1 IP, 0 H, 2 K, 0 ER. Even the reporters had gone home.

He'd thrown nine pitches. Savannah had told me that. He'd made a point not to mention it. He'd mentioned everything but those nine pitches, as if that one inning were a mark of shame. But look at the line: zero hits; two strikeouts; zero earned runs. He was flawless. I've searched, but there are no recordings of the game, no film, no secreted kinescopes languishing anywhere. There was no record of what his mechanics looked like except for what existed in my mind from that day on the back lawn in Bluepoint, my tire strung up, his curve acing it. I'd wanted a record of it, though. To see all the small stuff. To see Charles as he came into the game, as he walked across the grass, cut in late September with a pattern of diamonds, or zigzags, so that from the sky, if you were to cross overhead in a prop jet, you'd see something ornamental, something decorative, without knowing that a thirty-three-year-old from Birmingham was about to have his mettle tested. To see, at the least, how he'd got that last out. Did someone get ahold of Charles? Did his curve fail to break? And then did someone try to punch the gap? The optimist in me would like to think so. The optimist in me would like to believe that their manager, or their bench coach, or the owner, or maybe even their catcher, had seen something unfeasible in Charles's delivery, or in his curveball. Or that some guy in the bull pen noticed some flaw, languishing there with flaws of his own, shucking peanuts to keep busy, smoking out in the open just because he could and because it was boring to just sit out in the pen, waiting for someone to fuck up bad enough that they might call him in. But if Charles's curve failed to break and someone really got a good whack at it, and if, when that happened, the center fielder made a good grab and saved some runs, then his having never pitched again, never getting another try — all of that would make some sense to me. Any decent pitcher can get a few outs in a meaningless game. The alternative — *We've got Hank Aaron coming soon, and two colored boys is one too many* — is a more likely scenario. I knew that. But that was why I wanted to find film of it. To see how good he was. Nobody else here in Ebbington seemed to know that. It seemed to me that they all believed he'd had a long career. That he'd actually played for Milwaukee for longer than nine pitches. He'd stopped keeping it a secret and started allowing a lie.

What then? Had he stuck around in Milwaukee a few days, hoping they might change their minds? He'd bought that car, the Packard. In September 1949, driving south from Wisconsin to Alabama, or from Wisconsin to Mississippi, or from Wisconsin to Georgia, where Savannah was waiting with her mother, he'd have been carrying *The Green Book* with him. *The Negro Motorist Green Book.* This would have told him where he could stay on the road, who'd serve him, where there were toilets to use, even though up in Wisconsin, or even in the north of Illinois, he wouldn't have had to worry about any of this, about what his wife, who read all the newspapers, called Jim Crow, but what he liked to just call *all that bullshit;* but then, getting closer to home, all of it would have mattered, the bravado gone

260

suddenly, and he'd reach into the glove box, find that little green thing. He'd have gotten it at the Esso station back home, the old guy there checking his oil, saying, "You travel *anywhere,* son, you need this." In the backseat, he'd have had his uniform folded up, packed in a box as secure as one carrying the Hope Diamond. He'd have stolen some things from the locker room. Souvenirs, he'd tell his wife. Gifts, he'd tell Savannah. *Because they liked your daddy so much, sweetie.* In private, he'd think that the least they could do was to let him take some stuff home. In the trunk, a program from his big day, a resin bag, a glove autographed by all the guys nice enough to sign a colored boy's glove, some man's bat, just some anonymous guy's bat. Crossing from Indiana into Kentucky, he'd have had to watch the sun, be careful to get someplace decent for the night, be careful not to be out too late in the pretty country north of Lexington, where there were horses everywhere, where there were so many hills. With the book on the dashboard, he'd slow down to thumb through the listings, the Packard in the right lane, doing fifty. Just fast enough to go someplace. Just slow enough not to get stopped. Slow enough not to be bothered.

■ ■ ■ ■

Charles arrived at Gaithersburg Grounds in a rusting Dodge Dart, honking his horn, playing the ham, tipping his cap. He'd dressed himself in a Braves uniform that looked, to my eyes at least, like the real deal, the tomahawk across the chest, the cursive lettering. We were close enough to Milwaukee that the sight of the uniform brought out some genuine cheers. The memories were still fresh. The team had moved to Atlanta only six years earlier. Now the Brewers were in Milwaukee, with a better name for a town built on the back of beer. The Braves had come to Milwaukee from Boston, just the way I'd come to Iowa. A part of me had expected Charles to be driving the old Packard: the headrest on the front seat, the bench inside where Savannah had sat, her hands tugging me. *I like being with you. Anyone ever say that to you?* But there was no way a guy like Charles would still have that car. By now, I was sure, he'd gambled it away.

Far out in center field, playing from a wooden park gazebo, a brass band started up, New Orleans–style, the trombone woozy, loose, sliding up to every note, the trumpet chirping, a guy on a four-string banjo banging out some sloppy chords. It was "Sweet Georgia Brown," the Globetrotters song. It wasn't a bad comparison, I thought. Whatever this was that we were about to see, it wasn't a baseball game. As Charles crossed the base paths, he jumped the chalk — that old superstition of never touching a crack. The crowd hollered for him. In my notebook, I wrote: *Slim = hero?* He seemed unfazed. A second tip of his cap was out of the question. Ballplayers acquire this certain frozen determination early in their career and never lose it. Retired ballplayers have to find someplace to put it, and if you don't like to golf, it just lives in you, revealing itself at the worst moments. This was why I always hated interviewing old pitchers for the *Spectator.* If I'd challenged them somehow by saying that maybe there were young pitchers doing something better than they themselves used to do it, invariably they'd get a cold, locked-in, sniperish glaze in their eyes. And then, of course, I'd have ruined the interview. But in Charles, this coldness was different. In him, it seemed desperate. Like trying to fit together two pieces of a broken fishing rod. The ovation here was more an act of appreciation, of solidarity, maybe even pity. How had he ended up here, of all places? A thousand white faces. Maybe fifteen hundred. Had he always been their big-leaguer? Had he told his customers from the start that he'd pitched in the big show? Serving coffee, flapjacks, waffles fresh from the hot iron, had he leaned in, giving them their forks, their syrup: *I see you're looking at the sports page. Wanna know something? I used to pitch for the Braves. Yep. The Braves.*

Charles had become an old man. I don't know exactly what I'd expected to find. In the diner, he'd appeared more or less as I'd remembered him — long, somewhat handsome, with a hint of a devious smile. His hair was gone now, but even young men go bald. He was fifty-six. In the daylight he looked even older. His gait was awkward — his legs seemed stiff, his hips locked. His uniform hung from him. At the mound he kicked at the dirt, bounced a rosin bag three times in his open hand. At the backstop, a high school boy was wearing catcher's gear. As they were about to begin warming up, a man in a suit stepped out onto the grass to talk to Charles.

"That's Barnum," Davis said.

"Like the circus?" I asked.

He smirked. "Exactly. This whole thing was his idea."

"It wasn't Charles's idea?"

"Slim's? No. I don't think he'd ever just ask somebody for money."

"Really?" I said.

"Oh yeah. Slim's way too proud. Barnum came up with the idea. You know, all these guys out here, they all talk. Most of them think that Slim's bullshit. That he never pitched anywhere in the big leagues. I mean, it's not like there were that many black ball-players. Why wouldn't we have heard of him?"

"He played," I said. I thought about those nine pitches. Obviously he was telling people it was a hell of a lot more than that. "I know it."

Davis shrugged. I wasn't sure whether he believed me or not.

"So Barnum just came up with this whole thing. It's kind of like casino night at the church. Plus, everybody knows Slim likes to bet. It's like the only thing people know about him."

Charles was kneeling patiently on the pebbled infield, rubbing his right hand against his left shoulder, clearly trying to stay warm. The wind picked up, flinging dirt into his eyes. He winced, spit, rubbed at his face. He looked despondent and humiliated, and occasionally I saw him clutch the ball,

265

squeeze it, and fit his longer fingers across its seams. Is that what became of old Negro Leaguers, I wondered? Had they all turned out this way?

The first batter came up with a swagger. Barnum announced his name — Peters — and Peters obligingly bowed at the waist. Barnum stood behind the catcher, a plastic bucket at his feet. Peters put his five dollars in. Barnum barked out to the crowd: "Pot's at five, people. Pot's at five. If you want in, sign up with Lucy." He pointed to a white-haired woman wearing an apron decorated with sloganeered buttons. Peters, meanwhile, stepped confidently into the batter's box.

"This guy's an idiot," Davis said, not exactly whispering. "Owns a sandwich shop. Nice enough, I guess. Great sandwiches." Peters took three choppy practice swings at the air. His legs were a mess, his knees too stiff, his back foot loose on the dirt. Charles stood on the mound, waiting patiently for Peters to settle. He held a new baseball in his mitt, massaging it, working his hands around it. Barnum commenced the exhibition by blowing on a whistle — like a gym teacher, or a basketball referee, or a traffic cop. A whistle, though, has no place on a ball field. When Charles finally pitched, I saw what others around me must have only imagined. That old delivery: pumping, striving, his kick already so old-fashioned. Here was the man I'd seen in Bluepoint, acing my tire. His curve struck at noon and fell at six. It was likely all he had left, just this one pitch, and no one could hit it. Not Peters, who tried. He took the first pitch far too late and looked like a fool, swinging at something that wasn't there. His second and third strikes swung him around like he was a boy swinging his dad's bat. No matter who came in to face Slim, everyone suffered the varied magic of that pitch: a fast curve that broke at your eyes and dropped to your toes like somebody had batted it out of the sky, a swatter to a fly. A slow pitch, like something tossed as an explanation — *Here, this is a curve, take it nice and slow* — nearly broke some men at the knees. The batters tried, but each was spun around, made to seem useless, blind, impatient, their chastened strength an illustration of Slim's brilliance. The power hitters — the bigger guys, the cops, the firemen — swung far too early. And the contact men, the skinny guys, the men who Davis told me were the eye doctors, the dentists, the county livestock inspector, all waited too long. He made quick work of everyone. Soon, Barnum announced that the pot had four hundred dollars. Eighty guys up and down. I hadn't been counting, but Slim got nearly everyone on three pitches, sometimes four. The rare man got contact on the ball; the lucky managed to slice something foul.

After a certain point, it all became a farce. Nobody could get anything close to solid contact off Charles. The local high school team showed up, a bunch of scruffy kids in their uniforms, cocky in the batter's box. But they'd never seen a pitcher like this, someone whose stuff became invisible somewhere between the mound and the plate. It was clear that he was the best man of the bunch, even now, even at fifty-six. In his mind, he was at Wrigley or at the Polo Grounds or in the Bronx, and he wasn't pitching to some washed-up Little Leaguer from some Iowa hamlet, some man who'd given up his aspirations two decades earlier and who worked now driving a forklift or pressing tin or washing the killing floor of a pork processor. No, Charles was twenty still, with a rubber arm and boundless confidence, and he hadn't ever had a daughter, hadn't been to Massachusetts or even heard of Bluepoint or the Emerson Oaks or the Wise family. He was just a pitcher with a curveball no one could touch. I thought of

Lem, in my father's car, four months before the end of his life, telling me that Charles was no good. And I thought of Savannah that night, standing with her bandaged knee, with those buckets behind her, Lem giving her all his money. *He gonna find it. He got a nose for money.* In my notebook, I wrote: *Why were you living at the Emerson Oaks? Why didn't you and Savannah move somewhere else after the fire? Why did Lem tell me that you were "no good"? What did he have against you?* And then I simply wrote Lem's name in big, bold letters. I underlined it, and then: *What do YOU think happened in that prison?*

I started to ask people if they knew Savannah. "She's Charles's daughter," I said. "Do you know her? Do you know if she lives around here?" I got nothing. Even Davis, whose knowledge of Ebbington seemed beyond challenge, pleaded ignorance.

"A daughter? Oh, I have no idea," he said.

"She's probably my age," I said.

"Fifty?" Davis asked, humorlessly.

"No." I coughed. "I'm thirty-eight."

"Well, what's she look like?" he asked. "I mean, I assume she's black? Charles is the only black person in town. There's black folk a town over. But —"

And here he stopped. He didn't ever go a

269

town over. He didn't need to say this. I could tell. I knew the look on his face.

"She looks like Charles," I said, trying once more. I said this even though I knew it probably wasn't true. Not now.

"Sorry," Davis said, shaking his head. "I don't know her."

And then I asked him. "Could you ask around for me? I'm looking to talk to her."

"What do you want with her?" he asked me, which was, after all, the key question.

"We used to know each other," I said, pretending to be interested in this strange charade of a baseball game going on just feet from me. "That's all."

My anxiety about seeing Savannah had become something physical now. Sweat dropped onto my pad. Only when my foot cramped did I realize I'd been tapping it for an hour. Writing felt suddenly oppressive. To fix a grip on my pen was impossible. If the line between insane behavior and plain old stupid behavior involves some small bit of regret, some awareness of one's own lack of reason, I felt I was hovering at that intersection: afflicted and obsessed and maybe a little creepy, but convinced, nonetheless, that I ought to be here. Savannah was here in Iowa. I knew it. I was sure she was here. If her father was here, she'd be close by. I felt this the way that someone who wakes at night to see their candlesticks moving believes in their heart that a ghost is in their room, the way that my father believed that the crash of Boston Airways had been his fate. I'd looked for her name on so many hundreds of dispatches from the AP wire. And now I was looking at her father. She was here.

Eventually, Davis pointed to a bright red spot along the centerfield fence. "See that?" he asked. "That's Lauren."

"That's your girl?"

He winced. "Right."

"She's pretty," I said.

"Too pretty."

"No one's too pretty."

"That's crap. You sound like my mom."

"You're mom's probably right."

"She's miles out of my league."

I squinted. "Does she know you exist?"

He laughed. "Sure. But I'm kind of hoping for a little bit more than that."

"Go talk to her," I said. She was standing behind the fence, clapping. She was cheering, I noticed, for Charles.

"See: that's the problem."

"Can't talk to her?"

He shook his head. "No. I get all clammed up."

271

"I was like that," I said.

"She's got this messed-up father. Everybody in town knows it."

"What's wrong with him?"

"Drinks. Gambles. You name it. I want to do something, but I don't know how to go about bringing it up."

For a moment I thought of telling Davis about my own father, but instead we both watched Charles mow down two more guys — both firemen, both huge, each of whom swung like his life depended on it.

"I guess we should've believed Slim," Davis said.

"Window goes back up. Everybody's happy."

Davis was lost, though, his attention redirected, as if by a magnet, to Lauren's position along the center-field fence. Her hair, caught up in some wind, blew up against a billboard for Peterson's Oil.

"Go try it out," I said, nudging my head toward Slim.

"No way," he said.

"Go for it," I said. "What's the worst that happens?"

"I humiliate myself."

"It'll give you something to talk to Lauren about."

"True," he said.

"So if you humiliate yourself, I don't see how you'd be in a worse place than you are now."

"Also true."

"If you hit him —"

"Oh, I won't."

"Do it. Come on." I put the ten dollars I owed him flat in his palm. They were my last ten dollars. I closed his fingers around the bill.

He was opening his hand back up when we heard it: the loud *thwack* of a wooden bat slamming into one of Slim's pitches. It was a high fly ball, carried far back into the corner near the left-field foul pole. Everyone around us got to their feet to see if it would clear the fence. Sportswriters often call contact like this a towering shot. It's one of those useless, meaningless aphorisms we all use when we're lazy. But in this case, because the ball dinged itself against the town's water tower, the adage became, for the first time in my experience, something true.

The kid who'd hit it was still standing at home plate. He was young, maybe not sixteen, a dusty Cubs cap pushed back on his head, so that his hair poked out on the back and on the sides. I wondered how it'd happened. Had Charles just gotten tired?

Had his age caught up to him? Had his curve failed to break?

"Who is that?" I asked.

Davis shook his head. "Somebody who just won a lot of money."

He gave me his name, but I didn't write it down. It didn't matter, because a moment after the ball landed in the parking lot on the other side of Gaithersburg Grounds, Charles Ewing figured out who I was. I couldn't say why he hadn't noticed me the day before when I'd been right in front of him. Maybe it was because he'd been exhausted. Maybe it was because he found it easier to place me now that something terrible had just happened to him. And something terrible had just happened: he'd had the money he needed to fix his window, and now it was gone. I saw the flicker of recognition flash across his face. He ripped his hat off, stepped off the mound, and pointed at me. "What are you doing here?" he yelled. "Can't you just leave me alone!"

FOUR

"Of course I don't have five hundred dollars on my own," Jenny said, coughing into the telephone. "What kind of stupid question is that?"

It was midnight now, and I was back in my hotel. I'd come straight back here, even though a half-dozen people had stopped to tell me that Charles wanted to talk. One man grabbed my shoulder: "Hey, guy . . . hey, guy, Slim says you two are old acquaintances. Is that true? You? Really? Hey, guy . . . I'm talking to you. Why are you walking away? Slim says you two need to speak." But I just kept moving. Whatever hope I'd had that he'd forgiven me had vanished when I'd seen how angry he was.

There'd been a message from Jenny waiting at reception. *CALL HOME,* it read, the capitalized letters put there, so said the receptionist, because Jenny had demanded it. Across the line, she sounded as if I'd woken her — drowsy, hoarse, a dry cough snapping at the receiver. "You need to come home," she'd said. "I'm tired of you being out there. I need my boyfriend home." But I wanted to know if we had any money. I wanted to help Charles fix his window.

"What about your paycheck?" I asked. "Have you been paid yet this week?"

"Not yet, Hilly."

"I called my bank," I offered. "They weren't any help. I'm already overextended."

"You maxed out your credit card? Another one?" she asked me. She'd begun to yell now. "Are you kidding me?"

"I'm not proud of it."

"How does Arthur Wise's son max out his credit cards? I don't understand that."

"By using them," I said.

"Very funny, Hilly. How many is that now? Four?"

I paused a moment. "Five," I said.

"What do you need five hundred dollars for, anyway? I thought you already had your ticket home?"

"I need the money," I said. "For incidentals."

"*Incidentals?* What does that mean?"

"Listen," I said, sighing into the phone. "Do we have five hundred dollars or not?"

"What's happened to you? Are you in

prison or something? Do you need a lawyer? Have you been on a bender for the past two days? What happened to my boyfriend? My lovable, normal boyfriend?"

"I'm in my hotel room," I said. "Everything is fine. I'm still normal. I just need five hundred dollars."

Five hundred dollars would fix the window. He'd never take my money if I tried to give it to him. We were alike in this way. He'd leave that blue tarp up at the diner forever if it meant that he didn't have to take my money. I understood that. So my plan was to give it to Davis, tell him to give it to Charles, to pretend it was his. Or his father's. I didn't want the credit. I just wanted him to have his window back. After that, I was going to go home. Coming here to Ebbington had been a mistake.

Jenny's breath through the phone was thin, rushed, suspicious. "What is it? Did you meet somebody else out there? You did, didn't you? Your father was right."

"No," I said. "I didn't meet anybody."

Before I'd left, we went through our normal routine where she followed me to the cab, even though her hair was wet and tied up behind her head. This was one of the reasons I loved her — she did things like this. She insisted on making our own traditions. She'd put her hands on my cheeks. "Don't talk to strangers," she'd tell me. "I'm a full-grown man," I'd say. "You don't have anything to worry about." Then she'd say, "I'm gonna miss you, Hilly. Hurry home."

"You want to know something, Hilly?"

"Please," I said, exhausted. "What? Tell me."

"You know, your dad sent me that cake this morning —" she started.

"You told me."

"He also sent some money. That's why I wanted to talk to you."

I sighed. "Of course he did."

"I didn't know if I should tell you. But I told him the fridge needed to be replaced. And that the roof was leaking. And he sent the money along with the cake."

"Send it back."

"I feel like I'm in some bad gangster movie, Hilly. It's *ten* thousand dollars," she said, whispering the amount of money.

"Oh God."

"It's all in hundred-dollar bills. A *hundred* hundred-dollar bills. All this money is stressing me out. I keep thinking somebody's gonna rob me. Like, somebody knows it's in here somehow, and they're just gonna come in off the street and hold me hostage and *rob* me. And I'm having an awful hard time listening to you begging me — *me* — for five hundred dollars. That's about what I make in a month, Hilly."

"We can't touch that money. That's not on the table."

"Actually," she said, laughing, "it's on our kitchen table right now. I'm looking at it."

"What I meant —"

"I know what you meant," she said. "But I think you might need to get over yourself."

"It's more complicated than that."

"It's not complicated, actually. It's embarrassing. It's childish. Here we are, living in this crappy little apartment. And you've got millions in the bank. Millions!"

"It's not that much," I said.

"Actually," she said, "I did a little digging around."

I could hear the shuffling of papers. I thought of what I'd hidden away — photographs of my father and mother; press clippings; letters from Robert; every statement from McKinley & Sons. I kept all of it in a closet inside a locked trunk, one of the few remnants of my old life that I kept around. It was the trunk my mother bought for me when I'd gone off to college. She'd cried when she wrote the check for it, telling me that she found it hard to rationalize the notion that she was paying to have her baby move out on her forever.

Jenny cleared her throat. "According to the good bankers at McKinley and Sons, you've got quite a lot of millions, actually."

"I've told you. That's not my money," I said.

"The statement has your name on it."

"It's my father's money."

"Mmm," she said, making with her mouth the most circumspect sound I'd ever heard her make. "I think that's bullshit."

"If I take five hundred dollars, say. Just five hundred. And I spend it. You know what's gonna happen?" I asked.

"No, Hilly. Tell me."

"My father's gonna show up. That's what's gonna happen."

"Oh God. That sounds *awful*. Just *awful*. He's just gonna show up. Your dad. Oh no!"

"He gave you ten thousand dollars in cash. Like in a gangster movie. Just like you said. You don't find that suspicious?"

"Honestly, Hilly. It's one in the morning here. And you're calling me desperate for five hundred dollars. So, in fact, I think you're the suspicious one." Silence. She coughed. From a thousand miles away, I heard a car honk its horn out on Mount Vernon Street. Then I heard the sound of car keys jingling in the phone. "You know what? I'm going to go into the city in the morning. I'm just going to drive to McKinley and Sons, and I'm going to have them wire you the money your father left. 'Cause it's just sitting there. And, I mean, look at you: you're in some crappy hotel in Ohio with no money, calling me in the middle of the night."

"Iowa," I said. "I'm not in Ohio."

"I'm tired of this. We don't need to take all of the money, Hilly. We can even leave most of it. But let's do the right thing. Let's take some of it. Let's get a nice house somewhere. Let's move on. You and me. Let's move on with our lives."

This startled me. To hear it put this way. Suddenly, it was the truest thing I'd ever heard. I sat quietly for a moment.

"I'm coming home," I said.

"Good," she said.

"I miss you. I shouldn't have come out here. You're right. There are broken windows in Boston."

"And black people," she said, laughing.

"It was a mistake. I don't know what I was thinking."

"I'm still sick, by the way. Thanks for asking," she said.

"I'll take you to the doctor tomorrow afternoon."

Behind me, someone was knocking on the door to my hotel room. My credit card, I thought. Not again. In two decades I'd gone from our house on Riverside Drive — all forty-five rooms of it, with our butlers, our chauffeured limousines, our dinners overlooking the Hudson, lobsters and foie gras and cuts of beef the size of small children — to this: having some waiter take kitchen shears to my charge card.

"Jenny, I'll call you in the morning, OK? I'll call you from the airport."

"Hilly?" she asked. "What do I do with this money? It's just sitting here on the table."

"Leave it."

"Seriously?"

"Leave it and we'll figure it out together. You and me."

Again, someone knocked on the door. This time Jenny heard. "Hilly, who's at your door? It's so late!"

"It's going to be the hotel clerk cutting up my credit card," I said, resignation in my voice. "I'm pretty sure that's who it's gonna be."

"You sure you don't need me to wire you some of this cash?"

"I'll be all right," I said. And then I told

her I loved her and hung up the phone. Finally, I thought. She was right. We'd move on. Coming here might have been a mistake, but it was the perfect kind of mistake. The mistake that might finally get Savannah out of my system. Maybe coming here had helped me kick the habit.

Another knock. I had the door chained. My editor had told me always to chain my door in a hotel because people sometimes forget which room is theirs, and because the last thing you want during the night is some drunk trying to jimmy open your door, convinced that his key is broken and that you're sleeping in his bed with his wife. I heard noise behind the door. The people at my bank in Beacon Hill must have had a change of heart and denied my extension.

But when I opened the door, it wasn't the hotel clerk. And it wasn't Charles Ewing. I'd had the quick flash that he might have sought me out, however unlikely the possibility. But a young woman was waiting there. "I'm sorry to bother you," she said, her voice full, imploring, young. She was the girl Davis had wanted to impress so badly, Lauren Becker. "You're that reporter guy, right? You're doing that story on the diner, yeah? The guy from Boston?"

Lauren was pretty — prettier than in the

picture that Davis had shown me. She was seventeen, nearly as tall as I was. She was in a black cable-knit sweater that hung nearly to her knees and that she'd rolled up to her elbows. Her face was thin, and in the glow of the hallway lamp above us, she seemed unbothered by anything, despite the fact that she was here, and despite the manifold other evidence of what Davis had hinted was a terrible home life: the skin on her fingers was picked bare and red; small iridescent slivers like a musical staff were raised on her left arm, halfway between her wrist and her elbow. This was a decade or two before I'd ever heard of anyone doing this — cutting — and I thought nothing of it. Her eyes were clear. I noticed then that she had a duffel at her feet; blue, canvas, her initials stitched on by hand.

"I'm sorry to just come up here like this," she started, her voice quiet. "I didn't think the guy at the desk would actually give me your room number."

"You're Davis's girl," I said.

This made her frown. "I'm not his girl," she said. "I'm his friend."

I recognized something in Lauren's posture that I'd had myself since the moment I arrived in Iowa: the silent hope that someone might come out of nowhere and give me what I was looking for. My father had taught me that when someone wanted something from you, their body would always betray their motives. She twitched twice, an uncontrolled pair of little beats of her head, as if to some song playing somewhere. *Tap tap.* And she kept looking past me, into my hotel room. She couldn't look me in the eyes.

"I heard you were looking for Charles's daughter," she said, simply. "Davis said something."

"I am," I said. "Do you know her?"

She nodded. I felt my legs wobble. My conversation with Jenny might as well have been ten years ago.

"You do?" I managed.

She bit her lip bashfully. "I do. So, you really want to find her, huh?"

"I've been looking for her," I said.

"That's what Davis said. He said you were asking around. Said you seemed like you really wanted to find her."

"I was. But nobody knew her."

This didn't seem to surprise Lauren. "Is she in trouble?"

"No," I said. "I used to know her. That's all. A long time ago."

"You're an old friend?"

"Something like that."

"That's what Davis said."

"Look," she said. She reached into her back pockets, both of them, and took out two separate handfuls of money. "I've got seven hundred dollars saved up. It's basically everything I've ever made working at the grocery store in town. So I can pay you if you need me to."

"I think you've got it backward," I said. "Normally I'd pay you for the help."

"I was thinking we could do a trade," she said.

"What would we be trading?" I asked.

"I need to get out of here. To leave."

"Where do you want to go?"

"Anywhere," she said. Again, she pushed the money toward me. "I have seven hundred dollars. Where can I go for seven hundred dollars?"

"That's why you're here?" I asked. "You want me to help you run away?"

All of a sudden she seemed panicked that I might not help her. Coming here to talk to me, to knock on my door at midnight, in a part of town that had only the highway and some gas stations — coming here must have been so difficult for her. A girl her age could feign precociousness and maturity all she wanted, but this scared her. "I just heard you were asking around for her." She paused. And then, she said her name. "For Savannah. And I just thought, you know, I could show you where she is. And you could help me."

"Put away the money," I said.

"You can have it," she said. "It's all there. You can count it."

"I don't want it."

"I know you're rich and everything. But still."

"Excuse me?"

"You're Arthur Wise's son."

"How'd you know that?"

"You are, though, right? I mean — he's your father?"

"I'm not rich," I said. "He's rich."

"I just thought we could trade," she said. "You take the money, and I'll take you to her."

"Look —"

"No. No." She reached out and put the money into my hands. "Don't say no."

In a way, Lauren seemed a lot like Savannah had, the first time I met her — frightened, embarrassed. Jenny was always telling me I had a thing for women like this. When I'd met her, it was at the restaurant in Beacon Hill where she still worked. That night, as she was clearing away a table, I saw that she'd started to cry. I went over to

287

her. One of her brothers had suffered an injury in the unofficial incursion into Cambodia. A land mine had knocked him out, and he'd woken up strapped to a gurney in a medevac, banged up but alive. Jenny claimed I had a rescue complex. A need to take care of people, even if they could take care of themselves. When she told me this, I laughed her off. Not for the first time, she was right.

"How do you know Savannah?" I asked Lauren. "How do you know where she lives?"

"She's a librarian," she said. "In the town over. I go there sometimes. It's better than the one we have in town. People are actually quiet in there. It's a good place to study. So I take the bus. My dad works near there. Sometimes he forgets to pick me up."

"He forgets?"

"Yeah. He'll just forget."

She opened her eyes a little wider, as if to tell me that this was the sanitized version, that saying that her dad just forgot about her sometimes was only the beginning.

"So sometimes, she'll just take me to her house, 'cause it's not far."

"Savannah does this?"

"I can take you."

"How do I know you're telling the truth?" I said.

For the first time, she smiled. She opened the mouth of her duffel and took everything out of it: her clothes, a few books, some makeup, a handful of tampons, a compact mirror with a princess sticker on the lid, a small wadded ball of hair elastics. It was terrible to see all of this. Terrible to see her underwear fall off the pile, into the dirty hotel hallway, and the quick, shy way she retrieved it. And it was terrible to see the last thing she pulled out. It was a black plastic cap gun. At first I couldn't tell it was fake. Which was the point. When she put this down, she looked up at me. "It's a toy," she told me. "If I'm running away, I need to be able to scare people. Creepy men mess with girls. It's pretty realistic."

"It's a good idea," I said.

"Here," Lauren said. "Look." Again, her imploring hand thrust something toward me. It was a photograph. She gave it to me facedown, a white sheet with a blue stamp on it that read *Stockton.* I turned it over. It was me. And it was Savannah. That first day on the lawn, when her father threw the ball through my tire.

"You don't look too different," she said.

I started shaking. "Where —"

"It's you, right?"

"Where —"

"I figured you might not believe me. I used some of my money and got a cab to the library. I thought if I borrowed the picture —"

"Lauren —"

"You gotta help me, Mr. Wise."

"How —"

"Look," she said, "I stole it. OK?"

"From where?"

"From her office."

She got up on her toes and threw a crooked finger at Savannah's face.

"Her office," she said again. "I stole it from her office."

The picture's edges were torn, jagged, and there was still old glue on the back. Lauren picked at the polish on her nails. I couldn't stop staring at the picture.

"When I saw you today at the ballpark," she said, "I recognized you. Even before Davis said who you were. I knew it was you."

I managed a small noise. I was still shaking. I had the picture in my hand. I pointed at Lauren. "If you're lying —," I began to say.

FIVE

It was a small gray house on the edge of the soy field, the living room lights on, a crack in the wood on the bottom step. We'd taken the county road out of Ebbington, passing for ten miles through empty, flat country so stark, it seemed like land that hadn't been discovered by man, just the dark space between towns, empty, not yet farmed, not yet stuck with shops or strip malls or auto dealerships. Towns in Iowa crop up unexpectedly, sometimes in the crook of an elbow, sometimes on what passes for high ground. Everything there is postglacial, steamrolled by ice, carved by wind. Lauren knew the way perfectly. Countless nights she'd ended up here when her father was working late or drinking late and nobody came to the library to take her home. Savannah had done this. Taken the girl whom no one had come for. This was what Lauren told me as we drove down Route 112. She went to the library there because it was usually empty, and because she could get her work done without people bothering her. At school there were always boys asking her to go with them to a game on Friday nights, or to a movie. And at home, there was her father. She started to tell me something about him but stopped. "I'm running away," she said. "There's not really much else you need to know, I guess. I like the library. They let you stay as long as you want. People are nice to me there. Savannah's nice to me."

I parked in the dirt outside Savannah's house. This was Hove, Iowa, ten miles west of Ebbington. It was near one in the morning now. A yellow Chrysler sat in the driveway beside a row of potted tomato vines.

"This is so romantic," Lauren said. She'd been sullen on the way over, lost in her head, nervous about running away, but now that we were here, somewhere she was comfortable, she'd perked up.

"Is that what this is?" I asked.

"I wonder if someone will come back for me in twenty years."

"Maybe Davis will."

"Oh please," she said.

"If I told you how long I've been looking for her —" Lauren stopped me. She had the picture in her lap, the photograph

Charles had taken of me and Savannah in Bluepoint.

"I have an idea," she said, pointing at it.

"I was just about to give up," I said. "Right when you knocked on my door."

She smiled at me. I looked down at her arms — at the raised welts, the crisscrossed scars, the scratches.

"Are you nervous?" she asked.

"Very."

"Why don't we get out of the car?"

"Why don't we wait another minute?"

"Why don't we get out." She slapped my thigh. "That could be a good start."

"You think she's awake?"

Lauren looked out at the house. "Lights are on. I've heard that sometimes there's this phenomenon where people turn off the lights when they go to sleep."

"Are you being sarcastic right now?" I said. "Don't do that."

"Come on," she said. "Haven't you ever heard of levity?"

"I hadn't heard that word when I was your age," I said. "That's for sure."

"Look how nervous you are!"

"Is there a man in there?" I asked after a moment, having paused to try to figure out the best way to ask. "I don't want to go in there if there's some other guy in there."

Lauren smiled knowingly. "Not right now."

"You sure?"

She nodded. "How about we go up?"

I looked out at the house, the flat front of it, the siding streaked with grime and dirt. A weather vane on the roof was broken and lay collapsed against the chimney. The mailbox at the edge of the lawn had the name *Stockton* printed across it in faded marker. Savannah Stockton. Lauren went to the door, her moccasins scuffling on the flagstone. She'd brought her duffel with her. *So this is where Savannah has been this whole time,* I thought. When I'd been imagining her everywhere else, she'd been in the middle of the goddamned haystack, nearly in the dead center of the country.

"Hey," I called out to Lauren, whispering, hanging back. "Stop." I had nothing more to say. I just couldn't go any farther. Going farther meant getting closer to Savannah, which meant experiencing some level of terror far more extreme than the terror I'd just experienced with her father. The notion that I might be met with something other than anger seemed unreasonable now, wholly misguided. Lauren turned, lamplight at her back. She shot me a pitying expression, her lips in a mock pout. She'd put on a denim jacket and tied back her hair into a ponytail. It was easy to see why Davis had fallen so hard for her. She was pretty, but in a few years she'd be beautiful. She walked down the steps toward me and put a hand on my wrist.

"Come on. Let's go."

"Well, can you at least tell me what I should expect?"

Lauren had both of my hands now. "She is the most wonderful person. Which is something I think you already know."

Lights struck up behind the front door, twin pewter lamps slowly burning to life. Lauren turned expectantly, letting my hands drop, a smile forming on her mouth, her eyes the final thing to leave me, something close to mischief in them. From inside the house, there were footsteps — slow, cautious footsteps — of someone who's heard a noise out on her porch past midnight.

When Savannah opened the door, her foot was the first thing I saw. I'd been looking down, dreading the moment when she discovered me. I looked so much like my father now. His was the last face she'd want to see. Also, I wasn't unaware of how potentially terrifying it might have been for a white man to be making noise on the porch of a black woman in October of 1972, this being the year that George Wallace was shot, the year Angela Davis was acquitted, and the very week a full-fledged race riot had broken out in the cabins of the USS *Kitty Hawk.* Still, I didn't want her to see whatever expression happened to appear on my face — elation at finding her, confusion at seeing that she looked nothing like the girl she had been or, worse, some terrible combination of the two. I was taller than Lauren, and so I tried to position myself at the back of the porch, close to the step that led to the walkway.

Savannah's tiny foot: a striped athletic sock, one orange band at the calf flanked by two wider blue bands, some dirt on the toe. I allowed myself to look up slowly. I didn't know whether she'd seen me or not. After all this time, I was finally here. I'd finally found her. I felt every inch of my body — my heart going, my arms struggling to seem normal, my eyes refusing to blink. I wanted to take all of this in. To see everything. Her hair was cut close to her head. That was the first thing I noticed. That her hair was short. She was already gray at her temples. This was the second thing. We were older now. She had on a white wool cardigan and gray corduroys. A pair of eyeglasses hung on an orange cord around her neck.

"Lauren?" Savannah asked softly. She reached out and put one hand on Lauren's shoulder. Her other hand pulled tight the lapels on her sweater. "What are you doing? It's so late."

"I couldn't stick around any longer," she said in a sturdy voice that I admired. In barely an hour, Lauren had won me over. She kicked at her duffel bag.

"Oh, Lauren. I thought . . . you promised me you wouldn't!"

"I lied."

"Damn it, Lauren. And you came here?"

"Well, I also ran into this guy right here." She reached back for me and pulled me by the arm so that we were standing side by side. "And then my plans kind of changed."

Savannah looked up at me then. This wasn't Charles. She knew me the moment she saw me. If she felt any joy in seeing me again, I couldn't find it in her.

"How much did you pay her?" she demanded.

"Excuse me?"

She looked at Lauren and then back at me. She crossed her arms against her chest. "There's nothing here for you."

I tried to take a deep breath but came up short. A woman emerged behind Savannah, blinking herself awake.

"Lauren?" She was in a floor-length red nightgown, a bear stitched onto the breast. "What are you doing here?"

"She's running away," Savannah said, her voice flat, not annoyed but not pleased.

"Oh God. Oh, that's disappointing to hear. You'll be kidnapped by some trucker."

"This is Pam," Savannah said, although she wasn't looking at me. "Pam's my room-mate."

"And her coworker," Pam said, grinning at me.

"Hilton Wise," I said, my hand out to shake hers.

She squinted at me. "You look familiar," she said.

I saw Savannah smirk at this.

"It's probably my father," I said, although I hadn't wanted to say it. "We look alike. And people seem to know him."

"Wise. Wise. Wise." Pam repeated this like it was some bad version of a yoga mantra. "Oh, right. Wise. The airplane guy, right? He's the pilot? The recluse?"

"You're thinking of Howard Hughes."

"Oh," she said.

"My father sued Howard Hughes."

Pam laughed. "Oh. Wow. Far-out."

I nodded. "Right."

Pam waved Lauren inside, and then it was

298

just the two of us on her porch. Savannah looked straight at me now. "I heard you were here," she said.

"From who?"

"From my father," she said. "If Lauren weren't here, I'd call the cops on you," she said, stepping aside, her arm extended into her house. She let out a few fake laughs. "But make yourself at home."

Savannah's kitchen was an open space, filled with a butcher block table, copper pans hanging on hooks above a double-wide sink, and a stoneware vase filled with pink gladiolus. It was easy to see how cheerful it would have been, had it been afternoon. Someone had positioned a sunflower in a tall water glass on the windowsill. What I'd glimpsed of the rest of the house was clean, sparsely but tastefully decorated. There were photographs everywhere: some of Pam, but most of them of Savannah. This was everything I'd missed in her life: There she was on the Pont Neuf, a black American woman abroad. There she was in San Francisco, standing beside a giant fake pagoda. And in some of the pictures, there was a man: in a dress uniform, the cap on his head tilted back to block the sun, a broad smile. In work pants and a sweat-drenched white shirt, straddling the peak of a roof on a building, his hammer drawn. At a writing desk, square-framed glasses on his face, sitting behind a typewriter and an ashtray and a plate with a sandwich on it.

After she sat us down at her kitchen table — "Here," she said, telling me where to go, her cold hand brushing mine, the first physical contact between us in two decades — she didn't concentrate on me for more than a fleeting second, choosing instead to worry loudly over Lauren being here in her house at one in the morning, her long-threatened plan to run away now in progress. Nearly every five minutes, Savannah consulted her watch and tried to calculate just what level of terror Lauren's father might be experiencing. "Your father's probably already been to the cops."

"No way," Lauren said. "You think he's even left the bar yet?"

"He's probably terrified," she said.

"Are we talking about the same guy? Larry Becker? He's shit-faced. I guarantee you."

"Where were you even thinking of going?" Pam asked.

"Connecticut," she said, sitting up straight, saying it with a certain defensive emphasis added to the syllables, as if she knew that the name alone opened her up to attack. Which it did.

"Connecticut?" Pam laughed. "You want to run away to Connecticut?"

"My aunt lives there," she said. She seemed like she'd regressed seven years and was suddenly a ten-year-old. "She's nice to me."

"It doesn't matter," Savannah said. She had her finger up in the air, an idea on the end of it. "You know what's going to happen? Your dad's coming straight here. He never liked me. Never trusted me. I'll be the first person he suspects."

"Suspects of what? That's bullshit," Lauren said.

"What's bullshit," she said, "is you showing up here at one in the morning. A teenage runaway? Really? Isn't that beneath you?"

Pam, largely silent at the table, nursing an enormous cup of coffee and rum, a lit Winston streaming smoke from the grooved tooth mark of a ceramic ashtray, grunted in affirmation. "Totally, totally, beneath you."

"Oh please," Lauren said. "I think it's crap that you're both hassling me so much. Like, be cool!"

"You've only got about nine months left before college. You couldn't wait that long?"

"No," Lauren said, "I couldn't."

"What did you tell your father?" Savannah asked.

"What do you mean? I didn't tell him anything."

"So he's just going to come home and find you gone?"

"Something like that."

"So you can still go back," Pam offered.

"He's working the late shift. Or he's gambling. Or he's wasted. I stopped paying attention. He won't be home until the morning. And by then he'll think I'm in school. The plan was to get far away by then. Out of Iowa, at the least."

"What about your mom?" I asked innocently. Everyone, in response, glared at me.

"Her mother's not with us," Pam said, speaking softly.

"It's OK," Lauren said. "You don't need to whisper it. I'm right here. I remember that she died."

"I'll drive her," Pam offered.

"Please," Lauren said. She was close to crying. We all saw this. "Can't I just stay here tonight? We can talk about it more tomorrow. Please?"

It was near two in the morning when Savannah and I were finally alone. Lauren and

Pam were in the basement, setting up cots and sleeping bags. Savannah was on her third cup of coffee. Whatever had changed about her between 1952 and now, whatever gravity had done to her skin, whatever working at a midwestern library had done to her hair and her clothing, all of that disappeared after an hour in her kitchen, the present obliterating the past. As she wriggled in her seat, uncomfortable about this, about my being here in her house, about everything my face must have brought to mind for her, I tried to imagine her outside Lem's apartment door, standing sheepishly behind his hanging laundry, and the face that came to me was this face: thirty-six, graying, tired, annoyed.

She began to shred a paper napkin lying on the table. She'd wadded it into a ball, and now, sighing, looking up at me every few moments with derision, she'd begun to make confetti out of it. "What are you doing here, Hilly?"

I opened my mouth to answer, and she cut me off.

"That's rhetorical. Don't answer. I have a feeling I know."

She got up from the table and went to the cabinet to pour herself a glass of rum.

"I saw the business about your father's

diner," I offered. "The rock."

She hadn't turned around. She was looking out the kitchen window, into the black night. "Like I said. I had a feeling."

"I'm a reporter," I said, trying to clarify. "It's what I do. I report on race relations. Violence. That sort of thing."

She laughed aloud. "That's the worst job I've ever heard of."

"It's a job. It's necessary. Don't you think?"

"Newspapers, huh? I'd have thought you'd become a lawyer. Like your daddy."

"No," I said. "That was never on the table."

"He's on the news every day, it seems. Today, in fact."

"Nothing changes."

"Planes go up, planes go down."

I made a bad attempt at imitating the chiming, ringing, *cha-ching* sound a cash register makes.

"That's what I heard."

"Nixon —" I started to say, but she put her hand up.

"I know. I read the papers. I really didn't intend to start talking about this. Or *Nixon*. Let's drop it."

"That's fine."

"Good."

"I don't talk to him much anymore," I said. "If it matters."

"It doesn't matter, Hilly."

"I know it's no consolation, but I feel like I should say that I've never stopped thinking about what happened."

She turned around now, no trace of emotion on her face. "Let's avoid the melodrama. You've already shown up at my doorstep unannounced. At one in the morning. With a girl I know who wants to run away. It doesn't get any more dramatic than that. So how about we just go to sleep?"

"Whatever you want," I said, getting up from my chair. "This is your house." I thought again of Jenny. There was something in the tone of Savannah's voice that matched the way Jenny's sounded when she was disappointed with me.

"I have a husband," Savannah said then. "This is actually his house. He's away. Overseas. In Vietnam. I don't know where exactly. I can't get information. But that's something you should know. 'Cause . . . 'cause I don't know what's got you here. But I think I can imagine. Knowing you. Knowing how you were. All right? You got that?"

"He's the man in the pictures?"

She didn't bother to tell me I was right.

"You here to save me? Give me some more stuff you're not using?"

"No."

"You here to beg for forgiveness?"

"Maybe."

"Tough luck."

"But . . ."

"What did you think would happen?" she asked then, turning around, repossessed with some newfound energy, her hands quivering.

"I don't know. I just wanted to find you and see you again."

"Reconnection?"

"Maybe."

"Is it innocent?"

"What do you mean? Is what innocent?"

"Do you have a motive? That's what I mean."

"My motive was to see you."

"And then what?"

"I'm not sure."

"You gonna take me to the movies?

"Huh?"

"Buy me a motherfucking milk shake?"

"What?"

Now she was close to me. Both hands on her hips, both wrists covered with bangles, rings on all of her fingers, her foot tapping now. "Did you think we'd run off together?

Did you think it'd be romantic?"

I pursed my lips. She had begun to shake slightly.

"Did you think we'd just go off somewhere and make up for lost time?"

"Maybe," I admitted. "I think I hoped that."

"But I'm married." She flashed her ring at me. A small band, a small stone.

"I know. You said that."

"You didn't think that'd happen, huh?"

"I didn't think anything about it."

"You didn't get to fuck me then, so you want to fuck me now. Is that it?"

"Who's being dramatic now?"

"At least be up front about it. I see it all over you."

"You couldn't see that on me."

"Don't be a prude. That *is* why you're here. I know that. I just want you to admit it."

"It's more than that."

"Is it? I don't think it's ever more than that. With anybody. But if it is, then tell me. Tell me why you're here."

"This is awful," I said. And then, because I was drowning: "I couldn't begin . . ."

She blew air through her teeth. "OK." She took a step toward me. Same position: hands on hips, her feet tapping, bracelets clattering. "Fine. You've clearly got some delusion you're suffering from."

"It's embarrassing to even say it aloud."

"You can't be too embarrassed. You're here."

"You're interrogating me," I said.

"Just tell me, then. Spit it out."

"I just wondered about you. Didn't you —"

"Let's not do this."

"What?"

"Talk about *all that.* Ask each other these questions."

"Why?"

"Because your feelings will get hurt. That's why."

"You were the one —"

"What? I was the one to do what?"

"You were the one who kissed me."

"When?"

"Back then," I said lamely.

"Back in 1952?" she cried. "Back twenty years ago?"

I could barely nod. "You don't have to be cruel," I said.

"Would it be terrible to admit that I want to forget all about you?" she asked, her voice flat.

"If it was true," I answered.

She grimaced. "It's true to a point."

■ ■ ■ ■

In the basement, Lauren was sitting on her cot, pretending to read a battered edition of *Madame Bovary.* She was wearing a boy's T-shirt and a pair of flannel boxer shorts. Her legs were thin, stubble above the knees. There was pink polish on her toenails, and I could smell that she'd just applied it, that odor of the paint still hanging around in the air. She heaved the book onto the floor. As soon as I came downstairs I'd seen that she was crying. The marks on her arms were pronounced. "Emma Bovary is such a hussy," she said, trying to divert my attention. She dabbed at her eyes with the corner of her shirt.

I sat down on my cot. "Are you OK?" I asked.

My asking this question seemed to poke a hole in the dam. Now she was crying without trying to stop.

"It's just . . . not good here."

"We'll figure something out. OK?"

"I thought she'd be OK with it."

"With your running away?"

"Yeah."

"Look," I said. I put my hand out and took hers. She was cold. "I'll help you. OK?"

She looked upstairs. "Can we talk about something else? I'm just slobbering all over myself." A tiny smile broke through her crying. "How about we talk about you, OK? How'd you make out? Does she remember you the way you remember her?"

"I don't know," I said. "My first impression is no. No, she doesn't."

Lauren frowned at me. There were two small windows above us, dim light leaking through from the kitchen, upstairs. Shelves on three sides of the room were stacked with jugs of water, bags of rice, and canned vegetables. This, I realized, was a tornado shelter.

"She had that picture in her office," she said. "Remember that."

"I do," I said. "Believe me."

"Did you tell her?"

"I forgot," I said. "She, uh . . . she got kind of mad at me."

"She acts tough," she said. "But I think it's an act sometimes. She's a softy."

"To you, maybe. But for me, I think it was a mistake, coming here."

She was quiet for a second. She seemed alternately like a woman my age, a woman I might meet in a bar somewhere in Cambridge or Berkeley or Charlottesville, and then, with her pink toenails and her tiny legs, like a thirteen-year-old.

"Have you really been in love with her forever?"

"Sometimes yes. Other times no."

"You only get one of those in your life, I heard."

"Who told you that?"

"I don't know. Some magazine article, probably."

I thought of Jenny. "I think it's possible to fall in love as many times as you want."

She smirked at this. "Really? Is that why you're here right now, in this basement?"

There was a phone by the cot I was sitting on. *I should call Jenny,* I thought. *Tell her I won't make it home tomorrow, tell her to wire some of the money to me.*

"So, your father is Arthur Wise," she said. "What's that like?"

"Problematic," I managed.

"Problematic? Aren't you guys insanely rich?"

"I'm not rich," I said. "My father's rich."

"How rich is he?"

"Rich."

"Like, how?"

"Rich. Really rich."

"I've never really understood how you can get rich off plane crashes."

"Class-action suits. You find some reason

311

why a plane crashes, why it shouldn't have crashed; you uncover some memo somewhere saying that the airline knew about it, that they were covering it up, trying to stretch their profit margin."

"That sounds kind of grim," she said.

"Then there's the consulting work. Companies are so afraid to get sued by him that they hire him now to write up these indemnification clauses on the back of the tickets you buy. I don't know if that's the actual term. The fine print. Like: *If you happen to die, it's not our fault, your brother-in-law can't sue us.* That sort of thing."

"I see."

"To be honest, I don't really know how it all works. But he owns a lot of real estate, too. Obviously."

"Obviously," Lauren said, grinning.

"And commodities, I think. Oil futures. Various small companies. And insurance, probably. I think there's a part of his company that sells insurance. And whatever else I don't know about. He has his own law firm. Second largest in New York. Everything they bill, everything every lawyer in the firm makes, he gets a cut. He's just a waterfall of money."

"A waterfall."

"He wakes up and money just comes out

of the faucet."

"Wow. Money running out of the faucet."

And then, nervously flicking at a loose thread on the cot, I cleared my throat. I'd never discussed this with anyone before, certainly never confessed to a stranger the level of my wealth, however untouched the money was, however guilty and conflicted it all made me feel. Lauren was the first.

"There's this account for me that I never touch. And because of that, I guess you could say that I'm rich. Very rich, even."

"How much is in it?"

I shook my head. "Seventy million dollars," I said. "Or something close to that. I don't look at every statement. But last time I looked, it was seventy."

Lauren rocked back from her butt to her shoulders, laughing silently. She'd stopped crying now. "What?" she whispered. "Are you kidding me? Seventy million? What! I thought you were going to say, like, two million or something."

"I don't touch it," I repeated, and then I told this girl, this future runaway, this future millionaire herself, everything. About Boston Airways, Wren's Bridge, Bluepoint, Lem Dawson, Charles Ewing, and then about Savannah, her shack at Emerson Oaks, those buckets, the carful of things I'd

313

brought her way. And then: my father and mother and Robert Ashley, my house in Massachusetts, my job, covering race riots at the buckle of the Bible Belt. And Jenny. I said all of this without making any eye contact with Lauren.

When I was finished, all she said in response was this:

"Will you marry me?"

I smiled. "That's all you gotta say?" I asked. "My whole life story, and all I get is a marriage proposal?"

"Do you know that you could buy the Empire State Building for that much money?"

"Let's go to sleep. You've got a big day tomorrow. You have to finish running away, don't you?"

"No," she said, laughing. She stood up and got on the floor at my feet. "You're marrying me. That's what we're doing tomorrow. Marriage. Chapel. Priest. Gift registry at Dillard's."

"I'm Jewish," I said, "so we can't have a priest."

"Rabbi. Fine. I don't care. I can be Jewish."

"You'll have to convert."

"I love Barbra Streisand."

"Good night," I said.

"I can learn to cook."

"Good night, Lauren."

"Oh, right. You probably have a private chef."

"Good night."

"New plan. You adopt me. I become your daughter."

"Seriously," I said.

For a minute we were silent. On the other side of the thin wall beside my cot, the furnace churned. Finally Lauren turned to me, her face edging into a faint slant of moonlight.

"Will you help me get out of here?" she asked. She'd started to cry again. Just a little. A drizzle. "No joke. Will you? I need to get out of this place."

"If that's what you want."

"Thank you, Hilly," she said. "Thank you for helping me."

"No problem, kid. Thank you for helping me."

"Seriously. I'll never forget it. Friends for life. Promise?"

Six

By morning Savannah had decided that Lauren was going home. There wasn't much discussion about it. I'd come up the stairs with Lauren to find Savannah in the kitchen, looking like she hadn't slept much, her arms crossed against her chest, her gaze unwavering. Savannah pointed at us. "You get ready," she said to Lauren. "And you," she said pointing at me, shaking her head. "I don't even know what to do with you."

Lauren started to cry and shot me a helpless, silent look.

"Don't worry," I said to her. "We'll figure it out."

"You promised, though," she cried, before running back down to the basement.

Now I was alone again with Savannah.

"It's not much of a surprise, now that I think of it," Savannah said. "You find yourself some helpless young girl with a bad daddy. Try to save her."

"She found me," I said.

"You're always trying to save people. That's why you're here, right? Save my father's window?"

"What's so terrible about that?"

"It's insulting," she said. "That's what's terrible. Let him save himself. Let me save myself. And let that girl down there — let her figure her life out. She's a kid."

Savannah kept herself as far from me as possible. When I moved into the kitchen, she switched places with me and went out toward the far living room window. She was in a lilac sweater, a turtleneck, a gold crucifix up over the lip of the fold. Her feet were bare, and I noticed that she had matching silver bands on the fourth toe, the ring toe, of each foot.

"It seems like it's a pretty bad scene over there. And I think there's enough evidence —"

"Listen, Hilly. It's my house. I'm not getting involved. I'm taking her back. She's leaving for college in nine months. She can wait that long."

Implicit in the way she was talking — without eye contact, without any trace of softness in her voice — was the simple fact that she wanted to get rid of me after she got rid of Lauren. Behind her, out on the

317

soy plantation, a tractor painted in Hawk-eye gold motored past the window. I feel obliged to note here that the man on the tractor was black, as was a young woman standing in the field, watching him, a floppy straw hat shielding her face. As were two teenagers with burgeoning miniature Afros gossiping nearby, both of them in flared bell-bottoms. As were some farmhands who emerged as I watched, coveralls on, shit-splattered Wellies up to their knees. Later that day, I'd realize that all of Hove was as black as Ebbington was white: the men at the Esso station, the men flipping pancakes at the Liberty Café, the women selling wedding dresses on Frederick Douglass, the letter carriers, the butchers, the dentists, the judges, bailiffs, defendants, prison guards, hardware clerks, electricians, general contractors, ball coaches, chemistry teachers, portrait photographers, confectioners, even the elderly fellow who built caskets, the name of his establishment slightly too cheery for me: Bleavin's Heaven Boxes.

Five minutes later we were all in Savannah's safari-model Land Rover, an odd car for a librarian, an odd car for anyone in Iowa in 1972. It was John Deere green, with enormous tires that rose to my hips. She told me that her father had given it to her a few years earlier. She called him Slim, like everybody else did. "He won it gambling," she said, yelling over the engine. "The same way he gets everything he has. Apparently he thought it was funny that I have this car. You know: because you'd usually drive this across the savanna." She raised her eyebrows. "I look like an idiot in it. But it's what I have."

The roof of the thing had been removed, as if to make it easier to spot tree leopards or olive baboons, and then it had been reattached poorly; as we drove, the car seemed likely to separate in half if we hit a big enough bump. We went out on Route 112, back toward Ebbington, away from Hove, the grain elevators whiter and grimier in the daylight. Lauren sat up front, sullen, occasionally weeping into her duffel.

"I hate you," she said to Savannah, more than once.

"You put me in a compromising situation," Savannah said.

"Spare me the lecture."

"I can't help you with this. You've got to get through this on your own."

I thought Savannah was joking when she said this, and so I laughed.

"Oh my gosh," she said, turning to me. "Could you be any less helpful?"

"At least he listened. Clearly *you* just don't want to help," Lauren said. "It's not that you can't. It's that you don't want to." She tried to suck air into her lungs between her crying fits. "I can't believe you'd send me back to that house! You have no idea how awful it is to live in such a terrible place."

But of course, Savannah did. And after what I'd told Lauren last night, she should have known better than to say that aloud. To her credit, though, I saw through the side-view that Lauren's face became an instant wreck of regret. If there was anyone who knew, it was Savannah: that hut, shack, shed, hovel, at the Emerson Oaks; those buckets; the roof, lying in pieces in the brush beside the house.

"It's awful, honey," Savannah said, sweet now. "I know. You've told me."

"I haven't told you *every*thing," she said.

"What else is there?"

"He's terrible. He's just awful. He's a *bigot.*"

Savannah shrugged.

"He is," Lauren insisted. "You should hear his mouth. I can't even be there. He's hideous."

Savannah did it again, gave a small shrug, as if Lauren's father's being a bigot wasn't anything she didn't already know about. "Look, nobody's perfect. Nine months. That's all you need."

"Then what? College? You think he's gonna pay for college?"

"No," Savannah said. "But my father didn't pay for college either. I took out loans. Like most people." She turned to me. "Not Hilly here. Hilly didn't need loans. But most people just go to the bank, sweetie. It's actually pretty easy."

"Loans." Lauren said this oddly, as if she hated the concept of debt, but also as if she hadn't ever considered that she could finance her own future. For her, the word was clearly an epiphany. She wore the realization transparently, relief settling over her, replaced just as quickly by the embarrassment of not having known this earlier. Then: a perfectly pitched adolescent scoff. "I know it's easy. *Jeez.*"

We got to her house soon after we crossed the town limits of Ebbington. Hers was a neighborhood of intersections, a grid dropped as if by helicopter down onto what must have been a family farm once, sold off to developers, parceled, surveyed, flattened. A wooden billboard announced the neighborhood as the Peterson Estates. "Estates" was something of a misnomer. The homes

321

here were flat, shorter than ranches, about as tall as Savannah's Land Rover, as if some big twister had cleaved in half any structure that dared to commit a second story. The predominant building material here was a type of fake brick that was in reality simply cheap concrete shaped into rectangles and painted red. When the weather shifted from cold to hot, these tended to shatter, and as a result the houses here looked as if they had seen the wrong end of some harrowing battle, the chipped bricks welted as if by machine-gun fire. Lauren sank into her seat as we passed that wooden billboard to her neighborhood, the *P* in *Peterson* done up, for whatever reason, in a calligraphic typeface that didn't match the rest of the name, graffiti smeared onto the wood, a bright yellow *suck it* conjoined to a pink peace sign. Her crying became hysterical now. I hadn't noticed that she was wearing any makeup until it was wetly smeared and streaked on her face.

Again, she spoke in short artillery bursts: "Fuck. You. Both."

I tried to give her some reassurance by way of the side-view mirror, but she was lost, already working the door handle as Savannah slowed to her house.

"I'm never talking to you again," Lauren

said to Savannah.

"That's fine."

"You can live with that?" Lauren asked.

"You'll thank me for this."

"You're arrogant," Lauren said. "People say that about you. People all over say that. You think you're so smart."

"Good to know. I'll keep that in mind the next time I see some *people*. I'll try to act nice and stupid for them so that everybody feels good about themselves."

Lauren sneered at this, wounded. Then, shaking her head, she got out of the car. I watched her get halfway up her walkway before Savannah turned to me.

"Get out there," she said. "Make sure her father doesn't think we took her. I don't feel like getting arrested today."

Her old man was out on the step before Lauren got to the door, his obvious concern not eclipsed by the withering disgust he directed my way. Lauren saw her father and stopped midway up the walk. I had the urge to hug her when I saw this. She took a small step backward. If I hadn't before, I now believed everything she'd just said about him.

"You the one who took my daughter?" the man called out to me. "Or the colored lady take her?"

Whatever Savannah thought of my job, whether in fact it was the worst job ever, as she had put it, years of traveling had provided me with an ability to deal with men like Lauren's father. He seemed, at first glance, harmless: corn-husk skinny, with tawny, smoke-blanched skin, teeth like gravestones toppled by vandals. Men like him lacked any pretense of self-consciousness; everything about him worked on instinct. He was in his socks. They were, I found it necessary to notice, Green Bay Packers socks, green and yellow, the logo on the toe. Tacked atop his upper lip, a big furry cat's tail of a mustache gave accent to everything he said.

"Turns out Lauren got sick last night at the library. Really messy, actually. Some sort of food poisoning. Isn't that what they said?" I tried to find Lauren's expression so that we could corroborate this instantly. "Anyway. That's what the emergency room doctors told us."

At this, her father froze. "Doctors?"

"They wanted to call," I said, finally catching a glint in Lauren's eye. "But she couldn't really get it together to give anybody your number."

Her father turned. "Is this true, Lauren?"

Lauren managed, thankfully, to nod. "It

was gross."

"And who are you?" her father asked me.

"Hilton Wise," I said, my hand out to shake his. "Friend of Savannah's. She's the one who took her over to the hospital."

"Wise?"

"I'm a reporter. *Boston Spectator.*" Another business card, the same officious exactitude in the way I whipped it out of my jacket pocket. I was getting good at this. Lauren disappeared inside the house. I saw, as the door opened, a swatch of high-pile orange carpet, a fat tabby lolling about on a love seat, more Packers gear (a woolly throw, ratty slippers, a soggy-looking green pennant). Also: the wooden cabinet to a television set, rabbit ears splayed east and west. On the set he'd put a frosted mug, losing its icy coat now, the beer just poured, the fizz still popping. It wasn't yet nine and he was drinking.

"I'm Larry Becker," he said, nodding at me. Then he peered out again at the Land Rover. "You with her?"

"She's a friend of mine," I said. "Like I said."

He was still squinting out at Savannah. "She bring my money?"

"Excuse me?"

"Did the colored bitch bring my money?

325

She should have brought me my money."

I stiffened. "What'd you just say?"

He grinned falsely. "Sorry. The colored woman bring me my money?"

I stepped aside so that both Larry and I could look over at the Land Rover together. I wanted to see what he saw, which apparently was her color first and her lack of his money second. When she saw that we were looking, she revved the engine, a huge noise, the whole neighborhood awash suddenly in the churning of this beast of a car, designed to tackle a safari, to outrun a gazelle, to withstand the horn of a rhino. Instantly, birds were jolted out from the bushes of the neighboring houses.

"How much money does she owe you, exactly?" I asked.

"It's her daddy that owes me."

"Charles?"

"Who's Charles?"

"Slim," I said, correcting myself. "How much does Slim owe you?"

Larry took a tiny spiral notebook out from his back pocket, the cover of which was green, with a yellow stripe running the y-axis. Everything about this man seemed designed to silence the fool who dared to challenge his devotion to the Packers. Flipping back a few pages, he landed on a sheet filled with a horizontal slew of numbers, each line crossed out in pencil and then replaced below it with another, bigger number. "As of today, with interest, Slim owes me eighteen K. But it's about to go up. 'Bout to go up real soon."

"K. You mean *thousand*?"

"Yes. *K* as in *thousand.*"

Now Savannah was waving me home to the car. Another growling bit of thunder from the Land Rover. When I turned back to Larry, he was studying my business card.

"Wise. Any relation —"

"He's my father," I said.

"You look like him, so I was thinking that." Larry chuckled, his eyebrows rising. His whole disposition changed, the toughness melting out of him. Now he was my friend. "I'm a big admirer of his. I won't get in an airplane 'cause of that guy."

"He has that effect."

Larry motioned to me with my card, asking wordlessly if he could keep it.

"Say, how's it that Slim owes you so much money?" I asked. "Eighteen thousand is a lot of cash."

"Well, he doesn't owe me, per se. I run a casino downtown. Under the phone building. Sort of low stakes, usually. Unless things get out of hand."

"Casino? You're kidding me."

"It's a sports book, mainly."

He was smiling now, bragging. Rather than come across as a gangster, which I think was what he wanted, knowing now that I was Arthur Wise's son, and probably believing some of the various rumors that floated around my father's success like a swarm of bees — that in order to pressure the airlines, he needed to exert influence on the unions that supplied the pilots and the baggage folks and the mechanics, and to do that he needed to muscle the various crime syndicates that people assumed ran those unions — Larry came off to me as a preening teenager, harmlessly pleased with himself.

"So did he get out of hand, or did he just run up a tab?" I asked.

"Little bit of both. He actually owes the money to some friends of mine. I don't bet anymore myself. Cases like this, where the sum gets high, when people get angry — I usually have to step in and be the bad guy."

"Why's that?"

"Because I'm in charge," he said, with another jolt of arrogance.

"Eighteen thousand isn't a little bit."

"You don't need to tell me. I was against letting him wager with us. Just kind of figured this might happen. Guy's got a problem. It's a miracle he even still has that diner. It's the one thing he refuses to put up."

"How's he gonna pay you back?" I asked.

"That's not my problem," Larry said. "But he's gotta. He knows. I know he knows. We all know. Even your colored girl over there knows. Besides. Yesterday was the due date."

Because he thought we were friends, he leaned in to me now. "You be sure to tell your friend out there in the car to be careful at the library, all right?"

"Is that a threat?" I asked.

He sighed. "Not from me, it isn't," he said. "But these people I know that he owes money to, they're mad. That's all I gotta say."

Back in the car, I turned to Savannah. "I need to see that library where you work."

SEVEN

The library was small, a compact building made from fieldstone. The only building of any substance for a mile — maybe more, maybe two or three miles — the library served at various times as a de facto town hall, a meeting place on July Fourth for paraders and floats and a color-guard squad, the unofficial headquarters for the Hove Little League, the Hove Rotary Club, the Hove Future Farmers of America, and also the only real, serious tornado shelter in the whole county. And in November, the Democrats were scheduled to have the first Iowa caucus here. This was what Savannah told me when we parked. I got out first, fearing already what I expected we'd find: another rock, some spray-painted warning, a lynched effigy of Charles Ewing dangling from the second story. Larry Becker had all but promised this was coming. If not now, soon; if not soon, then eventually. That none of this came as a surprise to me or frightened me very much attested to what had become part of life by then, a side effect of my having seen so many towns like Hove and Ebbington devolve into rock throwing, brick hurling, lynchings and firebombings, into tombstone toppling, grave robbing, and church burning. I'd seen burned churches in seven different states, held burned Bibles in my hands, photographed them, written about them. Every bit of hostility now was colored by this expectation of mine, politics bleeding all over everything.

But Savannah was unconcerned. "That guy's not dangerous. Neither are his degenerate friends." The library was calm, the only noise a shingle loose on the roof, flapping against the wood beams. Even in October there were gardens: an oval of red-dyed mulch spread out and ornamented by cabbage the color of the Arctic. Behind the building, rather than a play set or a ball field, there was a sculpture garden, everything made from leftover farm parts and rendered into representations of animals. (Sample piece: the John Deere *Deer* — disemboweled tractor parts, gesso, copper wiring, Firestone tires flattened and hung like drapery.) According to a small signpost ramrodded into the near tundra, the sculptures were made by local high school students. The garden stretched an acre, into the mouth of a cornfield, the crop gone by now, the tassels detasseled but the stalks still high. I let out a small, impressed whistle, which made Savannah grin.

"I like it, too," she said.

"It's nice," I said.

Considering the last hour, this tiny conversation was a small victory. Finally she'd said something to me that wasn't an accusation or something meant to hurt me. On the way over to the library, she was so quiet and so tense that I knew I'd made the right decision to tell Jenny I was coming home. I'd check the library and get on a plane that afternoon.

We went in through the front door, Savannah grabbing a huge key ring out of her purse and expertly finding the one that opened the building. She went in first. "My beautiful office is downstairs," she said, passing by a series of closed doors that she said led to a staircase. "We've got the children's books down there. And the microfiche. Those are new, those machines. We just got them. We had to scrimp for *years* to afford them." She still had on her bracelets, and when she pointed, they clanked together, making me think again of Jenny, home alone now. My ticket was out of Cedar Rapids. I'd be back home by dinner, and all of this — these years of obsessing, of searching — it'd all be over. With her key ring, Savannah unlocked the glass doors that led to the lobby and the circulation desks. She stopped periodically to unlock various cabinets and stacks and files, every lock requiring a different key, every key color coded on her chain. I followed her everywhere she went. The main reading room was dark, and I could see the fields out beyond the windows better than I could anything around me. The shelves were columns of shadow, and the study tables, the carrels, the check-in desk, were somehow darker, formless, shadows of shadows. She left me then, breezing off somewhere. A big building like this without its light can bring you back to your boyhood so easily; there is something about the unfamiliar that is located in childhood, when so much is still new, when the catalogue of experience is cheerfully short. Then: light. Fluorescents buzzing. From somewhere, the smell of a blackboard eraser. I was in Wren's Bridge High School, sitting at my flip-top desk. It was just a moment — oh! — and then the spell was broken.

Savannah stepped out in front of me, a

huge atlas in her hand. "Listen," she said, lifting the book. "I've got stuff to do. Everything's fine here. I promise. Those guys didn't do anything. He's just bluffing. Maybe you should go."

"So this is goodbye," I said.

"Let's not get all sentimental, you and me."

"I'll go call a cab," I said. "I'll come get you before I leave."

She smiled and left the room. I knew only two things: that Lauren had spent most of her childhood here, and that somewhere in the building there was an empty frame that had once held the picture of me and Savannah near the beach at Bluepoint. This was why I couldn't just leave. I had to at least mention this. There was a second floor, and for a few minutes, I thought I heard her up there, milling around, moving book carts. In a way, the Hove library was no different from the countless others that I'd been in: there is a certain sensory combination shared by public buildings constructed in the forties and fifties: wood dust and double-glazed windows and durable industrial carpet and the pleasurable smell of books decaying and yellowing. At the foot of a stairway to the second floor hung an oil canvas, at first glance like most of the other life-less oil canvases hanging on the walls here. It was a picture of our bluff: Blue-point. Robert Ashley's house. Sun on the roof. There was the sand, the dirty gulls, the boardwalk, and, worst of all, the big dune, right of center, swept smooth. I took two steps closer to the picture, knowing already what I discovered officially a moment later by way of a bronze plaque: this was one of Lem Dawson's paintings.

Over the years I had allowed myself to believe Lem a genius, a dead genius, a genius that one way or another I'd gotten killed. I didn't have any real reason to think this. In fact, I shouldn't have thought it at all. I'd misconstrued his reluctance to show me his work as the eccentricity of some great talent. But now I saw how wrong I'd been. The painting was awful. I noticed nothing but its considerable flaws: its seams, its poorly rendered sense of light, its skewed perspective, the sentimental way he'd approached the clouds, the birds, the shadow of the trees on the flat side of Robert's house. The waves were especially amateurish: they were puffy, dry-looking, like the canned snow spread around in shopping malls at Christmas. To see this, to see how very bad he'd been! I took a step back, then two, and then a dozen, thinking that distance would help, that perhaps Lem's paintings were like something by Seurat, the whole puzzle locking into focus at a certain point. This didn't help.

Was this the only picture that had survived the rain that last day in Bluepoint? I tried to discover whether the big baroque frame Savannah had picked for the canvas (which certainly didn't help matters) was concealing proof of water damage. Pictures in museums and galleries hide in their frames all the human evidence of their making: vise marks on the canvas edge, hand-hammered staples, cigarette ash, pencil markings, food stains. I wanted to take the painting out of its frame, but I wouldn't allow myself to even graze my finger across the wall where it hung; Lem's nervous voice came suddenly to my ear. I wanted, at the very least, to obey this wish of his.

Savannah screamed then. Or she screamed a moment after I heard something crash beneath me — something glass, something large. I can't be sure now. For a moment it was impossible to tell if the noises were related. I heard the fire alarm go off for a second, then stop. Two hideous shrieks, followed desperately by my name. "Hilly! Come! Hilly!"

When I found her, she was frozen on the

bottom step of the staircase that led down-stairs. She was shaking, and when I touched her shoulder she shuddered as if I'd shocked her. Ahead of us, the room was destroyed. This was the children's section — all on its side, every book tossed from the shelf, the light fixtures swaying, the bulbs broken, glass everywhere. We went a few steps in. Savannah bent to pick up the broken rem-nants of a children's mobile — Disney characters, meant to hang above the story-time lounge. Everything was crushed. Around another corner, the walls were streaked with graffiti, most of it nonsense, just painted stripes. By now, Savannah was crying. "This is terrible," she kept saying. "Terrible."

Finally, we got to the reference room. It was a square anteroom, off of which there were two hallways that led to a bank of of-fices. In front of us were the new microfiche machines, all of them bashed in, their moni-tors wrecked. At our feet were a few reams of tape, all of it pulled from its spools. The lights were wrecked here, too. When she saw this, Savannah collapsed. I caught her, helped her to a chair. Already, she was thinking of the money.

"We can't fix this," she said. "We just can't."

Whoever it was that Larry Becker was talking about, whoever it was that Charles owed money to, had spent a while in here wrecking the place. I felt a breeze then, wind against my hair, and I heard the faraway sound of a lawn mower or a tractor. The reference room had no windows, though. The wind was coming from somewhere else. Savannah felt it too, the wind rustling her hair.

"There's wind," she said. "There shouldn't be wind. Why is there wind?"

"Does your office have windows?" I asked her. "Because that's probably where they came in."

She pointed at the hallway to our left. "Down there," she said.

I went down the hallway. There was a trail of broken glass on the carpet that led to Savannah's office door, swung open now to reveal the damage, the window smashed through, everything upended, her desk stripped of its drawers, papers in a storm's wake, a typewriter turned on its face, pictures and diplomas and certificates smashed and torn. I was right. This was where they'd come in. Sitting in the middle of Savannah's desk was a bomb. For an instant, I froze. I thought of what Jenny would think if I were killed this way — what kinds of questions she'd have, the awful truth she'd discover. I allowed myself to get closer. I'd covered bombs now for five years. I'd seen the wreckage. I'd been knee-deep in burned wood and books. I'd gone to the Boston Police Department and received hours' worth of tutorials on how to behave if I were to ever see a bomb. But of course, I'd never seen a bomb before it blew. In the movies there was always a clock. Or a mess of wires. There was ticking. But here, there was nothing. It was just an old car battery wrapped in silver duct tape. I thought it was a fake, left here to scare the hell out of Savannah. This had nothing that a real bomb had — wires, a packet of shrapnel. No clock. No ticking. Even though I was sure it wasn't real, I backed out of the room and closed her door. I wasn't going to take any chances. Before I ran back to get her, I saw that whoever had done this — Larry Becker, or his buddies — had painted a big green dollar sign on her door.

The first police officer who arrived was the same cop who'd wanted to introduce me to Charles my first night in Ebbington. Hove, it turned out, had to rent its police department from Ebbington, an arrangement that was profitable for the cops, but one that made nearly everybody in Hove uneasy and distrustful. The first thing Savannah told him was that she was Charles's daughter, that this same thing had happened in his diner, that someone was out to get them. All of which didn't seem to matter very much to him.

"Are you hurt?" the cop asked.

"No," Savannah said, shaking her head, confused as to why the cop wasn't listening to her. "I'm fine. The building is a wreck, though."

"You need to go out to the Peterson Estates," I started to say. "You need to talk to a guy named Larry Becker."

But the cop flipped shut his notebook. "We're going to go in, take a look around. You stay here. Somebody will take a statement from you."

"No," I said. "Take my statement now. This is unacceptable."

Suddenly I was furious. Furious to have come out here and to have misjudged the situation so badly, to have found Charles and Savannah still so angry with me. Furious for letting Savannah take Lauren home to her father. Furious that my father had sent my girlfriend ten thousand dollars. Furious that Jenny had unearthed my bank statements. Furious to see the damage that

Charles was still causing in his daughter's life. Furious to see what a bunch of dumb gamblers had done in a public library. Furious to see some lazy cop blow me off.

"Look," I said, pointing at his notebook. "Write it down. Larry Becker. Peterson Estates."

"I know who he is," the cop said. "Why don't you go look after your friend over there and let me do my job."

He pointed outside, toward the sculpture garden. Savannah had walked off, sobbing, and was leaning against the big metal deer. Some of her coworkers had arrived and had gone to talk to her, to comfort her. Some more cops were on the scene, as well as a few guys from the local papers, everyone milling around, expecting to find more than they did.

I was right. The bomb was fake. The first officer on the scene had known this the moment he saw it. They hadn't even needed to call in a bomb squad. I wasn't even sure that they had a squad to call if they needed it, but nevertheless, the officer had just picked it up and walked it across the lawn to his cruiser. Of course, he was manhandling the evidence. He wasn't bagging the thing, wasn't tagging it for fingerprinting. The cops here saw this as a simple act of vandalism. I tried to tell whomever I could about Charles's gambling debt, about what Larry had told me, about the guys in Ebbington who were hungry for their money. One cop, an older guy, his hat pushed back on his head, frowned.

"There's a high school a quarter mile from here," he said, pointing out across the cornfield in which we were standing. "It's probably just some kids. They do this from time to time. Especially out here. I doubt this has anything to do with Larry."

I let the insinuation hang there. That the local kids had done this. The black kids.

Outside the parking lot, a pair of cops directed traffic. In a small town like this, even the hint of trouble brought a crowd. Already a line of cars snaked down the road. It was still morning, not yet noon. Behind me, Savannah was talking to some of her coworkers. They were talking about the money, I was sure of it. The building hadn't been wrecked, aside from a few windows. But the damage inside — the books, the furniture, the mobiles and microfiche machines — all of it would cost a fortune to fix.

I heard Charles Ewing's car before I saw him arrive. He'd driven up on the curb, circumventing the traffic jam. This was the same Dodge Dart he'd taken to Gaithersburg Grounds. It was a clunker. Certainly not anything he'd be able to put up in a card game. Certainly not anything anyone would want. I wondered whether he did this on purpose, to keep himself from gambling it away. He parked in the lot, beside Savannah's Land Rover. He'd come straight from work, his apron still on, the diner open, evidently, window or no window. He stopped with one foot up on the parking lot curb. Then he found me.

"Where's she?" he asked.

I pointed out to the garden.

"She's upset," I said. "But she's fine. The place is a wreck, though. Total wreck."

"I told that guy I'd get him his money," he said.

"Doesn't matter now," I said.

"Is it really that bad?" he asked.

"They broke a couple windows. Threw some paint around. Then just ransacked the place."

Charles shook his head. "Shit."

"You should go talk to her," I said. "She's in shock. They left this fake bomb in there."

He pushed me then, catching me by surprise, knocking me over. Suddenly he was standing over me. "The fuck you doing here, son?"

I tried to get up, but he had his foot on my chest suddenly.

"Seriously? All the places to come. You come here?"

"Let me up," I said.

"You just bad luck, Hilly."

"I'm not bad luck."

"You come around, horrible shit happens."

"I had nothing to do with this."

"Why don't I believe you?"

"Isn't this your fault?" I asked. "Isn't this because of your debt?"

Across the field, Savannah was still sitting against that deer, crying. Charles caught me staring out at her and let out a short, mocking laugh.

"What is it with you and her? Huh? She got her own life now. She's *happy.* She don't need you coming by, getting her head confused."

"I'm glad to hear that," I said, although I felt a childish thrill at the idea that I might *confuse* her, replaced with an instant wave of reproachful shame. "Can you let me up so I can go help her?"

"White boy trying to do good, right? What good that do except to get her uncle killed?"

The breath went out of me.

"I didn't have anything to do with that."

"Sure you did. If you never came into his life, into our lives, my brother-in-law'd be alive, painting still, he'd be here, probably, living in this town, doing something good with all that talent he had. Now he's dead. He's dead 'cause of you."

"I had nothing to do with it," I said again.

"Always coming around with your fucking charity. Black man couldn't possibly take care of his daughter without help from some rich white motherfucker. Isn't that it? Right? You gotta bring me by food! Milk! A ham! I couldn't *possibly* have done that myself?"

I managed to get to my feet. Either he let me, or I overpowered him. "Charles," I said, gasping. "Charles, it was more complicated than that. You know it was."

"Everything's more complicated for someone like you. Who gives a shit whether he read your daddy's mail?"

"I know. I realize that now."

"*Now's* too late, though. *Now* he's dead. *Now* you're just here bugging the shit out of me in my own fucking town. Truth is, you ratted on him, he went to jail, then some motherfucker put a knife in his neck."

"I was seventeen."

"You got any idea the kind of shit I put up with when I was seventeen? I never got nobody killed."

"I know," I said. "I'm sorry. I came here to apologize. To both of you."

He was glaring at me. One of the police officers came over to us, grinning at first, then giving me a concerned look that made me feel uneasy, as if he were asking me wordlessly whether this big, angry black guy was giving me any trouble.

"Hey, Slim," the officer said, and then Charles let go of me.

We'd attracted a certain amount of attention by this point, and so when I grabbed Charles by the shirt collar, nearly a half-dozen people stepped in to intervene, none of whom prevented me from completely losing it. "This is all your fault!" I yelled. "All of it. This is you. You! Not me. Your debt. Your gambling. Lem was right about you." Of course, what comes next is what made the papers, and what, even forty-some-odd years later, I am still known for, and what, periodically, close friends of mine will still tease me with after a few drinks.

"Eighteen thousand?" I laughed. "Eighteen thousand is nothing! I have a thousand times that much money! I have millions! I could buy this whole fucking town! I'm Arthur fucking Wise's son! You could have called me! Millions and millions and millions and millions! Did you hear me! I'm Arthur Wise's son!"

EIGHT

Somehow I was the one to put Savannah in her Land Rover, the one left to pick her up off the ground when the cops finally left the library. By that point, she knew what lay ahead. Months of budget battles to find the funds to fix this. Months where the bottom level of the library would have to be closed, the carpets cleaned, the walls repainted, the microfiche machines hauled off to the dump. Months of filing claims with the insurance companies. Months of asking for donations from nearby libraries to replace the books they'd lost. We were two of the last people to leave. I hadn't known whether to stay or whether to go. At a certain point, I thought I'd just hitch a ride to Cedar Rapids right then. What else could I do? Her father was right. I was bad luck. But by then she wouldn't walk, or she couldn't. She'd become so upset, so distressed, she couldn't do anything but sit against that big metal deer and weep. So I carried her across the field, the corn whipping at either side, the sun low now, birds out, cicadas buzzing. As I did this, she whispered into my ear. "Hilly. Why did you come now? Why now? Why not two years ago? Why not then? I hoped I'd find you. But you're late."

These were the words I couldn't forget while I sat in Billy McKinley's office a day later. They kept playing in my head, a loop of everything I'd ever wanted to hear from Savannah for the last twenty years. Everything except for that last line. I was late. Late for her; late for me. Jenny was at home, waiting, having indulged my extending this trip one more day. Savannah's husband was in Vietnam somewhere either in the north or in the south, she didn't know where. We'd missed each other, and now I was in Chicago, fifty-nine stories above Michigan Avenue, the city beneath us mired in a driving rain blowing west off the lake. Billy had the corner office, a desk the size of a Ford pickup, leather sofas the color of wet cigar paper. On the wall he had pictures of his six sons. I'd known Billy when we were teenagers; his father, Chet, was one of my father's first good friends in that moneyed world of the fifties, the first guy who'd never really cared that my father was self-made, that his money was new, that he didn't know the difference between Easthampton and Bridgehampton. Now Billy had pictures of his children on the wall. They all looked exactly the way Billy had looked when he was young: freckles, a pug nose, barely any chin, and red hair like the rust color of the sun when you look at it with your eyes closed. The McKinleys were two generations removed from the Irish immigrants who'd dug the subway tunnels beneath Manhattan, and there was some deep connection between my father and Chet because of this.

Billy didn't seem to have any real responsibilities that day except to ply me with liquor and try to talk me into investing some of my newly claimed wealth in financial instruments whose contents I didn't understand. At various times, various attorneys arrived with documents for me to sign (wire transfer forms, certifications of interest, incorporation papers). Before I knew it, we were shitfaced, it was three in the afternoon, and I'd eaten two porterhouse steaks that we'd had brought up from Smith & Wollensky. At one point, while we were talking about our childhoods or the automobiles our fathers had owned during the Truman administration or the years Billy spent waiting for me to finally come to my senses and claim what he called my "gigantic heap of cash," I mentioned something about my job, about how I needed an office like the one Billy had, full of leather and windows.

"What's it you do now?" Billy asked. "Newspapers, right?"

"Right."

"So, what? You own a few?"

I chuckled. "No, Billy. I write for one."

He was still confused. "Um, you write for one that you own?"

I'd installed Lauren in a hotel room two blocks over. Her father had been arrested before I left town, and without anyone to look after her, a family-court judge in Cedar Rapids had sent her to live with her aunt in Connecticut. She'd gotten what she wanted without having to run away. I'd reserved her the penthouse. By that point, I thought she deserved it. She'd never seen a room so big, a view so commanding (*The buildings are right here! Look, Hilly! I can see straight into that guy's apartment!*), or a bathroom that had both a bathtub and a shower, separate from each other. When I came back from the bank that night, I left a note for Lauren with the concierge. In it were instructions to access the trust fund that I'd set up for her. There was two hundred

351

thousand on deposit, enough for college and grad school and her PhD and whatever else she wanted. Five years later, I'd drive down from Boston to see her graduate from Yale. She'd do the student part of the commencement speech, shaking hands with Vice President Mondale before winking at me and sitting down.

"Don't open it," I told the clerk, a girl as young as Lauren, her blue eye shadow nearly blinding me. "Just bring it up to her. There's a note for her inside."

"Anything else?" she asked.

"I need somebody to drive me to Iowa," I said. "I'd do it. But I'm drunk. Can you arrange that?"

NINE

When I showed up at Savannah's house, ringing the bell at an even later hour than I had the last time, I didn't have Lauren to serve as my decoy. Instead, I had the photograph she'd stolen from Savannah's office. I'd dug it out of my bag before I'd left Chicago, held it in my hands on the limousine ride from the Loop, out of the city, out across the flatlands, through Joliet, out over the Mississippi, into Iowa on Route 80. Here was Hove at three in the morning: the moon had vanished somewhere in Illinois, replaced by some dim hint above the dark fields, useless on the streets that led from the highway to Savannah's front porch.

When she opened the door, I held up the picture, this picture that I'd been staring at for hours. In it, I'm looking off, away from the sea, away from where Charles had been standing, away from the catwalk staircase where Lem and my father had stood and argued. Savannah, though, is looking right at the lens. Maybe she'd become used to having her picture taken at the moment her father had lifted his camera, the moment the shutter snapped. There is something tired in her expression. Tired of him. Tired of Cape Cod.

She blinked at me. She was panicked. I realized then that she'd been expecting to find soldiers at the door with news about her husband. They were the only others who felt it necessary to come knocking so late.

"Hilly?" She breathed my name out in relief, her hand on her chest. "Hilly, what are you doing here?"

"I came back."

"I see that."

"From Chicago."

"It's the middle —"

"I brought you this." The picture flopped as I tried to hold it upright. Again, that blue stamp on the back side flashed at me. *Stockton.* "It's you. And it's me."

"Are you drunk?"

"Maybe." I straightened myself and brought my thumb and forefinger together, as if ready to pinch some salt. "A little. Not much. Kind of."

"Hilly." She stepped out onto the porch, looked left and right.

"She's gone," I said. "Lauren's in Chicago. She's fine. We took care of her."

"We?"

"The Wise family. She's all set."

"Oh Christ."

I took a step toward her. "I came back."

"Hilly?" she asked, taking the picture from me. "Did you steal this?"

"Lauren did," I said. "She stole it and she tracked me down with it. Smart girl."

"I thought it was lost." She looked at it for a moment and pressed it — pressed me — to her chest.

"She said you had it in your office. All this time."

"What did you come back for, Hilly?"

"I took a limousine," I said.

"Not how, Hilly. Why?"

"I drank most of the way. Like father, like son. Funny — if you pay enough, they give you the fancy limo with the full liquor cabinet. It definitely makes the drive go by a little faster."

"Hilly."

"I was all set to go home," I said, reaching into my jacket and removing a United Airlines ticket. "All set."

She looked out beyond me. Then, with a pitying frown, she took my arm. "Come inside," she said. "Pam's asleep. Keep it down."

The house was quiet, the arm of the sofa strewn with newspapers, a light on in the kitchen. A mug sat on the counter, filled halfway with tea. Beside that, a half-eaten biscuit. She took me inside, her hand still on my arm. At the sink, she filled me a glass of water from the faucet. "Best water in America right there," she said, a claim that I disagreed with after drinking it. She laughed quietly, her hand over her face. "Oh, you're too easy to mess with right now."

I held up the glass. "This is gross."

"Something's wrong with our well," she said. "Who knows what."

"I'll buy you a new well," I said.

"Oh really?"

"I'll buy your whole town a new well."

"That's sweet of you."

"We'll get you the best water in America."

"Will we, now."

"Sure. How much could a new well cost? Where do they have the best water? We'll get it, and we'll do it up right. We'll get water from Tahiti. You and me."

She smiled a bit uneasily and pointed at a small, unframed picture wedged into the woodwork of her cabinet. It was her husband.

"Oh, right," I said. "I keep forgetting."

"Conveniently."

"Right. Conveniently."

"Well, perhaps you shouldn't." She crossed her arms against her chest. She was wearing a black knit cardigan and sweatpants.

"You said that you waited for me," I started.

She looked down. "I did."

"I was looking for you."

She looked up again at her husband's picture. "I shouldn't have said that."

"But it's true."

She smiled. "It's true. But it doesn't mean anything now. I just missed having someone here with me."

"What's his name?" I asked.

"Why do you want to know about him?"

"Tell me."

"Hershel," she said. "His name is Hershel."

"Hershel Stockton," I said. "He's younger than you, isn't he?" I leaned in toward the small picture. He was in his uniform, his cap on. "He looks it. What is he, twenty-one? Look at you! He's almost half your age!"

She smirked. "You're aging me."

"Still. It's a big difference," I said.

She took the picture. "He's an academic," she said. "Or I guess I should say that he wants to be an academic. He's not suited for being a soldier."

"The draft get him?"

"He tried to defer it as long as he could."

"What would he say if he knew I was here?"

She scoffed. "What the hell do you think he would say?"

"How did you meet him?"

"Let's not talk about this. Let's get you to bed so that in the morning you can go back home."

"No," I said. "I'm not tired."

"Why do you want to know how I met him? What's the point?"

"Because I do. I want to know these things about you."

"Oh, Hilly," she said, placing Hershel back into the fold in the wood of the cabinet door.

"Tell me."

"I'd rather not."

"Please." I sat down on one of her stools.

"Marching," she said. "How's that? I met him marching."

"Marching where?"

"You're getting on my last nerve, Hilly."

"Indulge me." I took out my wallet. For the first time in my life, it was stuffed with cash. "I'll pay you."

"My God, you are awful."

"Hideous. Terribly hideous. I know."

"In Washington," she said. "I met Hersh at a march in Washington. A protest."

"Against the war? Or for civil rights?"

"For jobs."

"I didn't know you'd done that."

She threw up her hands as if to say, *What, in fact, do you really know about me anyway?* She went on: "We weren't the people with the ideas. We were the people in the background of the pictures. The people behind the people with ideas. Once" — she laughed into her hand — "once, the side of my shoulder made it into a photograph of Dr. King that ran in *Life* magazine. You probably saw it. It's a rather famous photograph. Maybe you knew it was me."

"Your shoulder? How would I have known it was your shoulder?"

"See?" she said. "It's late. I'm talking nonsense."

"I thought about you, too. I waited for you, too."

"Now you're talking nonsense."

"I was at a lot of those marches," I said,

which was an exaggeration. I had been to four marches, all of them long after Johnson had signed into law the Voting Rights Act, all of them small, shabby, disorganized things.

She uncrossed her arms. "There were always a lot of these Jewish boys who came down to march. To help. Always these skinny boys in these dark glasses."

"I never did that," I said.

"I always looked to see if any of them was you."

"You did?"

"I thought maybe you'd seen the picture and you just came down to help."

"The picture of your shoulder?"

She laughed. "It's crazy, right?"

By now she had turned away from me and was looking out the window at the soy field, lit by a solitary lawn light. This last confession of hers had been made without one glance in my direction, as if she couldn't bear to divulge it while having me looking back at her.

I kissed her when she turned around. She startled, pushed me away.

"What?" I asked. "No?"

"No," she said, shaking her head. She'd whispered it.

"Really? No?"

"Oh, I don't know." She locked her hands around my waist but waited a moment before she did this, as if asking for my permission.

"Well? No or yes. Which is it?"

"Yes," she said.

"Yes?"

"Oh fuck. No. No. No." She shut her eyes. "What am I saying?"

"Why? Say yes."

"I want to say yes."

"Then do it."

"I can't."

"Why?"

"Why?" She laughed. "You idiot. You know why."

"It's not so impossible anymore. You and me."

"It's not much better."

"But it's not impossible. People do it."

"People do all sorts of things that others find unnatural."

"I thought being unnatural was in fashion now."

"Not in Iowa."

"Come back to Massachusetts."

"I'll never go back there," she said. Although she'd said this so sternly, her hands were still around me. I thought I felt her tighten her grip.

"How about maybe?" I asked. "At least say maybe."

"Now you're just begging."

"So what."

"Don't beg. That's so unappealing."

"What is this? Showing up at your house at three in the morning, drunk. Is that not unappealing?"

"Although it probably says something awful about me, I actually find this kind of appealing. In a desperate way."

"I'm desperate?"

"Slightly. But you've always been slightly desperate."

"When was I desperate?"

"You were desperate when you were young. It seems to be a cycle, Hilly."

"What if you're with the wrong person?" I asked. "What if this young guy you're with is wrong for you?"

She let go of my waist, turned around. "Don't say that. I love him, Hilly. I married him."

"But you told me that you were waiting for me."

"I was," she said. "But you didn't show up."

"Why didn't you look for me?"

She took a step back. "It just seemed crazy. Like some crazy hope. It wasn't real."

"Obviously it was real."

"You can sleep on the couch," she said. "But in the morning —"

"What if I hang around here?" I asked.

"Here? You can't stay here. I have no room. And I don't want you to stay here."

"Not here. In town."

"My father would kill you."

"What if your father didn't kill me?"

"I might kill you."

"Would you stop me? Would you, I don't know, visit?"

"Would I visit?"

"Visit for coffee. Or dinner. Would you stop me?"

She thought about this for a long while. "I don't know," she said finally. A tiny, devious grin. "Can we talk about this in the morning?"

In the morning, I woke to the telephone. Pam took the call in the kitchen.

"Is Hilly here?" she asked into the phone. "Hilly Wise? I don't think so. Let me check."

I sat up as Pam came into the room. "Look at that," she said, tossing the phone to me, the cord unraveling in the air. "You are here." I rubbed at my eyes. At the foot of the stairs, one hand on the banister, Savannah stood sipping her coffee, smiling

363

at me. She wore a blue-and-white skirt. Her toes were painted alternately in pink and yellow. Behind her, dust was caught without gravity in a slant of sun.

I took the call lying down on the couch. Pam had put Stevie Wonder on the stereo.

"Hello," I said, cupping the receiver against my ear with the soft butt of my shoulder.

"Hilly, this is your father speaking."

Instinctively, I sat up and turned so that my back was to Savannah. I checked my watch. It was early in New York, but he was probably at his desk anyway.

"How did you know I was here?"

"I've called practically every house in this goddamned country looking for you this morning. But it's not a complete surprise to find you here."

"I guess I shouldn't be surprised that you have this number," I said.

Over the line I heard his cigarette lighter snapping, then a sharp breath. "Right. Well, Billy McKinley called."

"Of course he did."

Behind me, Savannah took a step into the kitchen. I turned, one finger up. *Give me a sec,* I mouthed.

"We had a bet going whether you'd ever come to your senses."

"My senses, huh," I said. "What did you bet on?"

"I bet on you, Hilly. I always bet on you. You're my son."

Pam had begun to do chores, to dust, to put some dishes away into a big wooden cabinet they had in the living room. She'd carried a few wineglasses out to the cabinet, and then, leaving the doors open, she went back into the kitchen to grab a few more. From the couch I saw, aligned on a high shelf of the cabinet, above a row of dinner plates, above a messy stack of coffee cups, an array of the knitted dolls that Savannah had shown me that evening in Bluepoint. There were three of them — the one that she had made, with its disproportionate limbs and its cockeyed facial expression, and the two that her mother had made, which were perfect in all the ways that Savannah's was awkward. Pam put the glasses back into the cabinet, and as she was closing the doors I realized that those three dolls were resting against Lem Dawson's old jewelry box. The box that I'd seen Savannah take from his apartment that last afternoon.

"Listen, Hilton," my father said. "I've got the girl out at Bluepoint."

"Who?"

"Ms. Whitcomb," he said, and because I didn't immediately answer, he said, "Jenny. I've got Jenny out here with me."

"Why's that?" I asked.

" 'Cause she's pregnant, Hilly. The girl's pregnant."

I closed my eyes. Savannah had sat down beside me now, smiling at me.

"You there?" he asked.

A breath. "I'm here." Another breath.

"I suggest you come home," my father said.

"Home," I said.

"Bluepoint, Hilly. I've got Dr. Silver staying with her."

"Is everything OK?" I asked. "Is she sick?"

"She's not sick, Hilly. She's pregnant. I just said that."

"Why's the doctor staying with her, then?"

"Because I'm paying him to."

"Right."

I heard my father breathing. He breathed a certain way when he was getting things done. "Do you need me to send you a plane?"

"You have your own plane now?"

A *tsk*. "You need a flight out or not?"

"That's fine. I can fly like everybody else."

"Suit yourself." He was already hanging up. "I'll expect you tomorrow, Hilly."

TEN

There were gates now at the entrance to the house in Bluepoint: heavy iron doors that swung, a lock where they met. And in front of it all, a security booth. Inside sat a man on a stool, a small Zenith going, a red thermos on the sill.

I'd arrived late, near nine, my flight out of Chicago delayed because of runway traffic, the taxi from Boston slowed by an accident on the Bourne, the last part of the ride through town hampered by the same driving rain I'd seen in Chicago. My driver was an Algerian man named Hamid. He'd been in the country eight months by then, and for much of the trip I'd had to direct him. This amounted to the most of what he'd seen of America so far, all of it in the dark. When we crossed over Cape Cod Canal, he whistled and grabbed the wheel, whitening his knuckles. "So far down."

At the gate to my father's house, he

slowed. "What to do now, boss?"

"Stop," I said. "They'll let us through."

"Why is there a gate?"

I laughed. "To keep us out."

"What is this place? Museum?"

"House," I said. "It's a house."

"For how many?"

"Two," I said. "Just two."

He clicked off the meter. Then he looked back to me, as if to question what I'd said, his right eyebrow arched in outrage. "Serious?"

"Serious," I said.

More money: the fare was enormous, and I gave him an equally extravagant tip. By that point I'd decided I was going to give it all away, all of what Billy McKinley had told me was mine, all that had taken so many hours to sign from my father to me, every cent in the long line that began somewhere in the wake of that plane from Boston Airways.

The guard was off his stool now, shining a flashlight in the car, on Hamid, on me.

"And you are?" the man at the gate asked Hamid. The guard had the local accent. On the Cape, it's more British than it is inland, the long vowels really long.

"His son," I said, speaking up from the backseat.

"Come again?"

Now the light was on me. "His son. I'm his son."

"Mr. Wise's son?"

"His son!" I yelled. "Hilton Wise." And then, to Hamid, as if we were buddies now, I whispered, "Why's everything gotta be so difficult?"

The guard consulted his clipboard. "I don't have you on the list."

"A list? Is this a nightclub? Call him."

"Who? Mr. Wise?" He laughed. As if it were the most ludicrous thing to think to call my father. "He's busy."

"Busy with what? He told me to come. Just make a call from your box, or whatever you have to do."

"There's a party," the man said. "Can't you hear the music?"

And faintly, just then, I could: a trombone sliding, then something like the crash of a snare drum. We were, I knew, a few hundred yards from the house. This used to be part of the flat road that ran between Robert's house and ours. Erosion had recast the shore, biting off a piece of everything.

"Please," I told the guard, "just make the call."

I had an Ebbington High baseball cap in my hand. It was the only thing I'd brought with me. There'd been a problem with my suitcase in Chicago, the latch inexplicably refusing to close. As if my clothes had wanted to stay behind in the Midwest. Rather than take it with me, I'd just left it there at the airport, my underwear and my khakis spilling out. But the hat: Savannah had laughed when she saw that I had it. I'd told her the truth when I had to go. "My girlfriend is pregnant," I said. Although I wanted to see disappointment in her eyes, some reason to stay behind, what I saw instead was relief. Relief that I'd finally be going.

Whenever I was asked, I said that I hadn't been to Bluepoint since I was seventeen. I complained about the traffic, or about being so busy that I didn't have the time to go out and visit. But of course that was all bullshit. In the off season, it was two hours from my house. I could get back and forth and listen to a whole ball game and have a pretty good night. I drove by here as often as I could, stopping at a spot along the road where you could see the crown of the roof, the weather vane, a slice of the water, Robert's little house, out on the dune. I didn't bother to turn into the driveway, hidden now by shrubbery, by birch, by two wooden stakes affixed with primitive security cameras.

So I knew about the additions. There were two of them, one built at the beginning of the Johnson administration, a giant glass wing designed by some Dutch wunderkind who was supposed to turn out to be the next big thing and who, for whatever reason, didn't. The second was more recent, a wing off the right flank, very much like the first, but less glass, more steel. The old cottage sat in the middle of it all, the gray siding, the red door, the old windows; he'd turned the place into a glass butterfly. I'd seen pictures of the interior in various architectural journals. Of course my father wouldn't deign to build something like this without getting a little press. Apparently he and my mother slept in their old bedroom. He liked the space, he said. It was small, cold, had the worst view. "It helps me remember where I started," he said in one of those articles, a blatant lie. If he were being honest, he'd have bought the place in New Haven, the place where we lived when the plane went down. That was where we'd started.

Hamid was looking at me through the rearview. "What's the matter, boss? You don't want to go?"

371

"I don't know," I said.

"This place is nice."

"It is."

"I've seen palaces not look so nice."

"I'll tell my father you said that."

"How about I stay. You drive my car."

I smiled. "I like to drive."

"See? Perfect arrangement."

"What's the typical day — eight hours?"

"Try double eight."

Some lights went up behind the gates, maybe headlights, maybe lamps on the lawn. I sat in the backseat, unmoving.

"My girlfriend is in there," I said finally. "She's pregnant."

Hamid nodded. "I understand."

"So. I had to come back."

"Come back from where?"

"I found someone I'd been hoping to find for a long time."

"Another girl?"

I nodded. "Another girl."

"You sure you don't want to switch places?"

"Maybe we should turn back."

"No. In a minute we go through the gates. There's a party. Like the man said."

By now my Ebbington cap was a crumpled ball in my fist.

"We should go," I said. "Turn back."

"Huh?" Hamid looked up. His eyes in the rearview were wide and judging. "You can't leave. You have a baby."

"Turn," I said. "Go back to the airport."

"You can't, boss. You have a baby."

"Turn. Please."

"I'm not turning."

There was a knocking beside me on the glass. A face straining to see inside the darkened window. And then more knocking.

"Hilly! Hilly! It's me! Robert! Open up! Mazel tov! Mazel tov!"

There is one last thing: before I left Iowa, I took a car out through Ebbington, past Foreman's Diner. I had the idea that I would go inside to talk to Charles, to make peace. But I couldn't go inside. After all this, I didn't have enough courage even to do that. There was a new window in place — I'd had a guy come overnight. Charles would've arrived to find it. This one didn't have the glazing, the lettering, but it was there. I had the limousine park, and I got out on the sidewalk and stood at the glass. When Charles recognized me, he smirked, then smiled in a way that seemed genuine. Then he waved me in. *There's an open seat. Sit.* He mouthed the words. I pointed to my car. Gotta go, I waved. *No: sit!* Stop betting, I mouthed. *Huh?* Stop gambling.

And then he threw me an imaginary ball, except that it wasn't imaginary; he had a piece of aluminum foil wadded up, rolled into a tight ball, and after a moment it was coming straight toward me, and even though I knew there was a window there, I began to flinch, it was coming so fast. Finally, it broke. He'd be dead in eighteen months, a car accident on Route 112, a few miles from the refurbished Hove Library, coming home from an exhibition of photographs of the Negro Leagues. Some guy in Kansas City had unearthed pictures of Charles and had started to tell the world what I've been telling you: that he was as good as it got. Apparently at the exhibit he'd been the main attraction, the belle of the ball, the big cheese. It was a single car accident, ice on the road, bad brakes on his car, decidedly unsuspicious. When, over the next few days, his obituary was printed, it carried with it, in the opening lines, that familiar refrain that was never as true as it was for Charles: *He may have been the best pitcher you never saw.*

In Bluepoint, Robert Ashley took me out of the car. "You look terrible," he said, holding me at arm's length, then hugging me

374

tightly. "Where have you been?"

I started to answer him, and he hugged me closer. I left the Ebbington hat in the car.

"It doesn't matter. You're here. You're home." Robert yelled out at the security guard. "Open the gates! Open the gates! Hilton Wise is back!"

When we went through the gates, Jenny was the first person I saw. She was waiting out on the landing in front of the old house, in the same spot where I'd once stood with my father the first time we came here. She was wearing a blue pullover and jeans and white flats. Her hair was down at her shoulders. She saw me, put a hand to her stomach, and smiled.

"Papa Wise," she said, running to me, jumping into my arms. "Papa Wise."

PART III

ONE

People are always surprised to hear that, as a rule, I don't fly. For most of my adult life I've had the opportunity to take advantage of all that Wise & Ashley has to offer, including their pilots. My closest friends, and even my children, think this has something to do with my father — our shared trouble, our acrimony, our inability to find peace. And I'm guilty in a way of enabling the fiction that this is true. The reality is different, quite different, and, although it's ridiculous to admit, and often humiliating, I'm simply afraid to fly, afraid of anything that has to do with air travel now, so afraid that for a few years I haven't done it at all. Europe — out of the question. Asia — so out of the question that I laugh when the prospect of a trip to Tokyo comes up. I used to need a few drinks. Then it was some Valium. Then it was a good deal of Valium. Now I just keep my feet on the ground whenever possible. Part of this is an issue of proximity. I've been around air disasters my whole life — if not actually physically close, then tangentially. Whole periods of my life can be marked by various crashes, fires, runway overshoots, engine failures. My very name, issued from the lips of a lawyer waiting in the Air India first-class terminal, is enough to earn a reproachful glare from the stewardesses there. We Wise men are anathema to airlines, evidently.

One night not so long ago, when I had no choice, I was on a flight from Washington to Boston. It had been delayed for hours on the tarmac, first for weather, then for traffic, then for some security concern at another airport. By the time we finally left, my sleeping pill had kicked in, as had the two small bottles of Gray Goose I'd used instead of water. I was asleep when it happened. We were over Wilmington, Delaware. I was in first class. A woman was bringing around freshly baked cookies. As soon as we started going down, she burst into tears. "Oh no," she said, losing whatever cool she was supposed to project. "This is it!"

We'd lost power in one of our engines. Apparently this was a temporary problem, a glitch, a dangerous malfunction that our pilots were trained to circumvent. As soon as they'd disengaged the autopilot, the plane started to move in ways that you never want your plane to move. It took the pilots ninety seconds to get us straight again — ninety seconds in which we fell, or, I suppose, we glided, and in which the one hundred or so passengers alongside me began to pray, weep, caterwaul, and, almost in unison, whip out their cell phones to call home.

A quick lesson in aviation: without power in the engines, the craft has no thrust. Remember Newton. Motion is like marriage: wherever you go, something's pulling you in the opposite direction. Opposite thrust is drag. Minus the engines doing what they do — namely, *thrusting* you through space — the drag on the craft causes you to lose speed. So as you're slowing down, you're also losing flow velocity over the wings, and as you lose flow velocity, you lose your lift, and lift, as it sounds, is basically what's keeping you up in the air. Because these things had happened, and because our aircraft's losing power hadn't caused the plane to roll or flip, the pilot had the opportunity to keep the plane level as it lost altitude. Which prevented us from spiraling nose first into the ground. Crashing nose first would mean — and this is probably obvious — a catastrophic explosion. I guess I knew all of this as I was going down. I'd been around it for so long that all the information flooded me. I wondered if landing flat was like doing a belly flop off the diving board. *Maybe it'll hurt,* I thought. *But maybe I'll live.*

The first clue that we'd all survive came with the subtle hiss of the air conditioner bleeding through the vents, and then, in quick succession, the gentle uptick of the craft's nose and the gleeful, snorting laughter of our stewardess, cookies still in hand. "Yes!" she called out. "Yes!" Had power not come back, and had the pilots done what pilots are supposed to do, provided they know how to do it, we'd have done what my father likes to call a "scraper."

"You come in on your belly like that," he told me when I called him that night, "the craft is basically ruined. The FAA and NTSB love to get their noses up in that shit, too, Hilly. It's their favorite fucking thing to do. No one's dead, the plane's fucked to hell, the carrier's just looking around, trying to blame somebody. I love those cases. I love scrapers."

I thought of this comment when, not even a year later, during the first month of 2008, my father found himself in a scraper all his own when his private jet crashed outside Charlotte, North Carolina. The jet was his favorite. He called it *Ruthie,* after my mother. A luxury manufacturer had custom-built it for him at their factory near Bellevue, Washington. He'd had the interior paneled with an endangered subspecies of Brazilian teak. In the latrine: an equally rare white marble. All the seats had been removed and replaced with a king-sized mattress fitted with beautiful silk sheets from Tuscany (this was in the back of the cabin), a series of leather couches (midsection), a mahogany desk outfitted with a laptop and a phone and a dozen bottles of scotch (also midsection), and two sleek reclining chairs (these were up front, near the cockpit). On the outside, the plane was clean, all white, the logo for Wise & Ashley printed on the tail fin.

Apart from the luxury of this plane, and apart from the not-so-small fact that he crashed and I did not, the big difference between what happened to me and what happened to him was that he was alone. There was nobody screaming, nobody talking to him, nobody gripping him to pray, as the woman beside me that night in Providence had done so urgently, saying, "Pray with me, son. Please. Pray to Jesus with me." He was in the plane all alone.

Irony wasn't the first thing that came to my mind. Because he is my father, and because we have shared this curse of a name, my first thoughts were of the newspapers, the internet, the blogs, the wet stream of information that attached itself to anything he did and ran with it. Bad press for him meant people showing up at my house, looking for interviews, comments, annoying my daughters, staking out my bushes. Getting to Bluepoint was difficult in 1952. By 2008 all it took was a few keystrokes on a GPS device. I'm fully aware of how terrible a thing this is to admit, but in my defense, I knew straightaway that my father had survived the crash. Robert Ashley had called me from New York, breathless, crying, nearly incapable of uttering anything except: *Crash . . . plane . . . he's alive . . .* Nearly every bone in his body had been broken except, miraculously, his skull and spine.

I was in Bluepoint when I got word, sitting in the study. It was a gray morning. There was rain over the water in a sheet, the clouds over the bluffs obscuring my view of Robert's house, empty now for the season. As of a few years ago, I have another view, a view beyond Robert's house, of a hotel out at Broad Neck. It's a big resort-style hotel that wouldn't seem out of place in Aruba or Los Cabos. On Cape Cod, the thing is hideous and awkward. They've built a fake lighthouse up behind the main building, and that morning its bleating LED light kept sweeping the shore.

Robert had to hang up, collect himself, and call me back ten minutes later, after what sounded like a half-dozen glasses of whiskey. He was a mess.

"They're saying he's alive. Did you catch that when I called before?"

"I did." I had my laptop open. A story on CNN's home page said my father was dead. "But you might want to tell publicity. Let them know he's alive. CNN says he's dead."

"How in the hell did he make it?"

"He's always been lucky."

"I should probably tell publicity, huh?"

"I just said that, Bob."

"He's alive, Hilly. How is he alive?"

"Should I come?" I asked. "Tell me which hospital, and I'll come."

"I'm going. You stay."

"I've got nothing to do. Why don't I come? I should be there."

"Stay. I'll call you when I get there. I'll be on my phone."

"OK."

"They have internet in North Carolina, right?"

I waited a moment. When he was eighty-five, Robert transformed into an avowed tech addict but failed to master some very general concepts.

"Yes," I said. "They have the internet in North Carolina."

"Good," he said. "I'll send you an email when I get more information."

My father wasn't famous any longer. He belonged to that odd group of forgotten men who were *formerly famous.* The sort of American who knew his face, or the face, say, of Adlai Stevenson, was dead now. Try showing someone under forty Stevenson's face and see what you get. The last stop for the famous people of my dad's era was the obits page. After the crash, I was alerted to the fact that his obituary was already written. All it needed was his date of death. They figured that he'd stopped making news. The crash upended that notion. Within hours, the front of the house was packed with reporters. So here he was, back in the limelight. Of the news anchors who filed stories, only Ted Koppel seemed alert to the potential poetic justice in all of this, and he gave the camera a certain rakish wink the night he delivered the news of the plane going down. The other anchors — Brian Williams, Diane Sawyer, Wolf Blitzer, even — simply read the prompter. *Famous in the fifties and sixties for landmark lawsuits against the aviation industry.*

Immediately, I got calls from my girls. They'd seen the initial report on CNN's home page. I have four daughters. Sammy was our first, followed by our twins Rachel and Elliot, and then my baby, Eliza. Having four daughters means living in a perennial state of reciprocal concern. I worry over them, and all of them combine their considerable power and charm and wit to worry over me. A day does not pass without one of them Skyping me, her pixelated, adorable face beaming back at me from my laptop. They do this constantly, especially since their mother passed. My girls are like the McKinley boys — they've spread out around the globe, all of them having kept the name Wise (three of them are married), each one a satellite of their mother and me.

My father's crash occurred eighteen months after Jenny died. She and I were married for over thirty years. Except for the very, very beginning, for reasons that are obvious, we were happy together. Occasionally, we were so happy together that our life took on that particular weightlessness that elides time, so much so that it would come as a shock to us to celebrate our tenth or fifteenth or twenty-fifth anniversary. She would laugh in a particularly sad way when time struck her, as if she were saying, *Oh, right, this all isn't just permanent, is it?*

Cancer took her, but she was gone long before that. Chemotherapy is what kills people sick with a malignant tumor. The person left afterward is not really the person, just the skin and bones. Part of the soul is shed at some point, along with all the hair. That comment may offend people, and I apologize if it does. I shouldn't speak in such generalities. So let me try again: chemotherapy is what killed *her*. For a while we believed it would work. We tried to think that such a *medicine* (the italics, obviously, are mine) really could work, that by wiping out the entirety of the body's complex set of defenses, we were making her stronger. So it happened that her soul was gone long before her body passed. Every drip of morphine carried her away. Drip, drip, drip; less, less, less. If she'd made it to January, we'd have made thirty-five years.

About her death, I'd like to say only this: when she went, we were all there, all of us — me and all our children. When it happened, when the last of it came and went, I didn't know what to do. What *do* you do? Those first moments afterward, the first minute or two, the ridiculousness of it all, the quiet, the new permanence. There were doctors there with us — just in case — and then, after a while, there was some murmuring about having the men from the funeral home come to take her away. But I couldn't, you understand? We had been together so long. People say that all the time. I know that. But what they mean, I think, is that they were together in the larger sense, together in their fidelity. Maybe I'm wrong about that. But Jenny and I were always together, always in close proximity. If she went somewhere, I went with her. We were conjoined. We had no jobs. We were here, after all. In Bluepoint. All this time. Where would we have gone? So, when the man from the funeral home wanted to take her away, I fought him, literally, with my hands. At one point, I called out: You're not just going to take my wife away so that I never see her again! You can't! You can't!

Maybe this book should include our time together. I'm aware that she appears as some sort of footnote. But, really, what's the point of reading a happy story?

I reacted to Jenny's death the same way

that I reacted to my mother's death, which came ten years earlier: I took apart the house. The impetus to begin the deconstruction here was not, as some have speculated, a means by which to aggravate my father and to reject his money, but, more simply, the result of death, of loss. It's a way to honor the living — to take away the space they knew, to let that go the way the dead have gone. The Ancient Egyptians believed this. And, in the absence of any coherent religious dogma, I believe it too. My father had long since deeded Bluepoint to me, and so he had no recourse to stop me when I had a team of contractors come out from Boston and literally pry away the first of the two additions. When he gave me the house, he claimed he didn't want it anymore, that he had other houses. This had always been his plan — to give it to me. He thought it would bring us closer.

More than anything, the house in Bluepoint was my mother's. She'd built it for herself, and after she was gone I didn't want it anymore. They took it out of the ground, first with huge sticks, the way you might pry open a jammed car door. Then they took it off the beach by cranes. Then they put it on an enormous truck and literally just drove it all away. The butterfly had one wing now. The press loved this. My father was found at his house on 107th Street by a team of freelancers hoping to do a story on his life. The video footage is funny to see: his shocked face. For the first time the news media were his friends. "Are you serious?" he asked. "My house? The goddamned idiot. You're kidding." When, finally, he is convinced that the story is true — a miniature television is proffered, the video shown to him — he curses me out. "My son the idiot! What an asshole! Print that. My son the asshole!"

TWO

Five months after the crash, my father came back to Bluepoint to live. He arrived one afternoon in a dark Mercedes, attended to by a team of nurses, all of whom were men, and all of whom were black. He had steadfastly refused any contact from me while he was in the hospital, rejecting my telephone calls, my letters, my emails, and, with the help of Sammy, my text messages. Part of this was that he didn't want me to see him in such a state — in traction, in casts, on a morphine drip. And part of this was that he still hated what I'd done to the house. So the first I saw of him was in a lifestyle feature in *People* magazine: PLANE-CRASH EXPERT RECUPERATES FROM HIS OWN BRUSH WITH DEATH. The article was the first volley in a PR blitz intended to stave off the hemorrhaging that followed the whole ordeal. Since Wise & Ashley had a client roster that represented nearly every major player in the aerospace industry, the crash had hurt business. Robert had told me that in the first week following the crash, they'd lost nearly a quarter of their business to rival firms. Thus: the blitz. The photograph accompanying the story in *People* showed him at the helm of a Gulfstream G550, one hand on the controls, one hand on his knee. He looked strong. In the picture he was wearing a leather jacket. And, because he refused to be photographed without one: a necktie.

He'd done much of his rehab at Duke University Medical Center, and then, when he was somewhat better and more agile, at Mass General, where all sorts of brilliant young Harvard students doted on him and came at all hours to his bedside to ask him advice on the markets. Again, I'd learned this from the *Boston Globe.* This was followed by stories in the *Times* (ARTHUR WISE GETS BACK ON HIS FEET,) stories in the *Journal* (SIXTY YEARS AFTER FAMOUS CRASH, ARTHUR WISE RISES AGAIN,) and a long, hagiographic profile on Bloomberg entitled THE WISDOM OF KING ARTHUR, which was so riddled with falsehoods and tall tales and bald lies that I couldn't finish it.

My daughter Eliza had left to get him,

driving her ten-year-old baby-blue Toyota Corolla and returning in the Mercedes. It was midday when they arrived, just after a rain, the road up to the house muddy, beach weeds coming up through the asphalt. I hadn't repaved the drive in years, and, watching the car trying to tackle the considerable bumps and craters and gullies between the road and the house, Robert shook his head. He was beside me on the porch. Bringing my father to Bluepoint had been his idea. The salt air and the relative quiet and the proximity to his granddaughters — these being the chief reasons. My father had to be convinced. He'd been gone ever since I took the house apart.

"That's going to make him crazy," he said. "All the bumps."

"You're the one who wanted him to come back here," I said. "You know how I've kept the place."

"Still. Maybe we should have spruced things up a bit. Paved. Landscaped."

Eliza got out first. She has always loved her grandfather. He doted on her when she was young, seeing some fire in her that he didn't see in me, or in any of my other kids. She shared his nose, his taste for rye, and some of his zest for the political tussle. When we needed someone to go get him, she jumped at the opportunity.

"Where's your car?" I called out to her.

She frowned and then pointed at the Mercedes. "Right here," she said. "He junked the Toyota without telling me."

Robert laughed. "At least his spending muscles didn't need to be rehabbed."

Then I heard my father call out: "What kind of asshole buys his daughter a used Corolla?"

I turned to Robert. "They didn't need to work on his mood either, I guess."

The nurses set out the wheelchair, but because it was muddy, and because the wheels, even without my father weighing them down, had sunk into the wet ground, the men had to carry him up to the porch. He was in a suit — Zegna, chocolate brown, a blue tie, a white pocket square, a pair of ridiculous alligator-skin shoes. It took two men to carry him, and as they did, he closed his eyes. I'm sure he felt pathetic at the whole ordeal, but he looked less like an invalid than like a king being carried by his subjects.

When they put him down, he wheeled around in his chair to get a look at the place.

"Look at this!" he called out. "Look at what you did to my house!"

"Good to see you, too, Dad."

"It's just the cottage! You got rid of everything!"

"Right," I said. "Since Jenny died. I'm
pretty sure you knew that."

Robert chimed in: "You knew that, Art.
We told you."

My father wheeled forward a few feet.
"The other wing! You junked both wings!"

"I like it this way," I said. "And I didn't
junk either of them. People bought the other
wings. They're living in them. It was way
too big for us."

He slapped the arm of his chair and then
winced. Both of his elbows had pins in them
now. "This is bullshit!"

"You hungry?" I leaned down to talk to
him.

"Don't infantilize me. Stand up. Stop
crouching."

I stood up. "OK. No crouching."

"Robert!" he cried. "Robert!"

Robert came around to the front of the
chair. Since the crash, he'd spent half of
every week with my father, using the firm's
new jet to taxi back and forth between New
York and Durham, and then, after my father
was transferred to Mass General, to Boston.

"Calm down, Art," Robert said. "Go easy
on the kid."

"Bob, I want to stay with you. In your

place. I can't do this here. I can't."

Robert looked at me as if waiting for my approval.

"It's fine in the house," I said. "Really. It's clean. It's airy. We've got your bedroom made up."

"I don't recognize you, Hilly," my father said. "You're an old man."

"So are you," I said, which, after a moment, made him laugh.

The truth, however, was that he looked good. He looked younger in the sunlight. Younger than I'd expected, at least. His face was still relatively unlined, still marked with that famous seriousness of his. Age, if it had done anything to him, had softened him. His features, which were my features, had become round where they had been square, especially his cheekbones, which my mother had always loved. He had a key chain in his hands, and absently, while avoiding looking my way, he fiddled with the keys. He looked out over my shoulder for a few minutes while he debated what to do. It had been raining for most of the last week, and the mud was a brownish gold near the street where the grass had thinned and gone bald and where the mailmen had left their shoe prints like fossil markings by the fence posts. It was a deep black by the house, smudged by eelgrass and filthy gulls and a pair of forgotten, rusted lobster traps, and so many scampering sandpipers running in a line between the bumper of my truck and the rusted hull of a beachside trash barrel. This was what my father seemed to be looking at, the truck.

"Is that your truck?" he asked.

"Yeah," I said.

"A Jew in a truck," he said, scoffing. "That's absurd."

"It's a good truck," I said.

"What do you do in it? Haul things?" He laughed.

"Sometimes."

"A Jew in a truck," he said again. "You're always trying to be someone you're not."

I looked at Robert, smiling. "If you want him, he's yours."

"Where's Eliza?" my father said, calling out for my daughter. "Eliza, honey!"

She came around. She is beautiful in a way that nobody in the Wise family has managed to be: effortless, uncontrived, gorgeous in no makeup.

"What's up, Grandpa?"

"What's up?" He laughed. "What is *up* is that I want to be brought over to Robert's house. Could you have my boys take me over there?"

She snickered. The nurses were standing around on the lawn, laughing among themselves. Eliza looked out at them and then back at my father. "Your boys?" she asked. "You mean the nurses? The men over there?"

"The black fellows. Could you? Please?"

"Dad," I said.

"Oh, I know, Hilly. I know. I'm using the wrong terminology, aren't I? What is it now? I'm never sure what's allowed and what isn't."

THREE

In the morning, I went by Robert's. My father was out on the patio with a carafe of orange juice, a chess set, and a laptop with the morning news splayed on the screen. He had, like Robert, successfully migrated from paper to paperless without any friction, unlike me, who stubbornly clung to everything my daughters told me was bound to disappear from the world: the *New York Times,* paperback books, stationery sets, 35-mm film, pickup trucks. Aligned on the edge of the patio were my father's loafers. His bare feet were crossed beneath the table, wet with sand and wiggling in the cool air.

"Sit down," he said to me, waving me toward his setup. "Come and I'll beat your brains out at chess."

"I don't play chess," I said.

"I could teach you," he said.

"I haven't had enough coffee. Otherwise

I'd be up for it."

"Otherwise nothing. Otherwise I'd beat your brains out."

I looked at the board. It was a vanity set, everything cut from good marble, the knights fashioned into perfect little horse heads, their eyes made with real turquoise. I'd lied, of course. When I'd worked at the *Spectator,* some Russians in the newsroom had taught me the game, and I was sure that in a few shrewd moves I could beat my father soundly.

I sat down. Robert was out in the yard, painting his fence. He did this every other year. It was an old fence, and occasionally the wind would break some planks and he'd have to fix those as well, the whole project usually taking him a week of solid work. For the past ten years — ever since my mother had passed — he and my father had spent more time in Los Angeles, where they had houses near one another on a golf course in Bel Air. This left the house here in Bluepoint often in need of repair. Now it was more than the fence that needed mending. The insides were falling apart: the floorboards were warped from humidity, windows were cracked, the electricity was spotty on the second floor, ceiling fans were caked with grime so thick that to let them spin was to subject yourself to a blizzard of debris. What I liked about Robert's house, especially when he was gone from the Cape and I was the only person here, was that inside, it was as if no time had passed. Everything was old; nothing had been upgraded — not the stove, not the furnace, not the faucet fixtures (these especially looked so old-fashioned to me), not the lighting, not the bookshelves, not the plumbing or the wiring or the cooling system. Aside from an expensive alarm system, some new windows, and a new roof, everything remained as it was in 1952.

My father, smiling, his lips wet with orange pulp, pointed out to Robert, who was kneeling in the sand, his khakis streaked with white paint. "Idiot," he said gleefully.

"Why's he an idiot?" I asked.

"Hire somebody. Don't do it yourself."

"He likes it."

"He's ninety. He shouldn't be working that hard."

At this, as if he'd heard us, Robert stood up, wiped something off on his pants, fished around for a hammer, and then promptly ripped off three rotted planks from the fence. Behind him he had his laundry out on the line. Still, after so long, he hadn't bought himself a washer or a dryer.

"You know how much money he's worth?" my father whispered.

"So what?"

"He's trying to prove something."

"You sound like you're competing with him," I said, taking a bishop into my hand.

"Even if I knew how to fix a fence, I wouldn't want to do it," he said. "Why does he even need a fence?"

"I didn't know you played chess."

"I learned in the hospital. They had all these tiny little Mexicans trolling around in there, emptying out my bedpans and whatnot. They taught me. They just wanted to hustle me out of my money, I think," he said. "I actually got pretty good."

His laptop beeped at him, and he hammered out something on his keyboard. Post-9/11, Wise & Ashley had been tasked with writing what my father was calling *doomsday stipulations* into the various contracts that airlines were drafting for their pilots, their stewards, their mechanics, their passengers. His left hand wasn't yet perfectly healed, and so he typed for the most part with just his right — a hunt-and-peck method that must have exhausted him; he'd been the first person I knew who could type as quickly as he thought, the sound of his fingers on the keyboard of his Underwood

403

like a team of carpenters assembling a house.

When he was finished, he looked up at me. He put his hands together. He had a big, gaudy Cartier on his left wrist. This was a new watch. His favorite had been ruined in the crash. There were liver spots, or sun spots, or simply a combination of the two, dotting his forearms, like a constellation's worth of tattoos.

"You seem well," I said. "All things considered."

"I'm in pain all the time."

"I wanted to visit."

"I was a mess. It was ugly."

"Still. I called. I texted, even."

"I got them all. But there were media in the halls. It was terrible, Hilly. You'd have been ambushed. And we all know what happens to you when you're ambushed."

This, of course, was a reference to my outburst outside the library in Hove, an event that my father, surprisingly, had loved. I'd been told he'd tacked a photograph of my screaming face onto a bulletin board in the cafeteria of Wise & Ashley, with a caption running beneath it that read: *Don't mess with the boss's boy. He's got millions. Lots of millions!*

I folded my hands across my chest. The

patio was quiet with just the two of us. The only sounds were of my father's wheelchair, which squeaked beneath him as he fidgeted, and the lolling of the ocean out behind us. Occasionally Robert would bang at a fence post, testing its firmness, or we'd hear him scraping away paint with a flat-faced chisel.

My father laid his right arm flush against the table. Running from the crook of his elbow to the joint of his wrist was a long red scar like a line of fishing tackle. After a moment, he noticed me staring.

"In the crash," he was saying, "a piece of something tore this open. It came either from the seat back or from the tray. I was lying there, looking at it. My arm, it was just torn open."

"That's terrible."

"I had this flash that I was back in the war."

"Really?"

"You saw that sort of thing all the time. People spliced open in the most unnatural ways. But, you know, as soon as it happened, I snapped out of it and I thought to myself that I should sue whoever had that tray designed. Then I remembered that we designed it." His laugh was dry, a cackle. "You fucking believe that?"

"I didn't know you were designing parts

of planes now," I said.

"Oh, Hilly, you were never really interested in it all. It bores you." He tapped at his keyboard. "Anyway, it doesn't matter."

He pushed the chair back from the table and rolled up one leg of his pants. Here was another scar. "This one," he said, running his finger across two inches of raised red skin, "this is from the surgeons. My heart, apparently, was blocked to shit. Plane crash probably saved me, they said. They took some arteries."

"I had no idea."

"Apparently they also gave me some bovine valve," he said.

"A cow?"

He nodded and then leaned into me. "I won't eat a steak now," he said, and chuckled. "You believe that? I can't. It just doesn't taste good. It's the fucking strangest thing."

"You should have at least taken my telephone calls," I said. "I mean, even one of them would have done."

He pointed at his teeth. "They had me wired shut, Hilly," he said. "I couldn't even get a word out. I sounded like somebody was holding me hostage and had me gagged."

"Still."

"Look at us," he said. "Together for five

minutes, and we're already on the verge of an argument."

"I'm not trying to fight."

"Your feelings are hurt. I can see it. You were always so sensitive." He pointed out at my house. "I mean — all that dismantling. People die. You can't just tear down the house because of it."

"Sure I can. I did it pretty easily. It's amazing what people will do for the money."

"That's not what I meant."

"You let Robert come see you in North Carolina," I said.

"Robert is my friend," he said. "He was there in the war with me. It doesn't bother him to see somebody banged up the way I was banged up."

"It would have bothered me?"

"Of course. You're so goddamned fragile. Your daughters are tougher than you are."

They were all out on the beach now, attempting to go swimming. In May on Cape Cod, the water is basically untouchable. When the waves rolled back, they all ran in up to their ankles, and then, like birds, they ran back ahead of the tide, shrieking and laughing. My father fished out his pack of Old Golds and offered me one. I waved him away. I'd been off them a year by that point, but I still wanted one.

"Were you scared?" I asked.

"When? When the plane was crashing?" He smirked, lit the cigarette, blew the exhaust all over me. "What the fuck do you think, Hilly? The plane was crashing."

"I mean, did you have faith the pilot would land it?"

"No. Not the way we fell. We had total power-down. The tail dipped. Usually . . ." he trailed off then.

"Apparently he did an amazing job."

"He walked away with only a few scrapes. Me? His boss? I wouldn't call that amazing."

I leaned back in my plastic chair. (Robert had a plastic patio set — he was frugal to the end.) Out on the shoreline, the sea grass was high and buzzing with yellow jackets or beach gnats, and a weak breeze blew at a wooden swing Robert had hung years and years ago from the one still-strong pine in the yard.

My father was looking out to where Lem Dawson's apartment once stood.

"You can't even see where it was anymore," he said.

"Let's not talk about that."

"Do you remember the first time we came here together?" he asked. "There was that poor dog trapped in the house. The old owners had left it. Do you remember that? And he came out to get it?"

"It was a cat," I said.

He grinned. "It was a dog. A collie. You were sobbing."

"I was not," I said. "Mom was screaming. Not sobbing."

"Screaming? No. She never screamed."

"She was screaming." Now I'd made him agitated.

"I probably have a photograph somewhere," he said. "We have so many photographs from that first summer."

"A picture? Of the cat? Who'd have taken a picture of the cat?"

"The dog? Who else? Dawson. Lem Dawson."

"You think he took a picture of that?"

"Maybe."

"You're wrong," I said.

By then, though, he had turned toward the street, his attention now on a white sedan that had parked in the dirt outside Robert's house. He grimaced and looked at me. "He needs to put up gates," he said to me. "And you need to put your gates back up. People have no sense of privacy anymore."

"I don't believe in gates," I said.

"Of course," he said. "What do you believe

in, Hilly? Seriously?"

A young man was out on the gravel. He was dressed casually — in blue jeans, a black button-down, a foolish-looking cap. He had a canvas messenger bag slung over his shoulder, white earbuds stuffed into a pocket and spilling out. I got up to meet him, my father by that point pecking away at his keyboard, a series of beeps drawing his attention from the driveway to his screen. Before I was off the patio, the kid had his business card out for me to take.

"Theo," he was saying, "Theo Cantor. *Durham Herald-Sun.* Wondering if I could get a minute of your time."

I took his card. "Look —" I started to say, knowing what the kid was here for, having had to deal over the years with a small amount of unannounced visitors coming by Bluepoint with their microcassette recorders and their notepads and now their stealth digital cameras.

"You're Hilton Wise, right?" Theo asked.

"I am."

"I'm writing a book on your father," he said. He had something else to give me — a piece of paper, which contained information about his project, documentation to back up his claim.

"I can't help you," I said.

"Of course you can. But I understand that you don't want to."

"Whichever," I said, turning around to leave while raising up the business card in such a way as to thank him politely for making the effort.

"I've just got back from Iowa," he said, calling out. "From a town called Hove. About forty minutes or so from Cedar Rapids."

I stopped, or slowed, trying not to look too conspicuous. Of course, my having been there wasn't a secret. The most famous moment of my life had occurred there. Even perfect strangers knew that.

"I talked to some people there who remember you."

"All right." I held up his card. "Got your info. Again, thanks for coming."

"The book's going to come out regardless," he said.

"Good luck with it."

"Would you at least try to work with our fact-checkers when the time comes?" he asked.

"I don't know. It depends what your questions are," I said. Again I held up the card. "But thanks for coming."

"You were a reporter," he said. "You know how this works. I've already basically got

411

the story."

"And what story is that?"

He reached into his bag and took out a photograph of a headstone. "Here. Come look at it."

"I don't have my glasses," I said.

"I took this picture myself yesterday. Just so you know I'm not here scamming you."

It was Lem Dawson's tombstone. He told me this because I couldn't really see it. Later, inside, alone, I'd see that the stone was a simple gray thing, weathered, the lettering worn and flattened, some dead grass around it, just the dates of his birth and death carved on its face. I had the picture in my hand, the wind at it, the paper wobbling and flopping in that way that heavy paper does.

"Where'd you take this?" I asked.

"Nearby."

"Nearby here?"

"Walpole. Near the prison there."

"I never knew that it was there."

He was writing all this down.

"That's all off the record," I said.

He looked up from his notepad. "Ah, man, it's already down."

"Tear it up."

"But —"

By now Robert Ashley had come out onto

412

the lawn behind me. He was squinting, drenched with white paint, a hammer in one hand and a chisel in the other. Theo took a step toward him, another business card at the ready.

"Mr. Ashley, my name is Theo Cantor. I'm a reporter for —"

"You get off my property right now, Mr. Cantor," Robert said, his hammer raised.

Theo stumbled then, his bag falling off his shoulder and, with him, into the mud. Robert took a step closer now. "There are channels, young man. Proper channels to go through to get ahold of me. This . . . this, coming here, arriving like this . . . this is not a proper channel. Do you understand me?"

The kid was resilient, though, and, watching him right himself, grab yet another business card (the previous one had fallen into the mud with him), I thought of all the young stringers I'd known at the paper years ago. I'd never really possessed the unchecked aggression that a good reporter needs, the ability to dive headlong into hostile, unknown situations, the drive to drag yourself up from the mud and grab another business card.

"I'm writing a book about Arthur Wise," Theo was saying. "And I'm just looking for somebody to answer my questions."

Now Robert lowered his hammer. "He's got no comment. I've got no comment. Hilly's got no comment."

Robert had succeeded in backing Theo up to his car, an impressive bit of menacing that made me remember Robert in his youth — the man who'd knocked my father unconscious with such savagery. Robert had always taken care of himself. If you didn't know, you'd have guessed he was seventy. A few minutes later, the kid was gone. My daughters were up at the house now, all of them trying to cheer up their grandfather, all of them with sweaters over their bathing suits, their hair bundled up atop their heads, all of them, in parts and in pieces, their mother.

I showed Robert the photograph of Lem's tombstone and he scoffed. "Jesus."

"You shouldn't have treated him like that," I said.

"You don't understand," Robert said.

"I was a reporter for a long time," I said. "I understand perfectly."

He was still holding the picture, glaring at it. He'd gone pale. In the last few months, Robert had become more of a public figure than he had in the preceding fifty-odd years. Suddenly there were news articles about him. ASHLEY EMERGES TO RUN FIRM HE HELPED START. (This ran in the *Economist,* with a very flattering picture of Robert standing by his desk in the office on Park Avenue.) He'd confided in me, with no small amount of pleasure and self-satisfaction, that the demands for press had been so great that he'd had to hire his own publicist. A very fine-looking young woman, he told me. A half century with his name on the door, and now he'd finally gotten his chance to steer the ship. Of course, at their age, he and my father were just figureheads. He gave me the picture of the tombstone.

"I can't have any other bad news come out right now. I can't have anything that we're not controlling. It's been open season on our clients since the crash. Any more bad news, we might just tip over. This is bad. A biography? People smell blood."

I didn't care about any of that, though. "Did you know that Lem was buried near here?"

He gripped his hammer. "Of course I did, Hilly. I bought the plot myself."

FOUR

There is no real town to speak of in Blue-point. The peninsula of the Cape narrows, so that the main thoroughfare exists simply as an artery between dunes, a stretch of road through the moonscape that connects Wellfleet to Provincetown. There is a place to buy liquor, a place to worship if you're a Catholic, and a building in which to pay your property-tax bill or to convene at noon with your buddies before heading off to the water for an afternoon of angling for blue-fish. A string of impossibly small beach cabins fronts the ocean, three dozen shacks, everyone packed together with an urban density, and the road there is nothing but a paved, flattened top of the sandy dam between the sea and the marshes preceding the schooners at the yacht club. And there are homes: ours, Robert Ashley's, and those of a few hundred lucky people. For cigarettes and burgers and oysters, or for late-night videos, rum drinks, a copy of the *Times,* a wind chime carved from petrified wood, a batik sundress, a straw hat, some sunblock, a copy of Yo-Yo Ma playing the Bach cello concertos, or for any of those things that people yearn for when they come to the ocean, one needs to head elsewhere. In Bluepoint, there is little to do but sit out on your deck, in your yard, or on the beach, beneath the sun, with a book or a glass of iced tea — or lie in a hammock with a radio beside you, broadcasting the Red Sox game. This is Bluepoint.

I'd lived here long enough that I was known in town as my own man and not as my father's son. In the history of my life, this was no small achievement. For years, I had no real occupation other than to raise my children and to look over the foundation I'd set up in order to give most of my money away. This part is boring — foundations, charities, galas, the good deeds rich people do to feel less guilty. So I'll just skip it. Sometimes I wondered what people here knew about me. It was difficult to tell. A photograph at our grocery — it's called the Trap, as in *lobster trap* — had me in a suit and tie, dedicating the local restoration society. And another photograph showed me shaking hands with Bill Clinton sometime before all the business with Lewinsky. Still: I was just another guy in town, and except for the occasional reporter, no one bothered me. All of this was true until my father came back. The news had spread, and neighbors had begun to send food to the house, with cards for him: casseroles, muffins, bagels, and — because someone had read that it was his favorite — a plate of smoked trout. Already two police cruisers had swung by, ostensibly claiming to be on the lookout for any trespassers but really just looking to meet my dad, get his autograph, take a picture with him. So now, for the first time in a long time, things for me seemed different. I'd gone into town to get dinner with Sammy the day my father came, and the waitress, someone who'd known me for probably thirty years, took my picture with her cell phone. When I asked why, she reached out and touched my arm.

"Well, you're famous, sweetie," she said. "That's why."

"But you've known me all this time."

"And now I want your picture. So what? Sue me?" Then, having realized that she'd just told Arthur Wise's son to sue her, she suddenly looked stricken. "No. Don't sue me. Please. I was joking."

■ ■ ■ ■

On his second day, while all of my girls were in the kitchen preparing breakfast, and their husbands were arguing about various golf courses and exotic vacation rentals and NFL quarterbacks, my father demanded to be taken at once into Boston. A branch office of Wise & Ashley occupied six floors in one of the new skyscrapers downtown, and he wanted to go into the office. It was eleven o'clock. He had eased his way slowly into the room, eschewing his walking cane for the rims and ledges of every windowsill and chair back he passed.

"I need to do some banking, and I need to get a conference call together," he said. "Who's up for taking me?"

"Why don't you have one of your nurses take you?" Eliza said.

"Out of the question," my father said. "They're all city boys. Not a one of them knows how to drive."

"Why don't you try logging on to the web and doing it that way?"

This was Todd, my daughter Elliot's husband. When he was younger, Todd had been a hair's breadth away from making the Olympic team as a shot-putter, his best attempt falling short by some tiny distance. Like most shot-putters, he had a frame better suited to assembling automobiles or foisting steel onto the mouth of a smithy than to playing the violin in the Boston Symphony, which is what he did now.

"I'm talking about doing real business. And moving real money, son," my father said. He has never learned the names of any of the men. He was, of course, dressed immaculately: black suit, shoes shined to a reflective sheen, a presidentially red tie. "You can't just log on and move the type of money I want to move."

"Yeah, Todd. Seriously." This was Ethan, Sammy's husband, always ready with a quip. He is my favorite, something he knows, something all of the boys know. There is a rule that one cannot have a favorite child, but there is no rule governing their spouses.

"Don't joke," Sammy said. "Eliza? You'll take him, right?"

"Are you sure you can't do it online?" Todd tried again.

"Jesus, Todd. Give it a rest," Sammy said.

"Like: how much could you possibly be moving?" Todd asked.

My father needed a place to sit, and there were no seats available. Lacking a chair, he pointed at Greg, who is Rachel's husband. Like Rachel, he is a fiction writer, something my father has claimed on various occasions, to their faces, to be a useless, vain profession.

"Give me your seat, Gary," my father said.

"It's Greg."

"Who's Greg?"

"I'm Greg."

"Since when?"

"Since always, Mr. Wise. Since always."

"Good to meet you, Greg. Now give me your seat."

Greg and Rachel, being the two artists in the family, keep abnormal hours, and they'd just awoken and were sips into their first cup of coffee. What remained of Greg's hair was spastically askew on his scalp. The room was laughing now. Even Rachel. But Greg stiffened. My father was hovering over him, and to show his impatience, he lifted the cuff of his left arm to consult the face of his watch, a different watch from the day before, this one covered in diamonds.

Seeing this, Ethan squinted as if he'd been blinded. "Bling! Check out Arthur's bling! How much did that watch cost, Arthur?"

"More than the house you grew up in," my father said, sitting down slowly, turning to Todd. "You," he said, pointing his way.

"You. Mr. Internet. Let me ask you a question."

"I didn't mean to pry," Todd said.

"No," my father said, taking out a folded piece of white paper from the inside pocket of his blazer. "Let's look. Let me ask you your advice, Todd."

"I'm an idiot; you don't want my advice."

"But I do. Maybe I can *log on.*"

It's funny how bonds form among spouses in a family, where the fault lines lie, where the allegiances are fostered. For whatever reason — an effortless confidence, his being a Jew, a genuinely cheerful sense of humor — Ethan escaped the Wise scorn. Todd looked helplessly toward his brother-in-law. Ethan, however, was unmoved. "Dude. Concentrate. The Big Man needs your help."

"Joke all you want," my father said, waving the paper at Todd. "But this is a printout of last night's various trading activities for some of our Asian partners. The Nikkei was a wreck last night."

"I hate when that happens," Ethan said. "All my Asian holdings get wiped out."

"I bet you do," my father said, not missing a beat. The paper was quartered, and my father flattened it on the table. Suddenly he had everyone's attention. Rachel and

Eliza leaned over, their glasses perched on the bridge of their mother's nose. "This here," he said, pointing. "This is a company called TurTec. Their manufacturing base is in Singapore." My father looked up to Todd. "You know that Singapore is a nation, correct?"

"Correct."

"Could you find it on a map?"

"Unlikely, sir."

My father smiled. "Right, well, their offices, for various reasons, are in Tokyo. They happen to make the polymer that coats the turbine on a jet that crashed in Brazil two months ago. Did you hear about that crash?"

"I don't know. Maybe I saw a headline on the web."

"Right. Well, many people died. Crashes in the Amazon are awful. Some of the areas of the crash site were unreachable. It takes eons for the recovery. Animals usually get to the victims before the medics do."

"OK. I'll make a mental note not to crash in the Amazon."

My father winced. "Try not to crash anywhere, son."

"Right. Good advice."

"This airline, the one that crashed, the one in question, it was Estonian."

"Estonian?" Todd asked.

"Another sovereign nation."

"Right."

It wasn't entirely clear why my father had begun to give the family a lesson about the business of Wise & Ashley. Part of it, I'm guessing, was atrophy: he'd been away so long from it all, he needed to work. And part of it, probably, was a sense he'd gotten, not unfairly, that he was being pitied. Nothing bothered him more than pity. All prideful men hate being looked at the way that Todd and Greg looked at my father. Pity, as my father saw it, existed in direct opposition to dignity, and my father had always received every ounce of his dignity from his work.

He went on: "Turns out, initial forensic tests indicate the turbine combusted in midair. Turbines usually don't just combust. Sometimes they fail. Sometimes a goddamned Canadian goose gets stuck in there. But they don't usually combust unless they've been hit by a missile. I'm sure you knew that, Gary."

Greg frowned.

"Now, apparently, some jackwagon on the internet's spread a rumor that the crash was caused because the polymer was defective, that its burn temperature was too low. A whole slew of lawsuits have been filed. Their

stock is falling. We, of course, represent Tur-
Tec and a host of their subsidiaries. First
thing we need to do is move money between
the companies, top to bottom. Otherwise,
they can't meet deadline to their vendors.
Suddenly, since this rumor started, there's
been a run on their funds. That's our job,
being that our finance division manages
their assets. Second: legal needs to figure
out our stance on some pretty thorny
jurisdictional issues."

"Of course," Todd said. "Jurisdictional.
That sounds confusing."

My father crossed his arms across his
chest and grinned. "The suit's been filed in
Washington State. Of all places."

"Washington? I thought this was all Asian,
and . . . um, Estonian?" Todd was trying.
By now, the room was manically enter-
tained. I felt for him.

"America's got the most plaintiff-friendly
courts," my father said. "Which means
juries give you more money. Which means
anybody who's got half a brain tries to get
their case filed here."

"But that's crazy," Todd said. "Were there
even any Americans on board?"

"No. But the seats were manufactured
outside Seattle," he said. "This is why you
need a lawyer." My father slammed his hand

down against the table. "Everybody wants a piece of the action once something goes wrong. Everybody thinks they deserve to get paid if somebody dies."

"So you're trying to get the case tried somewhere else?" Todd asked.

"Doesn't that seem fair to you?" my father asked.

Rachel spoke up. "Isn't this, like, exactly the opposite of what you guys did in the Boston Airways crash?"

At this I interceded. "All right, legal lessons are over for the day. If he wants to go into the city, let's get him into the city."

"No," my father said.

"Well, *actually,* yes," Rachel said. "In the Boston crash, you defended the victims. You found fault in the plane. Now you're defending the airline. Even though there might be a problem with the turbine."

"There's nothing wrong with the turbine!" he yelled.

She took out her cell phone. "The *New York Times* says —"

"You think I give a fuck what the *New York Times* says?"

"At least admit that you've flip-flopped here."

My father turned to me. "Hilly, what's wrong with these people? They're all idiots."

He turned to the men: Ethan, Todd, and Greg. "You're all idiots! Get a degree in something useful!"

Rachel went on. "I mean, that's fine, if that's what it is. But just recognize the hypocrisy."

"Hypocrisy!"

"Let's get up, Dad," I said.

"It's bald hypocrisy. People died in the crash. What's the difference between them and the people you originally defended?"

"Those people hired me," he said. "And now, the airline has hired me. That's the difference."

"So you just go where the money is?"

"Young lady." My father was pointing at her, his hand shaking.

"What's the strategy?" she asked. "You just gum up the works as much as you can? Stall the litigation until you get a settlement?"

"No!"

"You get the case tried in Estonia? Or someplace where there are . . . what did you call them? Plaintiff-friendly courts?"

"I'm tired," my father said, turning to me. "Your children are communists."

"Oh! Now we're communists!" Rachel was up on her feet. "You cannot — I repeat — *cannot* expect me to respect you when

427

you just toss around words like that. Do you even know what that means? If you ever got your nose out of all that Frankfurt School bullshit. If you ever stopped just regurgitating Marcuse —"

My father grabbed my wrist. "Don't you have a driver around here, Hilly? Can't your driver take me into the city?"

"I don't have a driver. I drive myself."

"Right," my father said. "In your truck."

"Exactly."

My father turned to Ethan. "Do you believe that he drives a truck? A Jew in a truck. Who ever heard of such a thing?"

Ethan laughed heartily at this, which broke the tension in the room — his big-bellied, kindhearted laughter. Robert came in just then, dressed to work on his fence, his pants streaked with white paint and sprayed with sawdust. He looked straight at my father. "Art, the nurses told me you're going to Boston. Are you crazy? You don't need to go in to the office. We've got *hundreds* of people working on TurTec."

"That settles it," my father said, pointing to Eliza. "You're taking me. Let's take your new car. Maybe if you're nice I'll buy your husband one, too."

Eliza frowned. "I don't have a husband, Grandpa. You know that."

"Right. I'll buy you a husband, then, too. According to Robert, we're probably employing hundreds of men who'd kill to be your husband."

My father whistled for his nurses to help him to his feet. Robert watched this with a marked expression of pain on his face, as if to see his old friend struggle so much to do something as simple as stand hurt his body as much as it hurt my father's.

"Art," Robert tried.

"Bob?"

"Art, stay. Come help with the house."

"Do what? Paint? I don't paint. You shouldn't be painting either. You're running the company now."

"We've got good men on the job."

"How many clients have we lost since the crash, Bob?"

"Art."

"How many? You know how many clients we lost on my watch?"

"Art."

"None! Not one fucking client!"

"We've got, literally, hundreds of people working on TurTec. This is covered, so thoroughly."

"This is why I never let you run the show, Bob. Never delegate something you can do yourself. Rule number one in our business."

"Come by the house, Art. We don't have to paint. Why don't you help me hang some pictures."

The nurses were helping my father put on his coat. All of a sudden he was cold constantly. Even in the summer. "Pictures," my father said, giggling, looking to Ethan. "Pictures. You believe this guy? *Pssh.* Pictures."

FIVE

Later that afternoon, I went across the beach to help Robert hang his pictures. Mostly they were paintings he'd bought while in New York and on a vacation alone in Paris. If he allowed himself any luxuries, this was it: fine art. His tastes were as catholic as my father's were unwavering. Among the new canvases was one by George Condo, of an evil clown. For a while we both marveled at it. Of course, there were experts there to do the actual installation. These canvases were far too valuable for us to handle ourselves. When Robert had asked my father to help him, what he meant was that he wanted help trying to figure out where to hang everything, a simple job, seeing as there were only a few rooms with enough clear wall space. Robert seemed especially upset that my father had left to go to Boston. I wouldn't understand this until later, but apparently some of these paintings were presents for him.

He had all the windows open in his house. The living room, where he and my father had fought with their fists, was bright and airy, and you could hear the waves. He had the radio tuned to the BBC World Service. A cinnamon candle flickered on the windowsill. I was of little help to him. He wanted to do all the real work. When the men got up on ladders, Robert got up on them, too. It was amazing to see him do this at ninety, refusing to slow down. My only job was to say whether the canvases seemed level or not, a redundant task, since later they'd go over everything with a laser level.

He was handing me a magazine when he collapsed. Seconds later, he had no pulse. He'd lost consciousness with his eyes open and something close to a pucker on his lips. As if he'd been thinking of kissing someone the moment he left us.

Right before all this we'd been talking football with the workers. The Patriots were getting set to start their training camp. We'd been talking about the Super Bowl, the David Tyree catch. In the history of devastating Boston sports losses, this was the worst. Robert was quiet for a moment, and then, having begun, I think, to feel that his heart was failing, he murmured something I didn't catch, and then, forcefully, he said my father's name. *Arthur.*

By the time we got word to my father, hours had passed. His cell phone was off. And my daughter's cell phone was buried in her purse. It was evening. We were all at the hospital at Broad Neck, in the near-empty waiting room, the televisions muted, a small skylight above us, streaked with rain and grime. There was a plaque with Robert's name on it not even fifteen feet from my chair. Evidently at some point in the 1980s, he'd paid for the place to be built, and now he'd been pronounced dead in one of its emergency rooms. When I got hold of her, Eliza told me that they were chartering a helicopter to get out to the Cape, and an hour after that we all heard the chopper descending to the roof, that *whoof-whoof-whoof* sound. I wasn't sure what my father knew or what he didn't know. The boys had taken charge of the situation, and they had been texting with Eliza, and she had been texting with them, and when, finally, my daughter arrived with my father, it was clear to me that she hadn't had the courage to tell him the truth. He was shuffling through the narrow hallway near the waiting room, past the reception desk, past the array of dormant stretchers and pharmacy trays and past the line of orderlies who had stopped in their tracks because they knew my father's face. He was dragging his left leg as he went. "Robert! Robert!" he cried. He was a mess — his pants had a stain on them, his shirt was untucked, his tie was loose, and he was trying to talk and sob and breathe all at once.

I got up to stop him, to talk to him, and he tried to push me down. "Where is he?"

I caught hold of Eliza's attention. She was panicked. She mouthed some words to me that were, in effect: *He's been like this the whole way.*

"Hilly?" my father looked up at me. "Hilly?"

"He's gone."

He turned around then. I guess I thought he was doing this because he didn't want us to see him. But what he was really doing was looking for someone else to tell him something different.

"Dad."

"Is there a doctor?"

"No. He's been gone for hours."

"Where?"

"Dad."

"Where?"

"Gone. Dead."

"No no no."

"It was very quick. I saw it happen."

"But I just went for the afternoon," he said. "I was coming back. Why didn't he wait?"

"Wait for what, Grandpa?" This was Sammy. Of all my daughters, she is the one whose heart exists in closest proximity to her soul. What I mean by that is that she is pure, and there is little of the noise in her that weighs on all of us: fears and shame and guilt and worry.

"Wait until I was home," my father said. He was grabbing Sammy's wrists. "He should have waited until I was there."

"I guess it just happened. That's what the doctors said. Nobody could have predicted it," she said.

"Is it true?" he asked. "Really? Is it true? Is he dead? He saved my life. He was such a tough son of a bitch. How could it be true?"

"Dad." I put my hand on his back.

"Hilly?" He looked at me as if he'd just discovered I was there. "Hilly. What are we going to do?"

"The company will be fine," I said.

He laughed then. And then: "The *company.*"

"Do you want to see him?" I asked.

435

He shook his head. Suddenly he looked frightened. "I couldn't do that. No. I couldn't."

"OK. They were keeping him in case you wanted to."

"Keeping him?"

"The funeral parlor will take him now."

"Hilly?" he said, looking up at me.

"Yes?"

"I was terrible to him, wasn't I? In the house. Earlier. When we left. Was he upset? Was he? Hilly? Tell me the truth."

Six

There are two incidents that I'd like to mention here.

The first is this: about eight years before Robert died, I saw Savannah in Washington DC. I was there for some work with my foundation. We hadn't spoken since I'd left Iowa. I'd sent her a few letters over the years, just short notes to say that I was thinking of her, that I hoped she was well, and each time they came back to me unopened. And then, when the internet made all of this easier, I tried to reach Savannah that way, without success. I could include a page here of all my unanswered emails. I'm such a sap that I always wrote her on her birthday. But I'm not sure what good that would do. By now, you get the point.

I'd come out of a steak house to sneak a cigarette. My daughters had all been on me to quit, but after a while, a habit becomes more than a habit and something like a part of you, like your arm. It was a Tuesday — summer, hot as hell — but she was wearing a black trench coat. She was heading south, near that part of the Potomac that bends around the Lincoln Memorial. That's where I guessed she might be going. She'd had a few books on Lincoln in the house in Iowa, and it didn't seem to me to be such a stretch that she might take the opportunity while in town to visit the monument. I was sixty-five years old. She was sixty-four. Of course, I followed her. At a certain point, she turned west, into the city, and I stayed close to her as she passed the Treasury and the Old Executive Building and at least a portion of the White House. She moved well. She had taken care of her body, whereas I hadn't. In her coat and her heels, she had a sophistication about her that I didn't recognize or remember. I don't think I had any idea what I'd say if I caught up to her. All I knew was that I needed to do it. So much had changed, even if at my core I still maintained the most childish, pure affection for her. What was left was . . . I don't know what to call it: kindness? warmth? love? My daughters belong to a generation which believes that sentimentality yields weakness, that expressions of love unadorned with irony are saccharine. How wrong they are!

438

They've mistaken the word *sentiment* for the contrived emotion they get from television and movies, and, sadly, they've refused to allow themselves to have emotion in public, or even in private, for fear that it isn't real, for fear that any overt display of *feeling* must be fake. To say that I went after her with confidence would be a lie; I went after her with sentimentality in my heart! My legs shook at the knees; my hands clammed with sweat. I thought of the last time I saw her. It was just an ordinary moment. We were on her couch, just where I'd gotten the telephone call from my father. I told her about Jenny and said I had to go. She said: *Yeah, I guess you do, don't you?* Then she'd looked at me, relieved that all my efforts to find her would end in some neat, orderly way.

For a few moments I lost track of her. There were crowds outside the southern wing of the White House — protestors, tourists, police officers on horseback. When I found her again she was entering the lobby of a restaurant. The buckle on her purse caught my eye as the sun hit it. The restaurant was called Evelyn's. It was a brightly lit, aristocratic sort of place, everyone in suit jackets and polished shoes. I stood on the curb near Blair House. This was Clinton's last year in office, and near me men were holding signs and hollering about Ken Starr and the blue dress and all that tawdry business, and for a long moment I stood there among them, trying to summon some confidence.

The front room of Evelyn's was wide and open and frigid, and there was a raw bar stationed off to the side of the door, filled with ice and oysters and crabs. This made me think of the house in Bluepoint, the kitchen specifically, and the dull shucking knife lying near one of Jenny's dish towels. Savannah was at the bar, sitting with a tall glass of white wine. She saw me and grimaced. I stayed where I was. Maybe she knew I'd been following her, or maybe she thought I'd just stumbled in the door and found her this way. She stood up, called over to the bartender, leaned across the two feet of maple that separated them, and raised her hand to pantomime a writing motion. The bartender was young, with the same black hair I used to have, and, watching them together, I had the thought that this could have been an image of the two of us together, years ago, if things had been different. When they were finished, the bartender nodded, and then she left, quickly taking her coat and her bag and going out through the back.

Earlier that afternoon I'd been given a citation for work that the foundation was doing, and all in all it should have been a happy day for me. I'd been received by the president in the West Wing, talked sports with him, told him that he was wrong that the quality of professional baseball was on the wane, told him stories about my childhood, met his wife and his daughter. Later, I got to see the First Residence. (To be open about it: I was offered the Lincoln Bedroom for the night, but I refused.) Those things bore me. The award was a fraud, just some certificate of thanks, an institutional dose of gratitude for being rich and not being an asshole about it.

The bartender was still writing when I came over. "That's for me," I said, pointing at the letter.

The bartender looked up, suitably confused.

"That woman, the woman who asked you to write this. She was a friend of mine."

"Oh, then," the bartender said, looking at me with a poorly cloaked expression of pity — or was it misery? — on his face.

He left the letter for me. It was written on the back of a cocktail bill, the old-fashioned kind, green and blue, printed on hard card stock, the print engraved and raised off the sheet.

It read as follows:

I have nothing to say to you. If you ever see me again, don't follow me.
Mrs. Hershel Stockton

Just before my dad's crash, I saw Savannah again. Or I thought I did. This was in New York.

From the back, anybody can look like her. Give me a tall woman with cropped dark hair and a wool coat, a purposeful stride, a good smile, and my blood pressure will spike. In New York, this happened whenever I visited, on the express trains that run the west side of the island, in Battery Park, in a window seat at Grimaldi's, in the American wing at the Met, at the meat counter at Ottomanelli's as I was ordering a pair of lamb legs, and once on the rock wall at Riverside Park, right near our old home. Three times on the Northeast Corridor from New York to Boston I've disturbed strangers, thinking they were her. Normally, I convince myself that my eyes are deceiving me, that Savannah is not so distinctive that I might see her clearly from five blocks, or from six rows away on a speeding train. A shrink once told me that this was a sign of love: that seeing the object of your desire everywhere is a primal form of wishful thinking. But I really did believe I saw her walking along the west side of Central Park. I was there to visit Eliza. I have an apartment I keep off the park: just a studio. It was the first truly warm day of the year, and I'd exited the subway early so that I could walk home in the good weather. I'd just turned seventy-three, and, aside from a nagging injury to the Achilles tendon on my left foot, I could usually walk a good distance before the pain acted up. (My wife would disagree if she were alive to read this; it was a skill of hers.)

I'd stopped at the corner of 81st Street, where the big, gleaming cube of the Hayden Planetarium sits alongside the park like an oversized paperweight plopped down onto the avenue. I'd just bought myself a bottle of water when the woman came bounding down the front of the museum's northern steps, turned right, and walked past me. She was consumed with her cell phone, thumbing some urgent communiqué into it, and her elbow clipped mine. A moment before, I'd been looking in the opposite direction, east, across the park, in the direction of the Metropolitan's roof garden, where a few days earlier I'd gone to see Rachel read from her book of short stories. For some reason I'd felt an odd compulsion to turn my head toward this woman. This happens from time to time: How do we know when we're being watched? How do we know to turn to see that? Although I've never been inclined to look to the universe for signs, I seem to constantly find myself interpreting the slightest coincidences — this woman's elbow grazing mine — as omens intended just for my benefit.

I limped across the street, and then with some effort I called out after her. First: *Hey! Hey, you!* Then: *Savannah! Savannah! Savannah!* And then finally: *Savannah Stockton! It's me, Hilly Wise! Stop!* Meanwhile, the woman had turned south and had begun to walk toward Columbus Circle. The city was in chaos that day. A delegation from Iran or maybe from Venezuela had come to town in order to deliver remarks at the United Nations, and the motorcade had snarled traffic east across the island. The intersection at 72nd was a mess of horns and shouting, none of which seemed to bother this woman, whom I still believed was Savannah. She took an iPod out of her purse and plugged the earphones into her ears.

I began to run after her. I did this as best

as I could manage, and for a block I managed fairly well. But then she really opened some distance between us, and I stopped. By now, the pain in my foot had become considerable, and I'd drawn some attention. Suddenly there were private-school boys everywhere. They were from the Dalton School, across the park. The boys were all wearing blue neckties. One of them stopped to help me.

"Hey, dude," he said, greeting me. "You having a heart attack or something?"

I was sweating and must have looked awful. "Could you stop that woman?" I said to the boy.

"You gonna die right here on the step, dude?" he asked again. "Dude? You OK, dude? You croaking or something?"

"No," I said, laughing. "I'm not dying."

He was probably fourteen, a freshman, his forehead marked with a horizontal line of acne, a mustache thinly struggling to exist on the top of his lip.

"Could you please go get that woman?" I said.

"Who?" he asked.

"That woman," I said, pointing. The street was filled with women. "That woman in the black coat. She's an old friend of mine, and I need to see her."

"She, like, a girlfriend or something, dude?"

"Something like that," I said breathlessly.

"Dude! That chick was your girlfriend? The black chick? Nice: chocolate-and-vanilla *swirl!*"

"Could you go get her?"

To see this boy run down Columbus! Like a goddamned missile. I sat down on a bench and started to nurse my foot, rubbing my thumbs against the tendon in the way I'd seen my physical therapists do. I wondered then, just as I wonder now, why I continued to feel the need to see her, why I saw her ghost everywhere, why she appeared to me in my dreams. Since Iowa, we'd been in contact exactly one time, and that was the encounter I began with.

A moment later, the Dalton boy was leading this woman down the street. I could see her hesitating, stopping in place on the sidewalk, and then the boy gripping her by the wrist. It was clear from a block's distance that it wasn't her, and I felt immediately shamed, both for the boy I'd sent running (his youth had prevented him from breaking a sweat) and for the woman, who was so confused, and who, we both soon discovered, spoke not a lick of English. Thinking on it now, she was too young to be Savannah. She might have been ten years younger than I was, and, to be honest, I may have known this even before I went after her. Such things are difficult to know with certainty in retrospect. I had just become a widower, and I had no idea how to be alone. If you pay attention, widowers do this all the time. They search. They get desperate. They can't be by themselves. They marry the wrong woman really, really quickly.

For a long moment, we all stood there, all three of us, silent. The woman, for what it's worth, did look like her. They shared the high cheekbones and the same coat.

Finally, the boy from Dalton pushed us together, one hand on each of our backs.

"Dude. Give her a hug or something. Don't be so shy!"

And so I hugged this stranger. The poor woman must have been so utterly puzzled. I gripped her lightly at first, and then harder, at the shoulders, my arms on her like handcuffs, and then — I shudder to admit this — I began to weep. She wasn't Savannah. If she was, I'd never have done what I did. But for a moment I pretended she was. And I wept.

But enough of the sentimental stuff.

SEVEN

I mention Savannah here because of a letter I received not even an hour after we'd held the service for Robert's funeral. It had been sent from the offices of Rutherford & Schultz, the New York firm where Lauren Becker was the star attorney. I'll reproduce the most salient part of the letter here:

In light of recent events, Mrs. Stockton wishes to transfer to you and to your father certain properties that are in her possession. She wishes to do so with assurances as to the threat of prosecution, penalties, or civil litigation. This letter should not imply that these properties were obtained illegally, or that my client's possession of such properties indicates in any capacity behavior that could be construed by you or your attorneys as criminal.

This was hand delivered to me just after I'd crossed the beach from Robert's house to mine, Lauren's signature inked neatly onto the bottom of the stationery. She'd added a yellow sticky to the papers that said, *Hi, Hilly! I miss you!* The process server was a young man, maybe twenty, head-phones jammed into his ears. He'd been waiting for me by the house, looking bored, idling between his knuckles an unlit ciga-rette that he couldn't wait to light. I'd been crying just a moment before all this. My face was red and wet, and when the poor kid gave me the letter, he looked stricken. "Who knows?" he said, giving me a weak slug on the shoulder. "It might be good news?"

I read it right there, leaning against my fence post, just as everyone was filing into my living room. The idea had been to have a small service, but, Robert being Robert, so many people had called to ask us permis-sion to attend. Some of these were acquain-tances or former associates at the firm, and some of these were old hands from the Truman administration, or the Ford admin-istration, or even the Clinton administration (by the end, Robert had become, quietly, what we'd now call a centrist Democrat). Some of these were judges before whom

449

Robert had argued cases and won, and some were the heads of various aviation firms whose finances Robert's litigation had greatly affected. And some of these were people whose life Robert had touched in some small private way: nurses, landscapers, beach lifeguards, shoeshiners, hotel-desk clerks, telephone-company men, HVAC installers, deckhands, auto mechanics, shell fishermen. We'd had orders to scatter his ashes at sea near the house, which was something we couldn't accommodate, owing to all sorts of regulations prohibiting the disposal of human remains inside a national park. Instead, we'd had a tiny stone erected on the cusp of the beach, just a little pretty rock with his name on it. We buried some of his clothes there — some of his lumberjack shirts and some paint-splattered pants. And we kept his ashes in his house, interred in a simple wooden box made from trees taken from his hometown in Kansas. It's important to note that my father arranged all of this. Newspaper reports afterward had the crowd near two hundred people.

My girls had been the ones to suggest opening up Bluepoint to anyone who wanted to come, and this was what we did, posting a notice on the internet, putting out

the word on the radio and on local television. My father had been the sole outlier
in our group, his claim being that people
would come simply because it was our
house and not out of any particular sense of
mourning. Later, of course, we'd discover
that he was right and that a good amount of
those who'd come had done so merely
because our house was open, when for so
long it had been hidden behind gates. And,
even though I wish it weren't the case, I did
see some people wandering around my living room, looking bored and disappointed
by my modesty.

Part of the reason for the crowd was the
media attention. Suddenly, on the evening
news, for instance, you'd see this trick where
they'd show a photograph of, say, my father
speaking to Spiro Agnew, the two of them
on the South Lawn of the White House, and
they'd zoom past Agnew and my father to
find Robert's face, obscured, maybe by
some Secret Service agents. Because news
photographers prefer fast lenses, Robert
would be in soft focus, and they'd need to
sharpen his blurry face into something
recognizable. Over all this, a news announcer would intone: *Always the man in
the background, Robert Ashley often had an
audience with America's most powerful men.*

451

He did more to shape America's policy toward how, and how safely, we all travel through the air than any man in the history of this country. My father couldn't tear himself away from the television — the first time, really, I ever saw him watch more than a few minutes of what he still in 2008 called the idiot box. I found him this way one night, the room dark, my father in a suit but barefoot. He turned to me, drunk, red-eyed, and said, "Have you heard, Hilly? The next time you fly, you should thank Bob for your safety."

"They just do this sort of thing," I said. "They're filling time."

"Those little masks that come down when the plane loses pressure? Robert fucking invented them. The black box? Robert fucking invented that, too. Haven't you heard?"

"Dad —"

"No, Brian Williams is right about him. He's up in heaven now, making heaven safer. You think he's inspecting the wings on the angels?"

Because he was in his chair, and because he needed help to get across the beach, my father was the last of the crowd to get to the house from the funeral, his nurses behind him, pushing, enduring his abuse. When he saw the letter from Savannah's lawyer, he assumed I'd been served.

"Who's suing you?" he asked.

"Nobody," I said, stuffing the thing in my pocket.

"Looks like you're getting sued. I know that look. I cause that look."

"Just some legal business for the foundation."

"Are they suing to have you removed from the board?" he asked, his best attempt at humor in days immediately eclipsed by the pain of having to be lifted from his chair and placed on his feet. With both hands on the nearest railing, he winced. His nurses were doing the work — one man had him by his armpits; another waited for him with an ordinary pair of wooden crutches. He had a cast on his left leg now. He'd reinjured it in the hospital hallway, walking when he should have been in his wheelchair. "If you need a lawyer, I know a few," he said, righting himself, still trying to joke, wincing again. Then, turning away from me: "I'll be in my office. Please try to keep these vultures away."

His office was now my laundry room. Jenny had done this decades ago, replacing the long wooden desk, the crates of wasted Underwood ribbons, the acres of caked Old Gold ash, with a sturdy washer/dryer combo and a system of white particleboard shelving onto which she'd put the usual gallons of softener and detergent, but also the various nautical bric-a-brac that my parents had collected. She'd been loath to do all of this. She'd loved my father in a way very few people loved him. He had, after all, gotten me to come home to her. She'd been the one who kept calling it his office, even after we'd been doing laundry there for twenty years. It wasn't out of the ordinary to hear her say, in that sweet, strange Baltimore accent of hers, "Hilly, I'm going to the office to do some laundry." All of her work was still there, the machines, the shelves, her terrible homemade needlepoint, her equally horrible watercolors, the plumbing up through the floorboards where my father had liked to place his tiny motorized fan. He still gravitated there. Maybe out of habit. Or maybe because the window there offered the most unobstructed view of the ocean.

By now, he had privately confided to me that he blamed himself for Robert dying the way he had, his logic being that the plane crash had scarred the company and thrust Robert into a position that at his age he couldn't maintain without suffering an undue amount of stress. I'd let him say all of this because he seemed so convinced by it all, and of course because I had no hope of providing any clarity to what by now was an obstinacy so hardened that a diamond could not have marred it. I guess I let him say this because I also believed it somewhat. Like any businessman, my father had wanted to cut costs, and he'd done so with his airplanes, which, if it were anybody but him, would've been simply a dangerous decision to make. For my father it was catastrophically stupid. But still: to hear him call it his office stung me a little bit. I may have been living here now. I may have raised my girls here. My wife may have died beneath this roof. None of this mattered. It was his. All of it. Still.

I followed my father and his nurses into the house, up the steps and into our living room. A group of three or four newspapermen were waiting to get a comment from my father. If there was ever an illustration of how my father's fame had faded, this was it. In his heyday, there'd have been forty people. Now there were four.

Here, for the very last time, I saw him conduct a press conference:

Q: Can you comment on Mr. Ashley's death?
A: (*after a considerable pause*) Robert was

my closest friend for sixty years.

Q: *What did he mean to you, Mr. Wise?*
A: (*laughter*) Next question, please.

Theo Cantor was waiting for me in my office, standing in the doorway, his notepad out, his neat, blocky handwriting filling the page. I'd gone there to put away the letter from Savannah's lawyer. "What are you doing here?" I asked, brushing past him.

"I was invited," he said. He flipped through the pages in his notepad. Wedged into it he had a cutout from the *Cape Cod Gazette,* the article folded so that the notice for Robert's memorial was visible to me. "A nice touch for you guys," he said, "if not a little surprising."

"Is that a newspaper?" I asked. "I thought your generation didn't know what those things were."

"Yeah, well, I had someone very old tell me what they were and how they worked."

Theo was a good-looking kid, a bit scrawny. His hands betrayed his anxiety: fingernails cracked, dried, bitten, torn off; one cuticle caked with blood. I expected this. Young reporters suffer all sorts of terrible nutritional deficiencies and physical trauma in the service of their profession.

This new generation had it worse, I thought, than my generation, the sudden boom of news outlets and web organs creating the unlikely scenario in which reporters were discouraged from writing too much or delving with too eager an eye into any subject; brevity had won the war. Theo, however, seemed different in this regard. It took a certain mixture of arrogance and ambition and stupidity to want to write the first biography of a very public man. My old editor at the *Spectator* used to call this particular quality *swagger,* and he'd claimed that it manifested itself in one of two ways: either as a fool's errand, haplessly chasing around your subject, digging in his trash, paying off his mistresses; or as an illness, a compulsion, a deeply illogical catatonia that kept propelling you toward your goal, even when the original purpose of it seemed obscured. I hadn't yet figured out where Theo fell on the spectrum.

"I was a little shocked you all agreed to this today," Theo said. "Given the general secrecy."

"You're in my office," I said. "You find any big secrets?"

"You got a moment to talk?" he asked. He was putting away his notebook, sliding it into a fashionable leather attaché and, in the process, removing a slim laptop.

"This is a funeral," I said. "I don't have time to play computer games with you."

"Why are you so hostile to me?" Cantor asked.

"Can I give you a piece of advice? Don't ever say anything like that. You sound weak. And pathetic. You're a reporter. People are going to lose respect for you. That's the arrangement."

He ignored me, cleared a space on my desk, opened his computer, and cued an audio file for me to listen to. Without looking up at me, he started to talk: "So, I started working on this book on your father, I don't know, a year and a half ago? Long story short, I've got a friend at the Air and Space Museum. You know? The Smithsonian? Anyway, a little while ago he forwards me this."

He pushed a button, and all of a sudden, a loud *whoosh*ing noise came from the speakers: radio interference.

"I don't have time for this," I said.

"I think you do," he said, his eyebrows raised. "Here. Listen."

A man's voice came across the recording then. *"This is* Bunny. *Repeat. This is* Bunny. *BA Eighty-Eight. This is* Bunny."

Cantor flexed and unflexed his fist. *"BA*

458

stands for *Boston Airways.*"

"Where did you get this?"

"I told you. Smithsonian."

"Is this the crash?"

"The moments before it. Air traffic recording."

"Right."

"They're very calm," he said. "It goes on. They're having trouble gaining altitude."

The call came across the air: *"Pulling up. Pulling up. Pullllllllllling up."* Silence. Crushed air. Then: *"Nothing. Still can't gain anything. Throttle's unresponsive."*

Theo stopped it then. "The crash isn't on there."

"No?"

"I brought this to you as a sign of good faith," he said, turning the file off. "I figured that if I were you, this would be a pretty important thing to have."

I wanted to keep listening to the recording. This was something Theo could see in my expression. He took a small thumb drive from his pocket and gave it to me. It was tiny, an inch and a quarter long, blue like the logo for Boston Airways had been blue.

"It's on there," he said.

"How's that possible? This thing is tiny."

He smiled. "Ask one of your daughters to show you how it works."

"Why are you giving this to me?"

"As a sign of goodwill. I said that."

"What do you want in return?"

"I want to interview you for this book."

"Look —"

"There's all this strange stuff in your father's story."

"Half the crap people write about him is bullshit."

"I know that. It's the other things, though. The things people haven't written about." He sat on the edge of my desk. "He won't talk to me. I've been trying for a year. Maybe more. He's just not interested in what I have to say. People get like that. They figure it doesn't matter. But it does. I'm crafting his legacy here."

I laughed. The comment was preposterous.

"It's true, Hilton."

"Hilly," I said. "Nobody calls me Hilton."

"Let me show you something else," he said.

He lifted his bag up onto the desk and took out a paper folder. In it, he had a letter from Savannah's lawyer, printed on the same stationery I'd just put away.

"This is from Savannah Stockton's lawyer," he said, closing the folder before I could finish reading it. "Basically, it says that she's refusing to talk with me."

"What is it you're after?"

"I want to know what happened to Mr. Dawson," he said. "She's his only living relative."

"He died in jail," I said. "That's what happened."

"I know that. But it's suspicious. So I'm interested."

"How do you even know about him?"

"You ever hear of a guy named Jerry Silver?"

"No," I said, losing patience. All of this seemed suspicious, and finding suspicion in innocuous encounters was something my father did, not something I did.

"You probably met him at some point or another," Theo said.

"Never heard of him."

"Classic corporate superstar. Owned New York's legal world until your father toppled him."

"Still not ringing a bell."

"Had his hands in everything."

"Get to the point, Theo."

"I've got his diaries. That's the sort of thing I do — research journals and diaries and all that. But there's this business in there about him coming to visit your dad. They wanted to poach him. Keep him from

461

doing what he did, which was ruining them. And there's this bit in there about Dawson. Apparently there was a party here, and they riled him up a little bit."

"Jerry," I said.

"Jerry Silver? This ringing a bell now?"

"Maybe," I said, remembering perfectly how Jerry Silver had drunkenly shaken my hand, and how, later, they'd all laughed at having woken Lem up in the middle of the night. *The Big Black Wolf,* they'd called him.

"Well, that's it. I found it interesting. Did a little digging. Found out your father had the guy arrested. Found out the guy was murdered in prison. I mean, what else is there to explain? You start writing a book about somebody, and you stumble on that shit? That's gold."

"Gold, huh?"

"If it's not gold, it's something close. It's *fascinating.*"

He paused then. I waited.

"Anything else?" I asked.

He laughed. "No! Does there need to be anything else?"

"I guess not."

"I've hit a brick wall, Hilly. And I don't mean that lightly. I mean, seriously. A brick wall. A hard, serious, impenetrable brick wall."

I shook my head. "Honestly, if you haven't gotten anywhere with this, I don't think I'm going to be able to help."

"You'll help if you'll talk."

"I was young," I said. "Lem was my friend."

"This on the record?" His pad was out suddenly.

"Sure," I said. I was tired. I needed a drink. I rubbed my palms against my eyes. My daughters were at the door now. All of them. All in black funeral dresses. Their husbands were behind them — Ethan and Greg and Todd. Sammy cleared her throat. "Daddy, you should thank people for coming."

I looked back at Theo. "Put that on the record. It's true. He was my friend. I have your card," I said. "I'll call you."

"I need something better than that." He pointed at the thumb drive. "I've got more stuff like that."

"Really?"

He nodded. "I've got pieces of the plane."

"Pieces?" This astonished me.

"We could trade."

I shook his hand. "I'll give you one hour. How's that sound? One hour. Nothing more. I'll call you."

"With the truth?"

"The absolute truth."

EIGHT

Of course, up to that point the absolute truth was far from the actual truth. I wouldn't know this until two months after Robert's funeral, when Savannah came to Bluepoint with her family. That she came at all was a surprise. It was a long haul simply so that we could exchange a small jewelry box.

The box: by now I knew that's what she had. Neither she nor Lauren had confirmed this to me. But I knew. I remembered seeing her take it from Lem's apartment long ago, and I remembered seeing it again on the high shelf in her pantry in Iowa. I had no idea what was inside. As I recalled, it was too small to hold anything truly scandalous. It couldn't hold a gun, or a camera, or photographs, or, given the technology of 1952, a recording device. It was the size of a fist, and a small fist at that. So that ruled out postcards, books, knives. For a while, I was convinced there were bullet casings inside, or maybe a single key that belonged to a safety-deposit box.

After I got Savannah's letter, I'd sent a response through Lauren asking her if she wouldn't mind coming back to Bluepoint to return it herself. It was a long shot, I knew, but I thought it was worth it just to ask. After what had happened in Washington DC, I hadn't expected that she'd agree to it, and at first she'd refused. She wanted simply to FedEx us the box and be done. But I pressed on. I had Lauren ask her again. "Say that I'd love to have her here. Tell her that." Lauren seemed dubious. "Why do you want her to come? Just have her send the box," she'd told me. Why did I want her to come? I just did. That's the best answer I have. But I'll try to do better: Part of me missed her; part of me was curious; part of me felt guilty for what had happened to her. And part of me — most of me — was lonely. I told Lauren all of this, and in what I thought was a last-ditch effort, I told Savannah this, albeit in much more generous language, writing her via Lauren, sending along with my note a photograph of my family: all of my girls, their husbands, and all our various dogs and cats. On the back of the picture, I wrote: *Bring your family,*

466

Savannah. It'll be fun. I signed it: *The Wise Family.* When she agreed, Lauren called me to tell me the news. "I won't say that she sounded excited. But she said yes. She'll come for six hours."

"She put a time limit on me?" I asked.

"Oh my. It never ends with you two," she said.

I'm tempted now to say that all of this made me aflutter with some adolescent stirrings, or that I was rendered sleepless with anticipation by all of it, or even that I fell into some fantasy over having her back here again at the house, distracting her husband so that the two of us could be alone — her in a sarong, her in some tennis whites, her in a black two-piece, her with enormous, buggy white sunglasses and nothing else, her and me on the beach, her and me in the back of my truck. But none of it is true. Something about the way I thought about her had changed. Before Jenny became pregnant with Sammy, if I thought of Savannah, it was like trying to concentrate on something dangerous. The old fear was gone now, replaced by shame — first for her uncle, and then for the way I'd left her standing in her kitchen in Iowa, and then for the way I'd followed her in Washington. And the allure of it all was gone, too. Time does that; it kills the mystique, replaces the boundlessness of wishing and hoping with some well-earned, necessary clarity.

Of course, there's a bigger reason why I didn't think about any of this. Not even five minutes after I got word that Savannah had agreed to come back to Bluepoint, Sammy came into my office with Ethan. They smiled and sat down and handed me a ridiculously overpriced cigar. "We've known for a while," she told me, not able to actually say what it was they knew. Laughter escaped her, and for an instant she was my tiny black-haired toddler again. "But then Robert died. And it didn't seem right to be happy." I got up to hug them and to cry with them, and for all of us to start jumping up and down for joy. My father wheeled to the door, having heard the commotion. "There's always time for happiness," I said into Sammy's ear. "Always."

And then I watched Ethan tell Arthur Wise that he was going to be a great-grandfather. His response?

"Good goddamned Lord."

Savannah arrived at Bluepoint on a Wednesday at the beginning of August, with her husband, Hershel, and her son, Charles. They came in a rented Jeep Patriot the color of a candied cherry, American flags stuck to the pair of antennas on the roof, approaching the house very slowly. Hershel disembarked first. I was out on the porch, waiting. He called out to me.

"Are you Hilton Wise?" he asked. "Or are we very lost?"

"I am," I said. "You made it!"

He came to the porch alone. I could see Savannah and her son through the windows of their Jeep. Hershel looked more or less the way he'd looked in those pictures that had hung on the walls of his house in Iowa. Of course, prior to seeing him again, I'd forgotten entirely what he looked like. He could have been my postman and I wouldn't have known. But that's how memory functions: the moment he stepped out of the car, some trigger clicked in me, and I could recall with vivid familiarity all those shots of him in his uniform. He was older now, of course, his hair perfectly white but his posture the posture of a soldier. He had the handshake of a soldier, also.

"It's good to meet you finally," he said, crushing my hand — really crushing it — in his. Even though he suggested some gladness in our introduction, what I think he really meant was: *So. This is the guy who won't stop bothering my wife.*

"Did you have an easy trip, I hope?"

"Terrible," he said.

"You're killing me," I said, looking at my hand. "Christ."

"My wife's a wreck over this," he said, squeezing, if it were possible, harder.

"That was never my intention," I said. "Please let go of my hand."

"I need you to promise that this won't be a bad scene."

"You have my word."

He let go of my hand then. With a big, cheerful, put-on smile, he waved Savannah and Charles out from the Jeep. Hershel turned back to me.

"My boy's got no idea about any of the history behind all this," he said. "He doesn't know anything about you."

"Understood."

She got out then. Immediately I saw that she was frail, ill, her body clearly ravaged by something. Hershel went to her, jumping off the porch and going to her, grabbing hold of her right arm. Charles — a spitting image of Hershel, despite sharing his name with Slim — got on her left. She moved so slowly. I wanted at that moment to rush inside, to call Lauren, to protest. Why hadn't she told me?

"Do you need a hand?" I called out.

470

"Oh, two helpers is more than fine, Hilly," she said sweetly.

The boy was looking around in much the same way that so many visitors have looked around the first time they arrive here — at the wide sweep of the shore, the waves, the bluffs and rocks and birds and high grass.

"This all yours?" the boy asked as they came near.

"It is," I said.

"Wow. All of it?"

"Not all of it," I said. "But most of it."

The boy had let go of his mother now, and while Savannah kept plodding forward, one slow step after another, Hershel had his attention fixed on the three steps ahead of them. *Stairs,* his expression seemed to be saying, *no one told me there'd be stairs.*

She had her head down, as if the dirt threatened to rise up to trip her. Each step came impossibly slowly, an act of bargaining between her brain and her legs. She was wrapped in heavy clothing made from brightly colored fabrics, a purple sash across her chest, an orange stripe from one shoulder to the other. Her hair was cropped short to her temples, dyed black, her neck loaded down with pendants and amulets and charms. The same was true of her wrists, the small bones there decorated by dozens of ringed gold bangles that clinked and shifted as she gripped her husband's hand. They worked in unison, like they were navigating a balance beam. When she wanted to, she brought both of their hands up into the air, each step studied, considered, carefully placed. And then, when she felt it necessary, she took Hershel's hand near to the side of her own thigh, as if to push down on it. All the while, I realized, he'd been whispering to her: *Step, there you go, step, there you go.*

By now the boy had wandered off slightly, moving from the walkway onto the wet ground so that he could see the water. I heard him whisper to himself, a light, impressed, unironic sentence that ended, clearly, with the word *damn.* Then he slipped his tiny black telephone from his pocket and began to take pictures of the shore, shifting his position a little after every shot so that later, I guessed, he could paste them all together. Funny even now, when there's no shutter to open and no light to pour onto a strip of film, that all of these devices should keep the sound of the camera intact as a memory: the click and roll and whisk and clap.

"Hilly," Savannah said, still looking down, her long, knitted purse swinging around from her back to her front, "is there some way we could get into your house without managing these stairs?"

"No," I said. "If I'd known . . ."

"That's fine, Hilly. It's just that this might take most of the six hours we've allotted for you." She said this sternly, her focus still largely directed at the ground but the skin near the corners of her eyes crinkled — not at me, I realized, but at Hershel.

"I have some people inside who could help you," I offered.

"Help me how?"

"They could lift you."

Hershel looked up at me with a certain anger on his face. But the idea made her laugh.

"Lift me?" she said. "Do you keep people on staff to lift *you* up the stairs?"

"Nobody is lifting you, sweetie." To me, Hershel's tone was harsher: "Nobody's lifting my goddamned wife up any stairs. Got it?"

She let go of his hand now, as if to scold him with it, and then, without his help, she lost her balance. To right herself, she put her palm flat against his chest. "Oh, stop it. Just *stop* it right now. We talked about this. Calm down. Right now. Like I'd let somebody *lift* me."

473

Hershel shook his head. He couldn't look at me. Savannah, however, turned to me and then moved to survey the view. Her lips pursed, and she closed her eyes.

"It's completely different," she said, turning back. She pointed out to the water. "The beach. The whole shape of it."

"Erosion," I mustered.

Charles had come back to the walkway. "Damn," he said loudly to me. "That's all I gotta say. *Damn.*"

"Hilly Wise," I said, shaking his hand.

"I know who you are," he said. "I saw you on the news."

Hershel stepped between us. He was still a big man, each of his shoulders larger than my chest. His chin had a point to it, as if it, on its own, were a weapon that could harm me.

"How're we gonna do this?" he asked me, his voice dropped low. He had a hint of coffee on his breath, and beneath each of his eyes he had evidence of the stress this visit had caused.

"How do you mean?"

"The steps?"

"What do you usually do?"

"Usually we're at home. Usually we have ramps. Usually we don't travel all this way to do something like *this.*"

474

"Oh, Hersh," Savannah said. "I *wanted* to come. Stop being such a drag."

We took her up each step slowly, deliberately: her son on one side, her grim husband on the other, and me, walking backward up the three tall steps of my house, my hands outstretched and lightly grabbing hers. It took a few minutes to do this, and the whole time she glanced up at me with a series of alternately brave and pitiful and lovely and sad expressions. They said, in short: *I'm here, I'm sick, it's awful, but I came.* And, although I might have been imagining it, there was one last expression, right when we'd gotten her through the front door, when, rather sheepishly, she batted her eyes at me as if to say, *Do you still like what you see here? Nobody sees me in here anymore. Do you?*

Because the entire family was either living with me for the summer or up at Broad Neck and generally close by, I'd had to tell them what was happening. Or at least tell them something. My father had been the one to spill to my daughters and to all of the boys the secret behind all of this, which he did in his typical fashion. "Oh, her? She's the black girl Hilly was obsessed with, isn't she? You don't know about her? She's coming? Let's hope he doesn't get his heart broken again." Of course, my father didn't tell my kids the whole story. This was our history, our shared secret. How could we have explained this whole story? Especially to Sammy? How could he tell her how I'd waffled that moment at the gate, how I'd considered staying in Iowa?

My father had thought of this, though. The way he'd put it, Savannah was just a girl I'd had a crush on one summer. That was it. A summer fling. After he let that out of the bag, everyone started to tease me. In the week leading up to her visit, there was nobody who didn't chime in. At one point, Ethan grabbed me by the elbow and offered to take the girls away for the week so that I could have Savannah alone at the house. When I told him that she was arriving with her husband and her son, he offered to distract them. Most of this was innocent, even if, beneath the surface, there was something patronizing about it all. I'd been lonely since Jenny died. Everyone knew it. I had no idea how to be a widower. It was something that carried with it no set of instructions.

When they were all inside the house — young Charles, Hershel, and Savannah — my family was waiting for them, and I introduced everyone. Savannah took each person's hand with both of hers, gripping it the way a priest might, meeting their eyes. "You all look so much like your father," she said when we were finished.

Call it what you want — worlds colliding, universes intersecting; both of these were clichés that Greg used — but the first few minutes were painful to endure. Reunions always are. All the small talk, all the innocent questions. For instance, Eliza asked: "So, what was he like when he was young?" And Savannah, looking to me, some mischief in her eyes, responded, "He was awkward. But very determined to be liked." My daughters, especially, enjoyed hearing this. Then, Elliot perked up: "Was he cute?" Savannah looked to Hershel, as if apologizing in advance, and then back to Elliot. "He *was*. Sort of. He was skinny. He needed to eat more. It never made sense to me that someone so rich could be so thin!"

My father wheeled himself into the room at some point during all of this, one of his nurses behind him. He hadn't been out on the porch when Savannah arrived because I'd asked him not to come. If she'd gotten out of the car and seen him first, then she'd have turned right back around. He arrived with his typical panache, dressed to the hilt.

"You know," he said, taking her hand, "I

never did get to meet you. You met my associate. Robert. But I never had the pleasure."

She smiled. "I did. He was a nice man."

"He was," my father said.

"I was so sorry to hear that he passed."

My father was still holding on to her hand, and then, having realized that she was ill, he seemed to loosen up. "You're banged up, just like me, huh?"

This made her laugh. "Oh. Well. I didn't survive a plane crash," she said.

Charles interrupted. "Wait. Dude. You survived a plane crash?"

"Dude," my father said. The word sounded particularly refined coming from his mouth. "Indeed I did."

"What was it like?"

Hershel, clearly having been briefed on my father's explosive personality, tried to stop this, and I looked to him, shaking my head, hoping to convey to him that we were all at a loss to control my father. If he wanted to talk to you, he would talk to you. And if he wanted to engage your son, who was, for whatever reason, ignorant of all that bound us together, then he would do that, too.

"What was it like?"

My father leaned back in his chair and

put both of his hands on his lap. He had yet another watch on his wrist, this one black, with some small blue stones on it. "It was terrifying, son. I realized I was going to die. And then I realized that I really didn't want to die. And then I had a moment where I realized how terrible I'd been to the people I loved the most. And then, well, I felt bad for another few moments, and then I waited for impact."

"Did it hurt?"

"Charles," Hershel said.

My father looked at me for a moment. Then he looked out the living room window, where the crest of Robert's roof was dappled by the sun. His clotheslines were still out. There were towels still clamped to the line, now stiffened by sea salt. My father had refused to let us remove them. The fence remained half-finished. My father put his hands together. "Of course it hurt. But, in the grand scheme of life, it didn't hurt that much. So much about life hurts so much more, son."

Savannah saw that we had one of my father's spare wheelchairs out in the breezeway, and after looking at it longingly she asked me if I wouldn't mind taking her out to the water. She did this while we were in the living room, sitting in the blue Florence Knoll chairs my mother had first bought for the place. The group excluded my father, who, after talking some more about his crash, his recovery, ordered his nurses to bring him back upstairs to his office. Thankfully, my children had assumed the task of conversation, Todd and Ethan beginning to debate automobile engines while every few minutes the young Charles made dismissive scoffing noises. And, Rachel and Greg having realized that the Hershel Stockton sitting before us — with his legs crossed at the ankle, drinking a giant martini as if he were gulping water after a tennis match — was in fact the same Hershel Stockton whose book on hermeneutics had apparently caused some implacable fissure between the two of them, one corner of the room became filled with that particular sound of academic pedantry which has always made my stomach uneasy. Flattery, as I knew well, was the easiest way to calm a man's suspicions, and so when Savannah asked me to take her outside, her husband was far too busy accepting praise to remember how much he distrusted me. As I stood up to get the wheelchair, I caught him saying the following sentences to Rachel: *"Solipsism, I suppose I was trying to claim, is the obvious logi-*

cal byproduct of all this technology. Is there a more clear example of this sort of dualism than in the gadgets we're all beginning to worship? I mean, I don't think so, right?"

Outside the wind was steady, the flags up at Broad Neck stiff and pulling inland toward Hyannis. I walked behind her, pushing the chair, the breeze helping me. Although it was August, the immediate, dead heart of summer, she had a chill. Elliot had given her a wool throw to put on her shoulders, and as we got closer to the water, she pulled it up to her chin. Resting on her lap, she had her purse, and inside the purse, I knew, she had Lem's jewelry box. We went for a good distance in silence, heading north, up the beach, away from Robert's house. She had big black sunglasses on her face, and every few minutes, as the gulls dove near us, or as the breeze whipped up paper-dry seaweed and tumbled it past, she hummed to herself, either out of the obvious pleasure of being on the water or because she was in pain. I couldn't tell, and I didn't ask. I took her out as far as the boardwalk went, the wooden planks being one of the few of my father's additions that I'd kept. After a few minutes of walking this way, in total silence, we got to the end of the path.

"What? No butlers to carry me?" she asked, teasing.

"I fired everybody fifteen years ago."

"Don't you want to know what's wrong with me?" she asked.

"Not if you don't want to tell me," I said.

"Oh, I don't believe that. You were always so curious."

"Are you dying?" I asked.

"Not any more than you are," she said. "Just doing it with a little less style."

"That's all I need to know."

"Really? Here I am, you're pushing me in a wheelchair, and you're not curious?"

"My wife died not so long ago," I said.

She nodded. "I read that."

"If it's not terrible to say, I think it would be awful for both of you to die so close together. That would make me especially lonely, I think."

She shifted beneath her blanket. I had said the wrong thing. I spun around to look back at the house, not because I wanted to but because it meant that I didn't have to see Savannah's face if she turned to see mine. What I saw out at the house was two of my sons-in-law taking Charles out to the beach. The boy was taking his shirt off, and then, to much less impressive and much flabbier results, Todd and Ethan were taking their shirts off. Then they all began to walk toward the water.

"Oh, Hilly, please don't tell me I came here to have you try to woo me back to you." She sighed and shifted uneasily beneath her blanket. "That would be so . . . so embarrassing for both of us."

"You didn't," I said. "I didn't."

"That's good."

"I shouldn't have said that."

"It's not that it isn't flattering, Hilly. Crippled women don't get come-ons very often. You were always very good at buttering me up."

"It's not what I meant."

"Oh," she said, giggling, "it is. We both know that."

Far off down the beach, I could hear Charles screaming as the cold water bit at his legs. I turned Savannah's chair around so she could see.

"We adopted him," she said. "His mother died in a fire, just like mine did."

"What do you mean? He looks just like your husband."

"Hersh is always pleased to hear people say that. But it's not true. He was a baby. A fireman saved him. There's a rather famous picture of the rescue."

We watched them for a while, the three

men in the water, and then, a few minutes after that, all my daughters in their black suits running and splashing and shrieking into the surf.

"They're all so pretty," she said. "Each one of them is prettier than the next."

"Certainly not because of me."

"Self-pity from Hilton Wise? How rare!"

We were talking without looking at each other. I was still behind her chair, my hands on the two grips on either side of her neck. In front of us was the water, the tide far out past the bluff, the damp, marshy ground pocked with sea-smoothed stones and the abandoned shells of hermit crabs and tiny beach snails legging their way to a tide pool.

"Can I ask you something?" I said, crouching to look at her.

"As long as it's not about you wooing me," she said; then she giggled again. "*Woo. What a word.*" Then, singing it, as if to the birds: "*Woooo!*"

"Washington DC. A few years ago."

She moaned and then laughed. "Ah! You followed me for so long! I thought you were crazy!"

"You didn't stop."

"Because I didn't want to stop!"

"But why? I mean, it was innocent."

"It's always innocent with you, Hilly. But

484

then something terrible happens. You're a disaster magnet."

I stiffened, and she saw it.

"To me, Hilly. To me. Obviously not to your girls. Just — with me, you always appeared in my life, and then something cataclysmic happened. You're like the flash before the bomb goes off."

"Did you just compare me to a nuclear bomb, Savannah?"

Another burst of dry laughter. "A little. I'd be a fool if I didn't believe it a *little*. I mean, nearly right on cue, I'd gotten this awful diagnosis. Literally fifteen minutes before. And then you just appeared."

"Oh, come on. That's a coincidence."

"I don't know. Later I laughed about it. But at the moment, it was freaky."

"What about the note?"

"Well, I shouldn't have left that. I felt bad about that right away."

"I still have it."

"Why am I not surprised to hear that."

"But why — ?"

"You ever wonder why I was in Washington? It's not like it's very close to where I live."

"Business?"

"Business," she scoffed. "I'm a librarian."

"Then what?"

485

She patted her legs. "I was there to see doctors. To get a diagnosis."

"But —"

"And so the next time you saw me, if you ever did see me, you'd have seen me like this. Which, as you can imagine, wasn't something I thought I would be able to handle very well."

I lifted my hands off her chair. "Right."

"You never think you'll end up needing someone to do everything for you."

"You sound like my father."

She looked at her watch. "I don't think I'll be able to stay here very long, Hilly."

"You're not having fun?"

"Fun? It's fine. But it's all very — I don't know, *heavy*. If that makes sense."

"It does."

"I showed Chucky the Emerson Oaks today."

"Oh."

"It's not there."

"I know."

"Neither, strangely, is the graveyard where my mother was buried. You should have heard Hersh. 'A black graveyard is like a pile of mulch to these people. Just dig it up. Plow it over.' "

"If I'd have known," I said.

"I know," she said, reaching out to pat my

knee. "You would have bought it or something."

"Right."

"Do you ever get tired of buying things?"

"I have a foundation," I said, stupidly.

"I know. I subscribe to the newsletter online."

I laughed. "See? I didn't know we did such a thing."

"It does *good* things, Hilly. You should be proud."

"Why don't you sound sincere?"

"Well, it's just that I fear that it's all because of this guilt you have. This guilt you carry around with you."

"It is. Partly."

She looked down at her purse. I saw then that she had a trace of dark-blue eye shadow on, which made me happy to see. "Do you know what it is I have to give you?"

"I have an idea."

She took the box from her purse. "You can take it now. But I want you to know that I didn't know what was in it for a very long time. Far after you came to see me in Hove."

"OK."

I took it from her. The sheen on it had long since faded. I opened the lid. Inside was a stash of papers, so many of them, all folded into impossibly tiny squares, the paper thin like tissues, the pile of it like so much origami.

"What is this?" I asked.

"Open them all later," she said.

"Are these letters?" I said.

"Later, Hilly."

The papers were so delicate as to be translucent, and it took me a while to remember what this was: tracing paper, the form of mimeograph that my father had used for so long.

"If I were you, I'd close it before it all blows away. Hersh would be so angry that we came all the way out here, only to lose them."

I could see, through one of the top papers, what I thought were the pillars of the *W* in the Wise & Ashley logo.

"Are these the Brooklyn Pages?"

"I don't know what that is, Hilly. But they are papers. I know that much."

"Have you read them?" I asked.

"Yes. I didn't for ages. And then I did. It seemed wrong of me to pry."

"And?"

"Well," she said. "I came here to give them to you. If you want to read them, you can. But, Hilly?"

"Yes."

"Please close the box, sweetheart. I haven't let anything happen to those letters in fifty-five years. It's very windy."

I closed the box. It made a clapping sound.

"Your guilt," Savannah began. "It's always been misplaced. I'm sure I'm not the first person to tell you that." And then, pulling the blanket up to her nose, the wool muffling her voice, she said, "I'm very cold, Hilly. Do you think you could take me back?"

I realize I'm required here to explain how I felt being with her again (suddenly uneasy), or to negotiate whatever curiosity I had about the stash of so much paper that had lived inside that jewelry box for the past half century, or even to give some summary of what that many years do to two people having suffered between them murder and racial violence and sickness and all the attending guilt that adheres itself to those things. But I felt none of that. I felt, pushing her, walking behind her, adjusting her blanket so that she didn't get too cold, a sense that I was, as they say, *in the moment,* a concept that up until that point I'd never truly believed to be a genuine state of being but rather just some gibberish cooked up by New Age healers and television evangelists. But for an instant, maybe more than an instant, something had lifted from me as I walked back along the boardwalk, toward my family, all of them toweling off on the dry, hot sand. We'd put the box on Savannah's lap, and as we moved back to the house, she kept both of her hands covering the top of it. Maybe I felt this way because I knew that soon there'd be no more secrets. Maybe I felt this way because she was here with me, and she'd met my daughters, seen what I'd left Iowa for that day, seen what I'd done with myself.

This isn't to say that Savannah felt the same way. Bound to the chair — her legs occasionally reaching down as we rested at the end of the last wooden plank, to tap at the board or to give us a well-meaning but ineffective little push with her toes — she made me stop halfway to the house.

"Hilly," she said, her voice rising. "Hilly?"

"What is it?"

"Where was it? Where?"

"Where was what?"

"His house? My uncle's apartment. I can't remember. It all looks so different."

I frowned and then pointed out, off the beach a little, to a spot hovering in the air somewhat ahead of us. "I think over there."

"You think?"

She craned in her chair to look back at me. I moved around to the front of her chair, crouching now. "There," I said, pointing at a wake-swirl on the surface of the water, an agitated spot of whiteness that looked as if it were dish soap poured into the sea. "Right there. That dot of white."

"That's it?"

"Yes," I said.

"It's just washed out?"

"Hurricanes," I said. "Gloria. And then, especially, Bob. Bob killed us. Half the beach just fell off that day."

"That's terrible," she said. "That it's just gone. Just like that."

"It was gone before that," I said. "My parents had it torn down. For years they had this awful glass thing. I took it down as soon as I moved back."

"Right," she said, tears in her eyes. "But at least the ground was still there. At least if he had come back, you know, if he had just come back one day to do another painting, he'd have recognized it. Now, it's just all different."

What do you say to this? To the way she just started to cry? What can you say? I wondered for a moment if she wasn't becoming delusional, if the illness that had crippled her body hadn't also crippled her mind. I stood up from my crouch and kept pushing. Eliza came running up to us, dripping wet, salt on her skin, grinning, golden. Then, a moment later, Hershel came out onto the patio, drunk by now, his ego inflated surely, his sport coat off, a vest beneath it. He whistled, out of joy, I hope, at the water and the birds and the waves. A moment after that, Charles took off running up the beach, toward us. Apparently this was the first time he'd ever been in the ocean. "It's so salty," he was yelling just as Savannah was telling me, with a note of sheepishness in her voice, "He's from Iowa, remember. We're not hicks. We're just land-locked."

An hour later they were all gone.

When I said goodbye to Savannah, we were alone at the edge of the driveway, the car running. I think we both knew that this was it for us. I was holding her up with both of my hands, in a position not unlike a very tentative slow dance.

"Can we see the spot from here where you found him?" she asked me.

"Lem?"

"Can you? When you caught him?"

I pointed to the taller of the two dunes out on the beach.

"Right there?" she asked.

"In between the hills."

"I kept that painting, you know." Then she smiled. "Oh, you know. You saw it. I forgot."

I smiled at the thought of the painting. "He was . . . how do I say this?"

"Not the very best painter," she said, laughing.

"Right," I said, nodding.

"Quite awful, in fact." She was laughing easily now.

"Terrible!"

"So terrible!" Now I was laughing, but she had stopped and was pointing.

"So that's where it was?"

"In between," I said.

"The night I came looking for you."

"An hour before that."

"I was so stupid to drive by myself."

"I know."

"Anything could have happened to me."

"I was irresistible. What could you do?"

"Oh please," she said, laughing. Then, turning the chair around with her toes: "I have cancer, Hilly. In case you wanted to know."

"You didn't have to tell me."

"It's slow moving. Some rare form. I don't even have to take chemotherapy. Just a pill."

"I'm glad for that."

"If I didn't tell you, I just know you'd

show up at my door or something, demand-
ing to find out."

"No," I said, laughing.

"Yes." She made a show of looking at her
watch. "Probably in a day or two. That
seems to be your habit. You'd want to buy
me a hospital or something."

"Are you getting good treatment?" I asked.

"Please stop trying to take care of me. I
can take care of myself. I have always been
able to take care of myself. I'm not helpless."

"I never said —"

"Even when you were a boy you believed
I was helpless."

I shook my head.

She nodded and reached to touch my
cheek. "Do you remember me then? When
you first saw me?" she asked.

"You were beautiful."

"I couldn't have been. I had nothing."

"There was twine on the buckle of one of
your shoes. Keeping it together."

"See? How could I have been beautiful?"

"Even with nothing you were beautiful," I
said.

"Give me a kiss," she said. "Before I
leave."

"A real kiss?"

She shook her head. I saw her eyes flicker.

"Damn, Hilly. On the cheek. On the cheek."

I kissed her. "Goodbye, Savannah."

"Goodbye, Hilly," she said. "This is for-ever, probably."

"Don't say that."

She winked. "Goodbye forever, Hilly. Be good, now."

NINE

Two days later, my father had the cast on his leg removed by an orthopedist he had flown in from Boston to Bluepoint especially for the task. The orthopedists at the hospital here at Broad Neck were, of course, up to the task, one man's cast being just as easy to remove as anybody else's, a saw in Cape Cod functioning the same way as one in Beacon Hill, and their sullen, embarrassed faces should have made my father feel foolish. But eight months of pain and immobility and constant checkups, eight months filled with the daily humiliations of his helplessness, of having his every move, his every whim, his every bodily function, attended to by a team of young men — all of this had worn on him. So he flew in his doctor. The guy's name was Billings, and he milked the affair, booking the President's Suite at the hotel, charging everything to the firm, and generally strutting around

Cape Cod like some long-lost Kennedy brother. This happened on a Friday, a date that had been circled on my father's wall calendar for a month. The circle represented the last step in his recovery, the bit of plaster that ran from his ankle to his knee the very last piece of the plane crash that had put Arthur Wise back in the news. Doctors told him that his body was as good as it ever was going to be. My father was to have a limp, left as a final insult, until the day he died, very much like the fake limp evident on some of the extant newsreels from the early 1950s. His nervous tic had become a real handicap.

He'd asked me to take him to the hospital that morning, changing his plans at the last moment. Eliza had been primed to drive him, and she woke early to do the job. Instead, my father came to find me in my study, hopping awkwardly into the room. "It's at goddamned Broad Neck," he said, sweat on his brow. "And . . . you know . . . that's where Bob goddamn died. You're not doing anything important, are you?"

Now we sat in the same waiting room where I'd waited that day for his helicopter to land. This made both of us uneasy. "You'd think they'd give us a different room, at least."

"This is a tiny hospital," I said. "There is no other room. This is it."

"A fucking *lounge* or something."

"There's no lounge. This is a hospital. Not an airport."

"Some place you could get a decent drink."

"Seriously?"

"All over Europe," he said. "A man can get a drink in a good hospital all over Europe. Totally respectable. Totally, one hundred percent legit way to pass the time."

"You want me to call out for a flask?"

He blew me off. "They'd probably arrest me," he said. "It's probably against some government regulation to drink in a private hospital between eight and nine in the morning."

Beside me there was a cubbyholed sort of ladder bolted to the wall and slotted with brightly colored pamphlets. I flipped through them — *Someone I Love Is Sick, What Do I Do?*; *Abdominal Tumors Explained*; *Migraines: Is It in My Head?* — hoping to find something applicable to my father. Perhaps a pamphlet with suggestions on how to deal with an all-encompassing, gnawing, mushrooming cynicism.

"Look at that goofy plaque," he said, pointing at the wall where Robert's name was engraved in bronze. "Goddamned saint."

"Why don't you read a magazine?"

"I'm in half the magazines," he said. "If I wanted to see pictures of me looking like shit, I'd look in the mirror."

"Why don't we go outside and get you a smoke?"

"Also probably against some goddamned rule."

"How about we play cards to pass the time?"

"I would fucking crush you to pieces."

Billings, we'd been told, was on his way over, and every few minutes we heard his name intoned over the intercom. Nurses hurried back and forth in the hall. Some other patients began to fill up the waiting area, most everyone glaring at us, some with more discretion than others.

"I used to love hospitals," my father said. "I'd sit in places like this for days to find a client."

"So this should be a fun memory for you."

"That was when I was young. Nobody I knew had been sick yet. Or died. I was such an arrogant prick."

"What's changed?" I asked.

"Very funny, Hilly."

"They let you smoke and drink back in

499

the hospital in New Haven?"

"Every minute, if you liked. They gave out ashtrays."

He rapped his fingers against the hard, yellowed plaster of his cast. Across from us a teenage boy surreptitiously took our photograph with his telephone, a fact my father was oblivious to.

"So," he said, "you finally got that girl-friend of yours to come give you a visit."

"Girlfriend?"

"Miss Ewing."

"Savannah's last name is Stockton."

"I was surprised to see you got her out here. I didn't dare tell the kids the whole story."

"I noticed. I appreciate the discretion."

"I saw she basically took off once she got a gander at how you'd aged."

I smiled. Again, Billings's name came across the loudspeakers.

"What was wrong with her, anyhow?" he asked. "She sick or something?"

"Cancer."

"Christ."

I nodded. "Apparently it's not the kind that kills you."

"Oh," my father said. "Well, that's good."

"I think so."

"She has a young boy."

"Seventeen."

"I was basically the same age when my mother died," he said. "She died right after you were born. But she met you. She squeezed your little foot." He stopped. I'd never heard any of this before. "Then I was off at war when my father died. It's terrible to lose your parents when you're young."

I thought of my girls, and my wife, and I knew that my father was thinking of them, too. "Your girls seem fine, though."

"It's nice that they have their husbands."

"All except the baby," he said, speaking of Eliza. Her name was Elizabeth, but rather than call her Beth, which my father had advocated, we'd gone with Eliza, which he thought sounded absurd, taken altogether: Eliza Wise. Still, it was nice to hear him say that she was the baby. Of course, to me she was the baby. That never changes.

"She seems good, though," he said. "Did she tell you?"

"Tell me what?"

"That I gave her money."

I leaned my head back. *"No."*

"I'm going to do it for all the kids. But I did it for her first. She's been so kind to me. For no reason."

"She's your granddaughter. That's a fine reason."

"Flowers twice a week. Pastries. Various gadgets. At first I found it cloying. Because I thought she was after something. If you want money from me, I'd just as soon you ask me. But then I realized that she was just doing it because she wanted to."

"Amazing, isn't it?"

"Certainly doesn't get that from me."

"How much money did you give her?"

"Oh, not much."

"How much."

"Thirty."

"Thirty thousand?"

He shook his head. He loved this. "No. Thirty *thousand.* Are you kidding me? You can't get anything for thirty thousand. A goddamned Korean car costs more than thirty thousand now."

"Don't tell me."

"She's my *blood,*" he said.

"I'll make her give it back to you," I said.

"Now why would you do that?" he asked.

I didn't have a good answer for him or, rather, an answer he hadn't heard me give him before — that too much money made you idle, rotted you, took away your ability to dream. He laughed. "Figures you'd get all lathered up. It's hers now. If she doesn't want it, I'd rather she bury it on the beach. I can't take it with me."

"You're not dying. Just because Robert died doesn't mean you're dying."

"Let her start a foundation," he said, ignoring me. "I already know she doesn't want the money for herself. All of your kids are like that. Amazingly. They all have churches for hearts."

"Still."

"Still nothing. Fuck still."

"Do her sisters know?"

"Probably. You know girls. Gossip is practically one of their food groups."

"Oh, that's nice."

Another chime, this one from above us, Billings's name pronounced with a sort of urgency reserved for tardy high school students. *Dr. Billings? Dr. Billings, if you're in the hospital . . .*

"Funny," he said, "that you had only girls. Girls always had such sway over you. And what'd you do? You went out and had four of them. I'm sorry you never had a son. There is something wonderful about a son. Makes you the last one, you know that?"

"The last what?"

"The last Wise man," he said, missing the irony in this, the stupid, old, foolish joke.

For the next few minutes, he took telephone calls, largely ignoring the regulations against having a working cell phone in a hospital waiting room, shrugging at the orderlies who stopped to bug him about it, as if to say, *What are you gonna do about it?* I wondered if he knew that I had that box, that I had the Brooklyn Pages. When he was off the phone for good, I wanted to tell him.

"If I ask you something, will you tell me the truth?"

"It depends, Hilly."

"Did you kill Lem Dawson?"

He stifled a cough. I'd surprised him with the question. Then a nurse came out into the waiting room and called for him. I helped him up to his feet. He looked at the crutches. "Throw them away," he said.

"You didn't answer me," I said.

"Still? You're still thinking about this?"

"Yes," I said. "I have this b—"

He was standing in front of Robert's plaque. He turned to it. "Saint Bobby. Oh, Bobby." Then he turned to me. "Let it go, kid. For the love of God."

"But —"

"What do you want me to tell you?"

"Tell me who did it."

"You think so little of me. Still. After everything. I guess I lost with you. I tried and I lost. I was always the villain. But you don't understand. There are things I'd tell a

504

stranger that I wouldn't tell you. And I hate that."

"That doesn't answer the question," I said.

He looked at the nurse and then he looked at me and then he looked at the plaque beside him, Robert's name in big capital letters. *This hospital exists because of the generosity of Robert Ashley, veteran, attorney, and a longtime resident of Bluepoint.*

"Seriously, Hilly. Let it go."

"No," I said. "I refuse."

Later I would think of what happened next as the only moment in our life together when he'd been completely honest with me, a fact I would revise and revisit and turn over and rejudge and deny for years. He grabbed my face with both hands, as if he were about to kiss my cheeks, and he brought my ear to his mouth so that he could whisper into it: "He wasn't supposed to be killed." Then he let go of me, but he was glaring, his eyes wide with what looked like terror. "*That* was an accident. Do you understand?" he asked me. "We would never do that. Never. Ever."

Billings came to take my father away. Ten minutes later he was free. He streamed through the waiting room, not stopping to look at me. He had another pair of crutches. The doctors thought he still needed some assistance. His limp was slight, more like a hint of a limp than evidence of any real injury. He was on his telephone. "Dad!" I called. "Hey! Dad!"

A limousine was waiting for him at the curb. The electric doors slid open for him, and he crossed onto the sidewalk, chucked the crutches into the bushes, and got in the car.

TEN

The interior of the Broad Neck hotel is a farce, more like a Ralph Lauren store than a whaler's bar, which evidently is supposed to be the idea. Thick white rope. Desiccated coral, sitting on a shelf. A patently fake starfish aligned beside it. Wistful fake Turner canvases hung over decorative fireplaces. Old, staged photographs of rugby squads and golf teams. Burnished sailing trophies on the side tables. Fish on the menu, but not the fish native to the ocean here, not cod or bluefish, but salmon, Chilean sea bass, shrimp. I was here to see Theo Cantor and found him at the bar, an empty mug of tea beside his left elbow, a half-finished grilled cheese on a huge plate, yellow notebooks arranged in a neat pile. I hadn't wanted to come. But he'd been bugging me, calling three times a day, leaving messages with all of my daughters. This was the evening my father had had his cast removed, twelve hours after he'd gotten into his limousine.

Before I reached him, Theo stood up from the bar. He was in brown board shorts, his legs an unseemly shade of white, the backs of his calves as hairless as my daughters'. "Hilly," he said, wheeling around just as I got within earshot of him. "I need to show you something."

"I don't have tons of time, Theo."

"Really," he said. "Come. Please."

He led me to a conference room off the lobby. A long table surrounded by tall, leather-backed chairs occupied the lion's share of the space. A small video projector sat on the table.

"Dug this up last week," he said, turning off the lights, turning on the projector. "I think it's important you see it."

"What is it?" I asked.

"Just wait," he said.

A moment later the screen — one of those small pull-down jobs you see in conference rooms everywhere — went dark. The image was coming from a digital projector, but it was clear that whatever this was had originally been shot on film. Suddenly there were the telltale marks of celluloid scratches, flickers, a lens flare, a jagged piece of editing tape rushing by. Then, a leader counting down to zero. Finally, an airport hangar emerged on screen. The camera is on the front of a car, or a golf cart, and we're going down a runway. It's winter. The trees are bare. You can see them in the distance, lining the pavement. Beside me, Theo was biting the end of a Bic pen. "I've watched this, like, a hundred times already. I just want you to know where I'm coming from," he says.

We're near water. You can't see it, exactly, but I know it's there. There are gulls hovering, and the wind, evident on a ribbon tied to something near the wheel well visible in the lower left-hand corner of the frame, is strong. I've lived by the ocean most of my life, and I can tell when there is water nearby. The car turns, and we see, just then, a bluff that for a moment I don't recognize. As the camera pans to reveal the plane, I realize this is Logan Airport.

The aircraft is so much smaller than I imagined. For a moment we see it being wheeled out of the hangar. A team of mechanics pushes the craft. There are four of them, all in dark jumpsuits. You can see one man, shot close up, say the word *Chickadee,* his lips and mouth and teeth flashing. The yellow of the nose is rendered a light shade of gray. Funny that you can sort of make out color in a black-and-white film.

Theo leans over the table. "Promotional video for the airline. I found a whole bunch of these in a warehouse in Rhode Island. After your father ruined the company, the owners locked everything away. Nobody's alive now, of course. Their grandkids didn't care when I asked to see what I could find. So now it's mine until somebody sues me to get it back."

A white flash on the screen serves as a cut. Now we're inside the plane. The interior is modest. Cloth chair backs. A runner on the aisle, with two bright stripes. Two seats on the left, one on the right. We go all the way to the back. This is where the crash originated. The engine on the left side stalled because of faulty wiring here. I know this because I remember listening to my father rehearse his closing argument for the case in our old kitchen in New Haven. The door to the restroom is ajar. So is the curtain to the small space where the meals were prepared, just two hot plates, a drip coffee maker, and an icebox. The cameraman wheels around to show the cockpit. But there is a man in the way, one of the repairmen. Theo, again, leans over the table, then he pauses the picture.

"Everybody always wants to know why

I'm so particularly obsessed with this plane crash. With your father. This is the answer," he said, pointing at the screen. "This is why I won't stop calling you."

"Who is it?" I asked.

"My grandfather," he said.

"Really?"

"Such a smart guy," he said, sitting down. "MIT trained. Air force instructor. Total genius, they say."

"He's young here."

"Baby face," he said. "He's thirty-five."

I looked. The man on screen seemed younger.

"See," Theo said, "he was the head mechanic on the flight. His first job. Moved the whole family up from Roanoke to Waltham to work at Logan. After the plane crashed, they say he was the first guy at the scene. They say he knew when it took off. Probably bullshit. He wanted to know what went wrong. Then your father came along. Basically, my grandfather took all the blame in the lawsuit."

"I see."

"Ruined his life."

I nodded.

"I mean, I don't want to get into a whole sob story," Theo said, continuing to chew on the end of his pen cap. "But let's just say it was awful."

"So this is your idea of payback?" I asked. "Writing this book?"

"No, no, no. He'd killed himself long before I was born. I never knew the guy. My dad barely knew the guy."

"My God."

"Right. Well. Every story the media did on your father, every time he was in the paper, that was like a drill boring its way into my grandfather's gut."

"Terrible," I said.

"I don't hold a grudge. My father . . . well, he holds a grudge. Big goddamned grudge. But, see, I'm just fascinated. You'd be too. It's my story. I have to get my story down on paper. You know?"

He was talking about the crash, his grandfather, my father. This is how American society works, he was saying. You take two men born in basically the same year. One man works his whole life, studies, learns the science of aviation, the physics of it, serves his country; he has a son, he gets a chance to work on an airplane, he paints the nose of it yellow because that's his wife's favorite color. Her nickname is Bunny. So the plane's name is *Bunny,* although the boys like the way *Chickadee* sounds instead. He makes a small mistake. He fails to check something tiny, something simple. Maybe someone was joking with him and he forgot to check it, and when he went back to his work, he assumed he'd looked at it, when he hadn't. After all, it's a new plane, and new planes like this just don't have mechanical problems. They have design problems. Or problems of human error. He's consumed with the guilt. Every time Arthur Wise rattles off the names of the victims, it's as if a cancer blossoms. Finally, a suicide. Fitting for an engineer, it's a hanging. A simple equation of force, height, mass. He does it in the basement. Gets up on a wooden box, kicks it out from beneath him. The box has the words *Boston Airways* printed on it. It's filled with manuals. After the crash, and until he died, all he did was pore over the manuals, trying to figure out what he'd done wrong. And then there's Arthur Wise. A plane crashes, families are aggrieved, lawsuits are filed, millions of dollars are made, a whole generation grows up in luxury. There's an equation, Theo was saying, that had his grandfather's life going in a downward arc and my father's life going up exponentially. Then, he says, there's you and me.

But I wasn't listening. While he was talking, Theo had stood and opened the shades.

In the past few years the town government of Bluepoint had installed some arcade games on the boardwalk, booths where you could get Italian ice or soft serve or fried clams or pulled taffy or neon plastic sunglasses or henna tattoos. That's when I saw you. I should say that it was the first time I saw evidence of you rather than say that it was the first time I saw *you*. That would come six months later. But it was your mother and your father, Sammy and Ethan, and they were walking together and drinking milk shakes, just out for a walk. Your mother had a T-shirt on, a white T-shirt, and it was tight against her body, and I saw just a hint of what would become her pregnant belly. A tiny bump: you!

Eventually Theo stopped talking, and we started the interview. The one I promised him. And as you might grow to realize if you ever read Mr. Cantor's book, I lied. I told him bald fictions. The business about Lem Dawson having a bad temper, and how that temper, in my opinion, led to a fight that led to his murder in prison? Of course that was a lie. Lem was so docile. It had been trained into him, a tool to avoid conflict. The business about my father's grief over Lem's death, about how he had wanted to lift the charges against Lem, about how he had wanted to give money to Savannah throughout her life? All a lie. I could go on. You get the picture. Perhaps you will think less of me for harming a man I had already harmed so badly. The lies are what went into that book you have on your shelf, that book you might grow to take to be the truth, and that's the reason for all of this. I don't know — if I hadn't lied, maybe I wouldn't have done this. This book. This story; my story. This is what you need to know about me and my father.

See: I'd thought he was gone for good when I got back from the hospital. He'd have gone to New York, I thought, to his house on Riverside that my mother had loved so much, or to L.A., to his house on the golf course in Bel Air, that house where he once bragged to me that he had lemons growing in the backyard. *Do you believe that, Hilly? Real fucking lemons!* But a few hours after he left the hospital, I heard his limousine arrive back at Bluepoint. Suddenly, without a cast or crutches, he was moving around with the vigor of a man half his age. I was in the study then, and I left him alone. When I saw him again, a few hours later, he was kneeling in the dirt near the fence that circled Bob's house. He had a can of paint beside him. A brush. A scraper. He was finishing the job.

I went out onto the patio. It was warm. It was almost September, and the days had begun to grow shorter. Far out on the water there were dolphins. "Look!" I yelled. "Dolphins! Dad!" But he didn't hear me. So I started over to Robert's house.

I had the box in my hand. The box with the Brooklyn Pages inside. When I was maybe a hundred yards away, I stopped to open it. I read just the first one. My curiosity allowed me just the one single glance. My father stood up. He had paint on his pants. He was staring at Robert's house. I unfolded the paper. It was the bottom layer of a carbon set, the sheet you removed if you wanted to save your correspondence. Lem must have filed all of these away. This must have been his plan. He'd show these to my father, and my father would give him money to keep them a secret, and he and Savannah would go. I thought of her then. Just as the wind began to come across me. Savannah at sixteen, smiling out from behind the hanging laundry. Behind me, up on her uncle's staircase. She had waved at me that last morning. How I wish I had waved back! How I wish I had done something, anything, other than what I did!

I looked down to the paper in my hands.

Here was a handwritten letter signed by my father. *"Robert, please stop worrying that I'm going to take this damn job and leave you. All the money in heaven couldn't separate me from you. I told you that last night. I am yours and you are mine. And no one knows about us. Not Lem Dawson. Not Ruthie. Not the boys from Silver & Silver. Not even god-damned J. Edgar Hoover could ever find out. That's what all this money gets us. What else is there to say: I love you. This — you and me — this is eternity."*

I put it down then. I thought I heard something behind me, and when I turned around, I swear to you I thought for a moment I'd find her behind me, Savannah, catching me the way I'd caught Lem, her face stern, still young, still healthy. Of course there was nothing there but the sea and the sky and our old family home. I closed the box. My father was painting the fence now. There were tears on his cheeks. I went to him.

ACKNOWLEDGMENTS

I owe a great deal to the people who make my writing life possible. For his continued devotion, his patience, his friendship, his endurance in the face of my anxiety, and his belief in this book, I remain forever indebted to my agent, PJ Mark. To Stephanie Koven, who read this book with such a keen, clear eye, and whose pink Post-it notes helped fix what was broken — thank you. For her smart, incisive, and indispensable work on this book, and for making it better with every pass, I owe an enormous debt of gratitude to my terrific editor, Reagan Arthur.

For the short lesson in aviation that occurs at the beginning of Part III, and for answering all of my various science-related questions, I'm indebted to my friend Dr. Matthew Lackner from the University of Massachusetts Amherst. Any glaring errors in the physics of aviation are mine, and mine alone.

And a great, genuine thank-you to Molly Antopol, Gwendolyn Beckley, Marlena Bittner, Marisa Caramella, Lan Samantha Chang, Kris Doyle, Mike Fusco, Katharine Gehron, Sarah Murphy, Michael Pietsch, Costanza Prinetti, Robert Sokolowsky, Becky Sweren, Ted Thompson, and Andrea Walker; to my family — Richard, Pamela, and Marissa.

And to my first and toughest reader — my wife: I love you.

ABOUT THE AUTHOR

Stuart Nadler is a graduate of the Iowa Writers' Workshop, where he was awarded a Truman Capote Fellowship and a Teaching-Writing Fellowship. Recently, he was the Carol Houck Smith Fiction Fellow at the University of Wisconsin. His fiction has appeared in *The Atlantic.* He is the author of the story collection *The Book of Life.*